Earth Magic

Three Moon Falls
Book Three

Katie O'Connor

Earth Magic

Three Moon Falls Book Three

Katie O'Connor

-Earth Magic-

-Three Moon Falls Book 3-

Published September 2024 by Snarky Heart Press and Katie O'Connor

(katieohwrites.com)

ISBN: 978-1-989816-82-0 (Kindle Edition)

ISBN: 978-1-989816-83-7 (Other Digital Editions)

ISBN: 978-1-989816-84-4 (Print Edition)

ISBN: 978-1-997548-11-9 (Alternate Print Edition)

Cover art by Raquel Lyon, Crooked Sixpence Book Covers

Copyediting by Terri St. Clair

Dedication

This one is for Abby Lokszyn.

Thanks for your patience in waiting for this one.

It's also for Lynn Gale, Michaela Brent, and Audrey Carnes.

Ladies, you keep going and working through the rough spots.

You are my inspiration.

And, as always, for Terri, my editor who makes my creativity readable.

About This Book

The last thing Hyacinth Hawk needs is to run into her childhood love, Earl Cooper. Unfortunately, she's a midwife, and he's her current patient's brother. A decade ago, he fled in terror when she showed him her ability to move earth and other objects with the power of her mind. She's mourned their relationship ever since. As much as they'd both like to revisit their feelings with the maturity of adults, evil is stalking Hyacinth's family, and she doesn't dare risk love again.

To Earl Cooper, magic is bunkum, sleight of hand, and outright lies. When his newborn niece struggles to survive her birth, he must put his entire faith in the woman he scorned for her magical powers.

Can they overcome their past hurts to find love again, or will the evil threatening their families and their hometown destroy them and everything they care about?

Chapter One

Hyacinth Hawk bundled the newborn and placed the tiny girl in her mother's arms. "Here she is, your sweet baby girl. She's beautiful." She wasn't, she was red and wrinkled like all newborns, but Hyacinth wasn't about to say that. To every new parent, their minute-old baby was the most beautiful thing they'd ever seen, and as far as newborns went, she was cute.

"She is beautiful, isn't she?" Meredith, the baby's mom, asked, her voice breathless with exhaustion and happiness.

Meredith's husband, Chen, kneeled beside the bed, a stupefied, sunny smile on his face. "She's perfect, isn't she, Meri?" He wiped the sweat from his wife's brow.

"Absolutely. Ten fingers, ten toes, and an adorable nose." A few minutes later, after finishing her tasks as a midwife, Hyacinth said, "I'm going to get Meredith some tea. It will slow the post-birth bleeding and help her heal. I'll make coffee for you, Chen." Taking care of the patient and her spouse was part of being a midwife. She adored the special bonding moments right after birth. They filled her heart with joy and fed her soul with happiness.

Leaving the happy family alone, she slipped out of the bedroom and into the kitchen. The morning sun brought a golden hue to the white cabinets and intensified the sunny yellow walls. Meri's entire house was bright and serene, but a sense of unease tickled the hairs on the back of Hyacinth's neck. There wasn't a reason for it, but she couldn't shake it. Intuition wasn't something to ignore, so she pushed it to the back of her mind and let her subconscious worry out what was bothering her.

After plugging in the kettle and starting coffee, she collapsed in a chair. She was exhausted. Meri's labor had taken eighteen hours, and near the end, Hyacinth had seriously considered calling an ambulance. Meredith had been growing weak, and the baby was becoming distressed. Channeling her healing magic, Hyacinth had pushed everything she had into mother and child, her strength carrying them through safely.

She fumbled in her purse hanging on the back of her chair and pulled out a small plastic container of her grandmother's energy balls. Each ball gave a short-term magical burst of energy. After she perked up, she would make herself and Meri a nourishing snack. For now, she inhaled the dark rich scent of coffee. The scent alone boosted her flagging energy.

She'd be here for a few hours, just to ensure there were no complications. She would watch over the mother and child, ensuring the family was fed and content before she went home. But first, hot drinks.

Blending teas was one of Hyacinth's healing gifts. Her family grew almost all the ingredients on the land they'd owned for generations and in their special greenhouses. Each herbal blend had a purpose. Of course, they made some blends simply for flavor. Today's tea was a special blend, including rosemary, yarrow, witch hazel bark, thyme, plantain leaf, and a bit of willow bark to alleviate pain. Lemon and mint were added to flavor it and make it more palatable. It wasn't delicious. Many of her patients said it was gross, but it was great for post-partum healing.

Like any medication, it was best used in controlled doses. She grabbed a tea bag with a pre-measured portion of tea and prepped a mug for Meri. While it steeped, she set a bag with more tea and instructions on the table. She ate another energy ball, an apple, and some of the chocolate she'd brought with her. What she needed was something more substantial. High fat and high protein to fuel her body's flagging reserves. She had expended more energy than she'd intended and performing magic always had a physical cost.

She stood in a shaft of late summer sunshine beside the sink. It was hard to believe it was eight in the morning already. Robins and chickadees called outside the open window. The wind ruffled the leaves on the weeping willow in the backyard. A blue jay screamed and was answered by another. She couldn't wait to be outside, barefoot, her feet touching blessed Mother Earth. Standing barefoot in the grass was a form of grounding, of refueling her body and soul with nature's strength and goodness.

Earth was her element. She drew her magic strength from the soil and the soil's produce. Simply being in nature made her stronger. She could, with effort, bend the earth to her will. More than once, as a petulant teen, she'd shifted the earth under the feet of someone who'd done her wrong. Thankfully, with age came wisdom, and she'd outgrown her spiteful youth. At twenty-seven, she had solid control over her temper and her magic.

She opened the fridge and pulled out the broccoli cheddar quiche she'd prepped earlier. She turned on the oven to preheat and started some bacon to go with the quiche and the fresh fruit salad she'd brought. The grapes, apples, oranges, and berries were from her family's orchard and greenhouses.

She would leave the homemade soup she'd brought for the family's lunch. The amount of support she provided depended on the mother's wants, needs, and budget. Meredith had asked for the works. Birthing support, two hours of observation after her birth, and a light but nutritious meal. In addition to all that, Hyacinth had brought some red velvet cupcakes and some bran muffins. Like her grandmother, she found cooking for others soothing to her soul.

Her instincts nudged her again. Something wasn't quite right. She stood quietly, listening to the sounds from outside, puzzling on her sense of unease. Finally, she shook her head to dispel her disquiet. Now should be a time of joy, not worry. Besides, intuition was her weakest magical gift, and it wasn't always reliable. It could simply be the exhaustion following a long night and a stressful birth plaguing her.

Prepping a tray, she paused to reflect on the miracle of the birth she'd just assisted in. She truly was blessed to have a career, no, a calling, that came with such joy. She wrapped her arms around herself in a hug. Despite her exhaustion, or maybe because of it, she was giddy with exhilaration from the miracle of birth she'd just assisted in.

The kitchen door thumped with a soft, almost soundless knock. She hurried to answer before whoever was in the backyard disturbed the new family. Meri didn't need visitors yet.

She opened the door and the caution she was about to administer died unspoken in her suddenly dry throat. Earl Cooper, her onetime crush, turned nemesis.

The smile on his face faded to a frown and his gray eyes turned stormy. "Hyacinth," he offered a cold greeting.

"Earl." Two could play the one-word game. She stood between the inside and screen doors, carefully keeping her eyes on his face, no matter how much her heart wanted to drink in everything about him. She looked at him and waited.

"Can I come in?" he asked after a long, uncomfortable pause. He reached for the door handle and lowered his hand before it got there. He was still nervous around her.

"Certainly, if you're quiet." She stepped back and let him enter. She could hardly deny Meri's brother entry.

He wiped his shoes and stepped inside. Without invitation, he hung his denim jacket on a hook and put his shoes on the small rack next to the mat. "How is she? Is the baby here yet?"

"Meredith is doing fabulously and your new niece is adorable. They're resting."

"Excellent."

She waited for more than a single word. Not sure where to take the conversation when he didn't go on, she asked, "How have you been, Earl?" She ignored his subtle outdoorsy scent because if she focused on it, old memories would rush in and swamp her.

"Fine." He looked all around the kitchen, seeming to avoid looking directly at Hyacinth. "Can I see them?"

"Let me check. Just give me a minute, okay?" She flipped the bacon, removed a few slices from the pan, and turned the burner down. She finished prepping the tea tray and added coffee for Chen. "I'll be right back."

She stepped out of the kitchen and into the hallway of the massive five-bedroom bungalow and took a deep breath. She closed her eyes and forced her shoulders to relax. She should have expected Earl to show up. He and Meridith were very close since their parents had passed when they were in their teens.

At nineteen, Earl had taken over running the family bookshop and supported his sixteen-year-old sister until she graduated tech school. She admired that he'd stepped up for her. Now, at twenty-seven, the bookstore was a roaring success with locals and tourists alike. The shop, with the unlikely name, Cooper's Capers, was just down the street from the metaphysical shop that Hyacinth and her sisters owned.

The two businesses couldn't be further apart. Cooper's focused strictly on books, primarily fiction; the type of books you'd want to read on your vacation. Cooper's was the quintessential old-school, no-frills bookstore with almost nothing but books and related items. Four Seasons Metaphysical was all about magic, Wicca, and witches. They carried books on all the major, minor, and new-age religions. They also carried everything a person would need to cast a magic spell and live a magical life; from herbs and candles to talismans and trinkets.

She didn't want to think about Earl anymore, but her thoughts were hard to ignore. He was still too handsome with those expressive gray eyes, and his neatly cut dark brown, nearly black, hair. He was clean-shaven today and her fingers itched to stroke his cheeks to see how smooth they were. Of course, when he had a five o'clock shadow or neatly trimmed beard, she wanted to test those as well. There was something about Earl that had called to her heart since she was a young girl.

She sighed and pushed away thoughts of his muscular body and sweet smile. She knocked on the bedroom door jamb. "Hey, guys. I brought tea and cookies." Today's treats were, unfortunately, store-bought, but the bakery's cookies were nearly as good as Gramma Pearl's cookies. She set the tray on the dresser, cleared the last of her birthing supplies from the bedside table, and moved the tea tray closer.

"Here you go. Are you up to guests? Earl is in the kitchen. I can send him away if you're not ready." A tiny, hurt corner of her heart wanted to make him wait to see his niece. She pushed the negative thought away and gave her best smile to the happy family.

"Can he come back? Maybe in an hour?" Meri's smile was apologetic.

"Sure. I'll let him know. Breakfast will be ready shortly. I'm just reheating some quiche."

"Thank you. We appreciate you acting as gatekeeper," Chen said.

She gave them a thumbs-up and returned to the kitchen. Earl was busy turning the bacon. "I didn't want it to burn," he said. "How's she doing?"

"Tired, but good. She asked if you could come back in an hour or so."

In a moment of weakness, she offered him breakfast. Her stomach plummeted to her toes and rebounded with a bellyache. She didn't want to be near him. Okay, maybe she did, but having him close made her long for things she'd never have.

"I'd love breakfast. How can I help? Should I just finish cooking the bacon?" His voice said he'd be happy to finish cooking it. "I'd like to hang around in case they need anything, unless you object?" His words were as much a statement as a question.

"Thanks." How else was she supposed to respond? "Just give me room to put this quiche in the oven. She could use the microwave, but the delicious egg pie, like most things, was better reheated in the oven. He stepped aside, and she slid the pan into the oven.

"Bacon and quiche?" he asked.

"Yes, I know Chen isn't a huge fan of bacon, but Meri loves it and she needs the extra calories. The fat and protein will stick with her longer than carbs."

"Was it a hard delivery?" His brow wrinkled, and she recognized his fear for his sister. His protectiveness was something she'd always admired about him.

"I won't sugarcoat it. It was tough. Over eighteen hours and at the end, I debated calling an ambulance. She's exhausted. I'm exhausted."

"You're exhausted?"

She didn't bother to explain how her magic worked. He knew about magic and that Meri was magical; he just chose to disbelieve. It was the reason they'd never gotten together.

Fifteen years ago, she and her sisters were sent to Three Moon Falls Christian Church. They were just teens, but spending time learning another religion was beneficial in understanding how to keep up good relations with their neighbors. It was there that she had her first serious encounter with Earl. They'd been in a teen Sunday School class together. She knew Earl from school, he was in her class, but they ran in different circles. He was a jock; she tended to be shy and spent most of her time in the library.

At church, they found themselves together, and she realized, not for the first time, what an attractive young man he was. Every week after church, they'd spend time together in the park. It wasn't long before she lost her teenage heart to him and brazenly stole a kiss. Her heart thundered just thinking about the moment. No man since had affected her the way teenage Earl had. Just being near him had her heart pounding. She pushed the memories away.

"Well, I've been here for eighteen hours without sleep, and I was up hours before that. Granted, it isn't as difficult as giving birth, but it's no picnic either. I've barely had time to snack, let alone eat a full meal. I'm sure you've put in long days at the bookstore."

She unearthed another tray from the cabinet and put napkins and silverware on it. As she wobbled a bit on her feet, the exhaustion finally overcame her. Grabbing the nearest chair, she sat down with a thump and rested her head on the table.

"Are you okay?" Earl asked, sounding concerned.

"Yes. No. Sort of."

"That's not an answer. Is there something I can do for you?" The forks he was using for the bacon clattered onto the counter.

"Maybe a glass of juice and a couple of pieces of that bacon. I'm starved and I need to refuel. Helping with a birth always sucks my energy."

The fridge opened and closed. A glass of juice appeared on the table beside her. A plate of bacon followed before she could muster the strength to drink the juice.

"Thank you." She chugged the juice and nibbled the bacon. The acidic juice hit hard on her nearly empty stomach, but her energy perked immediately. She sat up. "I really mean it, thank you."

"Did you magic my sister? I don't believe in magic, but my sister says it can extract a physical cost." His frown showed his confusion and that he was upset by the idea.

"What's it going to be, Earl? Either you don't believe in magic or you think I magicked her. You can't have it both ways." Memories assaulted her again. Weeks after their first kiss, the topic of magic had come up, and believing herself in love with Earl, she'd confessed that the rumors were true. She was a witch, and she did have magic powers. His sister was magic, so she thought he'd understand.

Boy, had she been wrong. He'd recoiled in horror and broken up with her on the spot. Devastated, she'd lashed out as he walked away, sending a small shockwave through the ground, which knocked him off his feet.

More than a decade had passed. Her heart still ached from missing him. She hated him. She needed him, and he would barely talk to her. This was the longest conversation they'd had in years.

"I don't know." Confusion and honesty colored his voice.

It took a second for her brain to leave the past and remember that she'd asked him if he thought she'd used magic or not. Something inside of her withered. She was used to people being skeptical, or thinking she was a fraud, but coming from Earl, it still hurt.

Rather than start yet another argument, she found a bowl for the fruit salad. They'd have some with breakfast and anything left over after Meri and Chen ate would make a good snack for them.

"Hyacinth, come quickly. There's something wrong with Anna," Chen's voice cracked in panic. Despite her exhaustion, her heart and body exploded into action.

Chapter Two

H yacinth bolted down the hall and into the bedroom, totally ignoring Earl, who was hot on her heels. "What is it?"

"She's all blue," Meredith cried, tears streaming down her face. "I don't think she's breathing.

Hyacinth took the baby from her and carried her to the teddy bear print padded change table in the corner of the master bedroom. She unwrapped her and laid her down. She felt for a pulse and found nothing. "Not today," she muttered under her breath.

"What is it?" Earl demanded, standing right at her back.

"Stethoscope, in my bag." She jabbed her hand toward her black medical bag. Earl was back at her side in seconds. She listened for a heartbeat and found nothing. "Call an ambulance," she demanded, dropping to sit on the floor with the baby between her legs.

Chest compressions on an infant were the hardest thing she'd ever done, save for pronouncing a baby stillborn. She started compressions, and willed baby Anna to live. Desperate, she called the Goddess for help. "Pray," she mumbled to Earl, even though he was on the phone.

In the distance, Meredith wept, and Chen demanded to know what was going on. She ignored them. There was no time for reassurances or handholding. Baby Anna needed all her attention.

She kept up the delicate but forceful compressions and dug deep within herself. She didn't know what was wrong, but the universe was mistaken if it thought that this baby was going to die. Not on her watch. She was already weak, and barely functional, but she had more life in her than this helpless baby. She dug deep, simultaneously using her magic to search for the cause of the baby's distress, and to send the baby healing and energy for survival. Either was enough to sap Hyacinth when she was healthy, but today she was already running on fumes.

"Earl, I need you."

Phone in one hand, he dropped to his knees on the plush beige carpet beside her. "What can I do?"

"I'm weak. I need your strength. Put your hands on my shoulders and give me your strength. Push your power into me."

"Wait, what?" He reared back.

She dropped her voice to a whisper. "If you want this baby to live, you'll put your hands on me and let me use your strength. Give Chen the phone."

Earl recoiled further in horror. What was she saying? She was insane. He stared at Hyacinth in disbelief. Before his eyes, the color faded from her face, and she became paler and paler. *Shit! What did he do?*

Magic was bullshit, right?

"Hurry," her frantic cry was barely audible.

Tossing the phone to Chen, he leaned over the baby to grasp Hyacinth's shoulders. He didn't believe in this crap, but by all that was holy, he'd try to give her what she thought she needed if it meant they might save Anna.

Looking at the baby would break his heart. Instead, he watched Hyacinth's face. Her brows furrowed together, and she bit her lip. She moaned like she was in agony. "Please, God," he prayed aloud. "Don't take this baby."

"Yes. Pray for all you're worth," Hyacinth whispered. "I need more. Push your energy into me."

What the hell did that mean? How could he transfer his energy to her? It was impossible. He suddenly thought of faith healers. That was all bunk, wasn't it? He'd read something once about a healer who claimed they could push their strength into a weak body. Was that what she wanted?

Drawing on his imagination, built by years of reading fiction, he imagined his strength and energy rolling through his fingers and into her body. Tingles raced down his arms and through his fingers. He almost jerked away in shock. Holy cow! Was this happening?

"Yes," she whispered.

"What's wrong with her?" He kept his voice low, so his sister didn't hear him over her quiet keening.

"I don't know." Her voice was thready, like she didn't have the strength to speak. "It might be her heart, or maybe just exhaustion after the long labor. Keep pushing."

He doubled his efforts. "Can you fix her?" he practically begged in the same discreet tone.

"No. All I can do is hold on until help arrives." Tears rolled down her face, and she slumped lower. She seemed...defeated.

He pushed again, visualizing his energy as a flow of water going from him to her. He could feel his energy sapping. Was this what magic cost? He couldn't deny magic any longer. Something was going on here. He was getting weaker by the minute. *Where the hell was the ambulance?*

"Oh. Her heart is beating," Hyacinth exclaimed. "I think she's stable. Sort of. Don't stop." She lifted her stethoscope and focused on the steady thump thump until she was certain there were no irregularities.

Damn right, he wouldn't stop. Not until this baby was in the hands of medical care. Gratitude for Hyacinth nearly overwhelmed him. She was doing this! Her powers were keeping Anna alive. He watched in awe as she stopped compressions, and with one hand on the baby's chest listened to her heartbeat.

"She has a nice even beat now. I'm not sure what happened."

In the distance, he heard the frantic wail of the ambulance. Thank God the hospital was only moments away. Shifting so he was flat on his butt on the floor, rather than on his knees, he kept his hands on Hyacinth despite his exhaustion and the feeling that he'd run two marathons back-to-back.

Minutes later, the paramedics roared in on a wave of calming confidence. They gently shoved him out of the way and hooked Anna up to monitors. "She's stable," a gray-haired paramedic said, her tone serious and soothing. "Doctor Carter is going to meet us at the hospital. What happened?"

"I'm not sure," Hyacinth said. "Her heart stopped but I managed to get it going."

They discussed what happened, both of them using terminology he was unfamiliar with. Just how much education did a midwife have? Apparently more than he had assumed.

They loaded his sister and his niece onto the stretcher. "You two need to fuel up," the paramedic said. "Eat and rest."

"Meredith, I'll meet you at the hospital when I can," Hyacinth said. "She'll be okay. You're in the best hands."

They were gone in seconds, leaving Hyacinth and Earl sitting on the bedroom floor. "I'm exhausted," he said.

"There might still be cookies on that tray." She gestured vaguely toward the bed.

He stood up and immediately fell to his knees. "What the heck?"

"Go slow. You need food and rest."

Cautiously, he knee-walked to the tray she'd pointed at and, pushing it in front of him, crawled back toward her. She grabbed a cookie and devoured it like a starving dog. He did the same. The sugar boost was instantaneous, and he perked up a bit.

She picked up the coffee mug and chugged down several swallows before handing it to him. "Finish it."

He stared at her. Drink from the same mug she did? What about germs? He wasn't a germaphobe by any stretch but really?

"It's fine. I don't have anything contagious." She waited until he had a mouthful before adding, "At least nothing that can't be treated with antibiotics."

He choked on the drink before laughing with her. "That was mean."

"Just lightening the mood. Help me to the kitchen, please." Working together, they managed to stand, and leaning on each other found their way back into the kitchen. She pulled the quiche from the oven and served them each a quarter of the slightly over-baked pie.

"Whoa, that's a lot of food," he commented.

"Eat it all. You need it. I need it." She flopped into the chair across from him and started eating. He watched in fascination as she shoveled the quiche in, stopping only to drink more juice. She stopped and looked at him. "What?"

"I've never seen anyone eat like that."

"I'm starved. Remember, I told you that before..." She blinked and wiped her cheeks as if she were crying. "Eat, you must be exhausted."

"I am. How does that work? Why are we so exhausted?" Meri had told him that magic had a cost, but he'd dismissed her claims as fantasy. Now, he'd lived magic, and he was nervous and wanted to flee.

"Magic, all magic, has a price. Saving baby Anna, helping her hold on until she stabilized, was the most difficult magic I've ever done, as a healer and in any other way."

"Doesn't magic take fancy words and magic circles like I've seen on television?" He kept eating, pausing after every sentence to take a bite. "You didn't do anything fancy."

"All those things, the wands, the circle, the herbs, the fancy robes, they are props that help you focus your intent. Healing is different. With every person I heal, I give health from myself. Then, I need to use nutrition and rest to build my health back up. Think of healing as being similar to giving blood. They take some away, and after a time, your body rebuilds what was lost. Does that make sense?" She got up and poured them coffee as she spoke. After doctoring both cups with generous portions of sugar and heavy cream, she sat back down.

"Today, without your help, I would have given everything I had to Anna. You feeding me your strength made it easier." She hoped her gratitude came through in her words. "Seriously, you saved us both. I could not have done it without you. You were amazing, beyond that actually, because a mundane, or a newbie can't usually manage to push their power."

"Mundane?"

"A non-magic person, like you. Although you could have some magic, your sister does."

"Me? No way, I'm not magical." Disbelief and fear rang in his voice. He dropped his fork and crossed his arms over his chest.

"Maybe not, but you managed to help me save Anna. I can't begin to express my gratitude."

"No, all thanks go to you. I'm befuddled by all this. It's whacked. But I know you saved her." He stared at her until she became uncomfortable. Finally, he spoke. "How far would you have gone? How much of yourself would you give a patient?"

"Honestly? I've never been in a situation like this before, so I can only judge by how I felt in the moment. I think," she swallowed a lump of fear and sadness, "I think that I would have died for her."

He stared at her; his mouth half open. "Really?"

"I'm telling you how I felt in the moment, but unless it happens, a person doesn't really know when their survival instinct will kick in. But until you touched me, until you joined in helping Anna, I was mentally prepared to put my life on the line."

"Jesus. That's crazy."

"If she'd been born in the hospital, the staff would have done everything to stabilize her. Honestly, her weakness was sort of a freak accident. In the hospital, it might not have been a big deal. Here, at home, the unexpected can be a problem. I did what I needed to do, and thanks to you, all of us came out unscathed."

"You call this unscathed?" He laughed wryly. "I'm so tired, I could sleep for a week."

"So could I, but part of my job is cleaning up the mess and preparing for their return home. First, I'll rest a bit and eat some more. After that, I'll do what needs to be done."

"I'll help."

They finished eating and took a nap on opposite ends of the long living room sofa. Hyacinth cleaned up the bedroom and the small birthing mess while Earl tidied the kitchen and made a pot of chili for the family before they both headed home.

Chapter Three

Earl made a cursory check of the bookstore and chatted briefly with his staff before grabbing a coffee and cranberry-orange muffin, and holing up in his office with instructions not to disturb him unless it was an emergency. He reached for his computer mouse. It wasn't on his oak desk. He searched the desktop and eventually found it in the bottom drawer where he kept his stash of honey mint candies.

"Jeri," he called. "Did you use the computer?"

She popped her head into the office. "Nope. Why?"

"I could have sworn I left the mouse...never mind."

"Losing your mind in your old age?" she teased.

"I should fire you."

"You love me. I keep this place running and you know it."

"Get out of my office, you ingrate. You should be thanking me for not firing you." Jeri had worked for his parents. She was close to retirement age, though she acted and looked much younger. With solid respect between them, teasing was part of their dynamic.

She stuck her tongue out at him and laughed as she walked away.

He shook his head. As much as she was a pain sometimes, she was invaluable, and he knew it. Maybe he'd better lock up the office from now on. He didn't want customers snooping around. Resolved to do just that, he began entering invoices so his newest shipment of books could be shelved.

It was impossible to focus, so he leaned back, and with his feet up on the desk, he mentally revisited the morning's events.

He'd barely seen baby Anna at all and never even talked to his sister and brother-in-law. Yet somehow, he had managed to help Hyacinth save Anna's life. Crazy! Before that moment, he had always sworn that magic was fake. A trick. He'd fought with his sister, Meredith, and called her a liar when she claimed to be magic. It went against everything his Christian upbringing told him. He owed his sister an apology. He'd give that apology willingly because his beautiful niece was proof enough for him. More than enough.

He probably, no definitely, owed Hyacinth one too, because like it or not, what she'd done today had been real. He just hadn't known it when they were younger.

They'd been teens and thought they were in love when she confessed that she was magic. He'd dumped her and refused to talk to her for years. For a decade, he'd been turning and going in the other direction whenever he saw her coming. He'd believed her either a liar or delusional and he mourned the possibilities they'd lost. How wrong he'd been to overreact. Had he thrown away love? He didn't even want to think about it. Regret was a lead ball rolling around his belly, weighing him down.

Where would they have been now if he had believed her? Together? Apart for another reason? The mistake made his heart hurt. How must she have felt back then? It was a wonder she talked to him at all. While she'd never been friendly, she'd certainly been more civil than he'd ever been.

"I'm still not comfortable with all that magic stuff," he murmured to himself, "but I can't deny it's real." He was going to have to learn more. Perhaps, once Meredith was settled in with the new baby, he could pick her brain. "But first, a nap." He yawned so loudly that his jaw cracked.

He leaned back in his desk chair with his feet on the desk, wondering how Hyacinth was doing. Was she recovering okay? He was tempted to call her; but where did he call? The Hawk's house, the shop? He didn't have a cell number for her. Slowly he faded into sleep, and his dreams were of young Hyacinth and how close they'd been. Even in sleep, his heart missed her.

Much to his surprise, Hyacinth was at Meredith's bedside when he arrived at the hospital. "Hi, sis. Hey, Chen. Hyacinth, I wasn't expecting to see you here." He pushed away the awkward feelings flooding him after his dreams of the past.

She was beautiful. Even with dark circles under her eyes and mussed-up hair, she was still the loveliest woman he'd ever seen. Her hair shone with a dozen shades of gold. Her blue eyes sparkled with joy as she cradled baby Anna in her arms. She'd changed her scrubs for form-fitting jeans and a fuzzy sweater. She was a sight for sore eyes. Dang, he missed her.

Nope. Not going there.

"How's Anna doing?" He looked back and forth between the three adults in the room, almost begging for a positive answer.

His sister grinned. "She's amazing. There is nothing wrong with her. She was just exhausted by her ordeal. I probably should have listened to Hyacinth and called the ambulance earlier. It was a mistake I won't repeat with the next one." Her grin morphed into a smile of gratitude. "Thank you both for giving her so much and saving her."

He blushed and looked away. What he'd done didn't feel like a big deal, but at the same time, he knew it had been a miracle. Could it be that God worked through Hyacinth's magic, through his sister's magic? Before today, the idea was unthinkable. Now he couldn't push the thought away.

"Can I hold her?" He needed to be close to his niece and to reassure himself that all was well after the morning's ordeal.

"Absolutely," Meri said. "If you can convince Hyacinth to give her up."

Anna's savior rose gracefully to her feet. "Pull up a chair."

He squished past the end of the bed, nearly brushing Hyacinth as he went by. The aroma of lavender tickled his nose, bringing back a flood of memories. He never could smell lavender without thinking about her. He sat down and she handed him the baby. His arm touched hers, and his hand accidentally brushed against her breast. The soft touch, combined with her fresh, earthy, and floral scent, sent a rush of arousal through him. Heaven help him. His body and heart wanted her back in his life.

No way was he going to let that happen. His mind and soul knew better than to repeat that mistake. Steeling himself, he built an imaginary wall between them. It was as solid as three feet of concrete and he was not going to cross it. Ever. But man, oh man, was he tempted to pull her close for a kiss.

Reluctantly, he turned his attention to baby Anna. Unlike earlier, she was pink and glowing with health. She was adorable. As near as he could tell, she had Meri's nose. She was bundled in a pink blanket and wearing a tiny pink striped knit hat.

"What's with the hat?"

Hyacinth laughed. "Newborns, especially those who have struggled to arrive, often have trouble keeping warm. The hat helps trap her heat, so she doesn't need to be in an incubator and can stay with her family."

"Cool." There was so much he didn't know about babies. Thank heaven he owned a bookstore and could find unlimited books to bone up with. He cuddled the baby close and Hyacinth gave him a few tips on keeping little Anna comfortable. Hyacinth knew a lot about babies. He almost laughed at the thought. Of course, she did. She was a midwife.

Abruptly he realized that he was still out of sorts and muddle-headed from their earlier energy sharing. He wondered if Hyacinth was always affected like this, and how she managed to deliver babies day after day if this was the outcome.

They chatted back and forth while admiring Anna. Meri's eyes began to droop. He stood up, careful not to jostle the baby. "Here you go," he passed her to her mother. "I'm going to head out. I'll come back later. Let me know if you need anything." He kissed Meri on the top of her head in the way that had always made her angry as a teen. Her soft smile warmed his heart until it was full to bursting.

"Thanks, Earl. Can you take Hyacinth out to eat? She looks pale."

He glanced over and sure enough, the color that had returned to the midwife's cheeks had fled again. "I can do that. Come on Hyacinth, let's go grab something to eat and celebrate the birth of my niece."

"I'll just go home, but thanks. Meri, I'll be back to check on you before visiting hours are over. Both you and Chen should try to nap." She bustled around the small hospital room straightening things, finally grabbed her jacket from the back of the chair, and said another goodbye.

He followed her into the hallway. She was still thin, but definitely womanly. Even as a teen, she'd had sweet, subtle curves. It dawned on him that assisting babies and mothers, especially when she used magic, burned a lot of calories, and probably helped keep her thin.

He took two long strides, so he walked beside her. "Come on, Hyacinth. Let's eat. What do you want? German? Italian? Pizza? Vegan?"

"Earl, I've told you for years to call me Cynth. Nobody but my parents and grandmother call me by my full name." Her tone was light but serious.

"Okay, Cynth," he put soft emphasis on the abbreviated name and tried not to think about how intimate the pet name felt. "Where shall we eat?"

"I'm headed home. Gramma Pearl will feed me."

"And what about me?" he forced a quiver into his voice. "I'm weak too."

She stopped abruptly and whirled to face him. "Are you okay?" She studied him from head to toe. "You look fine."

"I'm exhausted, even after food and a nap. I can only imagine how you must feel." He paused to find the right words. "Look, I was wrong. I apologize. After what I saw and experienced this morning, magic is real. Now, let me feed you, or I'll follow you home to make sure you're safe." He'd probably do that anyway after what they'd been through.

"Are you serious?" She rolled her eyes. "Fine. Let's eat. I'll meet you at Lloyd's Bar."

"At eleven in the morning?"

"Not to drink, for a double patty, bacon, mushroom, cheeseburger with sweet potato fries and onion rings. Lloyd makes the best burger in town, bar none." Her laughter rang out down the hospital corridor. "Don't look so shocked. I worked up an appetite."

He bowed low and gestured for her to lead the way. "I'll meet you there. It's not far from the bookstore, so I'll park there and walk over.

Don't order without me." He shook his finger at her. "Don't even think of skipping out on me."

"What? Are you afraid of being stood up? Is that normal for you?" she teased.

"First, this isn't a date. It's a thank-you lunch. Second, yes, it has happened to me, more often than I'd like to admit."

"That's a story I have to hear. I'll meet you there, but only because I want details."

He walked her to her car and made sure she was inside it safely. He recognized her exhaustion from the slow, overly cautious way she placed each step. She shouldn't have been at the hospital; she should have been at home resting. Once she'd pulled away; he walked the short distance to his car and headed for the bookstore.

It was four blocks from the store to the bar. Halfway there, he realized he'd made a mistake. He was more worn out than he thought he was and should have driven. There was a bench outside a shop called The Gift Box. He'd rest for a few seconds and carry on. Seated sideways on the bench, he noticed a tiny figurine in the window. About four inches tall, it featured a witch and an angel dancing hand in hand, their feet surrounded by flowers.

Hyacinth, Cynth, he corrected himself, Cynth would love it. Standing carefully, he went inside and purchased it. Thankful for the complimentary chocolates they had on the counter, which gave him a boost of energy, he made his way to the bar.

"That took a while," Cynth greeted Earl when he finally arrived. "Are you okay?"

"I should have driven straight here. I had to stop and rest on the way. How long does this exhaustion last?" He slid into the booth across from her and slipped out of his jacket, letting it fall to the bench behind him.

"You'll be fine by tomorrow. Take it easy for the rest of the day. I should have warned you. I'm sorry, I forgot."

"You did have a lot on your mind." He placed a bag on the table. "It was lucky that I stopped to rest outside The Gift Box. I saw this. Consider it a thank you for saving Anna's life."

"I don't deserve a thank you. If I had insisted on Meri going to the hospital when her labor went long, Anna would have been fine." It was tough when hindsight showed you should have acted differently. If she had gone with her gut and called an ambulance, there wouldn't have been an issue.

"You can't change what happened, and I know my sister is stubborn. She'd have resisted leaving." He nudged the package toward her. "Open it. You deserve it."

Suddenly, their relationship had gone from awkward, bordering on hostile, to friendly and forgiving. The shift left an uncomfortable ache in her stomach. Stress changed people. She understood that. But Earl's abrupt transformation was throwing her off balance. She wanted to believe in it but doubted it would last.

She took the small gold paper bag and opened it. She pulled out the delicate figurine. "Oh! It's adorable. Look at them." The angel started at the top as pure white and the witch deepest black; they morphed slowly from monochrome, through pastels, to full color by their ankles. It was as if the figures came together to brighten their world. "Thank you so much. I love it." She clutched the figure to her chest. It was whimsical and perfect. "Thank you so much."

"I've never seen anything like it," he said. "But when I saw it, I thought of you." He paused. "You might call yourself Wiccan, or a witch, but you're the angel that saved my niece. I'm glad you like it."

"Like it? It's wonderful. I love it." She got up and rounded the end of the table to give him an enormous hug. "Thank you." She blinked away a tear at the incredibly touching gesture.

"Anything I should know here?"

She spun toward the voice. "Mayor Quinton, hi." As always, the major was wearing wild prints that would look ridiculous on anyone else, while they suited her perfectly.

"I never thought I'd see the day you two were speaking to each other." She chuckled. "You've been avoiding each other for years. This is wonderful."

"Nothing to see here," Hyacinth declared. "I was just thanking Earl for this lovely gift. He gave it to me as a thank you for delivering his niece." She slipped behind the brightly clothed mayor and eased back into her seat, sliding away in so there was room for the major.

"How are mom and baby doing?" She sat down. "I won't be staying. But fill me in." She looked back and forth between Hyacinth and Earl. Mayor Quinton was magical, though the general town populace didn't know that. She was eager to have her magical and mundane constituents get along. Being up on local gossip and town happenings was important to her, and she made it her purpose to know everything about her constituents. Her philosophy had to be working because she'd been in office, virtually uncontested, for years.

Hyacinth looked at Earl. It wasn't her place to share any updates about his family. Even to the mayor.

"They're doing great. There was a moment of worry, but Cynth pulled baby Anna through. They're fine now." The gratitude in his voice filled Hyacinth with pride. Moments like this were why she'd chosen this career. Getting along with Earl, no matter how temporary it might turn out to be, was a blessing.

"That's wonderful. You two have a pleasant lunch and I'll see you both later. Tell Meri congratulations from me. I'll visit once she's home." She winked at Hyacinth and slid out of the booth. "Later."

She was gone before either Hyacinth or Earl could reply. Their server stepped into the space she'd vacated. "Earl, Cynth. Nice to see you both," Vienna, Lloyd's wife and number one server greeted them. "What can I get you?" She raised her eyebrow and the coffeepot in her hand in question.

"Oh, yes," Hyacinth exclaimed with a grateful sigh. "Coffee, please. Lots of it. Can I get water, and a menu as well?"

"Double that, please," Earl chimed in.

Lloyd's was as popular for breakfast and lunch as it was for evening activities like dancing and karaoke. Because of this, they kept coffee mugs on the tables until early afternoon. Vienna filled their mugs and chirped, "I'll be right back with menus." It took her less than thirty seconds to return and slide menus onto the table. "Take your time, I'll be back in five."

Despite knowing what she wanted, Hyacinth read the short menu, just in case something else of interest popped up. She debated the prime rib sandwich but went with her first choice of a loaded burger. She'd been dreaming of it for weeks. The double patty treat wasn't something she indulged in very often. But exhaustion and a need to refuel made it her number-one choice. She might even have the triple-decker chocolate brownie sundae for dessert.

Neither of them said anything for a long time after they placed their orders. She was content to be near Earl without fearing she'd set him off. He didn't have a temper, but before they worked together on baby Anna, he had zero tolerance for anything magical.

Finally, it was either talk or put her head back and fall asleep. "So, how are things at the bookstore?" she asked, doing her best to make it sound like a casual inquiry rather than a desperate need to delve into his life.

He looked surprised by the question. "Good. Very well. I've opened an online shop. I'm no Amazon or Indigo, but I do okay. Especially in used books. I started dealing in used books to help out the seniors at Athena's."

Athena's was a privately run senior care center. They had apartments for independent seniors who wanted to live in a close-knit community with staff who checked up on them regularly. Most of the residents were close to the poverty line and barely making ends meet.

"I donate a lot of books to Athena's library," Hyacinth said. "What prompted you to start taking used books in?"

He chuckled. "Honestly? A couple of the ladies came to me with the idea of trading several old books for new ones. I resisted at first. But the more I thought about it, the more I realized I could make it work. There's a big market for used books, both online, and with vacationers who don't want to spend a fortune on a holiday read." He sipped his coffee. "Initially, it was slow. I didn't advertise. I still don't. But it has sure picked up."

"That's awesome. What sells best?"

For a second, she could have sworn he blushed. He ducked his head and mumbled an answer.

"Did you say paranormal romance?" She chuckled at the irony.

"Yes." He sighed. "Give the people what they want. I guess. Those old gals love their witches. Who am I to deny them?"

"You know what, Earl? I'm impressed with your open-mindedness." She really was. There was a time when he wouldn't have even considered those books.

"In the interest of honesty..."

"And you always try to be honest. That was one of the things I loved about you." She winced at using the L-word aloud.

"Honestly," he continued, as if she hadn't stuck her foot in her mouth. "It was strictly a business decision. If they couldn't get the books from me, they weren't going to read something else, they'd buy elsewhere instead. It's pretty hypocritical of me, but it made good business sense." He shrugged. "And I have to admit that none of the ladies buying them have gone over to the dark side. They're still as sweet as ever."

She knew he didn't mean that as rudely as it came out. He was trying to have an open mind. Back in the day, he'd been open to most things, except magic. It was nice to see that, over time, he'd softened.

"Mrs. Franks is probably the sweetest woman I've ever met," Hyacinth said, glad they had something to talk about.

"Isn't she though? And Miss Mary is a pip. I can't believe she used to be the toughest teacher in the school."

They fell into an easy discussion about the ladies in the center and their quilting bees, bake sales, and idiosyncrasies. It was easy to see that Earl shared her fondness for the elderly women.

An icy wind blew in through the doorway when a short, red-haired woman entered. Hyacinth froze. She shouldn't be able to feel the wind this far from the door, and it was quite warm outside. Her fork dropped from her lifeless fingers and clattered to the table as she stared at the lone woman. Her aura was a swirling mass of darkness.

"Shit," she mumbled without meaning to.

"What?" Earl turned to follow her gaze. "Do you know her?"

"No. It's nothing. Just a shiver. Ya, a shiver. You know how you get those random shivers when you're tired?"

"Yes?" He sounded doubtful.

"I guess I'm more tired than I thought. We've been talking for a long time. I ate all that food, burger, fries, and rings. Then I ate cake.

I should be fueled up. I guess I need a nap." Words rushed out of her as she attempted to cover her sudden unease from the newcomer.

Whoever she was, Hyacinth had never seen her before. She radiated darkness. Either the stranger was evil, or she was controlled by evil. Hyacinth worked to hide her shivers and trepidation. Even Keres, the first man to attack her family, hadn't radiated evil and darkness like this. It rolled off her in waves.

"It was nice talking to you, Earl. But I should get home." She needed to warn her family. They'd been expecting another person to show up, looking for the talisman that had caused their family so much trouble already. They just hadn't expected it to be so soon.

She forced herself to pause. Maybe she was jumping to conclusions. Just because Keres and his son Matt Brown had been seeking the talisman, it didn't mean this woman was. There were dark witches and wizards in town. They weren't after the family or the missing talisman. Just because this woman's aura was off, it didn't mean she was a threat.

Still, she couldn't shake the unease washing over her in icy waves. She shivered again.

"Come on, let's get you home." Earl dropped some money on the table.

"I can pay for my lunch," she protested weakly, stumbling to her feet. Wow, she really was tired.

"We'll fight over it later. I'll drive you home. We'll make arrangements to get your car later." His tone was firm and forceful and strangely comforting.

Chapter Four

E arl held Hyacinth's elbow as they exited the bar into the bright autumn sunshine. He'd dropped all his cash on the table, hoping it was enough for the bill. If not, Lloyd would let him know. He wasn't worried about it. What he was worried about was Hyacinth. She'd been okay until she started shivering.

As they walked slowly to his car, he reviewed the moment she changed from okay to stressed. "What's really up?" he asked. "That woman came in and you went pale. Who is she?"

"I'm fine." She stumbled over a small dip in the sidewalk.

"Yeah," he said sarcastically. "I can see that. Don't lie to me, Hyacinth. I thought we were becoming friends again. Friends don't lie to friends." He still wasn't fully comfortable around her, but with his admittedly grudging acceptance of magic, most of his fear had fled. It seemed that seeing truly was believing.

"Okay. Fine," she snapped, glaring at him. "She was evil. I could see it. I could feel it. And my family has been through a lot of shit in the past few months. Maybe she's involved. Maybe she's not. But she literally made my skin crawl." She fumbled her keys out of her backpack-style purse.

They rounded the hood of her SUV; he opened the passenger door and helped her inside. "Can you get your seatbelt?" He closed the Explorer's door gently when she glared at him. As he walked to the driver's side he mumbled. "She's as stubborn as she always was." It wasn't true. She'd stood firm on a few things, but as a rule, Hyacinth was pretty easygoing. That character trait was probably part of her success as a midwife. As soon as he climbed in, he was assaulted by her familiar scent, the one that hadn't changed since high school, but had somehow matured along with Hyacinth. Melancholy washed over him, along with the scent of lavender.

He pulled out of Lloyd's parking lot after she buckled up. He drove toward the outskirts of town and after several blocks, he asked the question that was nagging in the back of his mind. Things he'd wanted to know for months.

"What really happened to that guy who died on your land? And to the guy who was burned?" There were a million rumors about the middle-of-the-night incident that happened last spring.

"You don't want to know," she mumbled and leaned back and closed her eyes. Her arms wrapped around her middle, a sure sign she was closing him out.

"Maybe I don't want to know, but I think, if we're going to continue seeing each other, that I need to know." Shoot. He hadn't meant to say that aloud. He was barely even considering the idea of seeing more of her. Being with her felt right.

She opened her eyes and glared at him. "Just like that, you assume we're going to start seeing each other?"

She had a point.

"I worded that poorly. Hyacinth, I find myself rethinking my past opinions. Today, I really enjoyed your company and would like to see you again. If you are agreeable. And, if so, I think that I deserve to know what happened."

"That's a lot of assumptions." She fiddled with the silver crescent moon necklace she'd worn as long as he'd known her. She did that a lot when she was thinking.

"True." He kept his answer simple. Hyacinth tended to think before she spoke. Still feeling slightly fuzzy-headed, he drove carefully toward her family's rural property. He waited for her to gather her thoughts and resisted the urge to push her to a decision.

"I'm open to friendship with you," she whispered after a very long pause.

He risked a glance at her. Her eyes were closed and a slight frown puckered her brows. Either from the morning's stress, the strange woman they had encountered, or his desire to reopen their friendship. Okay, relationship. Or whatever it was.

"After a decade of being sworn enemies, I'm not sure I'm ready for more than friendship. In truth," she continued, "even friendship is questionable at this point." She sighed. "You hurt me badly. We were kids, and I scared you by telling you about a world you didn't believe existed."

"I believe now."

"Yeah, well, being slapped in the face by something usually wakes you up." Her laugh was dry and without humor. "I'm not sure how much I trust you."

"Reasonable. Hyacinth, being with you today, reminded me how much I've missed you and enjoy being with you. There's a possibility for friendship and seeing where it goes. Seeing what you did with Anna today and the skills that you and Meri share makes me want to learn more and I will try to keep an open mind."

"But you have questions."

"So many questions." It was his turn for a humorless laugh.

"The man who was burned was Keres. He's a dark magician. He killed the man who was with him. Keres was magically burned by my sister Amber when he was trying to kill us all. Hazel nearly died. It was the only way to survive. It was, quite literally, our lives or his."

He felt the blood drain from his face. He didn't know what he thought happened, but it wasn't murder. *Magically burned? Could one of them control fire? Seriously?*

"Before you get all judgy, he was trying to kill us. We only did what we had to do to survive. It was self-defense. We were cleared in a magical court. Even the local police didn't press charges. Keres is alive in a metaphysical prison. He's been healed, though I understand he does have some scars. He's there for life."

"Jesus." He didn't swear often and the single word was more prayer than cuss.

"Remember when the falls blew up and killed all those people? That was Keres. Hazel nearly died fighting Keres's son, Matt Brown."

"Why?" He had a million questions. It was all he could do not to pull over, and demand answers. Instead, he drove the last mile and turned into her family's driveway.

"They said we stole something from their family. Not us, our ancestors. We didn't. He thinks we have some *magical talisman.* Ever since the accusation, we've been searching for the alleged item, and for any references our old family documents might have about it. So far, we've got nothing. Whatever it is, Keres wanted it and was prepared to kill us all to get it."

"That's terrible. And the woman in the bar? How does she fit into all of this?" He slowed for the last turn. Ahead, enormous wrought-iron gates barred the driveway. They were almost seven feet tall and covered with ornate, stylized flowers. They opened slowly as the vehicle approached. What good were gates that opened without help? Did they have a remote? He didn't see the control box. Magic? His mind shied away from the idea of magic gates.

"There is reason to believe that other people might know about the talisman. We don't have it, but if Keres and Brown thought we do, others could have come to the same conclusion. She could be here for it, whatever it is."

"Crap. That doesn't sound good." He glanced in the rearview mirror and the gates closed behind them. He drove down the long driveway. Ahead, he could see Hyacinth's grandmother, Pearl, and one of Hyacinth's sisters waiting on the enormous front porch.

"Still want to be friends?" There was the barest hint of vulnerability in her voice.

He stopped the SUV partway up the driveway before answering. "Yes?" He couldn't keep his doubt from his voice. They were a pair; both wary and uncertain of changing the long-held status quo between them. Then there was the whole talisman thing and the danger it could bring.

"Don't sound so certain." She laughed lightly.

His heart stuttered. He had always loved her laugh. "I'm certain. It's just going to be..." he floundered for the right word, "an adjustment."

"True enough, but we were friends before, and I think, I hope, we can be again."

Yeah, but could he keep from falling for her? It had taken years to recover from their breakup. It was five years before he dated and even longer before he trusted another woman. All the while, despite his confused feelings for Cynth and keeping himself away from her, he could not stop watching her. He knew who her friends were, what she liked to do, and how amazingly successful she was as a midwife. He practically knew everything about her.

No matter how much their breakup had hurt him, he still felt something for her, and until this moment, had hated himself for being trapped in time by his heart. He had dated, he'd even been in one serious relationship which he'd broken off because if he was being honest with himself, he didn't love the woman as much as she deserved to be loved. Part of his heart had always belonged to Hyacinth.

Maybe rekindling their friendship was a mistake.

If so, it was one he was cautiously willing to make.

He stuck out his hand. "Friends?" he asked.

"Sure thing." They shook on the deal. He held tight, loving the soft feel of her hand within his grasp. "Now, Gramma Pearl and Lazuli will have questions, and you won't get out of here without answering them. Do me a favor and don't let them intimidate you, okay?"

"No worries. I remember them well, plus I see them around town, and in the bookstore, all the time. I can handle this." *At least I think I can.* He pulled forward and parked at the top of the driveway near the house.

The house was no less imposing than it had been a decade ago. Two stories tall, with dormer windows in the attic, it had octagonal towering turrets on either end. Flawless white woodwork was balanced with brick trim. A comfortable, welcoming blend of colonial and Victorian styling, it looked as if it had started as one and had been modified later. It was both elegant and imposing.

He climbed out and jogged around to Hyacinth's side before she even had her door open. He helped her out and offered his elbow as support to walk the short distance.

"Pearl, Lazuli. Nice to see you again."

Pearl frowned. She didn't like her granddaughters dating anyone, and he'd hurt Cynth badly. He hoped that time had mellowed her.

"Earl Cooper, what have you done to my granddaughter?"

Nope, not mellowed at all. "Pearl, I didn't do anything to her. She's weak from saving my sister's baby. We both are."

Pearl frowned, and Lazuli hurried down the stairs to throw an arm around Cynth's waist. "What does that mean?" Pearl demanded.

"Gramma Pearl, I-we had a very hard delivery. Baby Anna would have died if not for Earl. He helped me save her. Then he took me to lunch."

The frown deepened, and Earl thought, just for a second, that he could feel her displeasure like a physical touch. "Something happened at lunch," he offered. "A woman was there. She scared Hyacinth senseless. Plus, she's still weak, so I drove her home, where I knew she'd be safe."

They helped her up the stairs and he stood face to face with Pearl. Her stare bored into his soul. "I don't know the complete story of your past, or recent events. I just want to say one thing." He paused, as if waiting for permission, though he intended to speak his mind anyway.

"What is that?" Pearl crossed her arms over her chest and tapped one toe. The old gal had to be in her sixties, and she was one of the toughest people he had ever met. Heaven help anyone who messed with her family.

He swallowed down a lump of nerves. "I messed up. When Hyacinth told me she was magical, I freaked out. I didn't believe in magic, yet I feared it. It went against everything I believed. I can't understand how I could be a non-believer and afraid at the same time. It doesn't make sense, not even to me. Anyway. I freaked out and dumped her. It was a knee-jerk reaction."

His stomach rolled. He scraped a hand through his hair and searched for the right words. "I hurt her, and I'm sorry for that. Now, I know magic is real. I know it down to the tips of my toes and deep into my heart. My niece would have died without her magical help. I saw it.

I did what I was told, and I pushed my strength into Hyacinth. Don't ask me how I don't understand it. But it made me a true believer."

Pearl's glare eased slightly, but he wasn't finished yet.

"A woman came into Lloyd's. She came in on a draft of icy air, and Hyacinth went pale and started to shiver. There was something about this woman that scared her and freaked her out so I brought her home. To you. To safety."

"Thank you," Pearl said. She nodded as if her words were a benediction from the pope himself. Earl accepted the action for the acknowledgment that it was.

"We should get her inside. She needs rest, and maybe some of those teas she's always drinking." He cupped Hyacinth's elbow and helped her toward the front door. With Lazuli's help, they got her inside.

For a moment, as he crossed the threshold, he felt like he was stepping through an invisible barrier. He shook the idea off.

"Huh," Lazuli said. "It let you in. You must be okay."

"What?" He nearly stumbled because her words aligned with what he felt. "What let me in? Do you mean the house? Are you nuts?"

"Nope, not nuts. Our house, in fact our house and the land immediately surrounding it, are magically protected. If the house lets you step foot inside, you must have good intentions toward us. Of course, if your intentions change, you won't get back in later." She smirked.

"I'll keep that in mind." Of course, he wasn't certain he believed in a magical house, but he had felt...something, and after the morning he'd had, who was he to doubt her claims? "Where shall we put her?"

"Over here on the sofa. She can have tea and then sleep off her expenditure of magic without moving."

They struggled to get Hyacinth to the sofa. She was extremely weak and stumbled twice on the short walk. They got her seated and he sat beside her, holding her hands.

"Stay with her, I'll get tea." Pearl rushed past them toward the kitchen. It had been years since he was in their house. It looked exactly the same. Sure, the pictures were different, but it held the same comforting feel. Overfilled bookcases, candles, pictures. Much of the furniture was antique and in excellent condition.

"Thanks for getting me home," Hyacinth said, squeezing his hands lightly. "I might not have made it on my own. This is so weird. I'm not usually this tired."

"You probably should have come straight home after the delivery," Lazuli said.

"I had to clean up the delivery mess and check on baby Anna. It's what I do." She closed her eyes and shifted on the couch.

Earl stood and scooped her into her arms. She wasn't heavy, nor was she light. He twisted and set her back down with her back against the arm and her legs stretched out. Lazuli slipped a couple of couch cushions behind her and said, "You'll be more comfortable like this if you fall asleep. Good idea, Earl."

Lazuli grabbed his hand and yanked him to the far side of the room. "Tell me what happened," she whispered.

Quietly, he explained the non-event in the restaurant, finishing with, "She just went pale and shivery. She didn't look okay, though she said she was, so I brought her home."

"She was, no is, super weak. It's a good thing you drove." She patted his arm like you would a good dog. He banked a chuckle because he knew she didn't mean to be condescending.

"She can hear you," Hyacinth mumbled without moving. Her head was back and her eyes closed. Dark circles under her eyes highlighted her pallor.

"Why didn't you come home immediately?" Lazuli asked just as Pearl bustled in with a tea tray.

"Sit," Pearl looked between him and a chair. "You need tea too, and cookies."

"I just ate lunch." He sat in the chair she indicated with a brisk nod. "I'm not hungry."

"Perhaps not, but you need refueling. Explain everything to me. Start with the delivery." She thrust a china cup and saucer at him and set a plate of cookies on the end table. "Drink, eat."

He sipped the tea. It was heavily floral with a bitter aftertaste which was not quite hidden by the hint of honey. Instantly, he felt a rise in his energy. He stared at the cup and the women watching him and took another sip. He didn't bother to ask what was in the tea. For as long as he'd known Hyacinth, she'd preferred tea to any other beverage and usually carried her hand-crafted teas. He might not be comfortable with magic yet, but there was a lot of information out there about the healing power of herbs. After all, a lot of modern medicine came from herbs.

"I arrived after the delivery," he said after a moment of thought. "We were having coffee when something went wrong. We rushed into the bedroom. The baby was blue." His heart pounded at the memory. He could almost feel the panic of that moment. "Hyacinth grabbed the baby and checked her. She did chest compressions." He swallowed hard. "Cynth got paler and paler and told me to push my energy into her." He shuddered just thinking about it.

"I didn't know what she meant. but I have a decent imagination, so I imagined my energy was water. With my hands on her shoulders, I pushed it toward her. It seemed to help."

"Well done." Pearl smiled widely at him. "Especially for a non-magical."

"He might have magic and just be unaware. His sister has skills," Hyacinth mumbled. "I don't know why Anna faded. I searched her and didn't find anything beyond exhaustion. But her heart stopped. I don't understand it." She sipped her tea. Earl hadn't even seen her take the cup.

"I thought the doctor said it was the strain of delivery?" He glanced at all of them. Were they hiding something? "Was it something else?"

"All I'm saying is it was weird," Hyacinth said. She devoured a cookie and grabbed another one from the plate on her lap.

"Don't be dramatic," Pearl declared. "You'll freak the boy out. It was probably nothing."

"Probably," Hyacinth agreed.

In that second, he knew they lied. They had their doubts. This was all too weird for him. Their history, baby Anna's issues, and the woman in the restaurant. He ran everything over in his mind. They were hiding something. The question was, what? The only certainty was that if there was something, it was magical.

In a flash of decisiveness at odds with his exhaustion, he decided to let them keep their secret for now. But he would tell his sister that there was a possibility that something odd, and maybe magical, had happened to her firstborn child so she could guard against it.

How did you guard against the possibility of it being something and have no idea of what, if anything, it might be?

How did he go from being a non-believer in magic to certain that magic was causing issues in his world? It defied comprehension. His head was spinning, and it wasn't from the tea or the morning's events. Having your entire belief system shaken up was uncomfortable.

"I think we need to be careful about where we go. At least for the next little while," Pearl advised. "You too, Earl. Keep your eyes and ears open for anything weird."

Weirder than magical witches?

"I can do that." Of course, he had no idea what he was looking for. He'd have to do some internet searching.

"I can recommend a few books if you need advice," Pearl said as if she read his mind.

Mind reading wasn't real, was it? He remembered his parents and their crazy ability to anticipate each other's needs. His mother was particularly adept at anticipating his father's words and needs. Was that mind-reading? Or was it due to being married for a long time? His heart clenched. They'd died too young with so much unsaid. So much knowledge lost. What a dang shame, and not just because they left two teenagers behind without guidance.

"That would be nice, thank you. I have no idea where to start." He gave her his cell number and email. He finished his tea and with a thousand unformed questions raging in his mind, making his head hurt, he said goodbye to them all and had Lazuli drive him home.

Chapter Five

H yacinth woke with a kink in her neck. She wrinkled her nose at the bitter aroma of her pain-relief willow bark tea. Slowly, she opened her eyes. The massive headache she'd had earlier had dissipated to a dull ache, which was a major blessing. She barely remembered coming home, only that Earl had brought her and had come inside.

"Oh good," Pearl said, "you're awake. How are you feeling?"

"Better-more or less. I need to change and go see the baby. What time is it?" She swung her legs to the floor and was overcome with a wave of dizziness. "Shoot."

"Stay still. I'll call Dr. Carter. She'll check you over before you go running about. Anna is fine. I talked to Meri a few minutes ago. Hazel and Amber have taken her some amulets and wards to give protection while they are in the hospital."

"Good. What time is it?"

"Nine in the morning. You slept straight through supper and breakfast. You need to eat. I'll bring you something."

"I can come to the kitchen. I need something for this headache. Something fast."

"You know willow bark tea is the best for that." She pointed to the steaming mug on the end table. "But I'll get you some painkillers." Typically, unless they were desperate, her family preferred natural remedies to commercial ones. Occasionally, they made an exception. "Do you need help to stand?"

"I think I'm okay." Moving slowly, she eased to her feet. The room was stable. She was still weak and her head throbbed intolerably. "I think I'm dehydrated."

"I can fix that." Pearl took her by the elbow and walked her to their enormous kitchen table. She lowered the blinds in the alcove where the round, oak, eight-seat table sat. Within seconds, she slid a glass of water, two pain tablets, and a slice of cake in front of Hyacinth.

"Thanks, Gramma. Maybe I should eat something more nutritious first." The cake was tempting. Too tempting, but she needed something more substantial. The cake was perfect for that instant boost, but it had to come with protein and veggies for long-lasting benefits.

"Meatloaf, mashed potatoes, and a side of baked squash coming right up."

She'd been thinking more along the lines of eggs and toast, but she'd never complain if someone else was doing the cooking and there wasn't a better cook on earth than her grandmother. Pearl's biggest magical gift was her kitchen skills. She could cook anything and always infused her food with good wishes for health and healing. It wasn't overt magic like her sister Amber's ability to control fire, or Hazel's ability to control water and talk to ghosts, but it was impressive and often very useful.

She created the energy balls Hyacinth took to every call. Those were a combination of herbs, honey, protein, fat, and magic.

"Eat up. You'll want to be finished by the time the doctor gets here." She paused. "I've called in Pansy Irons to give you the once over."

The biggest downfall of Hyacinth's healing powers was that they couldn't be used to heal yourself. Healing took energy, and you couldn't use your own without succumbing to weakness. Then there was the whole rule of never using magic for personal gain…that always backfired. Like the time she'd cast a love spell on a guy she liked. He'd become so crazy obsessed that she had to have someone else unspell him before he did something to injure himself, or her. Caution was always in order with magic. She'd learned that lesson the hard way.

"I don't need Pansy. I'm fine." *She was fine, wasn't she?*

"As long as you live in my house, you'll follow my rules, young lady." Pearl slammed her stirring spoon on the counter and stood with her hands on her hips, glaring at Hyacinth. "Do you understand me?"

"Gramma Pearl, I am twenty-seven years old. I am a grown woman." Despite her grumbling, she fully intended to let Pansy look at her. She was relatively certain she was just exhausted, but a second set of eyes never hurt.

Her sixty-five-year-old grandmother said nothing, she just gave her 'the look', and waited for a response.

"Fine. She can check me over, but I don't have to like it." Pearl turned back to the stove, but not before Hyacinth caught the barest hint of a triumphant smile. She bit back her own grin. Sometimes giving in was a total win!

She devoured her meal, her dessert, and a couple of cookies before pouring herself a cup of energy boost tea. Her sister Hazel had concocted the recipe with Gramma Pearl. It had a light, fruity taste. They grew all the herbs and most of the berries in the family greenhouses. The pineapple and kiwi came from a reputable, organic wholesaler.

The teas were concocted from old family recipes. When they began selling the teas, they had their kitchen upgraded to a commercial one and underwent yearly inspections like any other food vendor.

She had barely finished when the front bell chimed. It must be her medical help. Few people got past the magical gates of their land unless a family member accompanied them. Dr. Carter and Pansy were among those few people. Occasionally, for their summer and winter solstice celebrations and special parties, the family left the gates open. Earl had only been granted access because he was with her.

She moved to the living room when her grandmother went to open the door and welcome their guests.

"Hyacinth," the doctor greeted her. "How are you feeling? I hear there has been an incident." She pulled out her stethoscope. The doctor was in her mid-thirties and while she wasn't magical, she was known and trusted within the magic community. She was the mundane child of magical parents. Magic wasn't always passed down and while some of it could be learned, the doctor chose to focus her attention on being a conventional family physician.

She gave Hyacinth a quick once-over and declared her fit and ready to go. "Rest more, and don't expend yourself so much next time."

"If I hadn't, baby Anna would have died. I was lucky Earl was there to help."

"Still, you're no good to your other clients if you're off work because you overdid it." She waved her hand. "I get it. You're a healer, it's what we do and who we are. Sometimes we give more than we should. I've lost patients, and I know how it feels. At the time, I would have given my life for theirs."

The words, simple though they were, helped her process her fears about being inadequate. In the future, she'd be more adamant when recommending an ambulance. When push came to shove, she needed to remember that she was the medical expert, and in an emergency, she had the final say. Even if it meant a disappointed patient.

"Hearing you say that is reassuring. I was stuck and scared. Thank the Goddess that Earl was there to help out."

"Meri and baby Anna were blessed for sure," Pansy said from a chair on the other side of the room where she'd taken a seat when she came in. When Dr. Carter stepped away, she rose and took her place in front of Hyacinth.

"You know how this works, but just to keep this professional, I'll give you my usual explanation. I'm going to run my hands over your body, barely touching you. I'm feeling for dark spots, illness, and toxins. Basically, I'm looking for anything that isn't right. I'm using my mind, my heart, and my intuition to examine you. It won't hurt. You'll barely feel anything. I will examine your head for damage and darkness, but I will not, and cannot, read your mind or your thoughts. Are you okay with an examination?"

When she examined her patients, she used a similar explanation. Though she knew what was going to happen, the words were strangely comforting. She didn't need an examination; she was fine, but she agreed anyway. It would keep her grandmother off her back.

Pansy rubbed her palms together as if she was warming her hands. She was building energy to read Hyacinth with. She ran them gently over Hyacinth, concentrating on her heart and lungs, but not missing a single part of her. Once the body exam was complete, she rubbed her hands together again and threaded them into Hyacinth's tangled hair until they rested as close as possible to her scalp. After a moment of intense concentration, she stood back with a frown.

"What?" Hyacinth blurted.

"I don't know. It's weird. Your body is fine."

"But? I hear a but." She struggled to keep fear from her voice.

"But there's an...an I don't know what, in your brain. It's not a shadow. It's not an illness." She wrinkled her lips in concentration. "It's like the dark residue that's left behind after someone casts dark magic. It's like someone brushed across your brain but didn't really touch anything."

What the hell did that mean?

"Are you saying someone messed with my brain?" She jerked to her feet and paced the room. "I have guards up. I'd have noticed if someone was in there messing around."

"Maybe not. I don't think they did anything except maybe take a quick peek. Perhaps accidentally. Maybe they don't know they can read minds?" She sounded as confused as Hyacinth felt.

"Is that even possible? For someone to read minds and not know they can?" she asked.

"Of course it is," Pearl said. "People who are unaware of, or don't believe in, magic would likely think they were just very empathetic. Or believe they just had a talent for reading people. I dated a man once when I was young. He didn't believe in magic, and I didn't fill him in. People were less accepting back then. He had a bit of talent for reading people's emotions, and on occasion, their thoughts. He had no idea he was magic."

"That's incredible. But I guess it makes sense. In a weird way. The witch trials were hundreds of years ago. People would have hidden their abilities or just stopped using them altogether. Abilities and knowledge are easily lost. If the fear was great enough, people would stop all magic and never discuss it. Tragic in a sense, but understandable." Hyacinth mourned for those who had lost their connection to their roots.

"If this has anything to do with the woman I saw at Lloyd's, it was no accident. She had a totally evil vibe about her. Zero color to her aura. It was pure black. She reeked of negativity. She reminded me of those evil characters you see in bad movies. You know, the ones who walk by and plants die. She came in on a rush of cold air and chilled me to my soul. It was hot yesterday. Shorts and tank top weather. She came in on a chill. She made the air-conditioned bar feel cold. Even Earl shivered, though he never admitted to feeling anything."

"At the risk of jumping to conclusions, maybe we need to put out a warning to local magicals," Pearl suggested. "Let them know what to watch for. Everyone knows about what happened with Brown and Keres already. Forewarned is forearmed."

Dr. Carter frowned. "I hate to accuse someone without cause. I suggest you take it to the council and see what they say. But just for interest, and because I already know what happened, what did she look like?"

"She's short, about five-three maybe. Poker straight red hair. Very thin, but at the same time she looked strong. I couldn't see her eyes at all. She wore jeans and a black leather jacket." She shrugged. There wasn't much else to say. "I didn't get a good look at her face, but I'd say she's about thirty, maybe forty?"

"That's a start," Pansy said thoughtfully. "There aren't many red-headed women in Three Moon Falls."

"I'll call Leticia," Pearl said. Leticia Stone was head of the police department and a member of the Witch's Council as well as a voodoo priestess. She had skills unlike anyone Hyacinth had ever met.

She went to the kitchen to make the call, leaving the doctor and Pansy with Hyacinth.

"I think you should probably ground yourself," Pansy suggested. "You're an earth witch. Probably the most beneficial thing for you right now is to get in the dirt. Literally."

"I was just thinking that. I need to garden. Burying my hands in the earth will refuel me more than anything else." It was a wonder she hadn't thought of it earlier. When Amber had been attacked by Keres,

Hyacinth had helped her heal. She had expended so much energy she'd had to bury her hands in the earth to recoup the losses. Food alone would not have been enough.

Years ago, she'd done a healing. Immediately after, to thank her, her patient had brought her a potted plant. Sadly, she'd sucked enough energy from the soil and plant that it had died. It had shocked her to her core. That trauma had stayed with her, and it was odd that she'd completely forgotten to ground herself properly yesterday.

Life was about balance, and after Keres had sullied Amber's mind, Hyacinth had overdone her magic to save her sister. After scorching the earth to recover her balance, she'd planted several new plants and nurtured them to the best possible health. She gave back what she'd taken.

Today, she'd work in the greenhouses. Simple contact would be enough, she wouldn't need to destroy life to regain her strength.

Each of them had different skills and different ways to recoup their lost strength. Hazel was a water witch, she could control its flow, and even make it rain if the situation was dire enough. Despite being afraid of deep water, simply being in the water, like a pool, tub, or shower was strengthening for her.

Lazuli was an air witch. Wide open spaces and working with wood refueled her; though none of them truly understood why wood was her sanity and health rebuilder.

Amber controlled fire. Nature was her safe space. Working with candles, stones, and herbs rebuilt her when she felt depleted.

As for Gramma Pearl, she was a kitchen witch. The simple act of cooking for others was all she needed.

They had a mixed bag of skills. Some crossed over and some did not. Pearl could do a bit of everything, but she lacked extra strength in any skill.

"I guess I'll head out to the greenhouses," Hyacinth said after a moment of random thoughts. "The earth will do me good."

She said goodbye to their guests and thanked them for coming out to check on her. Once they were gone, she stood in the center of the room, letting the magic of the house flow into her pores. Generations of Hawk women had lived and practiced magic in this very room. That magic had seeped right into the house and ground, giving them their own magic. Eyes closed, feet planted firmly, she opened herself to the magic surrounding her.

She'd grown up in this house, lived here since birth, and sometimes forgot the blessing that the seeped-in magic truly was. She blocked out the sound of Pearl on the telephone, then of her puttering in the kitchen. The sounds were still there; she had taught herself to ignore them. Beginning to ground herself, she stood in meditation, focusing on nothing but the magic swirling around her.

Somewhat refreshed, she opened her eyes, and after a brief chat with Pearl, headed outside toward the greenhouses. She detoured past them and wandered through their orchard, her naked feet enjoying the feel of the grass beneath her feet. She studied the apple and plum trees before moving through their nut grove. Satisfied that all was well, she entered the greenhouse through the far end.

It wasn't just one greenhouse, though, from the road, that was all you could see. There were three seventy-five-foot glass enclosures put together in a U shape. Outside, in the protected space between them, were her late great-grandmother's rose bushes.

Inside, she walked past rows of herbs, stroking their leaves. She crushed a small bit of thyme between her fingers, enjoying its savory scent. This, this right here, was her happy place. It didn't have the same rush as delivering a baby and listening to its first cry, but it was special, and much more healing and relaxing.

She sat on the floor, her back against a raised bed of tomato plants, and reached up over her shoulders to drop her hands into the earth housing them. Insects buzzed around her. Flies and bees went about their business. Outside, a blue jay squawked and robins called to each other. Slowly, tension slipped from her shoulders.

She did nothing but sit there, soaking up the earth's goodness for at least half an hour. Then, she rose and pulled weeds and trimmed dead or damaged leaves from several plants.

Everything looked wonderful and healthy. The fear of the morning slipped from her mind as she gave in to the beauty around her. Feeling better, she headed to town to see her sister, Amber, at the family's shop, Four Seasons Metaphysical.

Chapter Six

Hyacinth parked in the back, behind the shop, and knocked on the screen door. Amber kept the door latched to keep out unwanted visitors. She hoped Amber would be quick. It was chilly in the shade of the building.

Sasha, the shop cat, strolled up to the door and meowed a greeting.

"Sasha, how are you?"

"Good as I could be." It never ceased to astound her that this small gray cat with the white sash across her chest could talk. She'd just showed up one day and started talking to Kody, Amber's fiancé. Of course, back then, he'd been their sworn enemy. Things sure changed in a hurry sometimes. "I'm thinking you should take me to the house for a visit."

"Indeed?"

"I can hardly spend my entire life stuck here in the shop, now can I?" She licked a paw dismissively.

"Can't you walk through walls?" She asked as approaching foot-steps told her that her sister had heard the knock.

"I can. When I choose to. But the house is miles away and you have never taken me there."

"You are a petulant beast."

"Wouldn't you be if they ripped your babies from your arms and gave them to strangers?" Sasha sat down and looked away as if to say, *I'm finished speaking with you.*

Hyacinth laughed.

"Don't be so melodramatic," Amber chided as she crossed the staff work area to unlatch the door. "You approved every one of those families. Come in, Cynth. How are you feeling? Any better? You look better."

"I'm fine now. Much refreshed. But we need to refresh the wards in here." She explained her weird encounter at Lloyd's and ended by saying. "I don't know if what I felt was real or not. It sure seemed real. I don't know who she is or what she wants, if anything. I hate jumping to conclusions, but in this case, I can't help myself. She may not be associated with Keres, but if word of the talisman has gotten out, we could be in danger."

"So, we ward up our homes and the shop, and find that damned talisman before someone else does." Amber twisted her long blonde hair into a rope and smoothed her floaty skirt. "I guess it's time to get to work."

Standing side by side, they studied the back shelves of the shop. "We'll need some dried honeysuckle and sage for sure." Amber declared.

"Maybe bound to wreaths of willow and birch?" She snapped her fingers. "Oh, what about some mountain ash? I've got a collection of trimmings from the ones in our yard. Since it's the North American cousin of the sacred rowan tree, it's ideal for wards.

"Perfect. We can make them pretty with dried flowers and different shades of blue ribbon. Maybe even a bit of black ribbon. Blue for protection and black to absorb negativity."

Hyacinth zipped home and returned with their grandmother and a cluster of mountain ash branches. "Hey, I forgot I had these," She held up a jar filled with clusters of dried berries from the tree she'd trimmed. "We can add these too."

A short time later, their sister Hazel who worked at Get Growing Greenhouses popped in. "Hi, I heard you were up and about. I thought I'd come to check on you."

"Don't you have bookkeeping to do?" Hyacinth groaned. She appreciated that everyone was concerned about her, but at the same time, she wished they'd stop making a fuss.

"Lucky for me, my boss thinks I'm amazing." Hazel had fallen for her boss, Dennis. They weren't married yet, but it wouldn't be long. "I'll make up the time later. It's not like it's month end or anything."

Hazel wiggled in at the end of the worktable and picked up some willow and ash branches, pausing to inhale their distinctive woodsy scents. It was only minutes before she had them tied into a double-ended fan shape. She passed it to Pearl for decorating. "Cynth, since you're on good terms with Earl now, do you think you could go over and talk to him about adding the bookstore to the ghost tour? I've got four other places lined up, including the old Walker mansion. If he signed on, we'd pay him a cut, and all he'd have to do is have one of his staff talk about the resident ghost."

"I don't know, I think that would be pushing my luck. We've only been speaking since we saved Anna."

"Come on," Amber begged. "Do it for the business." The family owned the shop together and everyone contributed what they could from their skillsets, though Amber was in charge.

Hyacinth didn't want to risk her burgeoning friendship. She'd always cared for Earl, even when she hated him for spurning her for her beliefs and heritage. Now that they were speaking, she didn't want to do anything to mess it up. She considered the request. In the end, if he was going to have an issue with her beliefs, she might as well know now, before she invested time in a friendship, and before she lost her heart to him again.

"I guess I could do that. I don't think he'll go for it." Before she realized what was happening, she was out the door and on her way down the street.

She paused outside the bookstore, looking in through the display window. Worry and fear tightened her chest. She closed her eyes and asked the universe for strength to tackle meeting him again.

"Hyacinth, what are you doing here?" Earl's friendly voice startled her back to the moment.

She spun around to look at him. "Um. I came to see you."

"Come inside. I just went to grab a muffin." He raised a white bakery bag. "I bought two, I'll share. I might even be able to scrounge up a cup of tea."

"I'd take coffee if you have it." She grinned. It was so nice to see him and not feel she had to turn and walk away.

"Coffee I can do." He opened the door and used the bag to gesture her ahead of him.

"What about a latte?"

"Have you succumbed to the dark lure of coffee completely?" he teased as they wandered between rows of shelves stuffed with books.

"Only occasionally. I find I'm not quite myself yet and could use the energy boost."

"That I understand. I've eaten more in the last two days than I do in a week. Please tell me that will stop before I weigh a thousand pounds." His light laugh rang off the open beam rafters. "Jeri, I'll be in the staff room with Hyacinth if you need anything," he called to his assistant manager. At fifty-something, she'd worked at the store longer than he had. She'd been his parents' right-hand woman since he was a kid.

Jeri popped her head around the end of the aisle they were walking down. "Hi, Cynth."

"Good to see you, Jeri." They embraced briefly. Jeri was a close friend of her grandmother and a frequent visitor to their new shop. "Amber said to tell you that the raspberry cream candles are back in stock. She's put half a dozen aside for you."

"Thank her for me. I'll be over later today." She smiled and walked away.

"I didn't know you knew Jeri." He led her into the staff area and set the bag of muffins on the round bar-type table.

"Are you kidding? I grew up here, just like you did. Just because I was home-schooled through elementary doesn't mean I never met people. She worked here when I used to come visit when you were working." She chuckled. And after their breakup, when she knew he wouldn't be around.

"Right. Sometimes she's such a part of my world I almost forget about her."

"I'm sure she'd love to hear that," she quipped. "Now, how about that coffee?" Then, when he was comfortable, she'd broach the subject of ghosts.

"Regular latte, vanilla, or pumpkin spice?" He mock shuddered as he slipped an espresso pod into the coffeepot. "It won't be coffee shop style, but it will be drinkable."

"How about pumpkin spice with a shot of vanilla?" She glanced at the counter beside the coffeepot where about a dozen bottles of coffee syrups stood in a neat row. "Someone likes fancy coffee."

"Jeri. Though sometimes I use a shot of flavor instead of sugar." He shrugged. "Variety is the spice of life." He didn't say anything while the brewer ran. After making two coffees he returned to the table and set one in front of her and made another trip for plates and knives and a dish of butter. "Help yourself."

They talked about nothing for a few minutes. Just as she worked up the courage to ask about the ghost tour, he spoke. "Meri says I need to buy wards from your shop and hang them up in here." His brows pinched together, and he fiddled with the knife he'd used to butter his bran muffin.

"Sure. If you give me a budget, I can work something up for you, maybe even today."

"I researched wards, but I don't get it. How can a bunch of sticks and herbs do anything?"

"Honestly, I don't know myself. I was raised to believe in magic. I've seen it with my own eyes. It's about the interconnectedness of everything on the planet. Think of making a ward as sending out a prayer. You build the ward and while doing so, you concentrate on what you want it to do, in this case, deter people with bad intentions from entering your shop. The energy you put into thinking about it and making it is sent out into the universe and lingers as protection."

"That's nuts. But if it will make Meri feel safe, I'll do it."

"Come on, Earl. You pushed your strength into me. That's a type of magic. Why can't I push my strength and intentions into something that hangs on the wall? Think of it as a prayer, with props." How many people had she said that to over the years? Dozens? Hundreds?

"So, if I wanted to make one myself, could I pray to God while doing it?" He sounded skeptical.

"Sure. There are a lot of Christian witches. They believe the magic within the universe is another aspect of God's divinity. If he created the universe and everything in it, why couldn't you tap into that for your purposes?"

He frowned so hard she thought he was going to get upset. She waited breathlessly for the explosion. Instead, he sighed.

"It's going to take me a while to come to grips with this." He blew on his coffee and took a sip. "Can everyone do everything? Can your sisters do what we did?"

"Yes, and no. They can share their energy. But their healing abilities aren't strong. They each have different strengths. Mine is healing and working with plants. I'm an earth witch. I work with and can, to a limited extent, control the earth."

"What does that mean?"

"I can shift earth or draw its power for my purpose."

"I find that hard to believe." He didn't sound upset, just confused.

"Remember when we broke up? You walked away from me and suddenly tripped over a root and landed on your face?"

"Yeah. How could I forget that? It ruined my dramatic exit."

She laughed at his pique. "That was me. I used the earth to push that root above the surface. It was mean and petulant." She paused. "And I'd do it again if I had the chance."

He laughed. "Who would blame you? I was a jerk. I'm sorry."

"I forgave you a long time ago." She had, but it just hadn't made it easier to be around him. "I threw life-changing information at you without warning. You over-reacted. We both screwed up." She sipped her latte, giving him a minute to absorb what she'd said.

"You really can move the earth? That's incredible."

"It takes a lot of energy, even a little push like that one can leave me out of it for hours. I wouldn't have made it home without my sisters' help. It's not something I do lightly. Since I've grown up, I only shift earth for practice. Never in anger. I need to keep my skills up. Performing magic is a skill, like archery or tennis. If you don't practice, you lose your skills. I am stronger now than I was then. It's like weightlifting. The more you lift, the more you can lift."

"How do you practice shifting earth?" He sounded incredulous.

"I shift dirt when I work in the garden. A bit here, a bit there. Dig a hole without using my hands and hold it open until I slip a plant in."

"Could you blow up something? Make dirt explode into the air. Or," he sounded excited, "blow up a waterfall?"

"Maybe, with enough practice? But I doubt it's even possible." His question did get her thinking about exactly how Keres had managed to blow the top off the waterfall. Had he used dynamite or magic? Did the police even know? Did it even matter?

She swallowed the last of her drink. "Look, I'm enjoying this conversation, but I came here for a reason, not just to catch up with you."

He frowned. "I'm not going to like this, am I?" He stood, paced the small room, and finally settled; his backside leaned against the counter by the coffeepot. Yup, definitely putting distance between them, physically and mentally.

"I have a business proposal for you." She paused to formulate her words, mentally giving her head a shake for not planning them before she came over. She wrinkled her lips and took a deep breath. "We, that is my family, our shop is organizing a ghost tour of Three Moon Falls. We'd like to include your shop." His frown deepened, and she held up her hand. "Hear me out." This was harder than she expected.

"You don't have to do anything, well not much. You get your staff to talk to the tour groups, probably ten people max. Your staff talks about your ghost. What it does, how often it is seen, any history you know about."

"We don't have a ghost."

"Jeri says you do. Your sister says you do." She swallowed back her irritation at his stubborn refusal to believe. It was high school all over again. "Look at it this way...the tour will have believers and non-believers. They come for the entertainment. You'll help provide that and it will bring people into your shop. The tours will take several hours and will include time to shop. It could mean more business."

"That sounds dishonest. Duping gullible people."

"Is it though? They've signed up for a ghost tour that includes shopping. They're getting ghost stories, shopping, and an evening of entertainment. We've even got the old Walker mansion on the tour. I know you've heard of them. On weekends, they're going to serve tea and cookies at our last stop." No one lived in the mansion, but it was a local tourist spot. Walker was one of the earliest residents of Three Moon Falls. He had made a fortune from logging and had built the house for his lady love. She refused to move to town. It was a classic jilted lover story. In the end, Walker had died at home, alone. The mansion had been bought and sold several times due to strange happenings. Eventually, a magical person bought it and turned it into a tourist spot instead of living there.

"I don't know," Earl said. "I don't like it. Can I think about it?" He crossed his arms over his chest and tucked his fists into his armpits.

"That's all I can ask." It was further than she thought she'd get. "Think about it. It could be a good revenue generator. Halloween night will be epic. We may have to hire extra staff to help with the tours that week."

He nodded, but his frown stayed in place.

Now was not the time to push the issue.

"I'm going to the Autumn Equinox bonfire tonight. Did you want to join me?" Her family would have their celebration at home after the town event. They'd celebrate a successful harvest in their gardens and greenhouses, as well as the end of summer. To them, it was known as Mabon and was one of their most important days of the year. They celebrated, in part, with food. It was, essentially, a Thanksgiving feast.

When he didn't answer immediately, she added, "It's a town event, not a witch thing." Though technically it was both. "There will be a wiener roast, hot cocoa, apple cider. I think the town is even planning some fireworks later in the evening. Sometimes we stay for those, sometimes we don't. I'll leave that up to you."

Personally, she adored fireworks, though she did have some sympathy for people with pets who became frightened. Their cats ignored the noise completely. Of course, their cats were used to strange things and she suspected they fully understood English and could talk, like Sasha the shop cat could, if they wanted to. Cats were stubborn and the type to withhold information.

"Sure. I guess."

Hyacinth laughed. "Don't sound so certain. Seriously, Earl. No pressure. No lectures. Just an evening out in the fall air. It's supposed to be beautiful and clear. Do you know Frank Perrum from the lumberyard? He's coming and bringing his daughter, Rosie." She let that sink in and added, "Kodiak Wilkins will be there, I know you took diving lessons from him. Dennis Belanger from the greenhouse is coming too. Practically the whole town will be there."

"Why not?" he said. "It might be nice to get out for a change. I'll see who will be around to work tonight. I know Jeri is off at five."

"Great. Let me know. Parking is always tough. Gramma Pearl rented a bus. We're meeting at the greenhouse at six." She hopped up. "Text me! I'll see you later. I have to check on Anna, and two expecting mothers."

"Bye. Thanks for stopping by."

She almost laughed at the confusion in his voice. It couldn't be easy to have your entire worldview shaken up the way his had been in the last few days.

Chapter Seven

E arl climbed out of his car at the greenhouse. He scanned the packed lot. Surely not all these people were headed to the bonfire. He was bombarded with a dozen loud conversations and repeated peals of joyous laughter.

A crowd of people hovered around a yellow school bus parked on the gravel pad meant as overflow parking. He spotted Hyacinth's grandmother right away. She was a frequent shopper at his store. She had a secret addiction to cozy mysteries and had sworn him to secrecy. Why it mattered, he didn't know, but he respected her request.

He grabbed his jacket and locked the vehicle before heading toward the bus. As he got closer, he recognized the mayor and the head of the local RCMP detachment in the crowd. Apparently, Hyacinth's family had some high-level friends. Three Moon Falls wasn't tiny, but it wasn't huge either. He knew a lot about her and should have expected her to be connected, but somehow it surprised him.

Her younger sister, Hazel, met him halfway across the lot. "Earl, nice to see you. I'm glad you're considering letting us include you in the ghost tour. If you decide to join us, and even if you don't, I can come talk to your ghost, or at least try to, and see what his history is."

Earl stopped dead. She could talk to ghosts? Opening himself up to magic was crazier than he had imagined. It was giving him a gut ache. "Can we just forget all that for the night? Can I just enjoy the bonfire without discussing it?" The words came out more abruptly than he had intended. He took a deep breath. "Sorry. This is all a lot to take in for a guy with my background. I need processing time."

Hazel blushed and bent her head. Her long brown hair drifted over her face. She pushed it back and looked him right in the eyes. "You know what, Earl? I can respect that. Let's go enjoy the bonfire. Hyacinth isn't here yet, but she should arrive any second." She slipped her arm through his elbow and led him toward the crowd.

The group was comprised of people from all walks of life. Everything from rich to poor. There had to be half a dozen nationalities. There were people from the church his father founded to people who had probably never set foot in a church. Apparently, this event drew people together.

"Have you met everyone?" Hazel asked.

"I know most by sight. I'll wander through and talk to people."

"Earl Cooper, are you trying to ditch me?" Her laughter rang out, and several people turned to smile at them.

He couldn't help but laugh along with her. "Absolutely." He pointed to their left. "Oh look, there's Dennis. You're dating, right? Why don't you go pester him?"

"You're not brushing me off that easily, but nice try. Hyacinth asked me to keep you company until she got here." She gave him a wink.

"Doesn't it bother Dennis to see you with another man?" He didn't think he'd like it if the shoe were on the other foot.

"He trusts me. If he didn't, we wouldn't be together. I trust him implicitly. I don't think you can be in love with a person unless you trust them. You don't have to know everything about a person to trust them. I'm not saying there aren't things about each other that we don't know, secrets if you will. But we trust that those secrets aren't going to harm our relationship."

He was shocked by the depth of her thoughts. She was young. Early twenties if he remembered right. She was several years behind him in school. "I never thought of it that way."

"Didn't your mom spend a lot of time with other men? She was a minister's wife, and I know she did a lot of consultations with your father's parishioners."

"True. Still, I hadn't thought of it that way."

"You can thank me for the insight later, because here comes my sister."

He glanced away from Hazel. Hyacinth approached from the right. She wore a snug red T-shirt, an unbuttoned red flannel bush jacket, and form-fitting jeans. Her hair was piled on her head in a messy updo. She was the sexiest damn lumberjack he'd ever seen. Holy crap. When had she gotten so beautiful? She was always lovely, but today, she was breathtaking. Literally.

His chest felt tight, and his nerve endings tingled. What fresh hell was this? In his head, he heard his deceased mother chide him for cussing, even if it was just mentally. Lord, if she knew he was considering dating a witch, she'd be horrified. He pushed the thought aside. He'd agreed to this outing, and he intended to enjoy every second of it.

"Hyacinth, you look lovely." Stunning was more accurate. Her smile turned from pretty to radiant. The late afternoon sun glinted off her hair, turning it shades of gold.

"Thank you. You're not so bad yourself." Her smile lit up the early evening dusk.

Suddenly, he was glad he'd taken extra care to get ready. He'd shaved and put on new jeans and a clean Henley. He'd brought his leather bomber jacket, though he doubted he'd need it. The evening was still very warm. He loved this time of year. Warm days and cool but not frigid nights. The only thing better would be in October after the first hard frost when mosquitoes vanished.

"What's the plan for the evening?" he asked. "This whole bonfire was new to him but his sister raved about it. He'd promised to take a ton of pictures to show her tomorrow.

"We hop on the bus, go to the bonfire, and come home later."

A megaphone squawked, interrupting whatever she had intended to say next. They both winced and pivoted toward the sound. Pearl stood on the bottom step of the bus's doorway.

"Okay, people. Time to load up." She paused until the resulting cheer faded. "The bus is yours for the night. It will make return trips to this lot every half hour from eight to midnight. After that, you're on your own to get home. Now, let's go celebrate and have the night of our lives. Blessed Mabon to you all.

"Mabon, Autumn Solstice to most people. It's one of the magical community's sacred days. We celebrate a successful harvest. But mostly, we party together. I'm not talking about a drunken brawl. It's a celebration. There will be cider and cocoa, though some folk bring stronger drinks, most don't. We dance and sing. Eat and drink. Chat and get to know each other." Pearl made a welcoming gesture and hopped down. "Let the party begin," she declared. "All aboard."

"Let's hang back and let the crowd go ahead," Hyacinth suggested. "The bus won't leave without us and we can avoid the rush."

"Sure." They hung back and made small talk.

"How's Anna? Do you see much of her?"

"Every day. Either I swing by the house or Meri brings her by the shop, though I wish she wouldn't."

"Why's that?" Cynth pivoted to look him directly in the eye.

"I worry about germs."

She chuckled. "You always were fastidious," she teased. "Baby Anna has all of her mother's immunity for the first few months until her own start to develop. She'll be fine." She placed her hand on his arm. "You're a good uncle. Don't let your overactive imagination stress you out."

"I don't have an overactive imagination." Not that he'd admit to it, anyway.

Her light laugh rang out and danced down his spine. "You have a ridiculous imagination. Do you remember when your class read *Lord of the Flies*? You saw conspiracies everywhere for weeks."

He groaned. "Don't remind me." He pointed to the bus. "Oh, look. We can board now." He took her elbow and led her forward. She shook his arm off and laughing raced onto the bus. Panting, he caught up with her at the very back. The bus was loaded to the max.

As the bus pulled out, a speaker cut in. *Witchy Woman* began to play. It was followed by *Season of the Witch*, *Elvira*, and the hauntingly primal tune of The HU's *Wolf Totem*. The crowd sang and chanted along and despite himself, he got into the spirit of the evening.

In no time, they were unloaded and standing with the crowd in an enormous circle around an unlit bonfire. A string of rope kept the crowd from getting too close and helped protect wayward children from the rush of heat when the blaze ignited.

"Okay everyone," Mayor Quinton declared over a bullhorn. "Channel your inner magic. Focus on the fire. Imagine it bursting into flame in celebration of a successful fall harvest."

Earl looked at Hyacinth. She winked.

"What?" he whispered.

"We're using magic to light it. The power of the group mind. The match she throws is strictly for show. We tap into everyone's intentions. It's good luck for the town."

"What?"

"Just go with it. Focus your intentions on an enormous bonfire," she whispered. "The harder everyone focuses, the better the ignition." When he frowned, she added, "Play along. It's just like when you helped with Anna."

He'd never heard of such a crazy thing, but then, he'd never have believed he could use his own health and energy to feed Hyacinth's while she saved his niece. He turned toward the pile of sticks and logs and focused on a growing bonfire, lighting up the night.

"In three, two, one..." the mayor called. She lit a match and held it high in the air. She tossed it in the air and the fire whooshed upward, though he could have sworn the match blew out before it hit the pile.

The crowd cheered.

"Gas," he muttered. Though he hadn't seen anyone pour gas, nor had he smelled it. He knew gas would dissipate in the air and cause a much bigger burst of flame as it seeped outward. Movie fires lit with gas and a match without a big whoosh were such bull-pucky. "It had to be gas," he said, arguing with himself. The acrid but comforting scent of burning wood washed over him, bringing back vague family memories that he couldn't quite bring into focus.

"Go with that." Cynth laughed. "Come on," she tugged his elbow. "I smell mini-donuts. Let's beat the rush."

The entire evening had a party atmosphere. There were food and drink booths. A truck selling burgers and fries. A few craft booths selling miniature and full-sized brooms, or besoms, as the women behind the table called them. Another sold corn cob dolls and corn husk dollies. It struck him more as a fall fair than anything witchy or pagan.

Suddenly, he stopped dead in his tracks as memories swirled through his head like a whirlpool of colorful images.

"What?" Cynth asked.

"I just realized I've been here before." He swallowed hard. "As a kid, with Mom and Dad. Before Meri was born."

"What's the big deal?" She seemed genuinely puzzled.

"My dad was a minister."

"So what? Look over there," she pointed through the crowd. "There's the minister of the Anglican church, the priest from the Catholic church, and the pastor of the Christian non-denominational church." The three men stood together, obviously enjoying themselves. "There is someone from every walk of life here." She pointed out a few Muslim and Korean families. She stepped closer and dropped her voice. "To them, it's a fall party, to witches and pagans it's Mabon, the Autumn Solstice. Chillax and enjoy yourself."

They danced to eclectic music provided by local musicians. Ate until he couldn't stuff in another morsel, shopped all the vendors, and had a couple of spiced ciders. He even tried a mulled wine that was better than he expected but wasn't something he'd want again. He wasn't much of a drinker in part due to his upbringing, in part due to never having developed a taste for it. He preferred beer to wine or hard liquor if he drank at all.

The highlight, aside from the dancing was a stage act by an illusionist who made things disappear and reappear. He cast Hyacinth a sidelong look.

"It's an illusion, not magic," she whispered. "Magic is everywhere, just not there." She thrust her chin toward the stage.

They were dancing when he noticed the fire had faded to nothing but embers. "Holy cow. The fire is nearly out." The crowd had thinned to a few stragglers.

"It sure is. Midnight is upon us. We better hurry or we'll miss the last bus."

"Who looks after the fire?" he asked as they strolled hand in hand toward the makeshift parking lot in a cleared field.

"There's a setup and takedown crew. Lucky for me, I did my turn last year. I only have to help about every third year. The whole festival runs like a well-oiled machine."

"Apparently so. The vendors are all gone. Too bad, I could use a drink. I'm thirsty after all that dancing. Thanks for being my partner."

"Anytime, Earl. But as for water, I've got you covered. Gramma always has coolers of drinks for the parched on the way home."

She leaned into him as they shared a seat on the bus. Much too soon, they stood beside his SUV in the garden center parking lot. He was loath to say goodnight. "I really enjoyed myself. Thanks for making me come with you. You've opened my eyes to so many things this week. I've got a lot to think about." He leaned forward to kiss her and, at the last second, pulled himself back. They'd barely reached civility and friendship. Kisses were beyond that and he knew that no matter how tempted he was, no matter how deeply he felt the pull, he shouldn't be kissing her.

He stroked a finger down her cheek. "Thanks for a nice evening."

She winced at the word nice.

"What I meant to say is, I really enjoyed tonight. I'd like to see you again."

She nodded, though he had the feeling it was more an acknowledgment than an agreement to see him again. Reluctantly, he climbed into his car and pulled away. When he reached the turn to the street, he looked back. She was staring in his direction. A horn beeped, and she spun around and walked away.

Chapter Eight

Surprisingly, for the day after the solstice, none of her patients were due. She'd checked in with all her patients by phone and everyone was doing well. That left her with nothing to do. Unable to sit idle, she spent the morning making gingersnaps and lemon shortbread cookies. She nibbled a few of each to ensure they'd turned out properly. She also whipped up a batch of magically fortified protein energy balls.

Leaving the energy balls in the freezer until her next birthing, she dropped cookies off at the mayor's office and the medical clinic and took the two remaining tins with her to the family shop. One for her sisters and one for Earl. She really shouldn't give him one. It felt too much like a relationship thing to do. But part of her wanted to.

The shop was hopping. Solstice celebrations often brought a wave of business. Both before and after. People prepped for their personal celebrations and then, people wanting to know more, came to the store.

She strode through the front door, nearly banging into an old friend. "Danica, how are you? I love your hair." This week, Danica had dyed her pixie cut bright orange. Last week it had been blue and purple.

"Thanks. Good to see you, Cynth. Shift anyone's world lately?" she teased.

"Haha. This witch doesn't shift the earth and tell. I missed chatting with you last night."

"Yeah, you were all wrapped in Earl Cooper. Didn't he burn you when we were kids? Are you sure you want to go there again?"

"Honestly, no. But he really is a decent guy."

"And the...you know." She made a flourishing movement with her hands in lieu of saying magic. "You said he's totally not cool with it."

"He's coming around. His niece's birth helped."

"Yeah, I heard Meri had a tough time. Hope she's okay now."

"Mother and baby are doing great." She wasn't imparting any secrets with the statement. Meri and Annie had been in the bookstore and the supermarket this morning.

"Well, I've gotta run. Mrs. Leaper is coming in for a blue rinse and a cut and set. If I'm late, I'll lose my tip. Let's have tea soon."

"You bet."

The next two hours were crazy. She helped a couple dozen people find teas or herbal beauty products. Her family had a full line of moisturizers, bubble baths, bath salts, lotions, and lip products. She helped an elderly tourist find some silver and amethyst jewelry for her daughter and helped another decide between several colors of ritual candles.

"Whew," she declared, leaning on the cash desk, and staring at her sister Amber. "Is it always like this?"

"Not always, but it's coming to the end of tourist season, and it was a solstice." She shrugged happily. "I'll take the business when I can get it." The shop was doing well, but the future was always uncertain.

"You should have told me. I spent the morning making cookies and lounging around in my pajamas. I could have been here."

Amber blushed.

"Do not tell me you're embarrassed to ask for help."

"It is my store, and my responsibility."

"It is *our* store. Sure, it was your idea, but we all benefit. I'm happy to help. Just ask and if I'm not on a call, I'll be here."

"I appreciate that. Now that it's quiet, I'm going to go take a rest for a minute. Gramma Pearl can handle the front alone for a bit."

"I'm going to pop over to Cooper's Capers and deliver some cookies."

"Taking cookies to your beau?" Amber teased.

"Not hardly. I had a good time with Earl last night. He's come around a bit. And I thought cookies would be a nice thank you. Plus, I owe Jeri a few, she located some used books I wanted. I need to pick them up."

Amber gave her a long, hard stare. "Watch your back, sis. He burned you once. He could do it again."

"Did I interfere with your relationship with Kody?"

"Absolutely, every dang day." She mock pouted the way only a sister could do.

"Deal with it." She grabbed the cookie tin from behind the counter.

"Hey, grab me a latte while you're over there. Jeri knows what I like. And watch your back!"

Hyacinth saluted and slipped out the front door. What was it with sisters that made them nag all the time? And friends too? She wasn't a kid. She knew reconnecting with Earl could mean getting hurt again. It probably would. But she'd loved him once, long ago. Hell, maybe she still loved him. Whatever she felt deserved time to manifest itself and to grow into whatever it was destined to become. The universe had thrust Earl back into her life for a reason, and she was going to see where it went. All she knew right now was that when she was with Earl, she was happier than she had been in ages.

She strode down the block, dodging tourists, a radiant smile on her face until she reached the bookstore. A sudden attack of nerves paralyzed her. What if he didn't want to see her? What if he'd only gone to last night's celebration to be nice? Or because his sister made him go?

"Okay, Hawk," she muttered under her breath. "You can do this. There's nothing to be afraid of." How was it that Earl Cooper was the only thing in her life that made her feel like she was out of her depth? A new potion, no problem. Fight with her family, she'd get through it. A challenging birth, she'd handled dozens. She was a strong, confident woman in all things.

Except for Earl Cooper.

He had the power to turn her into a doubtful teenager all over again.

She clutched the celestial pattern cookie tin in both hands until her knuckles went white and her fingers ached. It buckled under the strain. The slight popping sound brought her to her senses. Time to go in.

She took one step forward, and a chill raced down her spine.

She froze.

Her gaze darted frantically left, right, then behind her. It was the exact feeling she'd had at Lloyd's. Darkness. Evil. The crowd in front of her parted. There! Half a block down, a petite woman with bright red hair strolled toward her, a vacant look on her face. She reminded Hyacinth of an automaton. Or someone so out of it they had no idea what they were doing or where they were.

Until she looked up.

Frozen gray eyes stared right at Hyacinth stealing her breath. Her knees buckled and she slapped up a mental retaining wall. Her vision went gray. Her knees buckled. She swayed into the wall, spots dancing before her eyes.

Then, like the sun bursting out from behind a heavy cloud, everything snapped back to normal. When she looked up, there was no sign of the woman anywhere.

"Too freaking weird," she mumbled.

"Pardon?" A well-dressed woman with a Gucci bag stopped in front of her. "Are you okay, dear? You look a little pale. Maybe we should get you inside, out of the sun. Let me help you." She grasped Cynth lightly by the elbow and steered her toward the bookstore door, and then inside. While her empathy skills weren't the best, she detected no ill will from the woman.

"Excuse me," her savior called out. "I think this lady needs some help."

Jeri hurried over. "Hyacinth. Are you okay? You're as white as a sheet." She turned slightly toward the back room. "Earl, get out here." Her tone must have conveyed urgency to Earl. He was at their sides in seconds.

"Hyacinth, what happened? Are you okay?" He grabbed her other elbow and with the stranger's help steered her toward the office at the back of the store.

She pushed his hand away. "I'm okay."

"Are you sure dear? You were wobbling like a newborn colt and as white as salt. I was worried she'd pass out. Right there on the sidewalk. Thank heaven I came along, or she'd have fallen."

"Thank you so much, ma'am," Earl said. "We're very glad you were there for our friend."

"You know her then?" She tipped her head in inquiry.

"I do. We used to date. Her family has a shop just down the street. I'll see that they look after her once she's steady enough to move."

"I'm right here," Hyacinth objected. By the Goddess, she hated when people talked around her. "I'm fine."

Earl gave her a concerned stare. "Maybe so, but clearly you weren't. Your color is still off. You look like you did the other night."

"I felt the same way. But it's passed now."

"Oh, no. Have you been ill?" the lady asked, looking back and forth between them.

"Thanks again," Earl said. "Jeri, can you please get this lovely lady a drink in thanks for helping Cynth?"

"Come with me, ma'am. I can't thank you enough for helping out. She's the granddaughter of my dear friend." She led the woman out of the office toward the coffeepot. Cynth listened to Jeri prattle on until her voice faded out.

"What happened?" Earl asked, pressing a cold bottle of water into her hands.

"I saw her. She looked at me."

His brows scrunched up in question.

"I wend dizzy and cold. Then, she was gone." She shuddered. "It was so cold. So weird. She's colder than Keres or Brown were. Creepy."

"Should I call Pearl?"

"I brought you cookies." She thrust the tin at him, hoping to distract him from calling her family. She'd deal with them later.

"I love cookies," he proclaimed, taking the tin, and popping the lid. "Oh, is that lemon shortbread? Gingersnaps too." He paused and looked up at her. "You remembered my favorites."

Heat stole into her face. She hadn't done it intentionally. "You better believe I did. I wanted to say thanks for last night. I really enjoyed myself."

He devoured three cookies without dropping a single crumb. He'd always been uber neat. "These are delicious." He closed the tin. "I better save some for Jeri. Are you feeling better? You're still quite pale."

"I really am. Do you want to see a movie tonight or something?" She blurted. She'd been thinking about seeing a movie with him but hadn't intended to ask.

He looked as poleaxed about being asked as she felt having invited him.

He stuffed his hands in his pockets and rattled something; pulled out his keys for a second, stuffed them back in, and resumed rattling. Classic Earl thinking pose. In his youth, he used to fidget with the change in his pocket.

"I'm just talking as friends." She grabbed her water bottle and slurped nervously. "It's okay if you don't want to go." The bottle thudded to the table. "I get it. We've been enemies for so long and now I'm asking you to do something against your basic beliefs." She swallowed a lump of unease. "But we could be...well, if not enemies, maybe friends. Or something."

By the Goddess, Hyacinth just shut up. This isn't helping.

Earl stared at the floor. His gaze darted toward the door as if looking for an escape route. Finally, after an eternity of ten seconds, he said, "I think I'd like that." He flashed a nervous grin that didn't quite reach his eyes. "It's retro night at The Marquee. They're playing-"

"*The Breakfast Club,*" she blurted just as he said it. "Not really a guy movie, I guess."

"Mom used to watch it all the time. I never understood it as a kid, but I'm feeling nostalgic, so why not?"

"I haven't seen it in years. I'm excited." She was more than excited. She'd been looking forward to going to the movie tonight, but with Earl at her side, her heart was tripping happily, despite the nervous trepidation poking at the back of her neck.

"It's supposed to be nice tonight. Shall we walk?"

"Why not? I'll leave my car at the shop and swing by."

"Come early. I want popcorn."

"And licorice, soda, and chocolate, if I know you. You always had a taste for junk food."

"And you'll sneak in something healthy and eat half my popcorn," he teased back.

She didn't even try to deny it. As a teen, she'd tried to be healthy, but junk usually won. Lucky for her, Earl understood and willingly shared his treats. "Maybe I'm different now."

"I'll believe that when I see it."

"I can't believe you bought your own popcorn," Earl elbowed Hyacinth as they walked down the street toward their shops. "And chocolate too."

"Well, for one thing, I've got more money than I had back then, and I'm pretty sure nobody will squeal to Gramma Pearl about me eating junk. Though if they did, she'd probably give me the stink eye."

Earl shuddered. Oh, how well he remembered those looks. "I was always terrified of Pearl. At least until I was older. She's protective beyond anything normal. Not even Mama Bear protective. More like Mama T-Rex." He shuddered again. "After my folks passed, and I took over the shop, I was surprised when she came in the first time. She'd been a customer all along, but always with that steely-eyed stare. That first time, she was kind and uber-polite. It really surprised me. I thought she'd hate me forever. I mean, she never liked me, but after we broke up...boy! God, she terrified me."

"Yeah, you and me both. Don't misunderstand, she's a great grand-mother. But she was scary firm with us. Especially when we messed up and misused magic."

They walked along for several minutes, their pace slow, barely walking at all. As they walked by the park, he said, "Hey, let's go on the swings. I haven't done that in years."

"Me either. Race ya." She bolted towards the thick canvas swings.

He let her win and take the center of five swings. All through school, the center had been everyone's favorite.

"Beat you," she called, pumping her legs to raise the swing higher.

He stepped behind her, caught the seat, and heaved it forward, shooting her in an enormous arc towards the sky. Her delighted laugh stole into his heart. Lord how he'd missed her. Six hard pushes later, he climbed into the swing beside her.

Thoughts and questions tumbled through his mind. He wondered if he should ask her about the happenings in his shop. For years he'd ignored them or blamed his staff, but now...he wondered if there was more to it than he thought.

It took only minutes before he matched her speed and they swung in unison, as they'd done in the past. Eventually, they slowed until they were barely moving. He glanced at her. She was looking at him; her smile sweet and soft, her blue eyes sparkling with delight.

"Can I ask you something?" He put his feet down to stop the swing.

She shifted so she straddled her seat and gripped the chain between them with both hands. She rocked back and forth on her feet like she used to when she was nervous.

"Sure. I guess."

"You said my shop is haunted right?" She gave him her full attention and nodded. "Can ghosts do stuff like in the movies? You know, move things?"

"Depends on the spirit. Why?"

Okay, so that wasn't reassuring. He'd half hoped he was losing his mind. "I don't know. Stuff gets moved around. I find books open on chairs in the morning, though I'm sure I didn't move them and I always reshelve everything before I leave. Once or twice, I can chalk it up to misplacing something, but lately, it's become a regular event."

"And that worries you?"

"I don't know if I'd rather it be ghosts or me losing my mind. My staff swears it isn't them."

"Maybe your ghosts are trying to tell you something. Ours are quiet most of the time, but they do like to play jokes when they're bored." She chuckled. "When we first opened, one of them pulled a book off the shelf and opened it to a chapter on how to talk to ghosts. As if Hazel didn't already know how. They had a riot changing the temp in Kody's apartment too."

Not what he wanted to hear. Not even close. He was hoping ghosts just floated around looking all spooky or ethereal.

"Don't worry about it. If your ghost was up to no good, you'd know by now. Malevolent spirits don't hang around doing nothing. Some hang around because they choose to, most stick because they've got unfinished business. The evil ones are usually trapped by someone, or something undone. But those can be freed to cross over."

"And how do I know what mine wants?" He groaned. "I can't believe I just said that. Two-thirds of me still doesn't believe ghosts exist."

"I'll ignore that last part, but Hazel can talk to your ghost if they're open to communicating. Who knows, maybe they'll want to be part of the ghost tour."

It took two full minutes for him to process that statement. "And how would people see him, her, whatever?" When had his world gone full-on crazy? This discussion was certifiable.

"Ghosts choose who to reveal themselves to, and when. But, of course, you have to believe to see them. But the lore alone, telling their story, would be more than enough to make the tour amazing." She grinned at him. "But no pressure or anything."

They hopped off the swings and resumed walking.

"I'm going to have to think about all of this." He needed a subject change, fast. "I enjoyed the movie more than I thought I would," he blurted. *God, could he be any more lame?*

"Me too. You're good company. I like that you can watch a movie without a million smart-alecky comments. I dated a guy for a while who ruined every movie and TV show with incessant chatter."

Jealousy jerked him to a stop.

"What's up?" She stopped beside him; concern etched between her lovely brows.

"Foot cramp," he lied. No way would he tell her he was jealous of some guy she'd dated. "Did you date a lot?"

"Not that it's any of your business, but no. After we split, or rather you dumped me, I didn't date again for seven years. Since then, I've dated maybe six guys. It's not easy to date when you have big secrets. I revealed those once, and it cost me too much."

Guilt slammed into his guts. He gripped her shoulder and squeezed gently before running his hand down her arm and clasping her hand. "I'm sorry I was a jackass. You threw me for a loop. I mean, I had no idea magic existed, and you freaked the hell out of me."

"But your sister is magical, and I thought your mom was too."

"No way was Mom magic."

Her shrug was eloquent. "If you say so." Her tone implied she did not agree with him, not one bit.

Rather than argue, he tugged her forward, and they resumed their walk, holding hands. She didn't tug free, and he didn't want to let her go, either. Being with Hyacinth made him unsteady and uncertain, but deep inside, a soft river of peace and contentment flowed through his heart. She fit beside him like a missing piece of a complex puzzle.

Chapter Nine

Exhaustion dragged on Hyacinth's shoulders like a weighted blanket. She'd gotten a 2 a.m. call that Whitney Egan was giving birth and had rushed to her home.

Whitney was one lucky mother. This was her third pregnancy and her second set of twins. She'd popped them out in under four hours. Her husband was helpful and understanding, and her mother-in-law had taken the other children for a few days. She had nothing to do but lie back and look after her adorable new baby girls.

She'd been an easy patient, though Hyacinth was still exhausted. This was her third birth in two days. With several hours of aftercare given to each patient, she was beyond tired. She slid her medical bag, her backpack, and her empty cooler into the back of her Ford Explorer SUV, and climbed into the front.

She leaned back and shot a quick prayer of gratitude to the Goddess. By all that was holy in the universe, she was beyond tired and more than ready to sleep for thirty-six hours. Maybe longer. She rested her head back and closed her eyes. Two minutes of quiet and calm and she'd be on her way. Fortunately, she was close to the outskirts of town and home wasn't far down the highway. She briefly debated calling one of her sisters for a ride. After a brief rest in Whitney's driveway, she decided she was fine and headed home.

No sense in worrying her clients if they should happen to look outside and see her sitting there. Besides, she needed food and a long nap, not necessarily in that order. She was ravenous and needed to bury her hands in some soil to refresh her flagging energy.

Driving past the theater they'd been to last night brought a soft smile to her lips. She'd enjoyed herself immensely. The frown slid right back on. She couldn't allow herself to fall for Earl again. That way led to heartache and sorrow. Somewhere, out there in the wilds of Alberta, was the perfect man for her and it wasn't Earl Cooper, as much as she'd like it to be.

She passed the gas station. Speak of the devil. Earl was talking to Raul, the owner and mechanic. She waved at them, and they waved back. Earl's smile was wide and welcoming. She turned her attention back to the road just as a fat orange tabby cat raced across her path.

She slammed on the brakes and skidded toward a parked car.

"No. No. No!" She slammed into the side of the sedan with a bone-jarring thud. Her forehead slammed into the steering wheel, and everything turned black.

Sound came back first.

"Hyacinth, Cynth. Are you okay? Don't move sweetheart, the ambulance is on its way."

Agony ripped through her head. "Shh," she muttered. "Too loud." She cracked open her eyes. Daylight blinded her, and she slammed them shut. Sirens sounded in the distance, slamming into her head like the beats of a bass drum.

"Make it stop," she muttered.

"Hang tight, baby. Don't move until we know if you're okay. You're probably fine, but your airbags didn't deploy."

She swallowed the bile rising in her throat and tried to make sense of what was happening.

E arl stood inside the SUV door with his hands on Hyacinth's shoulders. Blood ran down her forehead and pooled on her scrub top. He knew head wounds bled a lot, but the sight made his stomach turn, and the coppery scent brought forth a gag.

"Don't move, hun. The paramedics are here."

"Okay, sir. You're going to have to move."

"I'll be right here, Cynth. Do what they tell you."

He stepped back and to the side, angling himself so he could see. His heart was shredded. What if she was seriously injured? She hadn't been going fast, probably not even the speed limit. She never broke the speed limit, and used to grump at him every time he did. The damage to both vehicles was way worse than you'd expect from a slow-moving fender-bender.

His guts dipped. Magic.

Naw, couldn't be. Everyone knew that vehicles were practically all plastic these days. That explained the extreme damage.

He fisted his hands to keep from rushing to her side as the medics wrapped her neck in a C-spine brace and assisted her to the stretcher.

"Cooper," an authoritative female voice demanded. "What happened?"

He pivoted to his right. "Constable Stone. She was driving down the street and suddenly swerved for no reason."

"How fast was she going?"

"Not that fast. Probably barely forty."

"Forty kilometers an hour wouldn't cause this much damage." The dark-skinned officer pinned him with a stare.

How could he feel guilty when he was telling the truth? "Ask Raul. We were talking when she went by."

She peppered him with questions, then went to talk to Raul. By the time she finished her short interrogation, the ambulance was pulling away. He climbed into his car and followed the ambulance. He'd leave the car for its tune-up later, and the police knew where to find him if they had more questions.

"I'm sorry, Earl," Amy Bartman said ten minutes later. "I can't let you in until the doctor is done with his examination. You'll have to wait in the waiting room." They'd gone to high school with Amy, who'd returned to town after getting her nursing degree.

His stomach churned. If Cynth was seriously injured, he didn't know what he'd do. No. she wouldn't be badly hurt, he tried to reassure himself. She hadn't been going that fast. He paced the empty waiting room, his steps loud in the eerie silence.

"Dude," Amy called. "Chill. She'll be fine." She left her station and walked over to him. "I didn't know you guys were together again." She turned the statement into a question.

"We're not. We're friends. I guess. I saw the accident." He tried to downplay his overreaction.

"Riiiight. Have you called her family?"

"Shoot. No."

"You do that, and I'll see if I can find out how long it will be until you can see her. She'll be fine, Earl." She walked past her desk and down the hall toward the exam rooms.

The emergency entry doors whooshed open on a puff of air. He glanced up as Hazel and Amber rushed in. "Earl, what happened?" Amber blurted.

"She was in a fender bender. Her airbags didn't deploy. She cut her head."

They peppered him with questions he couldn't answer. He threw up his hands. "Stop. You know what I know. She was driving past the garage, swerved, and hit a car. She was headed out of town, probably toward home." *What's taking them so long back there?* His stomach dropped and rebounded at the thought that this could be more serious than it looked. *What if she was seriously injured and not just slightly concussed?*

And why was he so concerned?

The ache in his guts was more than just concern for a neighbor or fellow businessman. It was...he pushed the thought aside. Nope. He wasn't falling for her again. This was gratitude that she had saved his niece's life. Yup. That's what it was.

Gramma Pearl and Lazuli rushed in, and he answered all the same questions over again. His temper was fraying, and it took everything he had not to snap at them to back off and leave him alone.

Amy calling his name was the sweetest sound he'd heard in forever. "Earl, Hyacinth wants to see you?"

"What about us?" Pearl demanded.

"Sorry ladies. She asked for Earl."

"How'd she even know I was here? Did you tell her?" he asked.

"Not me. But she asked for you, so you can go in. Don't stay too long." She turned toward Hyacinth's family. "She'll be moved to a room for overnight observation soon. You'll be able to see her then." She led him away, leaving Pearl sputtering behind them.

"Girl, you've got balls of steel. Nobody walks away from Pearl Hawk."

She shrugged. "I've learned that arguing doesn't help. Walking away seems to work. Hyacinth is in here." She pointed to the only closed curtain in the short row of open and connected exam rooms. All five of the other beds were empty. "Keep your voice low. She's got a headache."

"Thanks, Amy."

She smiled and walked away.

Amy's soft voice drifted into her cubicle. When Earl responded, her heartbeat settled. Knowing he was just outside her curtain was soothing in a way it shouldn't be. He parted the drapes and slipped inside without a sound.

"Hey, you," he whispered, sidling up to the bed.

He took her icy hand in his large one. Warmth rushed through her, easing some of her post-accident chill. She was still a bit in shock, but having him here helped calm her frazzled nerves.

"What happened, babe?"

Babe? Since when did he call her babe? They were just beginning to speak again. She cuddled the endearment close. "I swerved to avoid the cat."

"What cat? I didn't see a cat." His frown pinched his brows together.

"How could you miss it? It was the biggest cat I ever saw. Probably twenty pounds. It was nearly as big as that lazy dog you had in high school."

"Cynth, sweetheart, I was looking right at you when you swerved. There was no cat. Were you going home from work? Overtired, maybe?"

"I didn't hallucinate a cat, Earl," she snapped and yanked her hand from his to cross her arms over her chest. "I was tired, but not that tired. I was fully coherent. There was a cat."

He shook his head, and her heart plummeted. "I can ask Raul, but at the scene, he told Stone he didn't know why you swerved." He swallowed. "God, you scared me. Your hit was too hard, and your airbags didn't deploy."

She closed her eyes. *Magic. Freaking magic. It had to be. But who'd do something like this to her? And why?* "Thanks for coming."

"You want me to leave?" His voice echoed hurt.

"No." She grabbed his hand and pulled it to her chest. "I mean, we aren't a thing, but you came anyway. I appreciate it." She groaned. "When will these stupid drugs kick in?"

A nurse she didn't know came in and chased Earl out. "You can check with the main nursing station in half an hour, and they'll let you know where she is." The woman eased Earl aside and unlocked the stretcher.

She closed her eyes against her nausea as she was wheeled down the hall and into a room. Leticia Stone, in full uniform, her dreadlocks swinging, strolled in, as the nurse exited.

"So, you Hawks are in the thick of it again," she said by way of greeting. She pushed the door shut behind her and sat beside the bed. "Okay, unofficially. What happened?"

"I was heading home after a delivery. Tired, but not dangerously tired. A cat, the biggest cat I ever saw, darted in front of me and I swerved to miss it." She dropped her voice low. "Earl never saw it." A chill swept through her, realizing that it might not have been real.

"Your truck reeks of magic. Dark residue everywhere. Were you practicing dark magic?" Stone fixed her with a stare. "I have to report this to the council." The Witch's Council tracked unusual magical happenings and frowned on dark or black magic. They didn't act on reports unless others were hurt or injured.

"What? No! Never. You know me better than that, Leticia. I'm a healer. I'd never..."

"I had to ask, officially." Stone was a voodoo priestess as well as chief of police and an investigator for the council. "Unofficially, watch your back. Whoever did this didn't even try to hide the magic. I can't believe you didn't see it when you got in. Your SUV is covered in it. Right down to the engine. If it hadn't been for the cat you thought you saw, you'd have crashed anyway."

"I saw a cat," she insisted, anger spiking in her chest.

"If you did, and I'm not saying you didn't, the caster would have had to be close. Throwing hallucinations isn't easy." She scratched her head. "I'm guessing this is due to that damned artifact. You need to find it and turn it over to the council before someone else is hurt. I can't allow innocent bystanders to be injured in this war."

"War?" Hyacinth squeaked.

"Well, isn't it?" Her eyes narrowed. "First Keres, then Brown and Natalia. Now this."

"And there's this redhead I've seen a few times, too. Something about her is off." Magic casters could recognize each other by the slight glow they left. Both Keres and his son, Brown, had reeked of darkness similar to the redhead she'd first seen in the restaurant with Earl.

"Damn. Okay. I'll spread the word. Watch your back, and find that damn talisman," she ordered just as Pearl marched into the room, her eyes snapping like a firecracker.

She rushed to Hyacinth's side showing more concern than she'd demonstrated in a long time. Pearl wasn't cold. Quite the opposite, but she rarely let her emotions show with her grandchildren.

"Hyacinth, are you hurt?"

"Not much. Just a head wound and a minor concussion. My truck is trashed." Slowly she related the accident, ending with, "I was tired, but not that tired. Honestly, I've driven feeling worse. It was a normal day."

"We have to find that talisman and destroy it," her grandmother declared, completely echoing Hyacinth's thoughts.

"We can't keep fighting people looking for it, that's for sure. If we have it, why did our ancestor have to bring it here and not leave clues?"

"If it's as powerful as Keres seemed to think, clues are the last thing you'd leave. Though why they didn't turn it over to the council bothers me. Why keep something like that?"

While their family did have dozens of magical heirloom items, it still didn't seem right to be in possession of such a powerful and coveted object. Especially without knowing you had it.

"And watch yourself around Earl," Pearl warned. "It's odd that you reconnected just as all this started up. He could be involved."

She laughed until her head pounded blindingly. "Earl? He's still totally anti-magic, Gramma. He's not involved. I guarantee it."

Chapter Ten

"Can I go home today?" Hyacinth asked, pacing the confines of her microscopic hospital room. Three nights in the hospital were more than necessary and the stench of industrial cleaner was almost more than she could bear.

"That depends," Dr. Carter said. She was silent so long that Cynth finally turned to stare at her. "Have you had any more hallucinations?"

"I didn't hallucinate anything. That cat was there!" She stomped her foot.

"There were four witnesses to the accident. Nobody else saw a cat. Either you imagined it," she dropped her voice to a near-whisper, "or someone projected that image into your mind. Either way, I need to be reassured of your mental capacity."

Dr. Carter took amazing care of all her patients, magical or not. Having a certified doctor privy to magic made using magical treatments easier. They hadn't treated Hyacinth with much magic, she was the family healer, but her grandmother and sisters had taken the edge off her pain and sped the healing of the gash in her forehead. They'd left a bruise and cut to heal on their own to avoid raising questions about how quickly she healed.

"I'm fine," she insisted.

"I want to run a couple more tests. They'll only take a couple of hours. Then, if I'm satisfied that you're okay, you can leave."

She fumed through a CT scan, an MRI of her brain, and then an interminable wait of nearly two hours for the results.

"I don't know why I can't just leave," she grumbled to Pearl when she arrived for her visit. They'd been sitting with her in shifts only leaving her alone at night when the hospital was locked to the public.

She stared around her room. It was okay for a hospital, she supposed. Pink blanket on her bed. Three potted flowering plants rested on the bedside table. An adorable cat picture on the wall with a caption at the bottom. *A healthy outside starts on the inside.* The saying was a touch trite, but the cat was adorable. Her window looked out over a sunny park where children played in the distance. The staff was excellent but, by the love of the Goddess, she was sick of being here.

She was itching to be busy. Patients to check on, lotions and shampoos to create. She had a brilliant idea of a line of all-natural lip coloring with a beeswax base that she wanted to test.

Pearl shook her head. "There's no rush. You have no patients due. We need to be certain there are no lingering effects of your accident. I've called your cousin Cecily; she'll be here later today to take a look at you?"

"What?" She strode to the small locker in the corner to get her clothing. It was empty.

"Where are my clothes?" She whirled around to stare at her grandmother. Stealing her clothing was going too far.

"I took them home to wash. Hazel will bring something by when you are released. And you will let Cecily examine you. My cursory look wasn't enough. With all the trouble this family has had in the past few months, we need to be one hundred percent certain that whoever pushed that illusion into your head didn't leave anything else. Cecily is much more skilled than I am."

Cecily was a distant paternal cousin, from a family of three daughters. Aside from emails and phone calls, they rarely got together. She was, by far, the family's strongest empath and had an uncanny ability to find brain anomalies.

"By the Goddess, I wish snapping things into being was real. I'd snap myself some clothing." Anger slithered down her spine. It was bad enough that she'd let all three of her sisters, Gramma Pearl, and two of Pearl's friends, snoop in her brain. Now she had to let her cousin in. It could be an invasion of privacy of the worst sort. Sometimes, like today, it was necessary. What she wouldn't give to disappear and avoid this! Not that it would help, her family would just scry and learn where she was.

The doctor strode in. "Good news," she declared, "you can go home. However, I want you to watch for anything unusual happening and keep me updated. And I'll see you in my clinic." She handed Hyacinth an appointment card. "The details are there. Stay safe." She pivoted and left the room without waiting for an acknowledgment.

The door hadn't even closed when Hazel came in. "Brought you some clothing, sis." She rummaged in the floral print purse she carried. "But first, put these on. Smoky quartz, labradorite, and citrine bracelets, and this tourmaline pendant."

"Protective stones? Really?"

"You can't be too careful. Amber made them for all of us."

"I don't see yours," Hyacinth snapped as she put the bracelets on to appease her family.

Hazel lifted the hem of her leaf-print maxi dress. "Right here on my anklet. The best part, she added bells to mine." She shook her leg, and the bells chimed. "Totally dope."

Cynth rolled her eyes. Hazel loved her slang.

"What's the plan for today?" Hazel asked. "I have to get to work. Things to do. And I haven't seen Dennis since yesterday."

"I'll probably take a long walk and spend time in the greenhouse. I need to recharge. This place is suffocating me." What she didn't tell them was that she'd be walking without her phone. She couldn't handle them hovering over her one more second. She'd sneak off for a walk. Maybe stroll up to Chickadee Falls. It was the smallest of Three Moon Falls' waterfalls and was on Hawk land.

Gramma Pearl drove her home, and miraculously she refrained from lecturing all the way. Her only advice was, "Be careful. We all need to be on our guard until we find that talisman or relic or whatever it is everyone is after."

"Yes, Gramma. I will be." She was seething and needed to vent. Moving earth was just what she needed. "Drop me off at the green-houses, okay?"

Each of the three greenhouses had several doors. She didn't enter any of them. Instead, she wandered past them and around back into the space they surrounded, to the family rose garden. She wandered down the pathways between the bushes until her instinct told her she'd found the right spot. Settling cross-legged on the path, she removed her shoes and socks. She placed her feet in one garden and leaned back, placing her hands on the bare earth of the one behind her, and turned her face upward toward the sun.

Peace flowed through her, taking the edge off her jangling nerves. She let the earth's power flow into her feet, through her body, and out of her hands. She was a conduit for the earth's magic and energy. Though it was fall, hummingbirds moved from rose to rose, their wings making only the barest hint of sound. If she wasn't attuned to the earth, she'd never have heard them. Leaves rustled in the breeze, chickadees chirped, and bees buzzed past. It should have been relaxing.

Her brain jumped like water in a hot skillet. Who was after them this time? Was it Earl? She didn't think it could be him, but Pearl had planted that suggestion, and like a tenacious weed, it was hard to root out. Was there a future with him, or was this friendship destined to explode again? She'd been deeply wounded by the volcanic eruption between them in high school and didn't think she'd survive another.

Being an earth conduit took the edge off, but didn't soothe enough. She needed a full-on immersion in the forest. She slipped back into her runners and filled a reusable bottle with water from the greenhouse cooler.

Ignoring the nagging voice that warned her that she should tell her family where she was headed, she struck out across the back of their sizable property for Chickadee Falls. She wasn't the family psychic, that fell to Lazuli. Likely what she felt was simple guilt for ignoring her family's warning to stay safe.

Out of sight of the house, greenhouses, and other outbuildings, tension began sliding off her shoulders. Almost imperceptible at first, the birdsong, wind in the trees, and sunshine-dappled forest began to ease her nerves.

She slipped down a little used, almost undetectable path to her secret place. She'd stumbled on it years ago. It wasn't pretty. Quite the opposite. Generations ago, some ancestor had dug a massive hole in the ground and revealed an old riverbed of rocks and gravel. Much of the stonework on their fireplaces had come from here, as had the rocks in the stone-walled gardens.

She wasn't after rocks. She was after the pile of sand that had accumulated in the center. With her shoes and socks off, she grabbed the small garden trowel she left there and dug a hole in the sand.

Kneeling on the mound she'd created, she thrust her hands into the hole, closed her eyes, and visualized the sandy walls of her hole caving in and burying her hands. She stayed there, locked in the image until her hands and wrists were covered.

Then, in an abrupt change of image, mentally pushed all her tensions, worries, fears, and uncertainties through her fingers into the soft moist sand.

The earth rumbled and shivered. Not a true shaking, like an earthquake, but a shiver, like a chill running through her body. It was a venting and a re-centering, in a place where the negativity could do no harm. She pushed slowly so as not to overwhelm Mother Earth with the poison of her thoughts. She cast a prayer of thanks to the earth and the Goddess for accepting her woes and burdens.

When she stood back, the earth where her hands had rested was dark. Slowly the shadows ebbed, and sunshine and warmth crept back in as if she'd never been there at all.

Using her mind, she refilled the hole and smoothed the sand until no trace of her being there remained. "Leave it as you found it," she quoted her mother and grandmother.

She wondered how her mother and stepfather were faring in their search for a magic stealer. She couldn't wait to hear of their travels and searches when they were home for Christmas. In just a few months, their family would be whole again.

She stuffed her socks into her shoes, tied the laces together, slung them over her shoulder and padded barefoot on the gravel, not minding the sharp pokes of sticks and stones. She resumed her journey to the falls, where she could be alone with her thoughts.

The falls were entirely on private property and occasionally a hiker would find them, but with their land entirely fenced in, that was rare. As the crow flew, it was less than half a mile to the falls. In reality, she traveled a deliberately wandering path that was closer to a full mile.

On the way, she saw two elk, a moose in a low swamp, and three mule deer. Birds chattered as she passed, unworried about her presence. As the sound of the falls grew, bird song ceased.

She wasn't alone. Someone was there.

Leaning against an enormous poplar, she put her shoes back on. She needed to be prepared if her guest was up to no good. She probably should have brought her phone. Crap.

A man sat on a blanket facing the falls with his back toward her. She recognized him in an instant. Earl. What was he doing here? Her aunt's question rolled through her mind. Was he here with good intentions? Or was he a threat?

She paused and listened to the ramblings of her mind until her heart intervened. He was not a threat. He was the only boy she'd ever loved. If she were honest with herself, no man she'd ever dated came even close to Earl Cooper. He was her heart, despite his earlier disdain and fear of what she was.

By the Goddess, she loved him so much her heart ached for it.

He spoke without turning around. "I know you're there Cynth."

She had made no noise, not a single movement. He shouldn't, couldn't have heard her. "How did you know I was here?"

"I don't know. I just did. Come sit. I brought a picnic."

"How did you know I would come here?" She edged closer, somehow still leery of his presence. "How did you beat me here?"

"Dirt bike. It's over there. I've been here for an hour. Hazel stopped by and told me you'd been released. I knew you'd come here. This is your favorite spot." He patted the blanket. "Come. Sit. I brought peanut butter cups and Dr. Pepper."

"Oh, my gosh. I haven't had that combination in years. I can't believe you remembered." Suddenly, her heart did not doubt him, she joined him on the blanket.

"I remember everything about you. Including that little mole just under your right..."

"Do not go there!"

His grin was unrepentant. "Whatever you say." He popped open a soft-sided cooler and handed her the soda. He set out cheese, French bread, butter, ham, fresh strawberries, and three packages of peanut butter cups. "Eat. I know you'll need it."

"How would you know that?" She shrugged. "You're not wrong."

"I talked to Meri. A lot. Today I asked what she'd do if she was just released after an accident and maybe an attack. It was an attack, wasn't it? I mean, she told me the details about Keres and Brown and everything that happened." It was his turn to shrug. "Anyway, she said she'd go to her favorite spot and vent. Then she'd need food." He paused and gave her a serious and longing look. "And here I am."

"You amaze me." She opened the peanut butter cups and devoured one. The chocolate and peanut butter were deliciously sweet on her tongue. "So good," she mumbled around the crumbs. "Last month you wouldn't even look at me, and here you are, satisfying all my needs." Heat rose in her face. "Well, not all of them." To her absolute surprise and delight, he laughed.

"That day with Meri and baby Anna, you showed me that magic is real. And if God saw fit to save her with magic, it can't be all bad. What's the saying? There are more things in heaven and earth."

"Yeah, but I think that's *Hamlet*. Not the Bible."

He gave a dismissive wave. "Take it for what it's worth, Hawk. It's an olive branch. And speaking of Shakespeare...are spells like "Eye of newt and toe of frog, wool of bat and tongue of dog,'"

She slapped a hand over his mouth. "Don't even think it!" She glanced around fearfully.

He paled and pulled her hand from his mouth and whispered, "Are you telling me that's real? Like actual magic?" His eyes went wide with fear.

She burst out laughing. "No, but you should have seen your face. Priceless." She dropped onto her back cackling with witchy laughter. "Oh, Earl..."

Suddenly, he loomed over her, frowning. Slowly the frown morphed into a soft smile. "You're going to pay for that, witch." Witch came out almost like an endearment.

"Oh," she whispered. *Would he kiss her? Please! Goddess, I miss his kisses.*

He shifted so he was sitting beside her, one hand on either side of her shoulders. He lifted his right hand and stroked his index finger down her cheek. "By God, I missed you." He leaned closer. "Can I kiss you, Hyacinth?"

The uncertainty in his tone surprised her. One thing Earl Cooper never was, was uncertain. About anything.

She reached up, wrapped her hands around his neck, and pulled him closer. "Yes, please." He resisted her pull and stared into her eyes until she was certain he'd changed his mind. His serious expression slid away to be replaced by a slow smile.

"As you wish." His lips brushed hers, barely a caress.

Lightning rocketed down her spine. Her entire body tingled. Sweet heaven, this was better than in their youth. "More," she whispered against his lips. Another brush. Her heart stuttered. Unfathomable, unquenchable love swelled through her. This man was her heart. Her soulmate. Her everything. Years fell away. Dimly she wondered how she'd ever managed to kiss another man after Earl.

She deepened the kiss, tracing his lips with her tongue. Probing, tasting. Kissing him as she had as a youth. When she was breathless, she slid her mouth to the side. "Whoa."

"No shit. Whoa on steroids. Where did you learn to kiss like that? I may have to kill someone."

She giggled. "Are you saying you didn't like my kisses when we were kids?" She was joking, but deep beneath there was a kernel of doubt. Shouldn't her soulmate be thrilled with whatever she gave?

"When we were kids," he said seriously, "You stole my breath, turned me on, and made my dick a rock. But baby, as a full-grown woman with curves that drive men wild, you shake the very foundation of my world. You don't know how hard it is to stop kissing you."

She quirked an eyebrow and smirked. "Is it hard?"

He growled and kissed her again. Abruptly, he pulled back and offered her a hand. "As much as I'd love to continue this, you need sustenance, and it's too early in our relationship to give in to carnal needs."

"You sure about that?" She let him sit her up.

"Not even freaking close to sure. Shut up and eat before I lose all respect for myself and for you and take what we both want but aren't ready for."

Chapter Eleven

E arl handed Cynth a strawberry. "Eat this."

"Are you always this demanding?" she teased. The sun glinted off her blonde hair. She had it drawn up in a high ponytail. Stray ends stuck out here and there, probably snagged by trees as she came through the forest. Her face was unlined. She looked a darn sight younger than a lot of similarly aged women. Twenty-seven wasn't old by any stretch, but she could still pass for eighteen, except for the wisdom in her eyes. She'd seen a lot of shit, and it showed in her shadowed eyes.

"Are you always this argumentative?" he countered. "Tell me about being a midwife." He popped open a cola for himself. Its sugary sweetness gave him a jolt of energy that he knew wouldn't last.

"I'm part midwife, part doula."

"Part what now? Doo la? What's that?"

"Depending on the client, I work with many first-time mothers who need help transitioning to parenthood. I'll work with them for up to three months, until they're on their feet, and over most of their nerves. Of course, more experienced mothers rarely need me."

"Cool. Why not be a delivery nurse?"

"What's with all the questions?" She broke off a chunk of bread and slathered it with butter. A lot of butter.

"I don't know. Getting to know you, I guess. It's been a long while since we talked. A lot has changed. I'm running the bookstore now. My sister has a kid. A healthy one, thanks to you. You guys opened up your shop. I've learned that magic is real, and ghosts exist. So much has changed."

"So, is this a bare all conversation?" She sounded nervous and she picked at the seam of her leafy leggings.

"More a getting to know you. Consider it a first date?" *That sounded so weird.*

"Okay. I'm not sure it's a date, but whatever." Her shrug was both eloquent and elegant. Sometimes, I use my magic to boost a mother or a child. Like I did with baby Anna. I use magically boosted energy bites as well. I couldn't do that in a hospital. Nor could I treat with herbs, though most modern meds come from a natural base. To stay true to who I was, I had to go my own way. Plus, I can choose my clients." She leaned back on her elbows to nibble her bread.

"Ever reject anyone?"

"Yes. Cassandra Mills, Jenette Gibson." She named two of their high school's bitchiest cheerleaders who had been mean to everyone. "I just couldn't accept them. Most of my clients, though not all, are from magical families."

"There are that many? I thought maybe one or two."

Her bright laughter startled him. "Dude. Half of Three Moon Falls is magical. Maybe more. And don't ask me to tell you who. We keep our true selves hidden. The Burning Times linger in our genes. My turn." She smirked. "What was it like dating Jenna Greenspan? You guys went out a few times."

"Three times and how did you know? You were watching me, you minx." He chuckled.

"Nobody uses the word minx anymore. It's archaic."

"I'm a wordsmith."

"Yet you didn't know doula. And don't wordsmiths write? Aren't they authors?"

"Maybe I am. I love the written word. I do own a bookstore, you know."

She jerked upright and stared at him. "What? You write? Like actual books? No fricken way. You're joking, right? What do you write?" Maybe she'd read some of his work.

"I am published. As for what I write, that's for me to know, and you to find out, because if I told you my secret identity, I'd have to kill you. I'm Book Batman. Nobody can know who I am, except my publisher."

She laughed and rolled her eyes. He knew he'd never seen anything so lovely. She was as adorable and quirky as she had been a decade ago. Warmth swelled in his heart along with sorrow for all the time they'd lost. He cursed himself for jumping to conclusions and giving in to fear back then, but he still couldn't shake a deep-seated unease about all that might be possible with magic.

"Can you at least give me a hint?"

"I write cozy mysteries, and that's all I'll say. Only my family knows my penname. When I marry, I'll tell my wife." Funny how easily he could picture her in his home. Cuddled up with him on the loveseat in front of a fire, a baby in her arms. He pushed the image away. It was way too early to go there. Despite being here today and trying to learn more about her, he wasn't certain they'd work.

His mind jumped from place to place, topic to topic. He snorted at his own waffling.

"What's that snort for?" She rolled a piece of cheese inside a slice of ham and bit the end off.

"Thinking too much, I guess."

"You always were an overthinker." She chuckled. Suddenly, her eyes widened and she leaned closer. "Don't freak out," she whispered in his ear. "We're not alone. Someone is out there."

"How can you tell? I didn't hear anything," he replied, equally lowly.

"Me either. But I can sense them."

His imagination shifted into overdrive. His thoughts fluttered past like the wind-ruffled pages of a novel. Was this ESP? Could she read minds? What other senses did she have? His thoughts stalled at the idea that they could be in danger.

"Should we leave?" he asked. He sipped his soda to clear the sudden dryness in his throat. The sweet beverage landed in his stomach like an avalanche of muck and stone.

"Act normal," she said. She leaned away from him. "I think I want ice cream."

"What?" He gaped at her.

"Ice cream. You know, that delicious frozen treat made from cream and sugar." She lifted one brow in question, a skill he'd never mastered. She was the only person he knew who could control her brows that well.

It kicked in that she was giving a reason for them to leave mid-meal. "You know what? A hot fudge sundae would be amazing. Finish that ham and we'll head back. I brought an extra helmet. While technically not legal, it'll get us safely back to my truck."

She devoured the ham while he talked. As she popped the last bite into her mouth, she stood and stretched. "I love this place," she mumbled around the bite. "One more bite of bread and butter and we'll go." She turned a circle. "Just look at it. So peaceful." She waved to the waterfall. "The water falling, the birds." She spun toward the forest, exclaiming about its beauty and the animals she'd seen earlier.

He fixed the bread she mentioned and let her ramble and walk around, knowing she was looking for clues as to who was there. She moved to the creek, which miles away, swelled to a stream, and then into a river. She kneeled and rinsed her hands in the water. While she was mostly protected from view, he saw her pick up two fist-sized rocks and wondered why. As weapons, they were suspect at best. She kneeled there, rocks in hand, just above the water for a full thirty seconds. She tossed them back with a double clank and rinsed her hands once more.

As she turned back toward him, a female voice called out, "Hello."

"Show yourself," she demanded. "This is private property."

"Is it? I'm sorry. I didn't know." The redhead from the restaurant strolled into view, a walking stick in one hand and a pack on her back. "Mind if I join you?"

"Yes. This is private property. You can leave now."

"I already mentioned I didn't know it was private. I apologize." Though she said the words, she made no motion to leave.

He rose to his feet. "The lady asked you to leave."

"Oh, give over stud," she said in a lightly accented voice. He was terrible with accents, but guessed maybe Irish. She strolled closer.

He crossed his arms over his chest and stared her down. "Who are you?"

"Rylie. I'm visiting Three Moon Falls and decided to take a nature walk."

"Five miles from town and across two barbed wire fences?" Hyacinth snapped.

The entire property was surrounded by two fences, twenty feet apart, with thick shrubs between the fences. There were only three easy entrances. The main gate, a side gate a hundred yards down the road from the main, and the back gate he'd come through. He'd only gotten through because he remembered the combination from years ago. He'd have to remind her to change the code.

"I didn't think the fence meant anything."

"Look, Rylie, or whatever your name is. It's time for you to go," Cynth demanded.

The woman stared at Earl, ice in her eyes, and he repressed the urge to shudder. She was up to no good. Something about him had his nerves screaming. How could he be afraid of this tiny woman? She'd freaked Cynth out the first time they saw her, and the tension in her shoulders said she was no less freaked now. Unless he missed his guess, she was barely holding it together.

A tiny ripple rolled under his feet. Like a mini earthquake.

Shit, she was losing it.

The woman smirked. "You're the earth witch then. Good to know." Her smile was as slimy as day-old bacon grease.

"We will be reporting this to the police," Earl said. "Leave now and stay off this land."

"It's not your land, so why do you care? You're not a Hawk." Her eyes narrowed and Hyacinth sputtered.

"Leave now," she demanded. "No more games. No bullshit. I don't know what you're up to, but it ends here. The Witch's Council will hear about this."

"Those wankers? Pfft. I couldn't care less if I tried. They're just a bunch of wannabe gobshites with no real skill. But I'll go. For now. See you around, witch. And you, stud, if you're looking for some hot love, give me a call."

He swallowed back a gag as she waggled her fingers in a parody of a wave and turned back the way she came.

"We need to follow her and see that she does leave." Earl slammed the leftovers into their containers and back into his soft-sided cooler and quickly folded the blanket.

"Cynth, honey? Are you okay?" She stood motionless, staring down the path.

"What?" She didn't move.

He went to her side and clasped her shoulders. "Are you okay?"

"What? Yes. I'm just trying to figure out what she's up to. She reeks of evil. She makes my skin crawl. I don't understand why she came here."

"The artifact? Or whatever it is?" He scraped his hands through his hair and jammed them in the back pocket of his button-fly jeans. "This makes me nervous as hell, Hyacinth. Something needs to be done."

"Ya, well, I wish to hell I knew what to do or where to find the stupid thing. I'd smash it into a million pieces if I could." Her anger didn't surprise him. The woman was obviously a threat to the Hawk family.

He tied the cooler to the bike. "Let's go. We'll follow her out." Helmets on, they idled slowly after her. As they crossed the last fence, a rusty yellow Toyota screamed down the gravel road he'd come in on.

"Damn. I wanted to get her plate number," Cynth muttered.

"We know the color and unless I miss my guess, it's an ancient Camry. There can't be that many of those in town. Let's go report this."

They loaded the bike into the back of his truck. All the way to town, she chewed her lips and drummed her fingers randomly on her thighs. The fear and confusion on her face pissed him off. Nobody had the right to get under her skin like that.

Chapter Twelve

"Hyacinth, I was just about to call your grandmother," Constable Stone greeted them as they entered the police station. "Come back into my office." She looked at Earl. "Should your friend wait in the lobby?" she asked.

"Earl's good. He's involved in why I'm here." Besides, she felt a deep comfort knowing he was at her side. It made no sense, as he had no magic, but his being there stabilized her jumping nerves.

Constable Stone led them past half a dozen empty desks and a lunchroom. They went down a black and white tiled hallway to a private office at the back of the station. Half a minute later, they were seated across from her with the door closed. "What brings you here?" she asked, flipping her dreadlocks back over her shoulder. The beaded ends clanked together. She was in full professional mode.

"After I got out of the hospital earlier today, I went to Chickadee Falls to recharge. I met Earl there." She relayed the story of the afternoon, keeping it to the relevant parts and ending with, "I don't know who the redhead is. She said her name is Rylie, if you can trust what she says. She drives an old yellow Toyota, probably a Camry and she was trespassing. We've got a sign on almost every fence post. She knew I was a witch and knew my last name. This isn't my first encounter with her, and it makes me nervous and uncomfortable." *Understatement of the year.*

"I can see why. I'll have my men watch out for her and see what she's up to and, I'll make another report to the council."

Having Stone at her back was reassuring, but she couldn't help but feel that it wasn't enough. They'd have to add more protection to their land, their home, their store. They chatted a bit about how to do that.

"You said you were going to phone Gramma Pearl. Can I pass on a message?"

Stone considered the offer. "I might as well tell you. There was a break-in, and an attempt to release some of the detainees at the prison two days ago."

Hyacinth and Earl gasped in unison.

"That's not good," Hyacinth said.

"Understatement of the year," Earl echoed her earlier thoughts. They'd always had the uncanny ability to think like the other without having to agree on everything. Magic had been the unpassable barrier between them. Though a few bricks had fallen from that wall.

"I just heard this morning," Stone continued. "They were caught trying to free Keres. They've been detained, but it brings up the question of who is behind this. Keres doesn't seem the type to inspire loyalty."

"Considering he killed his cohort; I'd say not."

Earl turned green. "I forgot about that."

"Yah. When they attacked us, he murdered his friend, or whatever he was, to use his blood. Blood magic is powerful, and evil. He nearly killed us all."

"Shit. No wonder Amber attacked back." He swallowed audibly. "I'm going to need time to process this. We better get you to your family, so you can tell them about this afternoon and the escape attempt."

As they walked back to his truck, she said, "Sorry you got pulled into this. My life is crazy right now. I wish that things could have been different between us. Then and now." Her heart ached.

His frown cut into her heart, reopening old wounds that had barely begun to stitch themselves closed. "Well," he said, sounding philosophical. "She's seen us together, more than once. I guess I'm in it for the long haul." His rogue grin, though nervous, was a balm to her heart, soothing over the wounds, though not eliminating them.

She stopped dead, halfway into the truck. "Are you sure? It's been ugly these past few months. Honestly, things have been as evil as you used to think magic was, only worse. I won't blame you if you take a hike." She wanted to beg him to go now if he thought he'd leave. She couldn't take another betrayal like the last one. It would be the death knell to ever loving again.

He closed his door without getting in and came around to her side of the truck and spun her to face him. He traced a finger down her right cheek. "Cynth, I've regretted my actions for a long time. Admittedly, it wasn't until you saved Anna that I began to believe. But I acted like a ginormous asshat, and for that I am sorry."

Her heart stuttered even as she wondered if his words might be too little too late. She chose to hope for the best and gave him a soft smile.

He cupped both her cheeks in his hands and looked right into her eyes. "I never stopped caring about you, even when you scared the ever-lovin' shit out of me. Now that I know I was wrong, I want to see what this fire is between us."

"Amber's the fire witch," she whispered to hide the trembling in her heart and knees.

"Goofball. Don't try and distract me with humor. You rocked my world the first time I saw you in the grocery store with your sisters. Four gorgeous teenage girls and I only saw you, earth witch. You bewitched me. I fell hard. Now, you're stuck with me. Maybe this won't work out. We're not the kids we used to be. But for good or bad, I'm willing to try again to see where this attraction leads, if you are."

His eyes darkened with emotion as he stared straight into her eyes. She read his sincerity, but also his fear. Was it for him, or her, or maybe for the future? An answering fear ran down her spine, and she shivered. She tamped her magic to avoid stirring up the earth. Strong emotions could be dangerous if unchecked. Fear was one of the worst.

She smiled at him. "Earl Cooper, you are foolish. I'm game to try, but I can't guarantee the future or your safety."

"I'm okay with that. Sort of." He grinned and brushed a kiss across the tip of her nose. "Let's go talk to your family and make plans. A strong defense is the best offense."

"Really," she laughed. "Quotes from your old football coach?"

"The man was an inspiration."

"You always said he was a tool and totally suspect."

"I was a teenage jock and a jerk."

"And a book nerd, too." She couldn't help but smile. "Your contradictions were what attracted me to you."

He waggled his eyebrows. "I was attracted to your fine-"

She slapped a hand over his mouth for the second time that day. "Don't even go there, Cooper." Laughing she climbed into the truck and waited for him to join her.

"The shop or home?"

"Shop, I think. We can call everyone from there." She slapped her palm over her mouth. "Holy crap. They think I'm in the garden. Gramma Pearl will flip when she finds out I left the immediate yard."

"You are an adult, you know that, right?" he teased.

"You've met my grandmother. What do you think? Plus, we've agreed to stay close to our homes, the shop, or work. With all this magical mayhem going on, it's best to be safe. I royally messed up by going to the falls. Thank the Goddess you were there. What if Rylie had tried something? I mean, I'm a hundred percent certain she's magical. She's got the aura of someone who casts dark magic."

"Is this going to come down to witch-on-witch action? I mean, this sounds like a made-for-TV movie or something. It's insane." He checked his mirrors and pulled out of the police station lot.

They drove slowly through town toward the shop. She waved at a few people she knew and got a couple, 'What the heck' looks back. Clearly, her friends were surprised to see her with Earl. Not everyone knew their troubled history, but a few people did. She got a full-on glare from one of the women he'd dated in the past. She waved back with a smile and shoved the negativity aside. She had enough to deal with already.

She stepped through the shop door and inhaled deeply. The soothing scents of mint, sage, and lavender washed over her. From the day it opened, the family's metaphysical shop had been a place of peace and comfort for the entire family. Sasha, the shop cat wandered up and brushed herself against her ankles with a meow and a low rumbling purr.

"Hey, Sasha. How's it going?"

"Merrp."

"A cat answer? What, no talking today?"

Earl gaped at them. "The cat talks?" he whispered.

"Only when she wants to. None of our other cats talk to us. I'm not sure if they can't or just choose not to."

He shook his head. "Unbelievable."

Pearl was at the shop with Amber, almost as if she were waiting for them to show up. "You left without your phone," she chided. "That was foolish."

"I was on our land."

"Don't sass me." Her grandmother gave her the look she and her sisters called the stink eye. A bit of a squint, her lips pressed together in a flat line, and one raised eyebrow. It was no less intimidating now than it had been as a child. "Do not leave the house without it again. At least not until the mess is cleared up. In fact, keep it with you in the house. That goes for you too Amber." The last dictate was funny, because Amber was basically living with Kody in the apartment over the shop.

"Fine." Cynth put a wealth of petulance and frustration into the one-word response. "We need to talk."

"About what?" Amber asked, coming from behind the counter, her floral skirt swirling around her ankles and brushing across her sandal-clad toes. She cast a questioning look in Earl's direction.

"This involves him too," Hyacinth answered her sister's unspoken question. "Call Lazuli and Hazel. See if they can come." She turned toward Pearl. "Do you have my phone?"

She rummaged in her black canvas purse for a moment and extracted the phone and a package of her energy balls. "Eat some of these. You two are pale."

"I'll run to the bakery and grab snacks," Earl said and bolted out the door.

"Coward," Pearl mumbled.

"Come on Gramma. It's been years since he's been around. He's only just learning that magic is real and he's had some shocks. Don't be too hard on him. He's a decent guy."

"I've always liked him," Amber added.

"I'm still unsure about where this renewed friendship is going," Hyacinth said. She walked to a shelf and straightened a row of candles. She looked around taking in all the new stock. Some dragon figurines, extra bags of herbs. "Oh, are these smudge sticks new?" She picked one up and smelled it. "Oh, rose and sage. This will smell lovely when it's burned. Maybe we should burn one now."

"I try not to smudge during business hours. We have customers who can't take the smokiness. But later, after I close, I'll be burning one. You've got negativity running off you like water."

"It's been a day all right." She walked to the back of the store, flipped through some books, and straightened some Tarot and Rune kits. Keeping her hands busy distracted her overactive mind. She was back to feeling jittery and didn't like it.

Earl came back just as Hazel and Lazuli arrived. Andi, their part-time staff member and friend, was watching the store. The family, Earl included went into the back room. Pearl served tea and coffee while Amber set out plates and the treats Earl had brought.

"So, long story short," Hyacinth said. "I went to the falls. Earl was there. While we were talking, the redheaded woman showed up." Everyone gasped. "She says her name is Rylie. No last name. She pretended innocence, but she reeks of black magic and something weird."

"This whole thing is weird," Earl muttered under his breath, taking a seat at the small kitchen table.

Hyacinth ignored him. "But that's not the worst of it." She leaned back against the counter and gave that a moment to sink in. "We went to the RCMP to report Rylie being on our land, technically trespassing, but we didn't press charges. At least not yet. Leticia advised us to press them if she returns. Once is an accident, twice is deliberate." She shrugged. "At least the incident is on record."

"That's good," Hazel said. "I'll make sure Dennis is aware of her too. He can keep an eye out for us."

"Leticia was going to call you Gramma. There was a breakout attempt at the magical prison. People were captured trying to free prisoners. Including Keres and Brown. After being caught, they were incarcerated as well."

"Busted broomsticks and rotten toadstools," Pearl blurted. "That means someone else could be behind our troubles. I thought we were free of Keres. Then Brown and Natalia showed up. It makes me wonder who else could have found out about this cursed talisman. If someone is trying to free them, it could mean they were after their own interests and someone else's. This is getting complicated."

"We're in deep shit." Lazuli carried a cup of tea to the couch and dropped onto its cushion. "Deep shit." She stared at everyone, her frantic gaze landing on Hyacinth last. "We're all in danger. So is everyone around us." Her eyes widened. "What about the surrounding innocents, the mundane? What about kids?" Her voice rose to a squeak. "Rosie Perrum could be hurt when she runs away and comes over to the house. I couldn't live with myself if that happened."

"We have to find that damn amulet, or whatever the hell it is." Hazel slammed her fist into her other palm. "This ends. Now."

The fire and determination in her sister's eyes were exhilarating, and if she were honest, a bit terrifying. Earl had gone white as a ghost.

E arl stared around the room. It was a combination family room, kitchen, storage area, and workshop. It had a small but full kitchen, complete with a table and chairs. There was a padded chair and a sofa. Further away were piles of boxes of merchandise and work-benches. The place was homey and welcoming.

But, at the same time, something nagged at him. He almost felt as if he were being watched. It wasn't the scrutiny of Hyacinth's family, though they were definitely giving him questioning looks. Lazuli, in her sawdust coated jeans and denim work shirt, looked like she had a hundred questions for him. Hazel gave him a look that said, "What can you do?" She shrugged and turned away.

Pearl's expression oscillated between questioning and accusatory. She probably wasn't thrilled that he was friends with Cynth again. And who could blame her? He'd hurt Hyacinth badly when they were younger. In Pearl's place, he wouldn't trust himself.

This whole magic thing was tearing up everything he believed, but for the life of him he couldn't just walk away. At the same time, he wondered what the hell he had gotten himself into.

"So, there's a Witch's Council, right? Can't someone just call them and get them to deal with Rylie and find the artifact?"

"They're not like the regular police," Pearl said. She sipped her tea and carefully placed her cup and saucer back on the table. "We do our best to keep mundanes, like you, unaware of us. Some police stations, such as ours, have magical officers, but they're in the minority. The council believes in free will and until there is a major issue, they'll be hands off."

"But didn't they step in when you were attacked? Isn't that how those men ended up in magical jail?"

"Yes, on both counts," Hyacinth said. "But unless Rylie or some-one else does something extreme, they won't step in. It's like parents ignoring the normal day-to-day bickering of their kids. Let the little things go, and solve the big problems."

He jumped to his feet. "This feels like a big problem to me."

"Not yet," Amber said calmly. "But I can see it becoming a problem. What do you think Laz?"

Lazuli closed her eyes. Her expression morphed to serious and contemplative. She hummed lowly and pressed the tips of her spread fingers together and pressed her index fingers to her nose. Her thumbs slid under her chin. A soft current of air shifted around the room and stray tendrils of her hair swirled about her head.

Holy shit. Magic in action.

He stared, fascinated.

"I can't get any kind of read on the near future. Or the far future, for that matter. There's nothing to predict at this point."

"Wait? What?" He swallowed hard. "You can predict the future?" He stared at her, slack-jawed.

"No. Not like you're thinking. I get premonitions, glimmers if you will, of the future. Sometimes I see multiple, but different, views of the same event. Like possible ways things might turn out. Most of my visions are about other people, rarely about me."

"So can you see if..." he struggled for an example. "If someone was going to have a baby, what it would be?"

"Sometimes. I don't always get solid images and being able to call a glimpse of the future when I want it doesn't usually work. Most often, I'll be hit with a vision while doing something else."

"I can't even wrap my head around psychics being real."

"Don't worry over it. It's a lot to take in. If anything appears that you need to know about, I promise to tell you."

He nodded though he wasn't certain he wanted to know his future, except if they were going to get out of this talisman thing unharmed, because based on the stories of previous attacks, it seemed like something bad could happen.

"The best thing we can do," Cynth said, "is find that talisman and either destroy it or give it to the council."

"How do we do that?" he asked.

"We've been reading our family grimoires. That's magic books. Every witch in the family has kept one. We're working our way through them. One at a time. Looking for clues."

"Like a book of shadows? Like TV witches?"

"More or less," Pearl answered wryly.

"Cool. Can I help?"

The women looked at each other. Some kind of silent communication passed between them. *Could they read minds? Yikes.*

"We prefer to keep our grimoires just to family. No offense."

He raised his arms defensively and shrugged. "None taken." He didn't mention it out loud, but he was a damned good researcher. He'd scour the internet for information or clues. Though he had no idea where to start, he'd compile notes on their descriptions of previous attacks and start with that information. Hell, maybe he'd learn more about witches and magic. He shuddered...and maybe even ghosts.

"Since Earl is involved, we need to strengthen the wards in the bookstore. The ones we gave him mightn't be strong enough," Cynth said.

Hazel, the youngest sister, sighed. "It seems like we're always making protective wards. As much as I love making them, this is getting old." She rubbed her hands together with fake enthusiasm. "Let's get this done."

Chapter Thirteen

Traffic whizzed by as Earl and Hyacinth walked through the cool air toward his shop, protective swags in their arms. He broached the next subject preying on his mind. It seemed like one thing after another these days. First, he'd fretted over Meri's pregnancy. She'd been, until Anna was born, his last living relative. He thought he'd die if anything happened to her. Then came the problems when Anna was born. They still didn't know why she was so weak until Cynth saved her. Then, all this business with Rylie. And, to top it all off, the ghost in his store just wouldn't stop shifting things.

"Can I ask you something?" He paused on the sidewalk and looked at Hyacinth. The sun glinted off her hair turning it all shades of gold with hints of silver and copper. Her blue eyes looked interested but shadowed with dark thoughts. Her face was pale, and she had purple bags under her eyes. She was beautifully exhausted.

"Sure. Ask me anything. You already know my biggest secret."

The joke fell flat between them.

"I think the bookstore has a ghost."

"That's not a question, but Hazel already told you there is a ghost there. What's the real question? Do you want Hazel to try to communicate with it? To see why it's hanging around?" Her smile was soft and reassuring. "It can't be malicious or you'd have seen more signs by now."

"Ya. I guess. Can you ask her to come over?"

"Yup." She whipped out her phone and one-handedly dialed her baby sister and explained the situation. She caught up to them before they entered the bookstore.

Inside, Hazel rubbed her hands together with glee. "Awe-some," she declared. "Let me at her."

"Let me see how many customers there are first. Go on into the office, I'll be right there after I check in with Jeri." He felt half foolish for having Hazel come to the store, but he was at his wits end. Shifting books, customers tripping over air, coffee spiked with salt or enough sugar to give him diabetes. He'd had his fill.

He stopped to chat with Jeri about the day's business. Jeri reassured him that everything was par for the course.

"Except, the bathroom taps keeps leaking," she said. "I turn it off and it's fine, but the next time I go back it's dripping again. I turn it off.... You get the idea."

He rolled his eyes. "I can't believe I'm going to say this." He sighed. "It's probably the ghost."

Her eyebrows flew to her hairline and her eyes went wide. She glanced around the store. "Did you just say what I think you said?" She chuckled. "Holy crap. Earl Cooper just admitted that what I've been saying, and he's been denying for years was true." She patted her chest. "Be still my beating heart."

"Stuff it." He laughed and shrugged. "Maybe I'm a believer now."

"You don't sound certain, boss."

"That's because I'm not. The whole concept is strange." He kept his voice too low for the two customers to hear. "Magic and ghosts. It's all so weird."

"But super cool when you realize it makes you aware of all the possibilities in the world. I mean, if magic and ghosts are real, are werewolves and vampires? What about pixies and elves?"

Fear crept down his spine and he shuddered. "Do not draw me into your *Buffy* and *Supernatural* fantasies," he warned.

"Never." Chuckling, she went to check on the customers.

He joined Hazel and Cynth in the office. "What do we do? Is it like a ritual or something?" He was so far out of his element that it was a bit terrifying.

"Not initially," Cynth said. "It's not a big deal, really. Either she'll talk to us, or she won't."

"There are ways to summon a reluctant ghost, but I don't think we need to go there," Hazel added. She looked around the office. "Mila Adamovich, we'd like to talk to you."

"You know her name?" Earl stared at her. "How?"

"It's called research." Hazel laughed.

"Don't be a jerk, Haze. This is all new to Earl." Hyacinth squeezed his shoulder. "We've researched every recorded and rumored ghost sighting in the area," she told him.

"Who's researched?" Hazel asked, sounding annoyed.

"Okay. Hazel has done most of the legwork, and the writing. But we're all familiar with ghosts. Some people die and their soul moves on. Some are trapped by unfinished business. Some, like our shop ghosts, are stuck and don't know why. Maybe there's a greater purpose or an event they'll play a role in later. Some souls just refuse to move on. No matter what happens, if they hang around too long, they can lose their sanity and become vengeful or evil."

"And what do I have?" he asked warily, not certain he wanted to know.

"That's what we're here to find out. Come on out, Mila. We know you're hanging around." Hazel pivoted in a circle, searching the office. "You've been playing tricks, trying to get this doofus's attention." She jabbed her thumb toward Earl. "We know you have something to say and we're here to listen."

He still couldn't believe this was happening, but resigned himself to the reality of it. He couldn't deny what had been happening right in front of him for his whole life. "Do you know anything about her?"

"Her name, if my research is correct, is Mila Adamovich. She was the daughter of Ukrainian immigrants who settled here shortly after the town was founded. This space was their grocery store. I'm not sure about all the details, but her infant daughter went missing and was later found dead. Mila went crazy for a while but eventually returned to normal. Well, as normal as a woman who has lost a baby can be."

"Jeepers. That's horrid." He looked around. "Mila, I'm so sorry for what you went through. Can you tell us why you're still here? Is it revenge?"

Rose water cologne drifted through the air as a misty figure materialized near the closed office door. His heart pounded and he gasped. Terror clutched at his throat, almost stealing his voice. "Oh." He pointed. "There she is." Hazel and Cynth turned to look, but nobody moved closer.

Mila wasn't a young woman when she passed. She was gray-haired, well wrinkled, and wore a frumpy dress so faded it had no color. Her hair was covered with a kerchief and she had a string of tiny pearls around her neck. Sadness carved grooves in her face and tugged down the corner of her mouth.

"I...I...I'm not sure why you're still here, Mila," Hyacinth said. "But we'll find out why and help you however we can." She glanced at him. He nodded his agreement.

How terrible it must be to be trapped between worlds.

"Can you tell us why you're here?" Hazel asked.

Mila shook her head and slowly faded away.

"Does that mean she won't tell us, or she can't tell us?" he asked. He scraped his hand down his face and then jammed his hands in his front pockets. "Jeez. I can't believe this." His knees shook. He dropped into his chair and elbows on the desk, cradled his head in his hands. "I'm too old for this shit."

"Dude, you're twenty-seven," Cynth chided him. Light laughter filled the air.

"Which one of you is laughing at me?" He lifted his head and glared.

"Um." Cynth snickered. "That would be Mila."

"No way. No fricken way." He groaned. "Is it too early to start drinking?"

"Early, it's almost dinnertime. Probably past. I'm starved." Hazel smirked. "Let the drinking begin. I'm going to do more research, but right now, Dennis and I have a dinner date and I don't want to be late." She waggled her fingers and left.

"What now?" he asked, just as Cynth's phone chimed. She shrugged and pulled it out.

"Gramma Pearl wants my cousin Cecily to examine me. She's worried that Rylie could have messed with my head."

He blinked stupidly for a second. "For the love of Pete. What else are you going to spring on me today? This has been the day from hell, I swear to God."

"Bet you're having second chances about being around me," she said quietly. Her eyes were dark with anxiety and fear.

"I probably should be, but for some strange reason, I'm not." He came around from behind the desk and clasped her hands. He wanted to hug her to reassure them both but feared pushing her too far. Today had been an emotional rollercoaster of a day already. "I told you earlier, magic still scares the crap out of me, but you've proven to me that you're a good person. That's enough for me."

"But..."

"No buts, Cynth. I get it. Weird shit is going down. This terrifies me, but I'm not leaving you to face it alone. I might not be magic, but I know karate and kickboxing. I'm good with knives and familiar with guns. I'm hoping like crap that it doesn't get that far, but I'm still in."

She stepped closer and leaned her head against his heart. "You're a fool, Earl. You should run far and fast."

He couldn't admit it to her, at least not yet, but he felt stable and happy when he was with her. Like he could face the world. She soothed something in him, even as half of his body was constantly focused on her sweet curves and memories of the kisses they'd shared in the past.

"Let's go see your cousin. Maybe she can check us both over."

She looked up at him. "You'd let her do that?"

"Honey, I'm scared half-spitless. If people really can mess with minds, I want to know that mine's unsullied." He shivered just thinking about it.

Chapter Fourteen

"Come on then. Let's go back to Four Seasons Metaphysical." She loved saying the name of the family's shop. "We'll both get checked over."

"Is there a fee?" he asked and patted his backside like he was looking for his wallet.

"No. Most witches don't ask for payment for services."

"But you sell magical stuff?"

"We sell products for use in magic, and a few charms and tokens. Things like wards. But those are physical products. Healing is different. And don't mention my doula services. They pay for the doula, not the magic I might need during their care."

"Okay. I get it."

It was clear from his voice that he didn't quite get it, but she let it go. "We do, however, accept gifts. Some witches take cash if offered. I expect Cecily would stuff it in your mouth if you offered a gift of cash. But she'd likely accept a bookstore credit."

"How much?"

"What's your piece of mind worth?"

"Oh, that is such a non-answer." He shook his finger under her nose. "I'll figure it out." He slipped one arm around her waist and led her out of the store.

"It's so hard to believe I left the hospital before ten this morning. I feel like it's been ten days, not eight hours." So much had happened.

It was pushing six o'clock and she was starving. The snack Earl brought to the falls was interrupted and hospital breakfasts of mostly-cold oatmeal were inedible. She had nibbled her dry muffin and ate the peach, but ignored the rest. Even the coffee was vile and hospital rules wouldn't let her use her own tea.

"Do I know your cousin?"

"Probably not. Cec lives on a small farm just outside Edmonton. She doesn't come to town often. Usually, we go there for visits. You know, the glamor of the city and all that."

Hyacinth hid a smile. She sat cross-legged on the couch, her hands in her lap while her cousin hovered over her. Earl sat across from her, his hands fisted together, his eyes wary. "Chill, Earl. It's not a big deal."

Touching another person's mind could be a big deal if it was done without invitation. But in this case, she welcomed it. "She won't be able to read your thoughts. She'll just look for magical anomalies."

"Like shadows left behind," Cecily said. "There are people who can read minds, I'm not one of them."

Earl's expression relaxed, though he still looked at her red-headed cousin like she was totally suspicious.

"You ready?" Cec asked Hyacinth. They were alone in the back room with Earl. Pearl had left to make dinner for everyone, Hazel and Lazuli were back at work, and Amber and her fiancé Kody were out front, watching the store.

"Ready as I'll ever be." As much as she hated having someone poke around in her mind, it was necessary and she completely trusted her cousin and knew she'd never peek at anything she shouldn't, not that she had the ability. Gramma Pearl could sneak looks, to a limited extent, but rarely did so. Such intrusions were highly frowned upon by the council.

"Take some slow, deep breaths."

Cecily waited for her to take three breaths. "Here we go, keep breathing steady." She rubbed her hands together, gathering power from the air around her. As an air witch, like Lazuli, she could pull straight from the air. She placed her palms flat on Hyacinth's head, just above her ears.

"Oh, that tingles." She trembled a little. Cecily's touch was different than Gramma's friend's. Stronger. Cec moved her hands in slow circles, humming a joyful tune as she slid her palms from place to place. Her green eyes were lightly closed, and she bit her lip. While her touch was uber-light, her arms were tensed, and her biceps clenched. The tingling stopped almost immediately. The examination didn't take long.

Cec stepped away and sat beside Hyacinth. "I can't feel anything. There are no shadows."

Disappointment battled relief. She'd half expected Cec to find something. Why else had she imagined a cat on the road? If there were a shadow, it would explain what happened. It brought up a million questions, none of which she'd ask in front of Earl. He didn't need to be exposed to more than he already had been.

"Excellent," she exclaimed, rising to her feet. "Let me get you an energy ball." After some fresh squeezed orange juice and three balls, it was Earl's turn.

"You'll feel some tingling," Cynth warned him. "Like ripples of static across a TV screen would feel like. It's not painful, I just wasn't expecting it."

"And you can't read my mind?" He looked at Cec, doubt in his eyes.

Only someone who knew him as a boy would recognize the nervous tremor in his voice. Cynth detected it immediately. "She can't and she won't. I'll be over there, just focus on me and let her do her thing."

He sat on the couch, wiggled around, and jumped up. He paced the room and sat back down. "Okay. I'm ready."

"You've got this." She caught his eye and said, "I promise it'll be fine."

He closed his eyes and nodded.

Cec stepped in. "Here we go." She rubbed her hands together and placed them on his head.

He let out a girly squeal but didn't move aside from a small jump. "So weird," he mumbled.

Cynth admired his bravery. How many men could go through all he'd been through today without being weirded out? She wasn't weirded out, but she was tense and nervous. Something was coming. Something big and she wasn't sure her family was ready for it, let alone a mundane like Earl. She half wished they'd never started rebuilding their friendship. She was scared for herself, and terrified for him.

What had she dragged him into?

His first thought was that Cecily smelled like lemonade. Then, she touched him, and electricity danced over his skin. The pressure of her hands was almost nonexistent, but the electrified feeling stayed for the entire time as she moved her hands against him. He felt nothing else. He rather expected to feel her walking about in his mind, like when someone walked their fingers up your arm. Tiny footsteps or something, but on his brain. He was relieved that he didn't feel anything inside his head.

"You're clean too," Cec announced and stepped back. "I don't know what that woman was up to, but she wasn't in your heads that I can detect. Or, more accurately, she didn't leave any residue."

"Thank God for that!" he exclaimed wholeheartedly. He stood. "Cecily, thank you. Swing by the bookstore when you have time. I'd like to thank you by giving you a store credit."

Cec nibbled another energy ball. "Thanks, Earl. I appreciate it. There's never enough money for books. It was my pleasure to help out a friend of my family." She flipped her long red hair over her left shoulder and her green eyes glowed with pleasure at his offer. She was lovely, but beside Hyacinth's blonde hair and pretty blue eyes, she was pale in comparison.

He looked at Cynth and smiled. "I think I need some time to think," he said. She went pale and he quickly added, "Just a couple of hours. A lot of shit went down today. Not the least of which was all this." He waved his hands around his head. "Plus, you need time with your cousin."

He stood and went to Cynth and wrapped his arms around her. "You, my friend, look as exhausted as I feel. Go, get some rest, and text me when you feel up to it. Okay?" He pressed his forehead to hers and fought the urge to kiss her. It was too soon. He still felt guilty for breaking them up out of fear, so how could she have forgiven him?

Surely, she had some residual resentment. He'd bide his time and not rush anything that might develop between them.

She leaned back and smiled up at him. "You're a good man, Earl Cooper. I'll text you later. Or tomorrow." She popped up on her toes and brushed a kiss across his lips. "I like having you in my corner," she whispered before stepping back. "Go and relax. Call me if you need me."

Half an hour later, he was in his apartment over the bookstore. He'd put away the leftovers from their picnic while he waited for his pasta dinner to be delivered. He tended not to eat too many carbs, but sometimes, like tonight, he wanted comfort food and there was nothing better than seafood linguini and garlic toast to fill that need.

He cracked a beer, fired up his computer, and opened a spreadsheet. He entered the names Adam Keres, Mathew Brown, and Natalia Smith. Natalia had lived in Drayton Valley, and Keres in Edmonton, so he wrote that down too. Then he added the name of the landowner of the island where Hazel and Dennis had been attacked. On another tab, he made notes of the attacks as Hyacinth had explained them to him. Then, he started a computer search using all their names and their known locations. He'd likely need to eliminate things one by one, but the first step in any proper search was to begin with everything you knew, and admittedly, he didn't know much.

Chapter Fifteen

"He was cute," Cecily said when they were alone in the back of the shop. "Where'd you find him?" She waggled her dark brown eyebrows. "I mean, he's, like, hot." She fanned her face.

"I've known Earl since I was a kid. We dated in high school."

"Oh, my Goddess, is he the guy that dumped you?" She plopped onto the red sofa and propped her feet on the coffee table.

"The same. He's come around since he had to help me save his niece, who was dying, just minutes after she was born. Learning that magic is real has mellowed him. A lot." She sighed. "So much has happened in only a few days. Baby Anna being so weak, if I didn't know better, I'd say someone was trying to steal her life force, but that makes no sense." She explained the events with Rylie.

"Seems like Earl was with you every time. Are you sure he's okay?"

"Absolutely sure. I don't get any magic vibes from him at all. None. You know how it is. You can tell a magic user from a block away. They just have this aura. Light or dark, depending on what magic they use. Earl's as flat as it is possible to get."

"But you said he pushed his energy into you?" Cec reasoned.

"Did he? Or did I just pull it from him? It could be either. And we both know half of magic is in the intention. I'm not worried about Earl at all." And she wasn't. The fact that two people had suggested Earl wasn't all he appeared annoyed her.

"I don't get anything off him either. But, girl, I just hope you know what you're doing hanging around him."

"I'll be careful." She would be, but not because she thought Earl was more than he appeared, but because something was going on and she wanted to get to the bottom of it. They needed to find that damn talisman. Now!

"Anyway," she said, sitting beside her cousin. "How long are you here for?"

"I took two weeks off work. I had vacation days coming. You know, take 'em or lose 'em. I figured I'd hang out here. Check out the shop. Keep Amber company while she works. Plus, you've got the best greenhouses in the province, maybe the country. I need to get my hands dirty. Being a paramedic isn't all it's cracked up to be." She shuddered. "Some days are hard on my soul."

"Oh, honey." She wrapped Cec in her arms. "I know how you feel. Sometimes, the pain is so hard to bear."

They commiserated for a while and after supper went out to the greenhouses to unwind with dirt and fresh growing flowers.

Hyacinth was excited to see Earl again. She hadn't seen him for three days. She'd been too busy delivering babies to call. They'd texted a few times, but that didn't make up for face-to-face meetings. She was styling her hair when Cec and Amber strolled in.

"What's up, sis?" Amber asked. "We're going to a movie. Want to join us?"

Hell no. She had a date.

"Where's Kody tonight?" She looked at their reflection in the bathroom mirror. Though Cec was a redhead and Amber a blonde, they shared the same green eyes, and their noses were virtually identical.

"He's doing a beginner's class at the pool this evening." She smiled fondly when she talked of her fiancé. Love glowed in her eyes and her pink cheeks.

"That explains it. I'd love to go with you, but I have a date."

Amber grinned. "You go, sister. Enjoy!"

Cec was less enthusiastic, but aside from her slight frown, she kept it to herself. "Catch you later. Maybe we can have tea when you get home."

"Cec, I'd love that." Hyacinth finished her hair and dabbed on some lip gloss. With a quick double-check of her black jeans and gold sweater in the bedroom mirror, she waggled her fingers. "Catch you later, chicklets. I have to get to town to meet Earl at the shop."

She looked at Amber. "Who is watching the store?"

"Gramma Pearl and Andi are there tonight. Gramma's idea." Amber worked long hours as the shop was open until nine five nights a week, and nine to six on Saturday and Sunday. All the sisters spelled her off when they could. Hazel worked full-time at the garden center, Lazuli was up to her neck with woodworking commissions, and Gramma Pearl kept her eye on the shop and the family gardens. Everyone created supplies, candles, talismans, artwork, dried floral arrangements, and things like that for the shop. But they all found time to help Amber and her staff with the store's long hours. Kody and Amber spent a lot of nights working together after his diving was done for the day. They were interviewing for more staff, but nobody suitable had applied.

"I'll pop in later and check on things since I'll be in town anyway."

"You do realize I live right above the shop, right?" Amber teased.

"Only until your house is built." Amber and Kody had plans to build a house on the Hawk's family land. Hazel and Dennis would live in Dennis's house behind his greenhouses outside of town. Right now, neither sister was home often. It saddened Hyacinth, but her heart was flush with joy for her sisters' happy relationships. Honestly, she was a bit jealous, not that she'd ever mention it.

"Oh, hun," Amber hugged her again. "We'll be close. You won't hardly miss us at all. Especially after you get your own man." She patted Cynth on the butt. "Now, go get your man. Have fun and don't do anything I wouldn't do." She pushed Cynth toward the door. "Go. Go. Go."

Cynth raced down the stairs and paused at the bottom to wave. "Later, gals." With her truck still in the shop, she jumped into the '69 Camaro she had inherited and headed for town. As she drove, she fondled the protective pendant Amber had made her. They all had one. Each held a large central citrine, surrounded by their birthstone alternating with tiny faceted moonstones and obsidian. The entire thing was set in sterling silver on a thick, but delicate chain. It was bright, colorful, and soothing to touch.

Her heart skipped happily. She'd longed for this date for so long. Nearly a decade. Okay, probably longer than that. She'd adored Earl from the moment she saw him. He'd been kind, generous, and helpful to the kids around him. His friends and teachers respected him, and he was a bright colorful light in the church youth group they'd both attended. She hadn't been much on the group itself, though the moral tenants it preached were sound.

What she'd loved about it was watching Earl, then growing close to Earl once he noticed her. And later, after the meetings were over, spending time alone with him, and kissing. Oh, sweet Goddess, how she'd loved his kisses. She couldn't wait to kiss him again, even if it felt like rushing their burgeoning relationship.

Burgeoning. She giggled at the double entendre. If she was lucky, something would be burgeoning between her and Earl before long.

Earl was leaning on the brick wall of Casper's when she arrived. She sat in the car a moment, taking him in as he scrolled on his phone. In deference to the cool evening, he wore a leather bomber jacket and snug button-fly blue jeans. The top button of his shirt was undone, and he had one hand in his pants pocket. Sweet heavenly skies, he was delectable. Delicious. She wanted to skip dinner and devour him.

He looked up and caught her eye. His wink sent shards of lust straight to her lady bits. It was a danged good thing they were meeting in public. If they'd been at his place, she'd likely have attacked him on the spot.

"Get a grip," she muttered to herself. She waggled her fingers in a little wave and shut off the car. Her knees shook as she got out. Nervous chills danced through her spine. She didn't want to mess up this relationship.

Earl strolled toward her and held out his hand with a soft smile. "Hyacinth, you look lovely. That sweater makes your skin glow."

"Thanks." She blushed.

"Shall we?" He nodded toward the restaurant. "I made a reservation for a table overlooking the lake on the screened-in deck."

"Lovely. I haven't had a chance to eat out there yet." She took his hand and allowed herself to be led inside. Tonight felt very date-like. A slow, sweet warmth crept through her and lodged in her heart.

Where could they have been if fear and misunderstanding hadn't thrown them apart in their youth? Would they have stayed together?

Would they have parted for some other reason? Hyacinth suspected that they weren't mature enough for the long term and that the Goddess had played a hand in their breakup. The biggest question burning deep down was whether they could make this work long-term.

They were seated at an intimate table in the corner of the deck with an amazing view of the lake. The lighting was dim. Electric candles shone on each of the seven cloth-covered tables. Earl held her chair for her and brushed a kiss on her cheek as he eased her chair in.

Nine houseboats floated on the lake. The lake was dark, but their small lights bobbed here and there. The dock was lit with dim solar lights. The bobbing lights seemed like reflections of the brightest stars overhead.

The air was still and cool, but not cold enough to make her wish they were inside. A small wood-burning fireplace brought additional warmth to the deck occupants and provided more light without disturbing the romantic atmosphere.

"Wine?" Earl asked.

She considered for a moment. "No. Probably not tonight. I have to drive home. I'd adore a cup of decaf coffee." Their server arrived to take drink orders and drop off menus. It seemed like only seconds when he was back.

After perusing the menu she said, "I think I'll have the beef Wellington and the garlic mashed potatoes. How about you?"

"Aren't you vegan?" Astonishment rang in his voice and pinched his brows together.

"Not really. I rarely eat beef, but I love chicken. Except for bacon, I'm not much for pork. No special reason, it just doesn't appeal to me." She smirked. "Tonight feels like a beef night. Besides, I've heard it's amazing."

Earl opted for the lemon-dill cod and rice pilaf, and the server vanished again. The guy was so stealthy she'd almost swear he was using magic to muffle his approach. The thought reminded her to keep any discussion of the recent events for another time and place.

"Do you remember when Damien Archer dove into the lake naked?" Earl asked with a laugh.

"During the grade twelve final camp? Don't remind me. Damien was always a showboat. Though it has served him well. Have you seen his latest movie?"

"I haven't. Was it good?"

"I think it's the best of the franchise." Conversation flowed and they fell into their old pattern of taking turns asking questions after they'd hashed one subject to death.

Earl was attentive to her needs, handing her the cream for her coffee, and pouring water from the small carafe before her glass was empty. The actions themselves were simple, but the tenderness and support they engendered were more complicated and very welcome. This kind of treatment was what she'd been waiting and longing for. Her opinions and needs mattered to him as much as his mattered to her.

"I want to apologize again," Earl said, folding his hands between his body and his empty plate.

"Are we going there, again?" She raised one eyebrow. "In hindsight, I did spring it on you rather abruptly. I could have, should have, gone slower. I guess I thought that since Meri is magic, you'd understand." She swallowed some old resentment. "The apology is mine." Genuine regret pressed on her shoulders. She'd been wrong.

Earl's serious expression slowly morphed into a warm smile. "I think we should agree to forgive each other our youthful mistakes and move on. Let the past go and look to the future." He looked thoughtful and she knew he wasn't finished speaking. "I'm not the boy I was back then. I'm less arrogant and certain I'm always right. I've learned that there are other opinions, other ways of living. It's given me a greater understanding of others." He glanced around as if ensuring himself nobody was listening. "I won't say magic doesn't freak me the fuck out, because it does. But I'm trying to be calm and rational. I've seen the good it can do, which balances my fear of the bad it could potentially do."

"Most magic wielders believe in the mantra 'do no harm'. But I do understand your fear. I'm worried too." She shook off a deep abiding sense of unease. "I'd like to rebuild this friendship." She grinned. "I know, we've said that before. But, this time, I mean it." She thrust out her hand. "Friends?"

He shook with her and lifted his glass with his other hand. "Cheers to new and growing relationships."

They touched glasses. "To us." Warmth started in her heart and seeped through her entire body. She hadn't felt this good since she first realized she was in love with him as a teenager. She wasn't any less vulnerable now, but she was more realistic.

"Want to take a walk?" she asked. "It's cool outside, but the sky is so clear, and the stars are lovely."

After settling the bill, Earl took Hyacinth by the arm and led her outside. She didn't need his help, but he liked touching her, even through her sweater and jacket. He'd never admit it aloud, but he was a bit giddy to be with Hyacinth. She was good company and if he were honest, he'd really missed her sunny smile and cheerful personality. Her smokin' hot body was nothing to sneeze at, either.

Outside, he slid his grip down and tangled his fingers with hers. She didn't pull away, and he banked a pleased and satisfied smile. "Do you want to take the left path through the campground, or go right along the waterfront and shops?"

"Oh, tough call." She paused and thought. "Let's go waterfront. I love the way the moon glistens on the water."

This late in the year, all the waterfront shops were closed evenings. In the busy season, most stayed open until ten. They sold hot food, snacks, souvenirs, and beachwear. A couple rented waterboards. Down by the docks, there was a boat rental place and a charming candy store called the Sugar Shack.

The path was illuminated by flickering LED lights designed to replicate old-fashioned oil lamps. It was a little more romantic than he expected, but Cynth seemed to be enjoying herself. She chatted about her work, which was fascinating, and asked him questions about the bookstore and about baby Anna. They talked a bit about politics and agreed to disagree on a few issues.

"Oh, look," she exclaimed, pointing toward the lake. "Ducks."

Half a dozen ducks floated on the water, swimming in and out of the moon's reflection. "I wish I had my camera. It would make an amazing shot."

"You still have a camera? Don't you just use your phone?" She pulled hers out and clicked off a few shots.

"I do, for most things, but sometimes I feel that a camera would suit me better. With the right lens filter..." he trailed off. "I'll probably come back again and see if I can recapture this. With luck, ducks will be creatures of habit."

"It's good that you still take pictures. You used to really enjoy it."

She was right. He loved photography. She used to be one of his favorite subjects. He probably had a thousand pictures of her from when they'd dated. Wherever they went, he'd snapped images. She'd always looked her best outdoors. In hindsight, that was probably because she was an earth witch. Funny how perspective changes things.

"We could go get your camera now and come back. They might still be here."

He appreciated the offer. "Naw. I'd rather just walk with you if that's okay." Her brilliant smile was reward enough. They strolled past the last lamp and kept walking. The path changed from cement to gravel, and then to dirt and sand. They'd probably walked a couple of miles when they approached a bench on the side of the lake.

"Let's sit for a minute." She sat and patted the bench beside her. "It's a beautiful night."

"It is." He sat and could feel the heat from her body. "Are you warm enough?" When she nodded, he said, "Not many mosquitos tonight."

"She chuckled. "I'm keeping them away."

"What?" He stared at her. "You can do that?"

"For short periods, yes."

"Can anyone do that?"

"No. You'd have to be magic, and even then, not everyone can do it. Lazuli can't, though my other sisters can."

"Well, it's a pretty neat trick and I appreciate it. Thanks." He slung his arm around her shoulder and gave in to the urgent need to kiss her cheek. She snuggled into his side like she belonged there. The breeze shifted her hair and brought him a hint of her lavender scent. He'd never been able to smell lavender without thinking of her. Today it mingled with a hint of strawberry.

Sitting, snuggled up together, was creating havoc in his brain and elsewhere. He should shift aside, or something before he gave in to the urge to kiss her. She turned and brushed her lips on his cheek, and he was lost.

He pivoted and captured her in his embrace and stared down into her eyes. He paused for ten long seconds and lowered his mouth to hers. Gently at first, then more firmly when she didn't resist. She shifted closer and wrapped her arms around his neck.

Arousal rocketed through him. His heart thumped and his soul sighed. Damn. He'd missed her, missed this. Tempted though he was to give into the passion flooding his entire being, he kept the contact light and easy. If these feelings were worth growing, there was no rush, despite the lost time between them.

Allowing himself one sweet moment, he deepened the kiss, pouring all his hopes and dreams into the gesture before backing away slightly. He leaned his head against hers and sighed. "As much as I'm enjoying this, it isn't very private. I'm not one for PDAs."

Her sigh echoed his. "I suppose." She sounded as disappointed as he felt. "We could take this someplace private," she suggested.

He stood and offered his hand. Wordlessly, they headed back toward the restaurant.

"Want a ride home?" she asked after looking around the nearly empty parking lot. "I don't see your vehicle."

"I walked." She wrinkled her nose. "On a date?"

"Well, if I drove, I wouldn't need a ride home, now would I?" He chuckled. "This way I get to spend more time with you because you had to drive. It's miles to your house."

"Not if I stayed at the shop, which I've been known to do."

"Aha, then I'd get to walk you home. Seriously, it's a win-win situation."

"Unless I drive off and leave you here."

He clutched his chest in mock pain. "You wouldn't do that." His theatrics earned him a light breezy laugh. "Nice car," he said as they climbed in.

"Thanks. I inherited it. Not too many '69 Camaros around these days. I don't drive her often. Just enough to keep her in shape. I wouldn't want the seals to dry out. But with my SUV in the shop..." She sobered abruptly then shook her head. "Doesn't matter. I'll be back in my SUV before long."

He didn't want their date to end on a sour note so he told her dad jokes until she smiled freely once again. "Why do witches stay in five-star hotels?

"I don't know, why?"

"Because of the excellent broom service."

Her groan was worth a million dollars, so he threw out another. "What do you call witches who live together."

"No idea."

"Broom mates."

She snorted once, then laughed as she pulled up to the bookstore.

He climbed out of the car. "Good night, Cynth."

"Thanks for the lovely evening, Earl. I enjoyed myself, but I don't know where you get all those vulgar jokes."

"Those are dad jokes, and I keep them in my dad-a-base." He grinned and shut the door on her exasperated sigh.

She drove away, shaking her head and smiling.

All in all, a pretty darn good date.

Chapter Sixteen

It was late, but Hyacinth couldn't stop herself from heading upstairs to their family library of notebooks, diaries, and grimoires. She hadn't said anything to Earl, no sense freaking him out, but all night, the possibility, no the truth, that there was another magical threat in town plagued the back of her mind. She could almost envision her worry as little termites chewing away at the foundation of her mental stability. Shivering, she climbed the stairs to the third floor.

Cool reason and calm washed over her as she entered the family library. As she did every time she entered, she paused to take in the familiar comfort of the nearly circular space. The air was fresh, as always, and had an undertone of smudging sage. She opened one of the floral stained-glass windows for fresh air. Several of the walls were lined with books. There were six cozy chairs set in groupings of two with tables between them. Unlit candles adorned many of the flat surfaces.

Bookshelves lined the walls without windows. At twelve feet across, it wasn't huge but was still spacious and airy.

She'd spent hundreds of hours here reading up on magic. Sneaking a peek here and there at ancient grimoires, some so old the English was hard to decipher. The snippets of her family's past were fascinating. Almost no one outside the family even knew the library existed. Though Amber's fiancé Kody and Hazel's fiancé Dennis had been admitted to help search for clues about that damned talisman.

Research was why she was here rather than in bed. She wasn't psychic like Lazuli, but a dark sense of impending doom hung over her like an unshakable cloud. It poked at her brain like a burr in her underwear. She turned on one of the side lamps rather than the overhead fixtures and walked to the shelves. They were chronologically filed. The oldest was top left, each shelf was left to right, top to bottom, and then restarted on the next shelf. Covers ranged from black to white with everything in between. Most were green or brown, but there was an occasional bright purple or deep red. Several volumes were missing. Her family must have taken them to study. They were all older ones, from at least seventy-five years ago, which made sense. From what they'd learned so far, it seemed that one of their ancestors, long ago, had gained possession of a talisman somehow and had taken it when they fled Salem.

What it was, and where it was, remained a mystery. Though both Amber and Lazuli had had sparks of premonition about it: Amber's featured running water, and something wrapped in cloth. Lazuli's focused on danger to the family soon but contained no real details.

She stood before the first shelf and ran her hand across the magically protected book spines. Row by row. Halfway down the second shelf, she stopped without meaning to. She pulled the purplish-red leather-bound book off the shelf and stroked the brilliant yellow moon and stars adorning the cover.

Excitement and energy radiated from the book.

"Are you the book we've sought so hard?" she whispered.

She moved to a chair and silently cast a prayer. *Great Goddess. Mother Earth. Creator of all. Help me find the clues I seek. Help us be free of the evil plaguing our family and our town. Help us end this. Give us the strength to deal with what comes our way. As I will it, so mote it be.*

It didn't rhyme, it was just words strung together in her mind and mentally cast out into the universe. Again silently, she added: *We've been good custodians of the land, protective of the earth. We've been strong for our friends and stood up for injustice. We've done what's right and good. For you and for others. And we thank you for all the goodness and bounty you've gifted us with.*

Confident the Goddess had heard her plea and her thanks; she opened the book.

The paper liner inside the cover, the end page, had a clumsily illustrated image of a waterfall amid a forest. At the base of the falls, surrounded by churning water, it read Rosalie Amber Hawk and a blurry date. The month and day were unclear, but it looked like the year was 1892. That was quite a while after the family had settled here in 1886. The illustration was poorly wrought, but to Hyacinth, it resembled Chickadee Falls, where she'd been with Earl just days ago. Maybe it was only her imagination teasing her because of the recent trip and her desperate desire to solve this.

She turned to the first page and started reading. It was soon apparent that this was a journal, not a grimoire. Daily entries talked about crops and chickens and how it felt to carry a child at only fifteen.

Cynth couldn't imagine bearing a child so young. She was twenty-seven and had only recently started thinking of her future family. Times were different now, but fifteen was still a child. Yawning, she read on. Page after page. Rarely did Rosalie skip more than two days. She read until her eyes burned.

Someone shook her shoulder. Fight or flight kicked in. She swung wildly with her fist and connected with soft tissue.

"Settle down, goofus. It's me," Lazuli grumbled. "No need to punch me out."

Hyacinth blinked. Her sister stood over her with the journal she'd been reading in her hands. "What? I'm reading."

"You're sleeping. I got home late from finishing a commission, saw the light on and assumed someone had forgotten to shut them off. I never expected to find you here. Research?"

"Ya. Pointless research. Our ancestors kept boring diaries." She rolled her eyes and yawned again. Gosh, she was exhausted. It was no wonder she'd fallen asleep.

Lazuli looked down at the book in her hands and frowned. "I don't know," she said slowly, sounding uncertain. "It does have a vibe to it."

Cynth perked up, suddenly fully awake, all traces of exhaustion gone. "Really?" Her blood thrummed. She waved for Laz to give it back with a frantic finger wiggle. "Gimme."

"Nope. We're both too tired. We could miss something important. If it's here," she added pointedly. "We need to come at it with fresh eyes after we sleep. Let's have tea and a nice chicken and cheese quesadilla. The tryptophan will help us sleep."

"I suppose that tea will be Hazel's sleepy tea," she half-heartedly objected and stood up. "How do I know you won't read the book while I'm asleep?"

"How do I know you won't?"

"Because I'll have it," Gramma Pearl said from the doorway where she stood arms crossed over her chest, gray hair askew, and her rose-print flannel nightgown brushing her bunny-slippered feet. She frowned at each of them.

Hyacinth's guilt gene kicked in, though there was no real reason for it. "I had it first." She winced at how petty and childish she sounded. She pushed to her feet. "Snack then bed. The book can wait for fresh eyes."

Laz pivoted so Pearl couldn't see and stuck out her tongue. "Suck up," she mouthed.

Cynth flipped her the bird as they headed for the kitchen.

Earl woke at five-thirty and couldn't fall back to sleep. He got up and overrode the timer on his coffeepot. Since he wasn't sleeping, he might as well get back to the research he'd been distracted from. It never ceased to amaze him how life got in the way of life sometimes. While he waited for the coffee to brew, he inhaled a bowl of cereal with enough sugar to wake the dead. With luck, it would revive him, because despite being awake, he was still tired. Knowing the sugar wouldn't stick and he'd crash, he ate a few slices of cheese.

Coffee in hand, he fired up his computer on the kitchen table, which doubled as a desk in the small apartment. Though he had no idea where to start his search, he forced himself to avoid his emails and the shop's social media accounts. Recalling Brown's history of living in Drayton Valley and Edmonton, he started wondering where exactly he lived. That led to wondering where Keres lived.

He knew Keres had rented a place near town. Where else might he have lived? He called up land records and found the owner of the farm Keres had used. The man also owned a house in Three Moon Falls. He traced the farm owner as much as he could and came up dry. The seventy-year-old seemed to be nothing more than a retired farmer, so he turned his attention back to Keres.

Had he been a landowner? Did he still own land? If so, where?

He spent hours looking at land maps in the area. Something told him if he looked hard enough, he'd find that Keres owned property. There had to be an easier way to search than reading each map individually.

His second alarm of the morning rang, startling him. How had so much time passed? It was eight-thirty, and he had to open the store at nine. He jotted a few notes on his fruitless search and shut down his computer. Fifteen minutes later, he climbed down the outside back stairs and entered the store.

Before today, he'd have said intuition was a load of butt-kiss. But he was certain he'd find something in the land records. He just had no idea how long it would take. There was a little voice in the back of his mind telling him that Keres must have a place to retreat to. And if he planned to revive his wife, as the Hawk family suspected, it had to be private. Very private.

He was just halfway through the store when a thought stopped him. Holy crap-balls. If Keres was going to revive her, that meant she was dead, but unburied. He shuddered. Who'd want a dead body lying around?

"That's messed up," he muttered.

"What's messed up?" Jeri asked.

"Jeez. Shit!" he exclaimed, whirling round to face her. "What are you doing here?" he demanded.

She raised an eyebrow. "I work here?"

"Ya. Well. You didn't have to scare the crap out of me," he grumbled. "Morning."

"Good morning to you, too, boss. I thought you knew I was here and were speaking to me. So sorry if I startled you. I was just about to turn on the lights. So, what's messed up?"

"Nothing. Just thinking out loud."

"I see that you're hanging around with Hyacinth Hawk. Be careful. There's weird stuff happening, and it centers around them. Watch your back."

His hackles rose at the implication. "Hyacinth isn't doing anything wrong."

"I never said she was. But you need to know that there is potential danger there. I've known you since you were a kid. I love you like my own. The Hawks are my friends. I worry about all of you."

"Thanks, Jeri. I appreciate your concern. I know what has happened and I'm working on how to make the problem go away."

She gave him a questioning look and flipped on the lights. "But you have no magic."

"Research takes brains, not magic." Was he the only person in town who didn't know about magic being real? He shook his head. "Anyway. Let's open up. We've got books to unpack and sell."

She gave an impertinent salute and a cheeky grin. "As you wish, boss."

"Enough with *The Princess Bride* references."

"As...you...wiiiiish." She spun in circles and moved away, mimicking the epic scene where Wesley rolls down the hill declaring his love.

"You're fired," he called after her.

It popped into his head that Keres would probably need to call on all the elements to revive his wife. He had to look for a place with privacy and a good source of water. Air was everywhere, as was earth. Fire could be created, but water might be his key to finding his base. If he searched for islands or places along rivers...

Chapter Seventeen

"Hand over the book," Hyacinth said, mostly joking, when she stumbled tiredly into the sunny kitchen to find her grandmother and all three sisters seated at the table.

"Tsk. Tsk," Pearl chided. "Seat down and eat." She waved toward the family-style breakfast on the table. "Then we'll read together. That's why I asked your sisters here. Maybe an entry will trigger something for one of us that the others might miss."

The idea was sound, but she really had wanted to read it herself. Play the hero and come up with the talisman's location and save the day. Still, she couldn't disagree with Gramma Pearl's assertion that more ears were better. Trying not to pout, she poured herself a coffee and loaded it with sugar and cream. She'd feel the sugar crash later, but needed a boost now.

She'd slept fitfully last night with dreams of faceless evil, running from danger, and of wildflowers. Wild clematis that twisted upward, choking the life out of trees, to be precise. She slid in place at the smooth, oak, eight-seat kitchen table. Hazel slid a plate her way and Lazuli reached over to drop two sunny-side-up eggs onto it. Pearl added bacon and sausages. Amber flipped her two pancakes from the tabletop warmer. Apparently, her family was set on feeding her before they started. She didn't mind. Everything smelled delicious. Especially the bacon.

"I'll blow up if I eat all this."

"Nonsense," Pearl chided. "You'll need the energy. Thinking is hard work and you've been working hard lately. Your energy stores are low. I can see it in the dark circles under your eyes. You need good food and a day of rest."

"And instead, I get amazing food and a day of research," she said darkly. She didn't mean to be surly, but her dreams had left lingering shadows on her heart and soul. Something bad was going down and her family was smack dab in the middle of it.

She sliced off a bit of pork breakfast sausage and dipped it in maple syrup. Delish. "I'm worried," she admitted.

"Don't talk with your mouth full," Hazel chided. "But I feel you. This whole thing is totally sus."

"Sus?" Pearl growled. "What is sus?"

"Suspicious, or suspect," Hazel laughed. "I thought that was totally obs. Obvious." She laughed.

"You've been working with teens too long," Hyacinth said around a mouthful of delicious, fluffy pancake.

"Yup."

"Dang kids are too lazy to say full words," Pearl grumbled and picked up her floral teacup. She sipped and set it back down on the matching saucer. The cup matched five others and a teapot and had been imported from France by some relative back in the early 1900s. They treated the service with care, but felt that not using it was a waste of resources. Of course, they'd never give it to a child, and until the girls were twelve, they were forbidden to use them. "Doesn't matter," she added. "Let's get to this." She opened the journal and started reading.

Hyacinth finished her breakfast and listened with eager ears for the first hour. "Goddess help me, our ancestors were boring."

"I find it fascinating," Hazel countered. "It's an amazing look into day-to-day life. I need to read more of these in my spare time."

"Ha. All your spare time is spent making kissy faces with Dennis," Laz teased.

"Keep reading, please," Hyacinth said.

After another hour, they were two-thirds of the way through the book and Cynth was beginning to despair of finding anything useful. Someone knocked on the back door.

As one, the five women turned to look out the window.

Rosie Perrum, their five-year-old neighbor stood there smiling at them.

"Crap. What's she doing here?" Cynth muttered and went to open the door. "Rosie, what are you doing here? Where's your dad?"

"He's at work. But you need me, so I came over." She kicked off her shoes and climbed up to the table. "Can I have bacon, please?"

Hyacinth choked back a laugh. "Sure, I'll get you a plate. Do you want eggs too?"

"Ew, eggs are slimy. But I like pancakes."

Hyacinth got up and brought a plate to the table. Lazuli was texting someone, and it didn't take a genius to know she was informing Rosie's father, Frank, that his daughter was AWOL. Ever since his wife, Celine, passed away last year, he'd been searching for the right nanny. One who could engage and control his wayward daughter who liked nothing more than visiting the Hawk family.

"Were you reading that book?"

"Yes, we were." Pearl poured some juice into an empty glass and slid it toward Rosie.

"Keep going. This is a good one."

The Hawks looked at each other, at Rosie, then at the book. More than once, Rosie had said or done things that led them to believe she was their reincarnated great-grandmother. It was a family belief, no a certainty, that when souls reincarnated, occasional glitches happened and the new person was left with lingering memories. Like a sense of déjà vu or knowing things that you shouldn't. Rosie was convinced that there was something important in their books. A purple book to be precise.

"What do you mean this is a good one?" Hyacinth refilled her coffee mug before sitting down.

"I dunno. It just is. I remember."

"Well, there hasn't been anything unfit for small ears. Yet. I'll keep reading."

"Yay." Rosie clapped with her fork still in her hand, spraying pancake and syrup all over her pink floral tunic dress and navy leggings. "Oops." Cynth helped her clean up the spill while Pearl read.

July 5, 1892. I found an old glass vessel. Its lid is sealed and something rattles within. I am unable to fathom its purpose. It is the strangest yellow color reminiscent of a squashed buttercup. The glass is murky and I cannot see inside. I swear it feels evil. I can barely stand to touch it. I want it gone from my presence but know not what to do with it. I cannot bring myself to destroy it.

"Oh," Hyacinth exclaimed. "Is this it?" They shared an excited look. Rosie nodded knowingly.

What the hell? More and more I think she's Great Gramma Rosie. Gramma Rosie had died in a freak motor vehicle accident only days before Rosie's birth. It's so weird that Rosie's mom abruptly changed the name she'd picked before she was even pregnant and suddenly called her baby Rosie. Did she somehow know her daughter would be a reincarnated soul? Celine was just learning about magic and had very few natural skills.

There were too many questions and not enough answers to suit Hyacinth. She pulled her attention from her own thoughts and focused on her grandmother's words. Nothing was mentioned about the curious object for another two weeks, though there was an entry nearly every day.

Pearl kept reading. *"July 18th, 1892. I've decided to get rid of it. My mind hasn't changed, it is evil but something, some inner voice, tells me not to destroy it. I'm perplexed. If I cannot keep it and cannot destroy it, I must hide it where it will never be found. But what if it is needed in the future? Clues. I must leave clues."*

Chills ran down Hyacinth's spine. Half in the excitement of getting closer to finding the relic, but most in unnamed, faceless fear. She shivered with precognition. This was going to be bad. Worse than bad.

The rest of the book contained nothing of value. Though they did learn of the birth of a set of twin girls who were named Opal Rosalind and Pearl Jade.

Frank showed up to collect his daughter. "I can't apologize enough about this. I don't know why she keeps coming here."

"Maybe she feels comfortable. We've always treated her like family. She would have been family, like Celine, if she hadn't passed." Laz swallowed hard. She'd been besties with Celine since high school, and her death still stung. She placed a hand on Frank's arm. "I'm so sorry for your loss. Please know we'll keep Rosie safe every time she shows up."

"Thank you." His voice was gruff. "Come on, Rosie Posie. It's time to go."

"I want to stay with Lazuli." She crossed her arms and pouted.

"Rosie," his voice had that warning tone parents perfected so easily.

"But I love her, and they need me to find the other book."

"I don't know what she's talking about." He shrugged. "She's been yammering on about a book for weeks. Maybe longer."

"Well," Hyacinth said carefully, "we are looking for a book in the family library. Maybe she overheard us talking about it." *Or maybe she has some precog skills.* She wasn't about to tell him why they needed the book. Family business and all that.

"Rosie, why don't you come back tomorrow, after school, for a visit? We can look at the book together then. If it's okay with your father."

"Fine by me." He shrugged. "Are you sure you don't mind? I hate to impose." He answered Hyacinth's question, but his eyes were fixed on Lazuli.

Cynth wondered if the pair would ever act on the obvious attraction sparking between them. She gave a mental shrug. If it was in the cards, it would happen. Perhaps Laz felt some moral trepidation as Frank used to be her best friend's husband. The universe would handle it, but she cast a quick prayer to the Goddess for them to be brought together in love and harmony...if that was their destiny.

"Okay. Come on, squirt, let's go."

Earl jumped up from his desk. "Holy crap. I found it!" He hit the print screen button and sent the image on his computer to the printer.

Jeri stuck her head in his office doorway. "Found what, boss?"

"I've been searching for hours, and I found it. I have to run. Watch the store for me." He snatched the paper from the printer, grabbed his car keys, and bolted.

"Found what?" she shouted as he raced up the aisle toward the front door.

He ran down the block and burst into Four Seasons Metaphysical and blurted, "Is Hyacinth here?"

Andi spun round to look at him. "Hi, Earl. No. They're all at home." She shrugged. "Research or something. I guess they'll be back after lunch." She grinned. "It's great for me, I can use the extra hours. Did you want me to call her?"

He rejected the idea, even as she mentioned it. "No. I'll call her myself. Thanks though." As he left, he added, "Have a great day."

"You too!"

He jogged around the back of the stores and climbed into his car. He fired up the air conditioning immediately. It was unseasonably warm, and his car was sitting in full sunshine. He dialed Hyacinth and put his phone on speaker, then backed out carefully and headed down the alley.

He fidgeted in his seat as he waited for her to answer. The phone rang and rang and went to voicemail. "Damn." He headed down the highway. He frowned when he approached the Hawk property and saw the closed gates.

He pulled up and the gates opened. He scanned left and right and couldn't find a camera, but someone must have seen him coming. He sped up the gravel drive and skidded to a stop behind a line of cars. All the sisters must be here. The driveway was like a parking lot.

He leaped over a cat and thundered up the steps and pounded on the front door. "Hello? Hyacinth? Pearl? Anyone?"

The door swung open so quickly that he jumped back. Hyacinth laughed. "Earl, what are you doing here? How'd you get past the gate?"

"I thought you opened it. Look at this." He thrust the paper at her.

She took it and studied it. "I don't understand. What is it? It looks like a pick-a-square guessing game."

"It's a land titles map. I've been searching the internet. I had a hunch that Keres had to have a base somewhere." He tapped the paper. "It's right here."

She grabbed him by the arm and yanked him inside. "Come into the kitchen. Everyone's going to want to see this." She flung her arms around him and kissed his cheek.

Heat rocketed through him. The joy of her kiss surpassed the joy of having a lead. She stepped back, and he instantly missed her closeness.

"What's going on?" Pearl asked from the living room.

"Earl found out where Keres lives, lived, or something. Look."

He kicked off his shoes as Pearl looked at the map.

"Come in, Earl. Tell us how you found this." She walked back into the kitchen. "Hazel, make some coffee, please. And maybe pull out a tin of those oatmeal coconut cookies."

They looked the map over as he explained his tedious search process of going one land block at a time. There was probably a searchable list somewhere, but he'd gone this route instead. He'd also saved money by not buying maps from the county.

"So, what do we do now?" he asked. "He's in jail, right? Do we tell the police about this? Or the, what did you call it, the magic council? Witch's Council?"

"I think we go there," Lazuli suggested. "Check it out. Maybe he has more information on this talisman and what it can and can't do."

"That's a great idea," Cynth blurted. "When do we go?"

"Wait. You can't just go racing in and snoop around."

"You can't stop me."

"Probably not." He sighed. She always was impulsive and some-times a bit rash. "But I can come along and keep you from doing something stupid."

"How much land is it?" Hazel asked. "Will it be a big search? We can search a house easy enough but start adding in sheds, forest..."

"He has a full section of land. That's one mile by one mile. I can look it up on the web and see if there are any satellite images of the place."

The land turned out to be a few fields, a ton of trees, and at least a dozen outbuildings in addition to a large house.

"We can't search that alone," Cynth grumbled. "We're going to need help. I also think we shouldn't rush into this. Who knows what he had going on there."

"Maybe Mom and Dad can come back and help us," Amber said. "I know Kody will come, and probably Dennis. We could get Leticia, Danica, Mel, and Jerry, too."

Pearl looked very serious. Serious enough that Earl was certain she was going to slam the brakes on the idea. "I think we need to phone your parents and get their opinion. They're more experienced in these sorts of things. I'll phone tonight."

"Wait," Cynth exclaimed. "You have a phone number for them?"

"For emergency purposes only. This might qualify. We're getting into something big and I'm not sure we can handle it alone. At the very least, we need their advice."

"So, when Keres was trying to kill me, that wasn't reason enough?" Amber pouted.

Earl had a hard time deciphering if she was serious or not. To diffuse the tension, he asked, "What do we do in the meantime?"

"We keep reading." Hyacinth picked up a leather-bound book. "I'll read. You listen."

Cynth had a great reading voice. The words fell smoothly on his ears. She varied her pace and paused occasionally. She read about chickens, sheep, gardens, newborn babies, and a whole lot more. Half an hour later, he was hooked. He was a huge history buff, but he'd never read anything like this. There was everything from day-to-day basics to retellings of dreams, recipes, spell work, and fights with the neighbors.

They went through two pots of coffee and more tea than he could count. They took turns reading to give their voices a rest.

"Want a turn?" Cynth asked after everyone else had read.

"Sure, why not?" He took the book. It was warm from being held by so many hands and felt alive under his fingers. He'd almost swear it held its own magic. He read a few entries and paused to take a sip of his coffee. He'd switched to decaf two cups ago.

"I'm going to have to get rid of it now. Before the snow falls again. Last week's snow has finally melted. I'll not list where it is going. But somewhere, within one of my journals, is a clue."

"Ugh," Hyacinth groaned. "We already knew that."

"No," Pearl corrected, "we had a hunch it was in one of the books. Now we know it is in one of Rosalie Amber Hawk's books. That narrows down the searching."

"That's good, right?" Earl asked.

"It's wonderful," Amber said.

"Are you all named with family names?" he asked. He recalled Cynth talking about her Grandmother Rosie.

"We all have at least one floral name and one stone name. Lazuli is short for lapis lazuli. Jade, Pearl, Amber, Opal, Amethyst, Beryl, and one Jewel. And a floral or nature name. We had aunts named Fern and Ruby. You get the idea."

"That's fascinating. Is there a list?"

Hyacinth groaned. "Yeah, going back over three hundred years. Births, deaths, marriages, names. Sometimes occupations. We've got it all."

He was practically salivating at all the information. The historian in him wanted to see every bit and read every detail. "Fascinating."

"Who are you, Mr. Spock?" Cynth teased.

"Don't you dare cast aspersions on *Star Trek*. I don't dis your *Star Wars* fandom."

"Star Wars? I'm over that. It's *Bridgerton* and *Supernatural* all the way. Go, team Dean."

"As if. Team Crowley," he countered as he stood. "I'd love to stay and hear more, but I have a business to run. I could take a book or two with me..."

"Not on your life. Nobody takes a book from this house. Not even us. EV-ER."

"Gotcha." He looked around the room. "Anyone need a ride to town?"

"I'll take one if you can bring me home later. I'm on shift at the shop unless someone goes into unexpected labor."

"Sure. I'd like a few minutes alone with you."

Hazel mock gagged. "Get a room."

"Hyacinth loves Er-rel," Laz chanted.

"Get stuffed," Cynth retorted. "Dude let's get out of here. Before their stupidity gets us, it's probably contagious. She stuck her tongue out at her sisters.

"Girls!" Pearl chided.

"Sorry Gramma," they chimed in unison.

Chapter Eighteen

A week passed before Hyacinth saw Earl again. She stood on the step, waiting for him and enjoying the moist morning air. Last night's rain had moistened the dry ground enough that his truck didn't kick up any dust as he came up the highway. Her heart thumped happily when he climbed out of the truck.

"Good morning," he called and strode toward the porch. Dang, he looked good in a navy and black plaid jacket and dark denim jeans.

She stood and leaned against a porch pillar, enjoying the view as he came toward her. "Morning. How'd you sleep?"

"Terribly." He grinned. "I had constant dreams of a blonde-haired, blue-eyed witch. She haunted me all night."

He didn't look the least bit tired. "Liar," she said with fond tolerance.

"I did dream about you. Come here so I can kiss you."

She hopped down the stairs into his arms. "Morning," she murmured against his lips before giving in to temptation and kissing him until they were both breathless. "Dang," she whispered, resting her head against his chest. His heart thumped as rapidly as hers. They were going to have to do something about the fire burning between them. She almost quivered with anticipation of being his lover, though part of her didn't want to rush into anything.

"Ready to go?" He nuzzled her hair.

"Yup." She hopped back. "I made us a snack." She grabbed a small backpack off the steps. They climbed into his truck for the short drive to Raven Falls. "I haven't been to the falls since Keres blew them up. I'm curious about how much damage was done. The police only allowed access last week, once they were certain the falls were stable. Such a tragedy." She frowned. Two people had died when the falls blew up. Her heart ached just thinking about it.

"Why would he blow the falls up? Doesn't it stand to reason that if something was hidden there, it would be reasonably accessible?"

"You'd think so. But I'm not sure Keres was in his right mind. He was trying to revive his dead wife. At least that's what we think was going on."

They parked in a gravel lot at the base of the hill behind Raven Falls.

Three Moon Falls was named for the Moon family who were town founders, and for the three waterfalls located nearby. Chickadee Falls cascaded one hundred seventy-five feet into a pool on Hawk land, which fed into Spruce Creek. The creek flowed toward town. The second, Eagle Falls, dropped an impressive two hundred feet into Spruce Creek, which flowed over Raven Falls. Raven Falls dropped into an enormous half-moon shaped pool connected to Three Moon Falls Lake.

Eager to see the falls despite her trepidation, she hopped out of the truck immediately. Earl grabbed the small backpack from the box of his truck.

"Lead on." He gestured toward the path leading through the trees to the top of the hill and the waterfall.

"Why me? You know where we're going as well as I do."

"True, but I like to watch your backside, and I know it's going to be hot as sin in those jeans."

She wiggled her butt at him before taking his hand and leading him forward. They walked side by side down the gravel path into the forest. Once they reached the softer path between the trees, she stopped and shed her sandals.

"I don't know how you can walk on the forest floor without getting jabbed. I can barely mince along."

She laughed. "I'm an earth witch. The forest is my playground. Despite the pine needles and twigs, I can't recall ever being uncomfortable or getting poked walking here." They chatted idly until they reached the falls again.

"Why here?" he asked as he spread a blanket on the grass between the trees and rocky banks of the creek. In the distance, the thundering sound of the falls called to her. She was torn between checking out the falls and simply being with Earl. Her heart had longed for this for years, and she intended to savor every single moment with him.

"We used to come here all the time. Nostalgia, I guess. Plus, my instincts are screaming at me about this place. I'm sure the talisman is here somewhere. Why else would I feel such a powerful pull and compulsion to be here?"

He shrugged.

"I want to chill out here and check out the falls. Later, maybe we can drive down and check out the base." She eased down onto the blanket, and he sat with her.

"Let's have a snack first. I'm curious about what we may find. If there is anything to find."

Several people walked by as they sat there. A family came and went. A lone jogger passed by. Three women giggled their way by. Three teens in swimwear came and went, grumbling about not being able to swim.

"Who thinks they can swim at the top of a waterfall?" Earl whispered as they walked out of sight.

"No idea. Let's check out the falls before it gets any busier." The higher the sun rose in the sky, the busier the path became. They packed up their picnic and followed another couple down the trail.

They stepped out of the forest onto a small plateau with a stunning view of the lake below. Boats bobbed on the water in the sunshine. Families played on the distant beaches. Water skiers sped across the lake, swerving and curving between other boats. Everyone was enjoying the last warm days of early fall. Her great-grandmother used to call this weather Indian Summer, though now there was probably a more culturally sensitive name for it.

Earl slung his arm over her shoulder. "It's so happy down there. We should go water skiing like we used to."

"We went exactly once, and I hated every minute of it. I am not a water baby."

"What?" He looked astonished. "You said you enjoyed it."

"I was a stupid girl. I thought I had to like all the things you did. Even football. I can't tell you how much I hated watching football." She feigned a shudder.

"Oh my gosh. I am so sorry. You should have told me."

"Probably. But would you have listened?" She slipped her arm around his waist and leaned against the warmth of his side.

"Probably not. I'd have told you that it would grow on you."

"Kids." She laughed. "We were so young and hopeful. And naive."

"Well, we're older and wiser now." They walked along the edge of Spruce Creek which was nearly the size of a small river at this point. People picnicked beside the water. Kids played on the shore.

"Let's go over there. It's not so busy." She pointed to the far side. She stepped out onto one of the many large flat rocks in the water.

"Hyacinth. That's nuts. It's dangerous. Those rocks could be slippery."

The panic in his voice made her pause and look back at him. "Hey, it's okay. My sisters and I did this all the time. It's an easier walk than it looks. We're five hundred yards from the edge of the falls. Come on." She waved for him to join her. When he took his first tentative step, she hopped onto the next rock. Most of the rocks were an easy step from each other. Four times she had to hop to reach the next one. They both made it across without incident.

"How did I not know about that? About how easy it was?" He stared back over the creek.

"Easy. You boys were always doing guy things. Fishing, rafting, water skiing." She swallowed a wave of nostalgia. "My sisters and I would hide up here where it wasn't so busy, and we could play around and work on our skills. But there were many days when we wanted to be down there in the thick of things."

"I had no idea."

"There's a cool cave just over the hill here. Come check it out." As they walked through the trees, the sound of rocks banging together battered her ears. "Sounds like there's someone already here. But it's a public place, we'll take a peek anyway."

With him right on her heels, she stepped into the cave. It was brightly lit by an electric lantern sitting on a rock in the middle of the fifteen-foot-wide space. A trickle of water ran down the left wall. The air was moist and smelled of moss and dirt. Near the back, about twenty feet away, a woman was throwing rocks left and right, and muttering to herself.

"Hi there," Earl called out.

The woman whirled around.

Cynth recognized her instantly and was shocked that she hadn't felt the woman's bleak aura before she saw her.

"What do you want?" the woman from the restaurant, Rylie, snapped. "I'm busy."

"Just checking out the cave." *Did she think the talisman was here? Maybe it was. Cynth had felt drawn to the caves for weeks.*

"You've checked. You can go now." Rylie pointed toward the cave opening. Menace came off her in waves. Her aura went from nearly black to midnight, with zero light or color remaining.

Earl sat on a large boulder, looking like he had no intention of leaving. Cynth banked a smirk. He always got stubborn over the weirdest things. "This is a public place," he said casually. "I'm enjoying the cool after the heat of the sun."

"Get out of here," Rylie warned. "Before something bad happens."

"Are you threatening us?" Earl asked. "Cynth, what's the name of that cop your family is friends with? Isn't she a cousin or something?"

"Constable Leticia Stone. Not a cousin, but practically family." She pulled out her phone. "I'll just call and see if Rylie has the right to kick us out. I think uttering threats is a crime."

Blue light flew from Rylie's fingertips and splattered on the ground like sparks from a broken power line. She kicked a loose rock and glared. "Fine. Stay if you want." She picked up a pickaxe to pry some rock from the back wall. "I'll find it anyway, even with you here."

"Find what?" Earl asked as if he weren't interested.

"You know damn well what." She whirled around, hatred lighting her eyes. "I have to find it or else."

"Or else what?" Cynth asked. Rylie seemed more scared than anything else.

"Or else they'll kill me, you fecking moron." She dug through the rubble she'd dislodged. "It has to be here."

"Why here? Why this cave?" Cynth walked toward her. She scanned the surrounding area. For the most part, the inside of the cave was solid rock. It didn't seem a likely place to hide something.

"Because I've searched all the others. This is the only one left," she snarled. Sparks skittered down the pickaxe handle.

She whirled around with the pickaxe raised. "Get out. Leave me alone."

The earth trembled and small pebbles dropped from the ceiling.

Hyacinth blinked. She hadn't done that. Had it been Rylie? Was she earth magic? But what about the sparks? Did she have more than one type of magic, along with her evil malevolence?

"Calm down, Rylie. We're not going to hurt you."

"You can't stop me." The tip of the axe flamed white, then red, then orange. "I'll find the talisman if I have to kill you all." Her eyes glowed with hatred and the earth shook again.

"Calm down. We're in a cave. You'll bring the whole thing down on us." Cynth kept her voice flat and reassuring like she was talking to a feral cat or an angry child. "If it comes down, you're as trapped as we are. Don't do anything rash."

"Stop telling me what to do," she screamed, her voice ricocheting off the stone walls.

Earl flinched and Cynth barely managed to keep from wincing. She wouldn't give Rylie the power of knowing she was upset or worried. There was power in another's fear. She stuffed her phone back into her pocket. No way would the police get here quickly enough if Rylie went off the deep end. She needed her hands free to cast her own magic.

"I'm telling you, one last time, to leave."

Earl stood and walked to Cynth's side. He didn't say anything.

"I'll take out the mundane first." She said mundane like Earl was dog crap on her shoe. "Him first, then you. But I won't kill you. There are worse things. Like losing your magic."

Holy snot balls. Was Rylie involved with the magic theft? Was there more to her being here than the talisman?

"My boss will suck every drop of magic from your soul and leave you an empty, brainless vessel, Hawk. Mark my words."

By the Goddess, she was involved. She had to let the council know as soon as she got out of here before this got out of hand.

"Not happening, Rylie. You won't harm one hair on his head. Or mine. I'm stronger than you."

She circled toward Rylie, who shifted left, away from the wall. She kept moving, slowly and steadily. With each step, Rylie retreated.

"I'm not leaving," she barked. "I'll get what I came for."

"Why do you need it?" Earl asked. "What's it to you?"

"My employer needs it. I've sworn to get it, and I won't go back on my word." Her eyes darted back and forth between Cynth and Earl, like a trapped animal. Her fingers sparked again.

Cynth couldn't decide if the sparks were a threat or if Rylie was losing control of her magic. New magicals sometimes had trouble controlling their power. Especially if they manifested suddenly.

Rylie raised her left hand. "Get out, now," she screamed.

A bolt of orange light exploded from her palm, straight toward them.

Chapter Nineteen

"**S**hit!" Earl screamed.

A small rock jumped up off the floor, right into the path of the light. It exploded into tiny shards. The shards peppered him like a thousand needles. Cynth grunted.

Barely risking taking his eyes off Rylie, he glanced at Cynth. Tiny droplets of blood dotted her face and arms. She'd been hit too.

Panic swamped him, making him gag. *They had to get out of here. To hell with the talisman! He had to keep Cynth safe!*

"Come on, Cynth. Let's go. Leave this whack job alone."

"No!" Her voice radiated anger, whether at him or Rylie he had no idea.

This was crazy. Rylie had magic. She shot light, or fire, or something. It exploded a freaking rock. They had to get out of here before she hurt them. And what the hell was with that stone jumping off the floor? Had Cynth done that? He was not prepared for this shit!

"Listen to the mundane, witch. Get out before I take you out."

"Not a chance. I'm staying until you find the talisman. Then I'm taking it."

The earth trembled again, nearly knocking him off his feet. Jeez. One of these women was going to get them buried alive.

"Ladies, come on now. There's no need to fight."

"Zip it, Earl," Cynth snapped without taking her eyes off Rylie. "I told you about Keres. She must be in cahoots with him somehow. We can't let her have it."

She edged toward Rylie, who stepped sideways and shot another bolt of light.

Son of a...

His knees shook, only this time it was fear, not the earth moving. What had he gotten himself into by hanging out with Cynth? Every cell in his body wanted to cut and run.

But he couldn't.

A man never left someone weaker than himself in trouble. He helped out. He protected them.

Only Cynth wasn't weaker than him in this case.

Still, he couldn't abandon her. He'd stay to the end and do what he could. He wanted this fight over.

The ground shook again and small rocks rolled like marbles toward Rylie, and she stumbled as they battered her feet and ankles. *How was this possible?*

Rylie shot back a barrage of hot blue sparks. They scorched his skin where they landed. He swatted at them to be sure they went out. Luckily very few hit him because they burned like the real thing. The bulk peppered Cynth's skin and she grunted in agony but kept her focus on Rylie.

The pebbles and a few larger rocks rolled toward them. Rylie's face was a mask of evil concentration. Shivers of fear raced down his spine as his fight-or-flight instincts kicked in.

"Come on, ladies." He kept his voice calm, but inside he was screaming and running away. At the same time, anger at Rylie for attacking them burned brightly, right beside his anger at Hyacinth for not backing down and leaving. This didn't need to be a confrontation. "There's no need to fight."

"Shut up, mundane." Rylie raised both her hands and double streams of light raced toward him and slammed square into his chest like a truck hitting a wall. His air whooshed out in a rush.

He grunted in agony and went down. Hard.

Cynth screamed.

His head hit the ground, and everything went black.

"You bitch," Hyacinth screamed. Her anger shook the ground. She didn't care. She whirled up a storm of small particles, some too small to see, and spun them toward Rylie like she was sandblasting her.

Rylie's arms flew up to protect her face. Cursing a blue streak, she stumbled toward the cave mouth and outside. Cynth let the particles fall and dropped to her knees beside Earl.

"Oh, Goddess, let him be okay." She dropped to her knees beside him and lifted his head. A few drops of blood stained a sharp rock. Gently, she rolled him over. Thank the Goddess for her constant work moving pregnant women around.

"Earl, are you okay?" Her voice warbled as she examined the back of his head to determine the extent of the damage caused by his fall. The cut was small, only half an inch long, and it barely broke the skin, but a goose egg was forming beneath it.

She sent a text to her grandmother that she needed help and began searching deeper for damage.

He was out at least a minute before he shifted and groaned.

"Hold still, babe. You've got a lump on your head. I'm trying to knit the skin back together." She pressed down on his shoulder to keep him in place. "Help's coming."

"Let me up." His voice was icy.

"Stay still. Please." He glared at her, and she added, "Don't make me sit on you."

He rose on one elbow, wobbled, and dropped back down. "Shit."

"Dizzy? Head wounds can do that. Let me heal you. The bump is small, but I can feel that it goes deep. I can knit the skin and ease the lump, but you need more healing than I can provide." She focused on the wound and channeled healing energy into it. "I can ease the pain a bit." The fight had taken more out of her than she wanted to admit.

He grunted and mumbled something under his breath.

"Pardon me? I didn't quite catch that."

"Nothing," he snapped. His entire body went rigid.

Shoot, he was mad. Hopefully not at her. It wasn't her fault Rylie picked a fight. Slowly, one millimeter at a time, she brought his skin together. She worked until her vision went blurry.

"Crap." She dropped her hands from his scalp. She was too weak to do more. "Sit still while I eat something." She rummaged through her pack for the energy balls she never left home without. She barely had the strength to chew the first one. By the time she'd devoured six, she felt almost normal. Still weak, but better.

"Aside from Keres, I've never been in a magic fight," she confessed. "It's exhausting."

"Let's get out of here. Before she comes back."

"I don't think she will, at least not today. She'll be tired too. She'll come back when she thinks she can be alone. At least that's what I'd do."

She pressed her fingers gently to his scalp again and pushed more energy toward him. "How are you feeling?"

"Dizzy. Nauseous. Pissed." He was silent for a moment. "Exhausted. Weak like a newborn baby. Why is that? I've had knocks to the head before and never felt like this."

"Sleepy or exhausted?"

"Like I've worked hard all day hauling boxes or something. Not sleepy, just bone tired."

That was odd. A concussion would make him sleepy. Exhaustion meant something else. "When did it start?"

"I don't know? When I hit my head, maybe before. What aren't you telling me?" he demanded, twisting to face her and dislodging her hands.

"Remember how you pushed your energy into me? Some people can suck energy out of others to power their magic."

He muttered a string of curses that would make a pirate blush. He stopped abruptly and stared at her. "Are you okay?" He struggled to his knees, the effort it took plain on his face.

"Tired. Let me finish healing the cut at least. Maybe I can help heal the lump, too." She reached for him, and he backed away and touched his scalp.

"I'm not bleeding badly. I'll live." He placed his hands on her shoulders and gently pushed her off her knees to her backside. "You need food, right?"

She nodded weakly, and he grabbed his backpack.

"Oh, my neck."

"Whiplash. That big pack protected your back when you went over, but it let your neck snap backward. How bad is it?"

"Not as bad as after the car accident I had at university."

"That's good." She reached for him when he turned his head back and forth to test the stiffness of his neck. "Don't overdo it. Wait for someone to check you out."

A distant thump-thump-thump penetrated the cave. "Is that a helicopter?" He looked at her for confirmation.

"Sounds like it." They listened, motionless, until the sound came closer and finally stopped. Half a minute later, Leticia burst into the cave, Gramma Pearl hot on her heels.

"Everything okay in here?" Leticia demanded, hand on her gun, eyes wide and wary.

"We're good. Earl is hurt more than I can heal. He'll need proper medical attention." After confirming there were no mundanes within earshot, she added, "He took a blast of rock shards, one of hot sparks, and another of bright yellow light. I've never seen anything like it before. I don't know what it was."

After another look at the entry she added, "Rylie can throw stones, blast sparks, and throw streams of hot, bright burning light. I don't know what else she's capable of. But she was looking for the talisman."

"I'll get a team up here right away to go over this place with a fine-toothed comb." She held up a hand to forestall objections. "I'll use a discreet magical team. Men and women I trust implicitly. If it's here, they'll find it."

"What about the other caves? Maybe it isn't here, but the cliff below is riddled with caves." Earl asked, taking the words right out of Hyacinth's mouth.

"Good point. I'll cordon off the falls. Say there is an accident investigation going on. They'll believe it since the chopper landed here, and there's an ambulance crew coming. People outside are already gossiping about the earthquake." She fixed Cynth with a hard stare. "I assume that was you."

"Guilty." She was guilty, but didn't feel one second of remorse aside from feeling bad that people might have been frightened. She did what she had to do. "Rylie did the worst of it, but I did my fair share and will face whatever consequences the council gives me."

Leticia looked at Earl. "We're taking you out of here on a stretcher."

"I don't need a stretcher. I'm weak and hurt, but I'm not an invalid."

"Don't sass me," she said, showing her Cajun roots and sounding every inch like an angry Southern mama. "Any other day, I'd make you walk. But we need a victim to keep the story of a serious accident strong. Got it?"

"Yes, ma'am. I'm suddenly feeling very weak." He feigned a swoon.

That right there, his sense of humor and the ability to know when to shut up and listen was why she loved him. She'd fallen hard for him as a teen and never stopped loving him. Sure, she'd dated after they broke up. Hawk women only truly loved once, but they'd been known to find happiness and caring with another. That's what she'd been seeking while dating. Someone who cared for her whom she could care for as well.

A medic raced in toting a heavy backpack. "Stretcher's on the way," he huffed. "Where's my patient?"

Cynth pointed to Earl. "He took a blow to the chest, has some small burns, and a serious bump to the back of his head. I did what I could," she added, knowing the medic was another witch.

"Gotcha." He ditched his pack and began a thorough investigation of Earl. He peppered him with questions to determine if there was any cognitive damage. "Definitely a concussion, though it is mild." He put a C-spine collar on Earl. Best keep your neck safe until we see if there is any whiplash. If there is, it's probably mild, but best to be safe." He made a series of notes on his tablet. Asked questions and made more notes. Then he looked at Cynth. "Your turn."

"I don't need medical attention," she objected.

"I see burn marks on your clothing. You're wobbling like a newborn baby deer."

"It's mostly a magical hangover," she answered honestly, knowing Pearl had stationed herself at the mouth of the cave to keep the gathering crowd out.

"Make way," someone called.

Cynth looked toward the sound. Pearl stepped aside as two burly firemen carried in a stretcher. Two more medics were hot on their heels with another one.

"I don't need medical care," Cynth objected.

Pearl whirled around to glare while Leticia and Earl fixed her with no-nonsense looks.

"Fine."

The medic finished his exam, and they were both loaded on stretchers. "Who's going to pay for this?" Canada might have publicly funded health care, but trips in an ambulance weren't free.

"The council will pick it up since it's the result of a magical attack. Now lay back down and make like you're seriously injured."

An officer stuck his head into the mouth of the cave. "We've cordoned off the top and cleared people away for the stretchers. You're good to go."

Leticia gave him a nod of approval and the medics and firemen picked up the stretchers.

The trip downhill was bumpy and twisty despite their care. More than once, she bit back nausea. Following orders, she kept her head flat on the stretcher, despite her urgent need to get an advance view of the obstacles headed her way.

The sky was a brilliant azure. Fluffy white clouds floated past, mocking her exhaustion and the sting of her minor burns. Then, they were in the trees. Branches swayed back and forth over her, or maybe she was swaying. Earl grunted a time or two. She bit her lip to keep from complaining about the rough ride. She had to play her part to the hilt, just in case Rylie was nearby, watching.

Behind them, the helicopter took off and headed back to the pad behind the police station. Three Moon Falls RCMP detachment housed the area's only cop-chopper. While bringing it to the top of the falls was wasteful, it would help with the rumors of extreme danger in the caves. No doubt the council would pick up that tab as well.

The council had deep pockets. Hundreds of years ago, they'd started amassing funds through trade and investing. She wouldn't be surprised if some magical trickery had been used as well. Sometimes, with the council, it was, do as we say, not as we do. The council now had major cash and investment reserves, several mega-farms, and if rumor was to be believed, owned several multinational companies that dealt in herbal remedies. They had discreet offices all over the world. They were no different from any other world government, except they had no known members seeking their own wealth and power.

Chapter Twenty

T he trip down the mountain had been hell on Earl's stomach. Already slightly sick, being unable to see combined with the jostling had nearly made him lose his lunch. If they had eaten more than a snack before the incident, he'd have puked for sure. The embarrassment of being toted down hurt his masculine pride.

Oh, he got it. He fully understood why they had to put up a façade. There was good reason to protect mundanes, like himself, from knowing what happened. He could well imagine another round of witch persecutions, only the punishments would probably be less public. He expected that if they started, witches would simply start disappearing.

His Christian soul ached knowing that there were so many unforgiving and fearful people in the world. He hadn't been any better, but he was trying. Magic scared the absolute snot out of him.

He lay in his hospital bed, neck still wrapped in a confining cuff he wanted to rip off. They were keeping him for observation and treatment of his burns. The burns hurt like a mother. It was like having a dozen small burns from bacon grease. Not serious but distractingly painful when combined with his countless cuts and bruises. Doctor Carter had been in a couple of times checking on him.

He hadn't seen Hyacinth yet. He was worried about her, but he was also pissed that she'd got him caught up in her magical fight.

A light tapping turned his attention to the door. Hyacinth peeked her head around the corner. "Can I come in?"

"Speak of the devil."

Her brows knit together, and she stepped inside, searching for someone else. "Who are you talking to?"

"Myself."

She winced at his abrupt tone. He didn't want to hurt her, but he didn't know how to deal with everything that had happened. The morning's events were never far from his mind, but seeing her brought them slamming back home. He wasn't a coward by any stretch, but he'd been terrified by the battle.

"Are you okay?" She perched on the edge of the bed.

Steeling himself not to move away from her, he fisted his hands under the covers and counted to ten. "Physically, I'm adequate. Not good. Not horrible."

"And mentally?" The corners of her lips turned down in a worried frown that gnawed at his heart.

"Mentally? I have no idea where I'm at." He sucked in a breath and scraped both hands through his dusty hair, wincing when his fingers grazed the bump. God, he wanted a shower. "This, what happened today...this is exactly what I was afraid of years ago. I've never felt so helpless in my entire life. I was terrified." He swallowed down his man-hood. "I've never been that fucking scared in my life. Never. Except when I thought Anna might die."

"Fighting for Anna was the most scared I've ever been. Rylie worried me, but I wasn't terrified."

"No, you were loving it." The realization hit him like a slap to the face. "How could you enjoy it?"

She closed her eyes for a long moment, and he began to think she wasn't going to answer him. Finally, without opening her eyes, she said, "There's an exhilaration in using my power. Aside from shifting dirt around in the gardens, there isn't much call for earth movement. I like using my power."

"That wasn't *like* I saw in your face below the concern," he snapped. "You took actual pleasure in shaking the ground and throwing rocks."

"So what?" Her eyes flashed with anger.

"People could have been hurt. I was hurt. Doesn't that mean anything to you?" *How can she be so nonchalant about this?*

"I knew the cave was stable. I can sense the cracks and crevices in my mind. I don't know how I just can. Just like I know there were no secret holes or things buried. I sense them. A couple of microscopic earth shakes weren't going to bring down that cave or alter the flow of the water. We were one hundred percent safe. Except for what Rylie might do."

"I didn't know that," he snapped back.

"I didn't have time to explain it to you. I thought you trusted me!"

Hurt hung heavy in her voice and pushed at him, but he wasn't going to back down. "Is this what life with you would be like? Magic at every opportunity? Danger and death hiding around every corner? I can't live like that."

"What are you saying, Earl?"

"I don't know. I need time to think." He was confused. He'd seen her save his niece. She'd lifted and thrown rocks and shaken the earth. She was powerful, and beside her, he was powerless.

"I saved your niece's life. I kept you safe from Rylie too. Doesn't that count for anything?" Her voice cracked, and she twisted her hands together.

"I wouldn't have been in danger from Rylie, except for my association with you," he snapped, unable to control his anger. "And how do I know that whatever happened to Anna wasn't your fault?"

She leaped off the bed and backed away from him. The betrayal in her eyes floored him.

"How can you even think that?" Tears ran down her face and she raced out of the room.

Regret for her pain tore at him, but he wasn't sorry to see her leave. Curling into a ball, he tried to quiet his mind and ignore the pain in his chest and when Pearl came to visit him; he feigned sleep until she left.

Hyacinth didn't remember a single second between Earl's room and the shop. How she'd made it out of the hospital and hailed a taxi she didn't know. She crumpled on the back steps outside the shop, blinded by tears, trying to regain control of her equilibrium.

"How could he even think that if he cared for me?" she whispered. She pounded her fists on the steps.

Footsteps thumped down the stairs from Kody's and Amber's apartment on the second floor of the building.

"Cynth?" Kody asked softly. "What are you doing out here?" He stepped past her. "Are you crying? Oh jeepers. You are!"

She almost laughed at the panic in his voice. "I'm fine."

"You are not. Hang on." He took two steps to the screened back door of the shop and shouted. "Amber get out here, Something's wrong with your sister."

The shop's duo of ghosts whispered back and forth as they wondered what was going on. The door latch flicked, and the screen squeaked open.

"Cynth, what's wrong?"

"Earl," she managed on a hiccupping sob.

"Oh, my Goddess, did something happen to Earl? I heard about the incident at the falls."

"He's fine."

"Maybe we should take her inside," Kody suggested, as if she couldn't hear him.

"Good plan. Come on, sis." She grabbed her hands and tugged Cynth to her feet. "Time to go inside. Do you want me to call Gramma and everyone?" Kody held the door open for them.

"I've got to get to the office. I have a dive starting in half an hour. Call me if you need me. Love you. Take care, Cynth. It'll work out."

She snorted her disagreement, though she appreciated his concern and optimism. Amber had done well when she snagged Kody.

She found herself sitting on the small red sofa in the private portion of the shop's back room. Customers didn't come in here. Just family and friends. There was a small kitchenette, a sofa, a couple of chairs, and an enormous workspace for making candles, oils, and lotions.

"Spill the tea," Amber demanded. "What happened?"

Slowly, the words spilled from her as she related their morning, and then the devastating fight in Earl's hospital room. "He hates me. He's afraid of me!" She sobbed uncontrollably as Amber patted her back in a gesture meant to soothe. She pushed her sister away and stood, so she could walk around the workspace and kitchenette, touching things here and there. "I am such an idiot for falling for him again. I knew better. He'll never respect what I am, who I am."

"Do you have any idea how rare magical men are?" Ev, the oldest of their two ghosts said. "They're like one in a hundred thousand female witches. They don't happen often. There are other fish in the sea."

"Ev!" Kansas, their other ghost snapped. "Don't be mean. Earl's a good guy. Even his shop ghost says so."

"What?" Cynth cried, distracted despite herself. "How can you talk to her? You're supposed to be confined to the shop and the upstairs apartment."

Ev mimed zipping her lips. Kansas, a petulant teen who had died of an overdose, looked guilty. Cynth was always amazed at the real emotions they showed despite being trapped between worlds.

"Spill it," Amber ordered, staring directly at the translucent Kansas. "Don't make me banish you without fulfilling your purpose for being here, whatever that might be."

Kansas looked apologetically at Ev and shrugged. "It started after we helped Dennis save Hazel in the lake when your spell set us free. When you zapped us back here when the job was done-"

"Nasty trick that was," Ev grumbled.

"You weren't meant to be free," Cynth reminded them. "You were tied to this section of the building by fate, not us." She waved for Kansas to finish her story.

"When we zapped back here, we discovered that we could roam a bit farther. Not out that way," she nodded her head left. "But this way," she nodded right. "This way as far as the bookstore. We can't go any other direction. And believe me, we've tried. Many times."

"Well crap," Cynth muttered. "It wasn't supposed to give you freedom."

"Maybe fate wants it this way," Ev snarked bitterly. She'd slipped on water and died in the suite upstairs, above the pharmacy she owned and operated, and occasionally her anger at her fate showed through.

"Maybe," Cynth hedged. "More likely, we made a mistake."

"Tell us what the ghost said," Amber suggested, getting up to put the kettle on. "I want to know everything." There was a hint of a threat in her voice that made Cynth proud.

"Me too."

"Her name is Mila, but you knew that. She refuses to talk to people and won't tell us why," Kansas said. "She's stubborn."

"She doesn't know why she's trapped here and says she doesn't have a vendetta. She's forgiven the person who killed her infant daughter." Ev added. "But I've known a lot of ghosts since I've been trapped. There have been at least a dozen trapped in town, but not in a specific location. Some were tied to items. Anyway." She paused dramatically. "Some of them had missions related to their deaths. Larry died from a drunk driver. He was trapped until he prevented an accident involving a drunk."

Amber's eyes went wide, and she stared at the ghosts.

"You're saying Mila could have a purpose outside her losses?" Cynth asked.

"You better believe it."

"Interesting." The idea made her think of Anna. If someone had been stealing her life force, would they, could they, be willing to try again? Was Mila going to prevent that? Or was it something else entirely? Maybe she should warn Earl and Meri.

Earl!

She'd forgotten about him for a moment. He'd acted like a jack-hole again. Was this how it would be forever? Was there a chance he'd come around once this stupid talisman crisis was over? Would he always be afraid of her?

She rubbed the ache in her chest. Why did love have to be so complicated? And she did love Earl. She always had. Fresh tears welled, blurring her vision. Her exhaustion after the magic fight was part of it. Her emotions were always less stable and more unpredictable when she was tired.

"I need to eat. Let's go get something."

Amber wrinkled her nose. "Are we talking takeout or bringing something in? Going home for food?"

"I need comfort food and something to boost my energy. A million calories. Why don't we go to Pop's? A burger would hit the spot and Pop makes the best cheesecake."

"Wow! You are beat," Amber said. "You're the veggie queen. Not vegetarian, but darn close."

The teasing was familiar. She wasn't even close to vegan, vegetarian, or whatever. But she did love her veggies. Today, she needed fat and protein to rebuild her flagging energy and cheesecake to soothe her soul. The sugar crash after the cake would lull her to sleep when her mind wouldn't shut down.

"Sounds good to me. I skipped breakfast because..." Amber's face turned pink, and she spun away.

Cynth held up her hands. "Whoa. I so don't need to hear about your nocturnal antics with Kody. Gag." She mimed barfing while clutching her stomach.

"Anyway, Andi is here today. I'll just let her know I'm leaving and see if she wants something brought back." They only had three women working part-time for them, but they treated them well enough that there was a constant stream of applicants, even though they weren't hiring. With Three Moon Falls being a tourist town, many shops downsized their staff during the off-season, and with summer fading to fall, the cuts had already started. It was telling that the applications had starting coming in before the cuts started.

Cynth followed her sister through the store and in moments, they were headed west toward Copper Street and Pop's Burgers.

Cynth smiled when she entered. Pop's was popular with both tourists and locals. It had won several awards for Favorite Local Eatery. Tonight, it was packed.

Pop's was spotless and bursting with 1950s charm. Chrome and Formica tables. Red vinyl stools and benches. Black-and-white checkered floors. It was a blast from the past, right down to the pictures of the original Pop with Hollywood and local celebrities. Her favorite was Pop, posed with Rock Hudson and James Dean. Right beside it was the current Pop with Jensen Ackles, Jared Padalecki, and Jim Beaver, who had taken a run through town between filming episodes of *Supernatural* together. This Pop, the current owner, was the original Pop's grandson. His name was Albert, but everyone called him Pops.

Pops ran the place from behind the cash desk. He worked as hard as any of his employees and could do all of their jobs. It was a blessed day if he elected to cook for you because he was the best chef in town. He greeted them immediately.

Menus in hand, he ambled to their side. "Ladies. Good to see you." He led them to a seat near the register. The one often claimed as the best seat in the house because Pops was always eager to talk and could keep a secret. Everything he heard went into the vault and never passed his lips. "It's been a while. How's business in that new shop?"

They slid into their booth. Amber immediately filled him in on their success so far. When she finished speaking, he congratulated them and turned to Cynth. "I hear you saved Anna. Thank heaven for your quick thinking. You're a gift from God, for sure." He slid the menus onto the table. "Now, what can I get you?"

His praise was heartwarming. She smiled up at him. He was a decade older than she was and had fine lines around his deep brown eyes. His blond hair was artfully styled to look messy. His wife worked at Bev's Beauty. "How's the family?"

He smiled. "Those boys are growing too fast. I can't believe the twins are turning eleven and the baby is fabulous. She's learning to walk. I can't ever thank you enough for attending Amy's birth."

"You say that every time I come in. I'm glad she's happy and healthy, and you are very welcome."

"I'll tell you this. If we have another happy accident, we'll be hiring you again." His smile was enormous. "Now, can I get you something to drink?" He took their drink orders and walked away.

"I didn't know you delivered their baby." Amber gave her a questioning look.

"You probably don't know half of my clients." She sighed. "What am I going to do? I mean, my life is a dumpster fire."

"Your life is not a dumpster fire. You're having a hurdle. Earl will come around." Her voice was filled with conviction. "Kody did. Dennis did, and look at what his ex did to him. Earl is level-headed. I know this will work out. We need Lazuli here. She's the most psychic. She'd know."

No sooner had the words left her mouth than Laz arrived. "What's up ladies?" she asked, sliding in, and wrapping her arm around Cynth's shoulder. "Are you feeling better?"

"I'm fine."

"Girl, don't lie to me. I know better. I felt your pain all the way out to my workshop and called Gramma Pearl. She said to call Amber. I called the shop, and boom, here I am."

"Thanks for coming."

"Now, fill me in."

Again, she related her story, pausing only when Pops brought their drinks. "Here you go. Iced tea all around." He grinned. "I can't believe there are people who drink unsweetened iced tea. I need the sugar to keep up with my kids."

After he'd taken their orders and departed, Cynth asked, "What do you see?"

"Honestly, when I look at you, I get a sense of trouble, then happiness. I don't know what it means. There are no details, and I can't tell if it's a short-term or long-term vision." Her smile was comforting. "All I can say is that you will be happy again."

Cynth had the sense that Laz wasn't telling the full truth. Wherever possible, she preferred to let things unfold without giving away details. A few times, she'd saved a life by interfering or giving details, but in day-to-day life, she let things roll.

"That's a relief." It was a comfort, but her mind kept flipping and churning over everything that had ever happened between her and Earl. She relived every moment and every kiss from the moment they met. Goddess willing, he'd find his way back to her.

Before their food arrived, Hazel and Gramma Pearl joined them. A pity fest turned into a fun family dinner, and they all got a little tipsy on Pop's house wine.

As they made their giggling way back to the shop, a soft whine made Cynth pause. "What was that?" She tilted her ear in the direction she thought she heard the whine come from. "Shh," she hissed when nobody listened.

After a moment, their giggles subsided.

A whimper and whine followed in the near silence. She moved toward the sound, down an alley between shops and past a couple of dumpsters. She paused and listened. A weak yip directed her to a pile of boxes to her left.

She started to shift them, one to each side and as she tried to lift the last soggy box, the bottom broke free and a black and tan puppy tumbled out. "By the Goddess, who the hell would bury a puppy in the trash?" The ground shivered from her wrath.

"Bank it in. It's safe now," Pearl advised, sounding more sober than she should. Had their grandmother been faking drunk? She'd worry about that later.

"Hey, little one." She eased her hand forward and the pup let her stroke its chin. "Come on pup. I'm taking you home. We'll get you some dinner too." She lifted the mixed-breed dog into her arms and cuddled her to her chest. "What are you? Golden retriever? Poodle? That nose is all retriever, and that kinky hair is poodle for sure." She reeked of trash and poo, but she cuddled her close anyway. The Goddess had sent her, and she'd take care of her.

Her family crowded around for a look as they walked back to the shop. Kody met them out back in the staff parking area.

"After Amber texted, I called the vet," he said. "He'll see the dog right away and make sure she's okay."

"He's going to love us," Laz said dryly. "First a stray cat, then a fainting llama, now a stray dog. Added to all the cats at home, we're keeping him in business."

Kody drove Cynth, Amber, and the puppy to the vet, and for a short time, she was more worried about another living being than herself. Abruptly, she realized that this was how it should be. If she took care of those around her, the universe would take care of her too.

Silently, she spoke to Earl. *Okay, dude. I'm giving you time to realize what we had is important. I'm praying you realize that despite what happened yesterday, I'm not evil, I'm a good person who was in a bad situation because I love you with my whole heart.*

Chapter Twenty-One

E arl paced the small confines of his apartment and wished he had more space to roam. No matter how he tried to distract himself, he couldn't get his mind off Hyacinth. She was like a burr under his saddle and a thorn in his side. The incident at the falls had terrified him. He'd been certain they were both going to die. Hell, he'd spent the night in the hospital, and his head still ached like former world champion wrestler, Tyrus, had used his massive fists as drumsticks on Earl's head.

The hospital had advised him against overdoing the pain meds. He was taking them at exactly six hours, as prescribed. Maybe he needed to go back to the hospital. *What if they'd missed something? What if he had a brain bleed?*

He needed a distraction.

He called his best friend and his sister's husband Chen. Ten minutes later they were kicking back, feet up, ice-cold beer and hot pizza in hand.

"How's Anna? Meri? Work?"

"Anna's growing like a weed. She's up two pounds and is a full inch longer. It's scary how fast she grows."

"Dude, you're a doctor. You should know how fast kids grow."

"I'm a psychologist, and I do know how fast, but it's different when it's your own baby. It's personal and amazing." He shrugged like he was pushing off embarrassment. "Meri is good. Tired, but that's to be expected. I'm thinking of having Hyacinth check her over."

He bristled at the name. "Why not go to a normal physician? What does a midwife know about women's health?" Even as he asked it, he realized how stupid the question sounded.

"Probably everything. Pregnant and nursing women are her business. Dipshit." His laugh was pure friendly mocking. "She's been peeking in on Anna nearly every day, anyway. I don't mind paying her extra to see Meri. You shouldn't either. She's your sister"

"I just want what's best for Meri and Anna. That's all." And he wanted them as far from Hyacinth as possible.

"Is this about what happened at the falls? You guys were tight before then. I honestly expected to see you on your knees groveling to spend the rest of your life with her."

"As if I'd stoop that low."

"I did," he said without an ounce of shame or remorse. "Best decision I ever made."

"You're good for her."

"She's good for me. Together we're stronger. But seriously, bro. Is this about the falls? I heard what happened."

"Nothing happened. Minor earth shake. They happen all the time."

"Oh, bullnards. That woman, whatever her name is, and Cynth got into a magical fight. You were there. You were hurt. I heard you took a blow to that cement block you call a brain. It scared the living crap right out of you, didn't it?"

"Magic?" he asked, feigning confusion.

"Really? You're trying to BS me? You're dating one of the most powerful witches in the province. Your sister is a witch and you're trying to convince me you know nothing about it. Get real." He shook his head, and his slightly long hair flopped back and forth. He sipped his beer. "Meri said you'd be stubborn about this."

Earl waited for his friend to speak his mind.

And waited.

And waited.

"What?" he snapped, tired of waiting.

"Magic is part of the universe. I'm no brain surgeon, but I do know that most of the human brain is unmapped. Who knows what it is capable of? We only know what ten percent of it does. The rest is...well, the rest could be magic or something else we can't fathom."

"Fine. Magic exists. I've seen it. But it isn't natural. God didn't intend it to be there."

"So, you're saying God made a mistake?"

"I didn't say that!" he snapped. This conversation was making him nuts. He couldn't explain what he meant or felt.

"Yes, you did. Admit it, Earl. You have no idea what God's plan is for us. I'm not magic, but I sure wish I could do some of the things Meri does. She can levitate dishes and clean the kitchen without lifting a finger. All with the power of her mind. That's a miracle as far as I'm concerned."

"I didn't know she could do those things. I had no idea. None." He was flabbergasted. How had he been so oblivious? "That doesn't make what Cynth did right."

"What would you do if someone you love was in danger and might die? Wouldn't you risk everything?"

Earl stared at the pine coffee table, and then at the framed photo of his family on the wall. He looked anywhere, except directly at his friend.

"Wouldn't you at least consider breaking the law to save them? This is the same thing. You were in danger, so was she. She fought to save you."

"And you know this how?"

"Because she talked to Meri today. A phone check-in and Meri asked what happened." He went silent again. "As your brother-in-law and your friend, I'm telling you to open your eyes and your heart. There are more things in heaven and on earth..."

He'd said those very words only days ago. Crap.

"It's okay to be unsure, or nervous. Hell, I thought Meri was crazy when she started talking magic. As time went by, I thought it was a quirk or something. Eventually, I started noticing odd things. Like she'd catch a glass I was sure was going to shatter. She proved herself, and her magic to me. I'm torn between excitement and trepidation for when Anna turns five. That's when magic manifests if you have it. My girl's going to be amazing. I'm a wee bit jealous too." He grinned. "Open your mind before your heart is broken."

He finished his beer and put his feet down.

"Now, I'm going to leave you to ruminate. You've got a lot to think about. Try to ignore your fear. Fear often holds us back from something wonderful." He plopped his bottle on the table, said goodbye, and left Earl alone with his turbulent thoughts.

He grabbed a second beer and took a sip before setting it aside.

He was happiest when he was with Cynth. She brought him a calm peace that he hadn't experienced since their first breakup. But her power worried him.

He stood up and strode to the door. He had questions, and she was the person to ask. She'd probably gone home since she was released from the hospital. He'd go there.

"What do you want?" She crossed her arms over her chest and glared at him. "How did you get past the gates?"

"I thought you let me in." *How else could they have opened?* He still didn't believe they were magic. She looked better. Her hair was damp from a shower, and her clothing was free of blood and debris. But he was struck by the pure exhaustion in her eyes and the shadows beneath them.

"Magic. They block out the unwanted."

Whoa! "Did you just read my mind?"

"I can't do that. I can sense emotions, and the question was written all over your face." She tapped her foot on the front porch. "What do you want?"

"I'd like to talk, if that's possible."

She paused so long that he was certain she'd say no. His heart plummeted to his nuts. Freaking out again had probably ruined his chance at building anything with her. His mom had always accused him of reacting without thinking. Maybe she was right. He turned to go.

"We can talk." Her voice was so soft he could hardly hear it. "Let me get some drinks. I'm still dehydrated. Wait here."

He waited, wondering if she was as nervous as he was. Doubtful, but possible. Time froze. Or at least it seemed to. Finally, she came out, two frosted glasses of dark brown liquid in hand.

She passed him one. "Root beer. You still like it, right?"

He couldn't stop his smile. He'd half expected some vile tea as punishment. Clearly. she was more kindhearted than he'd be inclined to be. "I do. Thanks."

She took a seat on the porch swing. He looked uncertainly at the other seating options. "I don't bite. You can sit with me."

Careful not to upset her drink, he lowered himself to the swing with a full foot between them. She pivoted to face him, and he turned slightly toward her. "Do you read minds?" he blurted the first question to pop into his head.

"Didn't we just discuss that? No. I can sense emotions, that's it, though I do read auras. My power is in moving earth, and growing things."

"Could you kill me?" *Shit, he hadn't meant to ask that.*

"Probably. I could cause an earthquake. Or maybe stuff your mouth with dirt. But I wouldn't. I'm a peaceful soul. Violence is abhorrent to me. What happened at the cave was...unusual."

"Would you use your magic against someone?"

She snorted. "You know the answer to that. I did it to save us. I think Rylie possesses the skill to take us out. What you saw was self-defense. If you meant, would I hurt you, the answer is no. I'd never use my magic against you. I'm a nurturer. I nurture things, I don't harm them. Not animals, not plants, not people. I rarely kill a bug. Except spiders." She shuddered. "I hate spiders."

He chuckled. Her hatred of spiders was legendary, though usually she begged someone else to put them outside where they belonged. "You're not done with Rylie yet, are you?"

"I would be if I could be." She sat quietly, staring out over the lush flower gardens dotting the enormous lawn.

He wondered who mowed it.

"I don't think Rylie is done with us," she said. "And, honestly, I don't know why she seems to pop up whenever I'm around. It's odd.

Keres went after Amber. Brown went after Hazel. I guess Rylie is my nemesis. Wow, that's something I never thought I'd say." She glugged half of her drink and let out an unladylike burp. "I won't fight unless I'm forced to. I'm going to read more journals and find the clue we read about."

He mulled her words around. "Why is Meri magic and I'm not?"

"Magic is passed down by the mother. Some men are magic, but most aren't. It takes a magical father and mother to produce a magical male. But it isn't a guarantee. Even when it happens, most men, even if properly trained, aren't as powerful as women. As yet, research doesn't know why."

"People are researching this?" That was shocking. "Let me guess, the council?"

"They're not just about law and order. There's a twenty-story office tower devoted to record keeping. That includes old magic tomes and digital records. There's the policing side of it. There's a group that tracks rules. We don't have many laws, but there are a few. There's a prison and a medical division devoted to research. The council was founded long before the witch trials ever started. Afterward, it grew because secrecy became paramount. The ironic thing is most of those sacrificed in the trials, worldwide, weren't even witches. Most were innocent civilians."

"Ya, I've read that. What a tragedy." He wasn't bluffing or trying to win favor. When she'd first told him she was a witch, once he calmed down, he'd done some research, and had done much more study recently.

"Consider the council like a professional and a research group combined. And they're aware of everything that's happened here. Keres, Brown, and even Rylie. They'll be informed of what happened today. I'll have to answer questions and maybe pay a penalty."

"Like what?" He'd had no idea how enormous and comprehensive this was.

"Prison can be an option, cognitive retraining, a fine, or being forced to wear binding jewelry for a while."

"Like an impaired driver not being able to drive without blowing first. I'm impressed." He sent the swing rocking gently with his feet and Cynth curled up against the back of the padded swing, her feet tucked under her legs.

"Anything else?" She put her head back and closed her eyes.

"Probably a million things. None come to mind right away. I reserve the right to question you more later."

"Granted. But I have questions of my own."

He couldn't deny her questions. "Go ahead." He leaned back and closed his own eyes but kept the swing swaying lightly.

"I need to know that I can trust you not to fly off the handle again. Give me time to explain before you start panicking. Do you trust me? Can I trust you?"

"God, that's a mouthful." He pushed them back and forth for a count of ten. "I swear on baby Anna that I'll try to keep calm and trust you."

"Look at me," she said quietly and shifted on the seat.

He opened his eyes and stared into hers.

"Say it again," she demanded.

She meant look me in the eye, and he totally understood. He couldn't meet her gaze and lie. "Hyacinth, I'm trying to get my head around this magic stuff and I swear on baby Anna, who, according to Chen, might end up being magic. I swear on my niece that I'll do my best not to act like an asshat. I'll try and trust you and give you time to explain."

She studied him until he was tempted to squirm, but he held her gaze, refusing to look away first.

"I guess that's good enough. Come," she patted the seat, "sit closer to me."

They swung in silence, and he tried to figure out what was wrong. Something seemed off. "Where are the cats?"

She laughed and the sound tickled down his spine and landed on his libido. "Pouting." She bolted upright. "I forgot. Come inside." She dragged him toward the front door. "There's someone I want you to meet."

Inside a wild-looking puppy careened toward them and jumped all over them. "Artemis, down," she chided.

"You got a dog?" He stared at her as she sat on the floor cuddling the oversized puppy. "I thought you were a cat person."

"So did I until I met Artie. She's adorable."

"Artemis, why do I know that name? It sounds familiar."

"Artemis is the Greek Goddess of animals, the hunt, childbirth, chastity, and vegetation. She's often considered a healer. I'm a healer…" she shrugged.

"It makes perfect sense." Artie left her sitting on the floor and sniffed him. She walked in circles sniffing and pawing as high as she could reach without jumping.

"Artie, down girl." She gently pushed on the pup's bottom until she sat. "Good girl," she praised. "We'll be taking obedience school as quickly as possible," she laughed. "Both of us need training."

Artie got up and started sniffing him again. "What's she doing? Why does she keep smelling me?"

"Don't ask me. I've been a dog owner for just a few hours. She's like that with everyone. Eventually, she quits and settles down. I'm not sure why she does it. The vet thought it was odd too."

"Where'd she come from?"

"I found her on the way home from Pop's. She was stuffed in a cardboard box under a pile of soggy boxes. Someone threw her away." She choked up as she remembered it.

"What?" His screech startled the dog, who yipped at him. "Easy girl." He stroked her back until she calmed down. "I can't believe someone would do that to such a precious girl. You are keeping her then?"

"She had no tags, and it's safe to assume since she was buried, that she was unwanted. I love her already." The soft maternal tone in her voice touched him and made him smile. She was going to be a great mom, and not just because of her career choice.

"She's lucky you found her."

"I think destiny sent her." She jumped up off the floor. "Come on, we were just about to read more of the journals. We're onto Rosalie's next journal. We're almost a year in without any hint about how she hid the talisman."

"Maybe it'll show up soon. She seemed in a hurry to be rid of it."

"Or maybe we missed it and need to review." She pursed her lips. "Whatever. Tea is ready and we're reading if you want to join us."

"If it will help end this, I'm all in. Take me to your teapot."

In the kitchen, he greeted each of the sisters in turn and they greeted him with cautious warmth. Pearl gave him the death stare. He wouldn't bow to her bullying. "Pearl, how are you?" Pearl didn't defrost one degree. She picked up the book and said, "Rosalie's hand-writing is atrocious." Then she resumed reading. It seemed that the cold shoulder was to be his punishment. He could live with that.

Rosalie went on and on about farm animals and helping deliver the neighbor's baby. There was a salve recipe for sore muscles that excited Cynth, and a cake recipe that seemed to lighten Pearl's scowl.

"Oh, this is interesting," Pearl said. "It looks like a verse of some sort."

"Water flows and nature divine.
I give up this which is not mine.
Powers hide it safe from harm.
Protect us from its evil charm.
Tumbling, falling, hidden keep.
Buried stone and water deep."

"Ugh," Hazel interrupted. "Why does it have to be a simple rhyme?"

"Rhymes make things easier to remember," Earl piped in, to everyone's astonishment. "What?" He shrugged. "I read a lot."

Pearl began reading again.

"One of three forever be.
Mighty flowing always free."

"Three could mean the falls," Laz injected.

"Are you going to let me finish this?" Pearl raised an eyebrow. Nobody spoke, so she went on.

"Wrapped in fabric.
There is no trick.
Buried in stone.
I shall not moan.
Out of my hands and hidden well.
In a water place, it shall dwell."

Silence reigned for several long minutes.

"Well, that tells us nothing." Hyacinth groaned.

Pearl turned the page. "Wait!"

"A Chickadee calls.
Water falls.
Let it be lest terror reign."

"Is that the clue?" Amber asked in unison with Hyacinth, both sounding equally incredulous.

"Would Rosalie make it that obvious?" Lazuli said.

"Obvious?" Earl asked. "Maybe it's just a distraction or poetic mumbo-jumbo."

"I didn't mean it that way. I meant she's only had one other poem-like entry. So, putting a clue that the reader knows is coming doesn't make sense."

"But the reader would have to luck upon the first reference to know that it meant something," Hyacinth said. "It was in another book. I only found it by some random instinct that I can't place. I was drawn to a shelf, and I took Rosie's insistence on a purple book to heart when I chose."

Everyone nodded in agreement with the coincidence.

"Let's look at it logically," she said. "Break it down line by line."

"Break it down," Hazel agreed in a singsong voice like she was some kind of pop star. Earl and Cynth rolled their eyes in unison.

"Obviously," Earl said, "It does refer to the waterfall. It mentions three, and cloth wrapped, and buried."

"It seems so simple. But it has to be in or near Chickadee Falls. Maybe under the water like in *Romancing the Stone*. Let's keep reading, maybe there are further clues to narrow it down."

They read for another hour before stumbling on what appeared to be detailed instructions. Cynth jumped up. "Let's go."

Chapter Twenty-Two

Waiting until morning to go back to Chickadee Falls nearly killed Cynth. She only slept two hours and spent half the night praying that none of her clients would go into early labor. It was barely six and she was on the front porch drinking her third cup of coffee, waiting for Hazel and Pearl to get ready, when Earl pulled up. Artie ran out to meet him. He squatted and fondled her tan head just the way she loved. Then he ruffled her black ears.

"I didn't expect to see you," she said when he joined her on the swing, Artie at his feet.

"Don't I get a good morning kiss?" he teased. "I barely got a good-night kiss."

They'd spent half an hour on the swing last night with Artie cuddled up beside them. They'd talked a lot before sharing a moving goodnight kiss. A lot of women wouldn't have forgiven him or would have made him dance through hoops to prove himself. She wasn't one for petty revenge, and her absolute faith in him was rock solid. She knew the boy, and she knew the man. She loved them both.

He slid his arm around her shoulders and pulled her close for a kiss. She didn't hesitate. She was taking him at his word that he trusted her and that he could be trusted in return. There was nothing to gain from playing coy. She cared for him, loved him, and didn't want to hide that. She leaned into the kiss, pushing her heart into every second of contact. He smelled like the forest and tasted of honey and mint. She pulled back in surprise.

"That's it?" he asked incredulously. "One little peck. A man could die from lack of lovin'"

"Are you still eating the honey mints I make?" She had designed them for him when they were young, and the treats were a popular item in the shop and online. It was years after they broke up before she could bear to eat them.

"They're my addiction. When I found them on the website, before your family decided to open a physical location, I ordered them right away. I'm surprised you didn't know."

"That rotten Amber. She's run the store since it opened. She never told me." She shook her head. "Traitor." Her sister probably thought she was protecting her. She may have been right.

"You know now." He rested his head against hers. "Are we going soon?"

"Right now," Pearl said, stepping through the front doorway. She patted the small pack she carried. "I've got the book in protective plastic. Hazel has water."

"I brought snacks," Earl added. "I couldn't pass up the smell of Dottie's Donuts. I grabbed donuts and muffins, and some bread and cheese, in case this takes a while."

Pearl nodded approvingly. After his second betrayal, Cynth knew it would take a long time for her grandmother to forgive Earl. She had a bit of a stubborn streak when it came to her family.

"I couldn't get through to your parents," Pearl told Cynth. "But I managed to get a message through telling them to come home. Whatever's going on, we need all wands on deck. Last I heard they were in Pakistan, headed to Kathmandu to talk to the council there."

"Couldn't they do that by phone?" Earl asked.

"The office is remote and has limited phone coverage. Even the internet is spotty." She didn't mention that the Kathmandu office was designed to be free of electronic tampering. It was the council's semi-secret base.

Hazel came out and the four of them began the trek past the greenhouses, into the forest, and to the base of the falls.

"I didn't realize there were hiding places at the falls," Earl said, a question in his voice.

"Tiny caves if you go behind the fall itself. They're hard to find, even in winter when the falls aren't flowing. We girls used to love to play in them and pretend we were cave dwellers or pirates storing bounty." Hazel grinned.

"I think that's booty," Cynth corrected with a laugh.

"I say booty, you say bounty." Everyone chuckled, and they walked in silence the rest of the way.

The morning was cool enough that Cynth was glad she'd grabbed her favorite hoodie, the one with long flowing arms and a cute hood. It looked like a cape with pockets.

"Where do we begin?" Pearl asked as Earl spread out a blanket. She read the poem aloud to refresh their memories.

"Is it safe to have that book out here? It's quite old. Don't you worry about damage?" he asked.

"Not at all. It's magically protected from damage," Cynth explained. "It couldn't stand to be underwater or buried for a long time, but regular use won't harm it. Still, we'll be uber careful."

Using the second poem they'd found yesterday, they began their search by stripping down to swimwear, despite the cold.

"I wish I'd thought to bring my trunks," Earl grumbled.

"You could strip to your underwear." Cynth waggled her eyebrows and leered at him.

"Ya. No." He looked at the cluster of women. "I'll wait here with Pearl."

Cynth chuckled. "Coward."

Pearl read the keywords aloud. "Behind a boulder, buried in water."

"Does that mean the boulder is buried, or the thing behind it?" Cynth worked her finger around the lower edge of three enormous rocks, looking for loose stones. She pried a few loose, but found nothing.

"It also says beyond the forest and veil."

"Well, the veil usually means the veil between life and death," Hazel said. "Maybe it means the falls? Could it be behind the falls, in those caves?"

"I wouldn't think so." Cynth stood and brushed water off her legs. "We spent hundreds of hours in them as kids. I don't remember getting any vibes back there."

"You should go in," Earl said above the roaring of the water. "Maybe your senses are stronger now."

Hazel, who was somewhat braver about water since her near-drowning, took the first cave, and Cynth stepped through the frigid waterfall to look in the last one. It was the smallest. They'd do the middle and largest together. The entry was tight, but the space behind was larger. She scraped both hips squeezing her way in. It was no wonder they'd rarely played in this one.

She'd barely passed the tight opening when her nerves jangled. "Holy shit."

She flipped on her phone's flashlight and scanned the interior. Near the back was a single large rock. Not a boulder, but larger than the others by far. Careful not to slip on the wet cave floor, she hurried forward, stepping gingerly over smaller rocks.

The tingle in her nerves turned to trepidation as she kneeled beside the rock. "Please be here," she muttered, though part of her didn't want to find whatever was giving off such dark vibes.

She dug in the small pool behind the rock, sifting through smaller stones and pebbles. Her hands slid over something smooth and slippery. Unable to see in the murky water, she traced the edges and removed the debris surrounding it. She pulled out an ancient jar.

"Holy, sacred rowan branches."

Careful not to drop the slimy jar, she hurried out from behind the water, calling excitedly. "I found something!" She waded across the stream and set the jar on the grass. Instantly, she missed the power it exuded and wanted to pick it back up.

Chapter Twenty-Three

"Don't touch it," she barked when Pearl reached for it. "I can feel the dark magic. My hands still tingle from holding it." She shuddered. "I'll open it."

Earl draped his jacket over her shoulders as she kneeled by the jar. Her hands shook so badly that she nearly dropped it twice. The lid was stuck. She banged it lightly on a rock, trying to dislodge it. Finally, she managed to twist it off. She poured the contents into her hand.

"This fabric feels like linen, but rough." She shuddered again. "So dark." She spread the miraculously dry fabric on the ground. Inside, a golden necklace studded with jewels shone up at her. She stepped back, glaring.

"Sweet Mother Earth, I can feel the power from here."

They stared down at the beautiful pendant. A central stone, maybe a ruby, was surrounded by twelve other stones. Two smaller garnets nested on either side of the ruby. On either side of the garnets were emeralds, followed by diamonds, labradorite, moonstones, and finally tourmalines. Each successive stone was smaller than the one beside it. They were all roughly square cut and set in gold bezels which hung from two rings. The stones glittered in the sunshine.

"I don't feel anything," Earl said. "But it is pretty."

"I get a hint of dark from it," Hazel said.

"Are you kidding?" Cynth gaped at them. "It radiates evil and repulses me. But at the same time, I want to grab it and run." Nausea rose in her throat.

Pearl and Hazel chattered away excitedly about their find and what it meant. She heard them like background conversation. Her entire being was focused on the necklace. She wanted it.

Hyacinth shivered as they celebrated their find with the feast Earl brought. Though the water had been icy cold in the dark, dank cave. It wasn't from cold; she was well toweled off and back in her jeans and hoodie.

"What's wrong?" Earl asked. "Are you cold?"

"No. I can't shake the feeling that someone's watching or something's coming our way. I've had this impending sense of doom for weeks, maybe months. It started a couple of weeks after Brown was captured. It comes and goes." She shivered again. "It's intense right now. I can't tell if it's the presence of the pendant or something else." Without realizing she had picked it up, she shifted the pendant from her left hand to her right, watching how the gems glowed in the sun.

"Let's go back to the house." Earl stood and started packing up the food. "We probably should have done that right away. We ran into Rylie here once already. Who knows who else might 'accidentally' stumble on the falls?"

"You're right." Approval rang in Pearl's voice. "We need to be more vigilant. Even I succumbed to the heady victory of finally finding this thing. Earl, I'd like you to carry it."

"Me?" His voice squeaked, and he took a surprised step backward. "Why me?"

"I feel it pulling me to try to use it. I'm sure the girls feel the same. We can't use it until we know more about it. About what it does and how it affects the user. It was hidden for a reason. You said you feel nothing, no power. It is safer for all of us if it is with you. For now."

"I can do that. I appreciate you trusting me." He held out his hand to Cynth who still had the pendant in her hand.

"I can carry it," she said, pulling it tight to her chest. "It's not like I'm going to use it," she almost snarled. *Why didn't they trust her to carry it? It was just a fancy bauble.*

"Come on, hun. What your grandmother says makes sense. Let me carry it." He approached her.

She backed up. "I've got it. Let's go." She started for the path without waiting for the others. They could catch up when they cleaned up their picnic spot.

"Hyacinth Hawk give Earl that necklace right now!"

Cynth felt the compulsion her grandmother put into her voice and recognized the hint of desperation. Her mind, used to nearly three decades of obeying that tone kicked in. It was almost physically painful, but she handed it to Earl.

"Thanks, hun."

"You're welcome." *Not*, she muttered under her breath. Some of the tension and unease she felt slipped away as he stepped back from her. "Holy crap."

"Holy crap what?" Pearl asked immediately. She strode up and looked Cynth right in the eye.

"I feel better. Was that thing affecting me, like making my feeling of doom stronger? As soon as Earl moved away, the gloom lightened. Was it causing the doom? Or was it strengthening what I felt?" She shuddered in fear and revulsion. "Keep that thing away from me. I'm never touching it again."

"Premonition is your weakest skill," Hazel offered. "Maybe it amped it up somehow."

"I don't know how you would charm an object to do that. It's beyond any magic I know," Pearl said. "We need to lock that thing up until we figure out how to use it properly, and how to destroy it."

"Won't the council pitch a fit when they find out it was destroyed?" Earl asked.

"The Witch's Council can kiss my wrinkled old ass," Pearl snapped. "Some things shouldn't exist, and I know this is one of them. Three people that we know of have come looking for it. When will it end? We figure out what it's for, record what we know, and destroy it."

It wasn't just the necklace's charm on her that told Cynth that it shouldn't be destroyed. How many other items of ill intent were stored in the magical archives? Probably hundreds, maybe thousands. They were created for a reason and should be preserved safely. "I'm not sure we should destroy it. It feels like it must have a purpose."

"For now," Earl put in, "We need to find a way to neutralize its pull. I'm worried people will sense its presence and come after it. What do you suggest?" He stuffed it into his pants pocket and pulled it out again. "I'm not sure I want this near my junk." He put it in his pack and zipped it up. "Let's get back to the house before this thing damages me."

They hurried back to the house. Once inside, Cynth asked, "How do we block its power?" Nobody had any concrete ideas aside from reburying it.

"What about a Faraday box?" Earl asked. "They're made of lead and stop electromagnetic radiation. Maybe one could block the magic too?"

"Where would we get one? Certainly not in town," Cynth looked at everyone.

"I have one," he said. "I'll go get it and come back."

"Why do you have a Faraday box?" she asked. "Aren't they kind of a tinfoil hat or prepper thing?"

"Yup." He didn't expand, he just left. The backpack sat on the floor beside the chair he'd been sitting on.

"I'll just put that somewhere safe," Cynth said.

"Don't!" Her grandmother and sister snapped as one.

"It's fine right there," Pearl added. "We do need to get your sisters here to see how it affects them. Haz, if you don't have to be at work, why don't you go to the store and send Amber home? We can't leave the store unattended. We can call Laz."

"Dennis won't mind if I don't go in. I told him I might be late this afternoon. I'll catch up on the bookkeeping later. It's not like it's tax season." She chuckled. "You're okay to watch her?"

"Hey," Cynth objected.

"You know I'm right. You can't be trusted with it. I feel the pull, too." Hazel glared at the bag. "You've got it worse than either of us."

"It'll be fine. I'll be fine." She crossed her arms over her chest and glared at her sister. *How dare she?* "I'm not even slightly tempted," she lied.

"BS." Hazel laughed. "If you're good with being alone with her, Gramma, I'll go."

"We'll be fine. We'll just sit here until someone else shows up. Double ward the door on your way out, please."

Cynth wanted to object to the extra precaution, but couldn't make herself. They only double-warded when they would be gone for days. The house's magic, magic that had seeped into it through years of its occupants doing magic in and near the house, created a magical protection for those inside that normally would be adequate. Through powers she couldn't fully understand, the house knew who meant them harm.

It had protected itself from break-ins, turned a hose on a small fire caused by lightning, and could do its own maintenance. She'd miss those skills if she ever moved away. Thinking about wards drew her attention back to the pendant. To keep from fixating on the bag and its contents, she imagined a life with Earl.

Could he, would he, consider living in Hawk Manor? What about kids? They'd never really talked much about that as teens. But he came from a background of strong family values, and he adored his niece. Surely, he'd want kids. Probably sons.

She sighed. Hawk women only had girls. There wasn't a single instance of them having a male offspring. Would that kill the deal if they reached the point of discussing marriage and family? She'd like a son. She'd always thought she'd try to find a magical boy looking for a home. Would that be okay with Earl?

She sighed again.

"That bag really has you tied up in knots," Pearl said quietly. "I'm hoping this box thing works."

"Actually, I was thinking about Earl and a future with him. What if he wants sons? What if no sons is a deal breaker? What if he won't adopt a boy when he learns I can only have girls? Maybe I should end it now." Goddess, the very idea made her chest clench like she was having a heart attack.

"Don't go borrowing trouble. You're young. He's young. You've got time to work things out if you get that far. Earl's a level-headed guy. He proved it today. He'll be reasonable."

"Wow, that was almost praise," she mocked.

"Well, he did. He might be flighty at times, but it seems like he's coming to his senses. His apology yesterday seemed sincere."

"You listened in on it?" She jumped to her feet and glared down at her grandmother with her hands on her hips. "How dare you?" Artie circled her feet whining anxiously.

"Oh, I dare." Pearl rose slowly and they stood, almost nose to nose, staring at each other. "When it comes to my family, I dare a lot. More than you'll know until you're my age with family to protect. You girls are like daughters to me. I practically raised you when your parents left on their mission. No, you weren't babies, but you weren't adults either. Sometimes, the teen years are the hardest and we got through them. Together." She inched forward. "That's how life is. Deal with it."

The door opened, but neither of them looked toward it.

"What's going on?" Amber asked, racing toward them without taking off her shoes. "Separate!" She shoved them apart. "Stand down."

Artie growled at Amber, but they stepped back from each other. "Sorry," Cynth mumbled.

"Me too."

"What was that?" Amber demanded.

"I think it's the talisman. It's glorious. But it seems to amplify emotions." Cynth backed away from her family and sat in the chair furthest from the bag.

"Considering what it appears to do, and I'm no less affected than your sister, it's a wonder Rosalie had the strength to get rid of it." Pearl shook her head. "You watch your sister, both of you stay away from the bag. Being near it is draining my energy. We need food."

"I have a better idea," said Amber, who glared at the bag. "Let's leave it here and all go into the kitchen. We're waiting for Earl, anyway. Should I call Kody?"

"It might be interesting to find out how it affects male magic. Should his grandmother come? She's in town for a few days."

"I don't know," Cynth hedged. "Do we want more people in on this thing? Isn't that dangerous? Doesn't it increase the risk of being found out?"

"Nonsense. Abigail kicked in her power when we fought Keres. She didn't even know us, but she's practically family now. Call him and have them come over. Maybe we should get Hazel to bring Dennis. Laz is on her way. This feels like a family thing to me. It took most of us to riddle out the clues, maybe we can riddle this out too."

There was something in Pearl's voice that told Cynth that her grandmother was deeply worried about the entire situation. She sympathized. She felt it too.

Chapter Twenty-Four

B y the time the others arrived, they had created a lunch buffet and had it spread on the enormous kitchen table. They pulled up an extra chair so all nine of them could sit. It meant crowding, but would be workable.

"Wow. The tension in here is off the charts," Kody said after greeting everyone. "Do you feel it?" He looked at his grandmother. "That bag is off." He shrugged. It had only been a few months since he discovered the magic powers his parents had blocked. He was barely learning to use them.

"That's evil you feel. I'd swear by it." Abigail looked pale and backed away from the bag. "I can feel it calling me." She fumbled backward until she plopped into a wingback chair.

"I feel the tension in the room like I walked in on the aftermath of a fight, but that's it. I get nothing from the bag," Dennis said. Like Earl, he had no magic abilities.

Lazuli stood quietly, staring at the bag. "I want to see it," she said. "But I don't want to touch it. I can feel its pull. It's almost like a voice calling to the magic in my cells."

"Jeez," Dennis said. "Magic is messed up." He grinned at everyone. "No offense." He hugged Hazel. "I still love you. This won't change that."

"I'll take it out," Earl said. "Dennis, stand by me and be ready just in case something weird happens." He handed him the Faraday box. "Get ready to put it in there." He looked at everyone else and warned, "The rest of you, stay back. As far as you can. I can't feel this thing's pull, but I know how it messed Cynth up. I don't want that to happen again." He waited until everyone did as he directed before he picked up the bag.

The second he pulled it from the bag, Laz jumped toward him. In a spinning move, Dennis whirled away and thrust the open box at him, and he slammed it inside.

The surge of power Cynth felt subsided immediately. The Faraday box worked!

"Give it to me," Laz demanded, still moving forward.

"Hells to the no," Earl said.

Cynth laughed at the dichotomy between his words and the serious look on his face. "Come on sis," she dragged Laz into the kitchen. Laz fought her every step. Finally in the kitchen, she pushed her sister down into a seat.

"Holy busted jigsaw and bent nails. I heard it. It called to me. A voice in my head." She shook her head in disbelief. "Don't open it again."

Everyone crowded into the kitchen. "Call the council and get rid of it," Laz demanded.

"We'll just keep it boxed up and away from you," Pearl said.

Abigail sat down. "I didn't hear it, but the second you pulled it out, I had a vision."

"What?" Cynth squawked.

"Grandma?" Kody stared at Abigail. "You have visions? Crap on toast. You never told me that."

"Kody, it would be unwise of me to tell you I have visions. But think about it. How did I know you were in trouble as a teen and how did I know you'd show up after you fought with Amber? You're a bright boy. Figure it out."

"Shoot. I always suspected but hearing it from your mouth changes everything."

"Be that as it may," Cynth interrupted. "What did you see?"

Abigail stabbed a finger at her. "You. Rocks. Shaking the earth. Some kind of magic fight." It wasn't clear. Just flashes of images.

"Was it a cave?" Maybe she'd seen the past not the future.

"No open land, for sure. It was familiar, but I couldn't place where it was. Definitely not your fight in the cave. I think what I saw is meant to come."

Fear rocked Cynth on her heels. She'd known something was coming. But a magical fight? No way. "Why is everyone attacking our family?"

"The talisman," Pearl said. "Besides, we're one of the top magical families on earth." She sounded smug.

"What? How do you know? Do you have contests?" Earl demanded; fear clear in his voice.

"It's not a measurement. It's a culmination of past and present magic skills. There's no solid ranking. It doesn't work like that because skills aren't even. But if I had to guess, we'd be in the top five at least. Maybe the top one or two." This time, her pride was unmistakable.

"Gramma Pearl? Really? And you never thought to mention it?" *How could she keep something like this quiet?*

"Our powers aside, I think these attacks are related to the talisman, the pendant. Keres specifically asked for it. Brown was his son. He also came here looking for something. Despite all that, I think this goes beyond them. I do believe Keres wanted to revive his wife, wherever he has her stashed, but I don't think he stumbled upon stories of the talisman by mistake. I think someone put him up to it for their gain. Maybe whoever got Keres to look for it was planning to steal it from Keres before he had a chance to use it." Pearl stopped talking as a stunned silence filled the room.

Earl was the first to speak. "Holy ham sandwiches and mustard on book covers." His odd attempt at clean cussing made them laugh and relieved some of the tension. "Speaking of which, fear makes me hungry. Mind if I dive into this delicious looking food?"

"Good idea." Cynth grabbed his hand and pulled him to the back of the table, closest to the circular windows that surrounded most of the table.

Lunch was tense enough that Cynth felt her nerves would snap and she'd burst out screaming and run away, never looking back.

"We need to study it," Laz said.

"How do you propose we do that?" Cynth snapped. "None of us can go near it. I think it's still affecting me a little, even in that box." They'd put the box into a freezer in the other room.

"Dennis and I could take pictures of it," Earl suggested. "Maybe there's a jeweler in town who could look at it and give some clues to its origin. With pictures, I'd have something to search with. Who knows what's out there that might be relevant?"

"You know, that makes sense." Hyacinth hugged Earl. "You're brilliant. We can't be affected by pictures, right?"

"Let's hope not. I think the idea is a good one. Thanks, Earl," Pearl gave him a genuine smile.

Whoa! Her boyfriend was gaining brownie points quickly. Pretty soon he'd redeem himself. Amid all the chaos, things were looking up.

"We might as well take pictures right away," Dennis suggested. "I've got a decent camera at my place. We can do it there."

"I'll come," Hazel said.

"As if," Cynth snapped. "None of us magicals are going. Just those two."

"Someone has to stand guard," she protested.

"We'll do it in the basement, with the doors locked, and the alarms set. We'll be fine. I promise." Dennis kissed Hazel on the cheek. "I've got magic warding now, remember?"

As if any of them would forget the attacks that had happened at his home and near his greenhouse business.

"It's settled then," Cynth said. "Earl, you should take your camera too. The more pictures the better."

While the Hawks, Kody, and his grandmother cleaned up, Dennis and Earl took the box and headed for Dennis's large, well-warded home.

Four hours later, they came back. The box was returned to the freezer, and the freezer was locked. Earl took possession of the freezer's key. Everyone gathered around the table to study the photos.

There were pictures of each of the thirteen stones, front, back, and from all sides. There were close-ups of all the stamping and text on the piece as well as pictures of the entire piece, front and back. All in all, there were nearly one hundred pictures to look at. They'd printed eighty by tens of each and had digital copies for ease of zooming in on details.

Cynth stared down at the front image of the entire piece. She started at the lone center ruby and touched each pair of stones as they went higher on the chain. Looking at it with pictures and digital images made it much easier to examine the talisman in greater detail without fear of its darkness messing with her thoughts and emotions.

Hyacinth listed the stones off. "Let's make a list of all the magical properties of the stones," she suggested.

"They're all real according to the jeweler. The setting is 24-karat gold. His best guess is that it is over nine hundred years old. He does admit that he's not an expert and gave us a couple of names to follow up with if we needed to. By his best guess, it's worth several hundred thousand dollars...at least."

Cynth whistled. "Holy birthing babies. I had no idea. I just thought it was pretty. Well, that and magic." Her attempt at a laugh fell flat.

Amber hurried to the library and returned with three volumes on the power of gemstones. She searched through them and made notes while the others studied the photos. Finally, she looked up.

"Listen up. I've collected the major traits of each stone. Ruby helps with circulatory and heart problems. It can alleviate pain and low energy. It aids in detoxification and can increase youth and vitality. Garnet is considered a lucky stone, and Goddess knows if you were bringing back the dead, you'd need luck. Emerald is a life-affirming stone and is also good luck. Diamonds can protect the wearer against thieves, fire, water, poison, illness, and sorcery. Labradorite strengthens psychic ability and provides protection. Moonstone promotes emotional balance and reduces anxiety and mental ailments. Geez, this thing is a recipe for the perfect evil tool. Of course it could also do amazing good in the right hands. Why do magic items always have to be dual edged?"

"With all good comes the possibility of evil. It's an unwritten law, or something." Cyn reminded them. "You'd need the emotional balance of moonstone for whoever you brought back. I think a revived dead person might not be in their right mind." She stared at the images, half mesmerized.

"Truth." Amber laughed. Moonstones have protective qualities as well. Tourmaline is a healing and stabilizing stone." She sipped her coffee. "There are lots of other uses and magical properties. I've just hit the highlights."

"That's a lot of information," Cynth said when Amber, the family gemstone expert finished listing off the stones' magical properties.

"How come she's the stone expert when your power is earth-based?" Earl asked.

"I've always wondered that myself." Cynth looked up long enough to smile at him. "Ironically, her power is water, and she knows rocks. After living with magic all my life, I've concluded that while there are patterns and rules to how it works, it doesn't always make sense. Just go with it. That's what I do."

There was more examination and searching to consider, but she was exhausted. "I think I'm going to stay in a hotel tonight," she said. "I want to get away from the stone. Laz, you should too."

"I don't want you alone," Earl said. "Why don't you stay in my guest bedroom?"

"Laz and Gramma should stay at Dennis's. Dennis and I can stay here and guard the stone. It doesn't affect me at all when it's boxed up," Hazel suggested.

"I'll be at home, with Kody and Abigail," Amber said.

"I hate not being here," Pearl said. "But I think that's a good, safe plan."

Chapter Twenty-Five

"Welcome to my home," Earl said as he waved Cynth into his apartment. It was pushing seven when they arrived with Artie in tow. He was exhausted from the emotional upheavals of the day but still wondered what she thought of his mom's solid wood tables, glass globe lamps, and a Persian rug. All were in fabulous shape, so he'd kept them. He'd boxed up most of her trinkets after Meri moved out and had started to make the place his own, but he liked the blend of past and present, including his grandfather's ancient gramophone.

"This is so cozy. I don't think I've ever been up here," she said, looking around.

"Probably not," he said as Artie scurried around sniffing everything. "We didn't spend much time with our families back then. Make yourself at home."

She placed her bag at the end of the hallway she assumed led to the bedrooms and took a seat on the oversized plush sofa that dominated the living room. "I adore the lamps. No way this was your mom's," she teased, patting the sofa.

"It wasn't. The old one had been around since I was ten. Two years ago, it was falling to pieces. I like this one, it's wide enough to sleep on, and it fits my long legs. It's deep enough to cuddle. Not that I've been cuddling anyone," he added hastily.

"Earl, we were apart for a decade. I'd be an idiot if I thought you hadn't had a girlfriend in that time. We live in the same town. I know you dated, and in some cases, know who you dated." And she'd hated every woman, even those who had since become her friends. Jealousy was an ugly beast she'd tried not to embrace.

"Ditto for you. Though I don't think you dated much."

"Well, first there was school. Studying to become a midwife and doula wasn't easy. Then, once I had my practice established, I got busy. I'm still busy. I don't have time for dating." Nor had she wanted to, but that was another secret she'd take to her grave.

"Then what's this we're doing?" He asked, sitting at the opposite end of the couch.

"Dating," she said with certainty. "I appreciate that you don't grumble about my work hours. They're always sporadic."

"You forget I'm a preacher's son. Dad and Mom were always off visiting some family or helping out in bad times. I know what life is like when you dedicate it to others. Meri and I were often left to fend for ourselves."

"That must have been hard."

"No harder than you being raised by your grandmother while your folks were off fighting evil. I learned to live with what I was dealt and to trust in God. Which makes my sister being magic a huge kick in the pants." He pointed to a cardboard box in the corner. "Meri dropped that off. She said it's Mom's journals and that I need to read them."

"Are you going to?" She asked with soft understanding. "It might be tough."

"Meri said she only cried a couple of times. And she's an emotional wienie. I might cry, I might not. But frankly, I'm afraid of what's in there."

"I don't think the past can truly hurt you. Bruise you a little, but not injure you. We could do it together. Sometimes there's comfort in sharing with friends."

Was she right about sharing? The day had been ridiculously emotionally taxing already. "Maybe? I have made peace with their deaths, but still..."

"I get it. I have no contact with my birth father. He gave me the Camaro and that's about it. Mom's husband, Trevor is like a dad to me, but I would have liked to know my real dad better. Mom cared about him, about all four of our fathers, but she only ever loved Trevor."

She had warned him years ago that she and her sisters all had different fathers. She'd worried there was a stigma attached to it, and maybe at the time there had been. Now, she didn't seem to be bothered by it. He was glad she'd found that peace.

They commiserated about their families and fell into silence. "Beer?" he asked abruptly.

"Wine if you have it. If not, beer will do. Thanks."

"I'll get wine for next time." He came back with a cookie sheet covered in a tea towel. On it was a bowl of pretzels, a dish of cashews, and two unopened bottles of Pilsner. He set the tray on the table, popped the tops off, and handed one to her. "Cheers."

"Should we read from the journals?" she asked a few minutes later. "I'm curious about your mother. She was always so kind and helpful, but still a bit scary." They shared a chuckle.

"I guess we could." He really didn't want to know what was inside. After Meri's insistence that he read them and her assertion that their mother practiced magic, he was nervous about what they'd reveal. His stomach roiled and he set his beer aside.

"Want to start at the beginning by date, or just take them at random? I can read aloud," she suggested.

She had a wonderful reading voice. Grade twelve English had been his favorite class. While he'd hated reading aloud himself, he'd loved listening to her. She'd been a bit of a teacher's pet and was often called on to go first.

He tamped down his anxiety knowing that the longer he put off the dragon of opening his mom's journals, the larger the anxiety would grow. In the two weeks since they'd arrived, the journals had grown in his mind from a small box to a massive cargo container. How could a sixteen-by-eighteen-inch box hold so much uncertainty?

"I'd appreciate that. It's hard for me to open the box, let alone the books."

She brought the box to the table and stood over it. She opened it and pulled out a bundle of paper and set it aside. "It's well packed." Another bundle followed. "Oh, this one is heavy. There must be something in it. Should I unwrap it?"

"In for a penny, in for a pound." If his mom had hidden it, he didn't want to know what it was.

She folded the paper back carefully. "Oh, it's a stand for something. It looks like pewter." She examined it from every angle and gave it to him. It had a round, flat, felt-covered base with three floral patterned prongs raising from the base. It looked like it was designed to support something.

"It's pretty. Definitely Mom's style." He set it down and waved toward the box.

Next was a plain white, four-inch square box. Before she could offer it to him to open, he told her to go ahead. She pulled out a perfectly clear glass ball. "Is that crystal?" he asked.

"I think just glass. But glass can be effective for reflection."

"Reflection?" *What did that mean?*

"You stare into the ball and either let your mind go blank or focus on a problem or a question. The distraction of staring opens your mind to new ideas and ways of looking at what you're thinking about or avoiding. It's a meditation technique."

His stomach clenched. *His mom had had a crystal ball. Holy smoke damaged books.* "This is turning my whole world upside down. I wonder if my dad knew about all this."

"I bet we find out in the books." She pulled out a floral print book. "There's nothing on the cover to say what it is. Shall I?"

Swallowing a yoga ball-sized lump of trepidation, he nodded. She studied him for a moment, sat down, wiggled a bit, and made herself comfortable before opening the book.

"Oh, she's covered it herself. See." she showed him the inside. It was neatly done, but obviously not professionally. "She did some sewing in her spare time, didn't she?"

"Ya, a lot of mending for the church thrift store. Things that could be fixed and sold."

"Okay. Here we go. July 17th, 1997." She looked at him. "Isn't that your birthday?"

"Yes," he could barely force the word out.

With one last sympathetic glance at him, she began to read. *"I'm thrilled. Okay, that's not strong enough. I'm ecstatic. Caleb and I have tried for four years to have this child. God has finally blessed us with a perfect baby boy. We're calling him Earl Caleb, after his father, and after my father. He's perfect in every way."*

"I didn't know I was named for Mom's dad. She didn't talk about him much, and I never met him. That's cool." Cynth's smile lit her entire face, and he didn't need her to say that maybe his fear of the box was unjustified.

"I had a home birth. Yanna, a local midwife came to help me out. Caleb wasn't able to be there as he was attending a dying parishioner. Of course, he's a bit squeamish, so he was probably relieved to escape. He doesn't like the idea of men around when a birth is imminent. He's so old-fashioned sometimes. Besides, Yanna gave me some herbs to ease the pain and help the birth along. I'm not sure he'd have approved."

"She treated us with herbs all the time. From her family's recipes. Why would this be different?" The herb thing was weird, but it was nice to know he was wanted and loved. He knew it from his memories, but seeing it on paper, or rather hearing it, made it hit home with a warmth that chased away some of his worries about the box.

There were only one or two entries most weeks, and many were a single sentence, so journal time jumped quickly. She read for another half hour before she found anything else interesting. Why were journals so dull sometimes?

"Caleb and I argued today. We might be headed for separation. He'd never agree to a divorce. I've given it a lot of thought. Way too much. I haven't slept in weeks. I've lost fifteen pounds because I can barely eat. I'll stay in Three Moon Falls because while I'm pissed at Caleb, I can't separate him from his son. He is a good father. He dotes on Earl and loves taking him with him on church calls."

"He was a great dad." The words fell soft, almost silent in the room. The pain in them hit Cynth square in the heart. It must have been terrible to lose your family and be thrust into the role of provider at such a young age.

"I liked your parents. They were always kind." She reached out and squeezed his knee. He gripped her hand in his for a second and then slid his under hers. It was, in Earl's own way, a gesture of thanks for the support.

He nodded toward the book, and she resumed reading.

"Myrna says not to jump the gun. Caleb will come around. Caleb hasn't said anything, but I've been spending some time with Lily-Beth Hawk. She's been helping me hone my skills. Her medical knowledge is out of this world. She's taught me about herbs, and controlling my power so I can shift larger things. She nags me to refuel so I stop losing weight, but eating is difficult when my entire world is crumbling. As for Earl, he's a happy child who rarely fusses for no reason. My heart longs for a daughter, but unless something changes, that won't happen."

"That's my mom. Our moms were friends. Cool." She smiled at him. Somehow, it lessened the strain his mother's words were causing.

The next entry was dated a week later. *"I've moved out. I'm renting a bedroom in Mrs. Shumaker's basement. It isn't much. It's dark and small. But it's a place to sleep. I go home every morning to be with Earl while Caleb goes to the church to work. It breaks my heart, but I've promised him to never let our son see my magic. If I do, he'll take Earl away from me."*

There were a long series of entries about the joys and pains of her new life. "Today was a horrid day. Bad enough I'm tempted to cuss. I've never been so scared in my life. I was sitting in the park near the church, enjoying the sun while Earl slept in his stroller. He's been fussy lately. I think he senses the trouble between Caleb and me. He only sleeps when I walk him."

Cynth turned the book toward him. "Look at this. Is it a teardrop?" On the bottom of the page were several spots that looked like the thick journal paper had been hit with drops of liquid.

"Keep reading," he said, his voice thick with emotion.

"I was sitting watching some children play, but I was too far from their parents to interact with them. People are asking about our separation,

and I'm sick of answering questions. I sat there, and a man approached me. He wore a long black coat, like an old west cowboy would wear. Something about him set my nerves on edge. He gave me the heebie jeebies. He started asking questions about Earl, and if I planned to have another child. I swear to God and the Goddess, that my soul screamed for me to run away. He was young, maybe twenty, and I saw him five more times in different places as I walked around town doing errands. I think he was following me, and I'm scared."

Cynth and Earl shared a concerned glance, and she went back to reading. The next entry was dated a week later. *"By all that is holy, this has been one hell of a week. Yes, I just cussed. I can't help myself. Every time I went out after the day in the park, I saw that man. I was coming to the church to drop Earl off when he stepped in front of me on the church's sidewalk. He asked to hold Earl and when I refused, he grabbed my hand. It was the weirdest thing. I'm still shaking. My knees went weak and my mind went foggy. I started to faint. I swear to God! I screamed and Caleb came running out and chased the man away."*

"Once I calmed down, Caleb brought us home and said that I was to move back in. He hugged me close and kissed my temple. I'm not sure what that means, but I'm hoping it's a sign he still loves me. I know he cares for Earl. But I need him to love me."

"That's so weird. It's like what happened to Hazel and Amber. I think the man might have been magic and was testing her magic."

"Jeepers. She must have been terrified. How did I miss all of this? I mean the magic. She never told me about it, but Meri knew." He stood and walked back and forth in front of the windows. He paused, parted the curtains, and stared outside.

"She kept her promise to Caleb and never told you. Maybe she didn't ever promise not to tell Meri. Obviously, they got back together and stayed together. Should I read on?"

"No. I don't think I can take anymore. This is enough for one night. I will be reading the rest for sure. Just not today. My world's been shaken enough."

He sat right beside her, and she leaned into him, savoring the warmth and safety of being at his side. "I hate that magic messes things up. Why can't it be easy?"

Earl's chest rumbled with his laugh. "Babe, I wish I knew." After several long and contented moments, he broke the silence between them. "This whole mom being magic is a total kick in the pants."

Chapter Twenty-Six

E arl didn't expect to sleep despite being exhausted and emotionally overwhelmed. Surprisingly, as soon as sounds stopped coming from the spare room where Cynth slept, he drifted off and slept right through to his alarm.

He showered quietly and stole into the kitchen to make coffee and breakfast. He was ravenous. Did emotional stress make you hungry? He snorted, "More like I'm eating my feelings." It didn't matter because he was hungry, so he'd eat, and he'd feed Cynth.

The sausages were browning, the mini quiches in the oven, and the bread was ready to toast when she slipped up behind him and wrapped her arms around his waist. "Good morning, Earl." There was a smile in her voice.

He spun around and embraced her. She looked up at him, her eyes sleepy and her smile wide. He instantly caved to the sweet enticement of her lips. She tasted sweet, like mint and temptation. His heart soared, and he knew a blissful moment of contentment.

"What are you cooking? It smells almost as good as the coffee." He told her and she asked, "Is there anything I can do?"

"Slice up a couple of oranges if you want them. I'm good without. And if you could set the table while I finish these sausages, that would be amazing." He brushed a kiss across her cheek and turned back to the stove, though he'd rather stay in her arms. "I have to watch these maple sausages. They burn way too easily." He looked back at her and winked. "I'd rather be holding you."

"Me too." She sliced two oranges after he pointed her to the knife block on the counter. "Gosh, I love this kitchen. The big window, the white appliances. I know a lot of people went stainless, but with the light-colored cabinets and the gray countertop, the white suits the room perfectly. And I love that you kept your mom's silly cat clock."

"I hated it as a kid. It was too silly. Now, it's retro and quirky and a fond memory."

She grinned at him. "I like this side of you. What's the plan for today? I only have a couple of visits later in the afternoon."

"Work this morning. I've got some bookkeeping to catch up on. Then I have to go buy a rocking chair and a playpen."

"Something I should know about?" She picked up the knife to butter the toast that had just popped. He gave her a squinty look of confusion and then started laughing. His deep chuckle started her own lighter one.

"Heaven's no. I'm babysitting tonight. I have Anna for the evening. All night, if it goes well. Meri and Chen are having a date night."

"That's so sweet."

He shrugged. "It's what Mom and Dad would have done. Since they're gone. I'm stepping in where I can. Chen doesn't have family here. Though they plan on moving up from the States, eventually. A baby needs family."

"They do indeed. Lots of role models to follow, and many arms for cuddles." There was a wistful tone in her voice.

"I can't wait to have kids. How about you?"

"Absolutely. Yes. I can't wait to have daughters to cuddle."

"Just girls? No sons?"

She looked at him seriously. A touch of sadness in her eyes. "I would love that more than anything. But Hawk women only have girls. Never in our family history have we birthed a son. The name passes on because we keep Hawk as our last name. While there are many Hawks, none of them are men."

"I'm sorry you can't have a son." He stayed silent for several minutes while mulling the information over. "I think I'd be okay with all girls, as long as they're healthy. Or I might consider adoption."

"I've thought about that, too. Maybe an orphaned boy, or the son of a young mother who chooses to break her own heart to give her son a better chance."

A lump of emotion clogged his throat. He coughed to clear it. He felt half misty-eyed at her generous heart. Was it any wonder he loved her? "That's enough deep talk for the morning," he filled his voice with cheer. "Let's have breakfast, and if you're interested, we can go shopping." He carried their plates to the table and sat down at the round oak pedestal table.

"I'd need to be finished by two to get to my check-ins on time. But that sounds like fun. Let's do it." She brought over the plate of toast and joined him.

"Okay. I'll check in on Jeri and the crew this morning, and if all's well, I'll do my bookkeeping while you do your check-ins." He grinned. "Look at us, compromising on our busy schedules to spend time together. We're a good team."

Cynth looked around the space that had been her temporary bedroom. It had changed radically. The small dresser had been replaced with a change table and there was a playpen, complete with sheets and a few toys, set up in the corner. She'd be able to get to the bed if she inched sideways, and she thought it might just be the most adorable space she'd ever seen.

She leaned against the doorjamb and watched Earl fuss with the fitted sheet in the playpen. "You're a great uncle, you know that, right?"

He jerked upright and stared at her. "Why do you say that?"

"Look at all this. You've given over your guest room to the baby without hesitation. You're taking care of all Meri and Chen's shopping. I also know, via the grapevine, that you've paid for six months of maid and gardening services to lighten their load. You're a good man, Earl Cooper, and I'm proud to know you."

"Anyone would do the same."

"Would they? How many of your friends have siblings with babies or kids? Who else went to this sort of effort for them?" She paused. "I can tell you. None. One at the most. Right?"

He shook his head. "It doesn't matter. Other people are not me. Meri, Anna, and Chen are my entire family. I'll support them every way I can."

"See? Good man." She grinned at him and patted his shoulder. "When does she arrive?"

"Just before seven. Their dinner reservations are at seven-fifteen. They're going to Heaven."

"Wow. They were lucky to score reservations there. It's always packed." The high-end restaurant was a popular date spot and very hard to get into on short notice.

"I may have pulled some strings and booked a table just after Anna was born." There he went again, proving how much of a family man he was.

"You are adorable. I brought the stuff to make fish chowder for dinner. I figured since I'm bunking here, you'd appreciate someone else cooking."

"I don't think I've ever had fish chowder, but I love fish. I'm excited to try it."

"I brought some frozen fish stock from home. We make it in batches because it takes days to get it right. After that, it'll take about an hour. I'll make fresh biscuits to go along with it." She checked her watch. "Anna might be here by the time we eat. If she's fussy, we can take turns cuddling her while the other eats. Does that work?"

"Yup. Does this all seem okay?" he asked.

"What? The perfectly flat sheet, the cute toys, the change table, and the massive pile of diapers? Yes, Earl, it's perfect. Even if I don't mention the tiny bathtub and accessories." When his brows stayed bunched tight, a thought hit her. "Are you nervous about babysitting?"

"No," he snapped way too quickly.

"Oh, hun, you are. You'll do fine. I've seen you with her a couple of times and you've done fabulously. Tonight will be a cinch." She paused and raised her brows. "Besides, who better to give you unneeded backup but a woman whose whole life is babies?"

Somewhat calmer, he left her to make her chowder and went to work downstairs in the bookstore until Meri arrived. The chowder was simmering away when he returned, Meri, Chen, and Anna right behind him.

"Cynth, they're here." There was a tiny nervous shake in his voice.

She chuckled to herself; of course, she'd heard them enter the tiny apartment. The foursome joined her in the kitchen. Meri set a large flat box on the floor and Chen set the car seat on the kitchen table. "Smells good in here," he commented. "I haven't had chowder since I moved out. Mom made the best."

"There's plenty. We'll save you some and you can pick it up when you pick up Anna."

Meri started unloading the diaper bag, her eyes on Earl. She named each item like he was an idiot and had never seen diapers and butt cream before. Cynth hid a smile. Meri was even more nervous than Earl. Chen just looked impatient to go. "These need to be in the fridge." She handed Earl three tiny baby bottles. "Don't let them sit out. That's breast milk. I pumped for an hour to get it. I'm barely making enough, though it's coming in more every day."

Earl's face went white, then red, and he thrust the bottles at Cynth. "Ew. I don't want to hear about that," he grumbled.

Cynth and Chen laughed.

"Oh boy," Meri doubled over, chuckling. "Dude, it's natural."

"Ya. I know. But ick."

"Just go," Cynth advised. "I won't do the job for him, but I'll make sure Anna is safe. He'll relax before too long."

"I hope so," he muttered under his breath.

Meri whirled around. "Earl, stop being an idiot. You're my brother. You practically raised me. I trust you. We're both a bit nervous. I've never been away from Anna for more than the time it takes to shower. And I brought you this." She kicked the box she'd set down earlier with the toe of her foot.

"What's that?" He eyed it the way a rabbit stared at a snake. His look earned him an eyeroll from his sister.

"It's two protective wreaths. One for the back door to outside, and one to go at the top of the stairs between here and the shop. They're magically warded to keep everyone inside safe."

The look on his face said he hadn't reached the point where he fully believed in warding, and Cynth didn't blame him. Magic like that didn't seem real sometimes. "Relax, Earl. They won't bite. I had intended to draw some protective runes and sigils on the doorframes and windows anyway. After I asked if it was okay."

"Fine. I'll hang the wreaths, but they better not be all flowery and girlie." He opened the box and pulled off the top layer of tissue. "What?" He stared into the box, then grinned as he pulled out a square-shaped wreath made of sticks and leaves. Handing from the center was a six-inch model of a classic truck. "That's a 1968 Dodge D100," he exclaimed. "That's so cool. Not girlie at all. It even has cargo in the truck box."

"That's the magic part," Meri said. "It's filled with protective herbs. It's the male equivalent of a witch's glass protection bottle."

He gently set it aside and pulled out the next one. This one was round with a Model-T Ford in the middle. "Let me guess, the herbs are in the car?"

"Now you're getting it. I'm glad you like them."

"Come on, Meri. We don't want to miss our reservation. Let's escape before she wakes up." Chen tugged her by the hand toward the door. "See you guys later."

Before anyone could say anything, he bustled her out the door.

"Whew," Cynth said. "He's eager to leave."

"Ya, he told me that at home Meri only has eyes for Anna. He's feeling a little attention-deprived. When she's not with the baby, she's working on what he calls magical stuff. Whatever that is."

She waggled her brows. "That's for witches to know and for you to mind your own business. Let's take Anna into the other room and sit while we wait for dinner."

"Should we leave her in the seat?"

"She's fine in there for a little while. No sense poking the baby and waking her up. You wouldn't leave her in there all night, but for an hour, she's fine. Think of a long road trip. You'd leave her safely buckled in."

He carried her to the other room and set her on the floor. "Do I unbuckle her?"

"Just loosen it a bit. She's not likely to wiggle her way out of the chair this young, but it's best to be safe. Not everyone would leave her in, and many people would unbuckle. There's a lot of use of your instincts to being a parent, or in this case, a babysitter."

"Boy, am I glad you're here." After loosening the straps slightly, he perched on the edge of the couch, facing Anna.

"Earl," she snapped. "Sit back and relax. She's not going anywhere. Babies sleep for a couple of hours. She'll stir and cry when she needs something. She can even poop in her sleep."

He laughed. "Gross." He leaned back and she could see he was trying his best to act normal.

She stopped teasing him and they managed to have a relatively normal conversation. His nerves were cute and endearing. She adored that he was so concerned and desperate not to make a mistake. She was right, he'd make a good father.

"Is parenting going to be this hard?" he asked seriously.

"No. It's way worse. My friends tell me that it's like having your biggest fears and fondest wishes come true simultaneously while standing naked in a rainstorm holding an angry cat." He laughed as she intended and began to truly relax.

Two hours later, Anna was tucked into her playpen, the monitor turned on, and they were settled on the couch with the stereo on low. "This hasn't been so bad. I expected worse."

"She's a newborn. Unless they're unwell, they're pretty easy to care for." They fell into a relaxed silence. She studied him from the corner of her eye. She'd rather be staring, but didn't want to be rude. Truthfully, she wanted nothing more than to climb into his arms for a snuggle, and maybe more. Even if Anna wasn't there, she'd have resisted the temptation because deep inside, she knew it was too early.

Her guardian angel whispered for her to go slow, even as the devil on her other shoulder urged her on. "Do you ever think that it's funny how your intuition and your desires play against one another sometimes?" she asked.

"I've never really thought about it. I always thought intuition was more of a woman thing. Occasionally, I've backed out of doing something or changed my mind because something didn't seem right. That's not intuition, that's logical thinking."

Were some of the times she'd used her intuition just her mind using logic to figure the situation out? That's what rune stones and tarot cards were for, helping you focus your mind, so you could see the question on your mind from a new perspective. Sure, some individuals could see glimpses of the future with them, but that was rare.

Her thoughts swirled as the quiet music played on. Earl had his head back and his eyes closed. She couldn't tell if he was resting or if he was trying hard to hear every move Anna made. Trying to emulate calm, she pushed her thoughts aside. She shifted on the couch, turning sideways and leaning her left shoulder against the back. Then she tipped her head over and rested it against the plush cushion. A moment later, she scratched a persistent itch on her nose.

Then her toe twitched. She shifted in case it was a lack of blood flow from sitting mostly cross-legged. Her shoulder ached. She sighed and shifted again. Unable to get comfortable, and not ready to go to bed, she eased off the couch and slipped into the kitchen to plug in the kettle for tea. Maybe some sleepy blend would help her unwind.

She stared out the window, over the back alley. It was nearly full dark; the moon was hidden behind clouds. A horn honked in the distance. Something moved in the shadows. She stared at the spot where she thought she'd seen the movement. Nothing moved except the chill climbing up her back. She closed the blinds to a narrow slit, shut off the lights, and crept back to the window.

What was out there? She scanned left and right, trying her best not to move. Bryan Wilcox's Great Dane barked twice before he was called inside. She waited and watched. Every fiber of her being screamed in alarm. She froze motionless, except for her eyes, until her muscles ached for release.

"What are you doing?"

She screamed and clutched her chest. "Jeez, make some noise, would ya?" She glared at him, trying to catch her breath.

"What are you doing? What's out there?" He rubbed his hands up and down her arms, the warm heat of his palms penetrating her long-sleeved T-shirt and chasing away her chill. "Are you okay? You're shivering."

"Ya. I guess. I thought I saw something out there. I was trying to see what it was." She slipped away from his comforting hands and peered outside again.

"I'll go look."

"What? No!" She grabbed his arm. "We don't know who is out there, or what. It could be nothing."

"Or it could be a cat. Or a thief or Rylie. I know you won't relax until you know."

"Dammit, Earl. No."

He slipped out of her grasp and headed to the back door at the end of the kitchen. "Lock up behind me and don't let anyone in. If I'm not back in five minutes, call the police."

"Earl," she hissed out the door after him.

"Lock up," he whispered back.

Panic raced up her spine. She was as twitchy as hell. The man was idiotic. What did he think he was doing? This was going to end badly. She raced back to the living room and grabbed her phone and barely kept from pre-dialing 9-1-1.

Earl paused at the bottom of the stairs with his head tilted toward the fence across the alley. Cynth opened the back door a crack and listened. Lots of normal night sounds. A catfight screeched down the alley. Traffic swished on nearby streets. Somewhere, a streetlight hummed.

She crouched low on the metal landing at the top of the stairs, trying to see while hiding behind the barbecue. Something flickered across the alley right where she'd seen the motion earlier. She bit her lip to keep from crying out a warning. If someone was there, she needed to let Earl get close enough to find out who.

Unless they attacked first.

She shuddered in fear and clenched her fists. *Goddess, keep him safe.* Lips pressed together; she watched him speed across the alley without making a sound. Thank goodness for paved alleys.

Blue light flashed from the shadows straight toward him. "Earl," she screamed, thundering down the stairs. The blast hit him square in the chest and he stumbled but didn't go down.

"Hold on," she told him, grasping his hand. She sent a pulse into the earth and gave it a shake. Hopefully, nobody except their enemy would notice. There weren't many earthquakes, even tiny ones, in Three Moon Falls.

Someone grunted. More light flashed. They dove to the ground. Her chin scraped badly across the dusty pavement, and she smelled the coppery scent of blood. Earl grunted and cussed. Two brilliant flashes came in quick succession with an enormous gust of wind. Their attacker. She shielded her eyes to protect them from the light and dust.

Their attacker raced away, leaving nothing but the sound of distant footfalls.

The light faded, and she blinked rapidly to clear the grit.

"Shit," Earl grumbled. "They got away, didn't they?"

"Yes. But I can get Leticia to come and check things over. Magic leaves clues as to who cast it and if it's light or dark magic. Maybe they'll have a familiar signature."

"It was Riley," he declared. "I smelled her."

"What?"

"Ya. I can't explain it, but she has this unique scent. Kind of like cookies, but there's this super faint hint of...I don't know, rotting garbage?"

"Gross."

He shrugged as they walked back to the stairs. "Shit. We left Anna alone." He was upstairs and inside in a split second, leaving her trailing only two steps behind. He paused at the bedroom door and listened. "She's still asleep."

"Open the door and check on her. Just to be sure. Maybe the noise woke her."

He gave her a quizzical look but peeked in anyway. He sighed. "Sleeping like a baby."

"Thank the Goddess," she breathed. Could this attack have been a potential diversion to get close to the baby? She was attacked once already. Cynth needed to hash this out with her family before she mentioned it to Earl. No sense freaking him out more than he was already.

A wave of exhaustion hit her. Adrenaline letdown and the burned energy of shaking the alley had sucked all her strength.

Earl did a double take. "You're cut. Let me clean that up for you." He hurried away.

She snapped a quick picture of her chin. Ouch, it looked worse than it felt.

Earl came back with a first aid kit.

She hissed when he cleaned the scrape. "Thanks. That hurt like hell but I know it'll help. Are you okay? Are you hurt?"

"Just winded. I'm fine now." He brushed some dirt off his clothing. "You did magic. Do you need to eat?"

"I do. And I need sleep."

Half an hour later, having refueled, she felt slightly better but still anxious. "I think I'll turn in." If she was in the room with Anna, she could protect her.

"I changed the sheets for you. You'll sleep in my bed, and I'll sleep with Anna."

Not what she wanted. Not even close. She couldn't protect them if they weren't together. They were helpless against a magical attack, and while the attacks seemed to be against her and her family, someone had gone after Anna once already. Nope, she wasn't leaving them alone. "Wanna sit together and watch her sleep?"

"You don't need to sleep?"

"Come on, Earl. Be realistic. You're not going to sleep either. We might as well be awake together."

His laugh was wry. "As always, you're right."

She couldn't stop her enormous grin. "Thanks for admitting I'm always right. I'll just brew some calming tea for us and meet you there."

"It's not going to taste like grass, is it?" he teased. "Maybe I'll take decaf coffee."

"You'll take tea and be glad you get anything." She missed bantering with him like this. She'd always loved that they could tease each other about their quirks.

"Yes, ma'am." He kissed her forehead. "See you in five. Can you listen for Anna? I want to catch a quick shower."

"You got it. I'm on baby duty." She saluted with her tongue out. He rolled his eyes and walked away.

"Ah," Earl sighed ten minutes later. "This is nice." They sat shoulder-to-shoulder with their backs braced on pillows up against the wall. He'd pushed the bed into the corner, against one wall to accommodate the playpen. She had no idea what he'd done with the second nightstand. Their laps were covered with a soft yellow and red quilt in a star pattern. The lights were out except for a tiny nightlight.

It was almost romantic. Eventually, she drifted off. She woke in the morning to Earl whispering to Anna. She pretended to be asleep and listened.

"Hey, little one. Awake already? You slept a long time. Almost three hours."

Three hours? He must have fed her once while she was still sleeping.

"Time to change your stinky butt. Boy, I wish Cynth was awake. She's sweet and kind. She helped you be born. But I think we'll let her sleep." He gagged a couple of times while changing Anna, who cooed happily. Almost soundlessly, they slipped from the room.

She waited a couple of minutes and joined them. Her heart clenched at the sight of him in the wooden rocker he'd bought for Anna. They cuddled together and his entire being was focused on feeding her. The soft smile on his face was tender and endearing, and she fell a little deeper in love with him.

Chapter Twenty-Seven

As Earl and Cynth stepped into the forest's shadows two days later, the bird calls intensified. Crows cawed overhead and chickadees hopped from branch to branch, singing happily. Earl sighed at the blessed coolness after the heat of the sun. If he didn't know better, he'd think it was the full sun of August, not the first weeks of October. The shade was cool and energizing, and the peace of the forest was soothing. Moist earth and pine scents drifted on the breeze.

He rubbed at the pain in his thigh. It was like the muscle cramps he used to get when he didn't stretch properly and overdid it at high school track meets or before football games. It had been nagging him intermittently for weeks. Two days ago, it had started to ache continually. He tried not to worry about it because the doctor couldn't find anything wrong. Now, he was certain the doc had missed something. Maybe he needed more tests. He'd schedule another appointment.

Up ahead, Artie barked at a squirrel but didn't chase it. The squirrel chittered back angrily. Hyacinth laughed at their antics. The bright beauty of her laugh was another of the endless reasons why he loved her.

"How was your delivery yesterday?" He clasped her hand in his, and they walked side by side beneath the canopy of leaves. It was shades of yellow and hints of red with a few hold-out green leaves still showing. Someday, he'd go somewhere where fall was a full riot of color, not just yellow and green.

Artie raced back to them and jumped up on him, nuzzling his thigh right where it ached. "Ouch. Down, girl."

"Oh, did she hurt you? Artie stay off Earl." Her town was mild, and Earl almost swore the dog nodded in agreement. "Sorry, she's usually better behaved. She rarely jumps up."

"It's nothing. Just a bit of an ongoing pain. Tell me about the delivery." He didn't want to discuss his issues. Today was meant to be a date. Both of them loved being outdoors, and what better way to get some alone time with his girl than to go on a picnic?

"Ongoing pain isn't something to be ignored." She gave him a questioning look.

"I've been to the doctor. We're working on it." The words came out with more snap than he intended.

"Well, if you want, I could check it out for you. I can heal things. I mean, I can't fix a massive wound, at least not all at once, but I can find problems and repair a lot of stuff."

"I saw you in action with Anna. You were fabulous. I can't believe what you did for her. I can't say enough times how grateful I am."

"You're welcome." She tugged him forward. "Through here." They stepped into a shade-dappled clearing with a small creek running through it. A mule deer doe and fawn looked up from feeding and resumed eating.

"Aren't they going to run?" he asked in an incredulous whisper.

"Not if we're quiet. Mule deer aren't as skittish as whitetails. I've spent hours here with them grazing nearby. Artemis lay down." The dog stared longingly at the deer but didn't bark or chase them.

"She's obedient."

"I can't explain it, but I feel that Artie and I have some kind of mental connection. Like she can read my mind, or understand what I expect. She's been the perfect pup since I found her."

"Wow." The idea of a psychic connection with an animal didn't bother him like it would have just weeks ago. He spread the blanket he had carried slung over his left shoulder and set down his soft-sided cooler. "Your table, madam." He bowed low and gave a flourishing wave.

Giggling at his showmanship, she sat and pulled him down with her. He took a moment to get comfortable and popped open a couple of bottles of sparkling water. They drank deeply and laid back.

"Look at that cloud. It looks like an open book," he said.

She agreed. "That one," she pointed west, "looks like a puppy chasing a ball." They watched the clouds rush by. The air was nearly still at ground level, but it was reshaping and pushing the clouds quickly overhead.

"Look, that one's an eagle," he exclaimed.

"Don't be ridiculous," she teased. "It's a crow."

"Eagle."

"Crow."

He rolled over and pressing his left leg over hers, tickled her side exactly in the spot he knew was sensitive. "I said, it's an eagle."

"Crow," she squealed wildly. Across the clearing, the doe stamped her foot and snorted in warning.

"Hush. You'll scare the deer." He stopped tickling and stared down into her eyes. The intelligence and caring in those deep blue eyes pulled him in. A deep part of his mind wondered what the precise color was. Azure? Denim? Navy? Deep sky? They seemed to deepen as he stared into them. So lovely. They were the eyes that had haunted his dreams for the years they'd been apart, and the eyes that heated his nights now knowing she was just a phone call away.

He shifted so more of his weight, but not too much, was over her. The thudding of her heart accelerated his own. He had to kiss her. Nothing else would satisfy the ache in his heart and soul.

"How did I get so lucky to find you again? You're kind, generous, smart, talented, beautiful. I'm sure I could find a word for every letter of the alphabet." He kissed the tip of her nose.

"Go ahead," she dared, her cheeks an adorable pink. "Hit me with your alphabetical list."

"You doubt me?" Her lips were soft under his. Her fresh natural scent rose to ensnare him. "Adorable." He kissed her again, long, slow, and deep, pouring his heart into the heavenly contact. "Beautiful." He ran his lips down the silky column of her neck and smiled at her sweet sigh. "Courageous enough to deliver babies and fight bad guys." He slid his lips along her swooping, heart-shaped neckline. She shivered under his caress. "Mmm. Delicious."

She grabbed his head and pulled him upward. "Kiss me," she demanded, raising her head to meet his.

"Enchanting." She swept her lips across his and traced them with the silken tip of her tongue. Every molecule of sense in his body headed south when she nibbled his lower lip. Several long, heated minutes later, they came up for air.

"Fun, gorgeous, heavenly," he panted between each word.

"Are you going all the way with this?" He was thrilled that her labored breathing matched his own.

"Definitely all the way," he quipped, his voice filled with innuendo.

"Mm. I'm okay with that."

"I knew you were *intelligent*." He placed a slight accent on the last word and dove back into the heaven they were sharing.

Naked and panting, they lay side by side, fingers entwined, staring up at the sky. "Joyous and kind," he whispered. After a short rest, he said, "I'm starved. Want something to eat?"

H yacinth turned her head to grin at Earl. "Boy, do I ever. I worked up an appetite. And while we eat, you can finish that list."

"I'm going to make you wait until our next date for the rest of them." He sat up and handed her some moist wipes and a small dry towel before slipping into his underwear. When she had tidied herself up, he took the wipes and towel and slipped them into a plastic bag.

"You don't have the words," she gloated. "You need time to think of them." She jabbed him lightly with her elbow.

"Ouch, witch. That hurt. Get over here."

She willingly gave in when he tugged her into his embrace after she had her panties and top back on. She nestled between his legs and threw his shirt over her thighs. "Feed me."

"You are insatiable."

"Yes, but you've passed letter I already. Try again."

"You'll get a swelled head. How about you pass me a sandwich instead?" He waggled his fingers, and she slapped a sandwich into his hand.

"I like that you use the beeswax wrappers instead of plastic." She opened her own sandwich and inhaled the delicious aroma of egg salad. "You remembered!" Egg salad with mustard, mayo, and a few green onion bits was her all-time favorite sandwich.

"Fine. Joyous, kind, loving, meticulous. Honestly, I remember everything from back then. Every conversation. Every outing. Everything you did, said, liked, or disliked. It's burned into my brain like it was forged in metal."

Heat rose in her face. It was weirdly thrilling and embarrassing that he remembered the past as clearly as she did. "Me too," she whispered.

She had nearly finished her sandwich when he started shifting behind her. "Am I leaning too heavily?"

"Naw. You're good. It's just this ache in my thigh. It cramps up sometimes."

She scooted out from between his legs. "I can look at it," she offered, worried that he'd decline. Nobody should suffer needlessly through pain. "Maybe it's just a muscle spasm or a deep cramp. I might be able to relieve your discomfort."

He massaged his thigh, running his hand up and down the leg alternately applying pressure and squeezing. His lips were pressed together like he was trying to disguise how much pain he was in. He groaned so low she barely heard it, but Artie rushed over and began sniffing his leg.

"What's with the dog?" His teeth ground together audibly. "She's been going after my leg all day."

Twice was hardly all day, but she understood what he meant. "I've heard that there are animals that can detect illness. Maybe she senses something. I wish you'd let me look at it. Maybe I won't find anything, but I'd feel better if I looked."

"Nagging," he said, obviously still working on his alphabetical list.

"Nagging is not a positive attribute, even if it is true." She let the subject go, suspecting he needed time to consider allowing her mind to search his leg.

"Okay. Take a look." Uncertainty and fear rang in his voice.

She pivoted to look at him. "It won't hurt, I swear."

"How does it work?"

She sensed the question was a delaying tactic and thought for a moment. "I'm not sure I can explain it. I have a sense of what's going on in a body. Unless someone is actively dying, I can't 'see' what's going on without looking." She made air quotes around the word see. "So, if I pass a random person on the street, I get nothing. When I look, with permission, my mind or my intuition sees things others can't. It helps if I put my hand on the affected area."

"Okay. Go ahead." His permission was hesitant, but he lay back as instructed.

"Are you sure?" She waited for his nod of agreement. "Okay, lay back and stretch out fully. I'm going to put my hands on your thighs and move them around a bit. It's good that you have no pants on. I get a better connection through naked skin."

"You don't have to explain. I trust you. Just go ahead." Despite the bravado in his words, she knew he was putting on a brave front for her benefit.

"Sorry, occupational hazard. I explain everything I do to my patients before I start. Here we go."

She shifted to the edge of the blanket and sat on her knees with the tops of her feet resting on the grass and took several long calming breaths to center herself. "Okay, here I go." She rubbed her hands briskly together to warm them and build up energy before placing one on either side of his thigh. She reached within herself, simultaneously focusing, and relaxing her mind and senses. With her eyes closed to eliminate distraction, she let her intuition guide her. She began at the knee and searched slowly upward, moving her hands as she went, being careful not to miss a single millimeter of his leg. She was two-thirds of the way up when she noted an anomaly. A single dot of something, she wasn't sure what, no bigger than a millimeter across. It was almost undetectable.

She must have made a sound because he twitched and said, "What? Did you find something?" His thigh tensed to rock solid under her fingers.

"Relax, Earl. It could be nothing."

"What is it?" he demanded fearfully.

"An almost microscopic anomaly. Let me finish. Whatever it is, it isn't enough to make you hurt. Besides, everyone's body has anomalies."

He made a sound like a growl but relaxed under her hands. She kept going. She found seventeen anomalies. Two were slightly different. Unless she was wrong, they had an echo of magic. Dark magic.

She sat back and rubbed her hands up and down her arms to dispel the chill the dark magic had given her. "All done," she said. She picked up her clothing and started dressing.

"Well?" he said. "What is it?"

"Honestly, I don't know."

"You healed Anna. Can you get rid of it?" He sat up and met her eyes. "The doctor didn't find anything."

"It's tiny. It reminds me of bits of pepper scattered over food."

He interrupted her. "What? How many are there?" He jumped up and grabbed his pants.

"I found seventeen spots. I might be able to heal it. But you have to know that two of the seventeen spots have dark magic residue. Someone has done this to you." She placed her hands on his shoulders and met his eyes so he'd know she was serious.

"What do you mean?"

"If they were all magic, I'd say you ran into some dark magic remnants. There's a theory being studied that dark magic residue can cause cancer."

"It's cancer?"

Crap on a cracker! She should have worded that better. She stood beside him and put her hands on his shoulders. "Earl, don't freak out on me. I didn't say it was cancer. It doesn't look or feel like cancer. It's just small clusters of cells that aren't quite right. There is no cancer vibe. I think we should go back to the house. If I tried to clean it up right now, I'd exhaust myself. I need more food, some tea, and then I'll need a mountain of food when I'm done."

He stared at her like she'd lost her mind.

"That's if you want me to try and get rid of them." She didn't push him for a decision. It was hard for a mundane to accept magical healing. She finished getting dressed, a little sad that their intimate time together had been ruined. While Earl dressed silently, she cleaned up their food and the discarded condom, packing everything but their unfinished waters neatly in his backpack.

He walked slowly along the tree line, touching a leaf here and there. Even back in high school, he'd paced when he was thinking. Tough exams had made him crazy because he was forced to stay at his desk. If fidget spinners had been around, he'd have used them during tests until they wore out. She folded the blanket while she waited.

"Why didn't my X-rays show anything?" He spun around to face her.

"Maybe because they're as small as pepper. They'd be easy to miss until or unless they grew larger. They have the same density as your muscles, but they feel different to my mind." She shrugged. "Maybe they're nothing. Maybe they're normal for you. I'm not a doctor. I'm a healer and midwife. There are a billion medical things I don't know."

He straightened his shoulder like he'd made a tough decision. "I trust you. Let's go get rid of the little buggers."

I n all her years as a midwife and healer, she'd never been this nervous. Her hands were shaking, and she felt sick to her stomach. Maybe she should call in another healer for this. She suggested it to Earl as they entered the house.

"No," he snapped. "You're the only person I want messing with my innards. If anyone's going to try and heal me, it's you."

"What's up? What's wrong with Earl?" Lazuli dressed in her usual jeans and flannel shirt asked, coming into the living room from the kitchen. She took a bite of the cookie in her hand.

Cynth explained the situation.

"I'll get the room ready while you fuel up. Is this an all-hands-on-deck thing?" She finished the cookie.

"That's up to Earl." She turned to him. "Sometimes, like when you helped me with Anna, things go better with assistance. "Are you okay if my family helps?"

"Hell yes! Call in the Armed Forces if it'll help." He paused. "Would Meri be of any help? She's magic."

"With the traces of dark magic, I don't think we should ask her. She's breastfeeding and I don't think we should risk contamination."

He blanched and dropped into a chair. "It's that bad?"

Curse her wayward mouth!

"I don't know. Despite hundreds of years of research, there's a ton we don't know. You picked this up somewhere or had it put on you somehow. Let's not put anyone else at risk."

"Then we don't use your family either."

Laz walked over and patted him on the shoulder. "We've got you, bro. We're around magic all the time. That gives us better insight into our bodies. Plus, we check ourselves regularly, like a monthly breast exam, only bigger. It's a maintenance upkeep thing."

Once Cynth and Earl had eaten as much as they could hold without succumbing to the need to sleep off the gorging, they headed upstairs.

Pearl, Hazel, Lazuli, Amber, Kody, and his grandmother, Abigail, were there. The family magical space was set up for the ritual. "Earl, you're with me, in the middle."

Her family completed the magic circle, lit some candles, and Pearl called in the Goddess and the healing deities of Asclepius, Hygieia, Aceso, Apollo, and Artemis. In a reverent tone, she asked for their assistance to heal Earl. She started a CD of light flute and chime music. One by one, everyone sat on the floor in a circle and joined hands.

When they were all seated, Hyacinth said, "By the power of earth, sky, moon, and sun, Mother Earth, heal your son. As we will it," everyone except Earl joined in, "so mote it be."

"Okay, Earl, lay back like you did in the clearing and I'll get to work."

"Um, what's with the bucket of dirt?" He eyed the large plastic container of earth that sat within the circle.

"I get my power from the earth. I'll work with one hand in the bucket to bolster my strength." Later, she'd have to refuel with food, and with a long rest in nature. Months ago, when she'd healed damage to Amber's brain, she'd failed to fuel up in advance and had scorched a whole section of earth to restore the strength she'd lost. With luck, this healing would be easier. The hardest part was going to be ensuring that she got all the spots.

"Okay. I guess."

"As I said, I get my power from the earth. I can control the earth to a certain extent. I take from the earth when I need it, and I give to the earth when I can. I can help plants flourish, or heal a body. The healing is both taking and giving."

She wanted him to know everything, but now wasn't the time to go into the minutiae of her magic.

"I'm still not sure I get this." He lay down. "But go ahead."

"Your trust means a lot to me." She leaned in close so no one else could hear and whispered, "I love you, Earl Cooper, and I'd never do anything to hurt you." She squeezed his hands and he returned the caring gesture.

"Here we go, everyone." She raised her flowing skirt high enough that she could sit cross-legged on the soft woven hemp mat she'd placed on the floor. The natural fiber would help with her strength. Her family began singing a low song Lazuli had written as a teenager. It was a tribute to the Goddess and all the gods and goddesses from the beginning of time. Abigail and Kody hummed along.

"I'm going to touch you now." He nodded and she put both hands on his legs and began her search. She found the first grain. "There you are, you sneaky devil." She placed one hand in the bucket of soil and absorbed its cool strength as she imagined the speck getting smaller and smaller and vanishing into the vast nothingness and entirety that was the universe.

She didn't know how the process and her imagination worked. She just knew it did. "One down," she declared. After five spots, she paused to eat one of Pearl's energy balls from the container beside her. She was barely feeling the effects of her efforts but knew to fuel up before she got weak. The family continued singing, and by now Abigail had learned the words and was singing along.

"This is like those rare, inexplicable cases when a cancer patient imagines their cancer going away and it happens," she said. "Only I'm doing it for you."

"Cool." His voice was barely audible.

"Are you okay?"

"So far, so good." Then, in typical Earl fashion, he added, "I need to research spontaneous cancer cures." His serious, but glib, response was reassuring. She gave him the laugh he wanted.

"Going back in. If you wanted to visualize the spots going away, it wouldn't hurt." In the end, after over an hour of effort, she found the original seventeen spots and two more. She eliminated them one by one, ensuring that each, especially the dark ones, was completely gone. When she was certain his leg was clear, she ate another energy ball. "I'm going to check your entire body. It shouldn't take long."

When she finished, she buried both hands in the pail while thanking the deities they had invoked. Her family got up and cleared the circle. Lazuli helped Earl stand while Amber and Pearl helped her to her feet.

"Time for food," Pearl declared.

"I've got it covered," Hazel said. "Dennis will be here any minute with takeout." She glanced at her watch. "Okay, in fifteen minutes. I gave my best guess at how long we'd be."

"Thanks, sis," Cynth said as she fought against the exhaustion dragging her down.

"I can't believe how tired I am, and all I did was lie there." He walked over to Cynth and hugged her. "Thank you."

"How does it feel? Is there a difference?"

He lifted his leg and rotated it left and right. He squatted with a wobble. "I don't feel anything now. Thank you."

"That's great. Let's eat. Let someone help you down the stairs, just to be safe." His frown said he thought he didn't need help, but he agreed to let Kody give him a shoulder to lean on.

Later, at the table, while they ate, she put forth an idea she'd had. "This might sound nuts. I think someone is attacking the people we're close to, and I think it's Rylie. Initially, I thought she felt evil, but I didn't detect much magic. Now, I'm not so sure. She's proven, more than once, that she's powerful." She paused. "Think about it. What I don't get is why Anna was attacked. It doesn't make sense, but I can't shake the feeling that it is connected to the other attacks, and that it all rolls up into that damned pendant."

She paused, realizing she didn't feel its pull. "Why can't I feel the stone?"

"Because I took it away," Dennis said. "Haze and I decided to hide it again. Everyone here is too drawn to it. We put it away until we figure out what to do with it."

"Or until we need it," Hazel added.

Cynth frowned at the couple, who sat side by side. Were they being honest, or were they hiding it for their own use? She hated not trusting her sister and hated herself even more for being doubtful.

Chapter Twenty-Eight

E arl watched Hyacinth cuddling baby Anna on his couch as he entered the living room. It was five o'clock on Sunday afternoon and outside the first, hopefully temporary, snow of the year whispered down.

"I'm glad we're inside. Whatever made Meri and Chen want to be out in this weather means we get to spend time with this sweet girl," she said.

"Me too." He set two mugs of hot chocolate on the coffee table. "I made yours with a scoop of ice cream instead of milk."

She looked at the mug. Miniature marshmallows covered the rapid-ly melting ball of ice cream "French vanilla?" she asked hopefully. She inhaled the sweet chocolate aroma as memories of their dates rushed through her mind.

"As if I'd put anything else in your cocoa." Ice cream in cocoa was an old date night tradition from their youth. "I worked through lunch, so I've already ordered us dinner."

"Thanks. I haven't eaten since breakfast, though I should have. I'm still catching up on my energy after that last birth. Between healing you and a stubborn baby, I'm running on empty."

"Well then, drink up. I'll hold Anna." He took the baby and settled into his rocker. "I'm sorry I sucked the life right out of you." He rocked slowly back and forth, staring adoringly at his niece.

"No problem. It is literally what I do for a living. I'm a healer. I heal people. It's my calling, my gift from the Goddess."

"I wonder what my gift is, or if I got skipped over. I can't imagine having a skill that qualifies as a gift. Maybe because I'm not magical." He highly doubted he had any special talent. He was, in all ways, quite ordinary and he knew it.

"It's not about magic. Everybody has a gift, though many people don't explore enough things to find theirs. Imagine if your gift was the violin, and you never tried your hand at music." He nodded his understanding, and she continued. "But you, you absolutely have a gift. You've got an innate ability to make every customer feel special and to find exactly what they need. You've got the research instincts of a bloodhound. Those are gifts."

Her praise both pleased him and made him uncomfortable. "Thanks, but they don't measure up to being a healer or throwing fire like Amber." There was no jealousy in his statement. No part of him wanted to be magic. Sure, it was cool, but it didn't mean he wanted those skills and all the problems that came with them.

Just look at how much crap Cynth and her sisters were going through because of that damned magic necklace. No thanks.

"Maybe you don't have magic," she said, "but how many times have you put together a dozen miscellaneous facts to reach an amazing conclusion? You kicked so many high school essays out of the park that you were accused of cheating."

He chuckled. "Boy was Morrison pissed when she couldn't catch me cheating. Not even when she made me write my entire essay without computers, and right in front of her."

Her phone vibrated in her back pocket. She pulled it out and looked at it. "It's Laz. She knows I'm on a date. She wouldn't call if it weren't important. I should take it."

She accepted the call. "Yo, Laz." She listened quietly for a moment, a worried frown on her face. "Okay. We'll be careful. Thanks. I'll check in periodically. Watch your back." She said goodbye and hung up.

"Trouble?"

She shrugged. "Laz, she's the family's most psychic person, has a bad feeling. She's certain that something is going to happen tonight, and she's most worried about us."

"What us? You and me? You, me, and Anna? Or us, like your whole family?" He didn't like not having all the information.

"Us. Mostly the three of us. But Meri and Chen too, and my family. She's scried, done tarot and runes, tried the crystal ball. She even had a friend do some voodoo divination. Even with all that, she can't get a bead on what's coming."

"That doesn't sound good." Hell, it sounded terrifying. "Is she always right?" He handed her the baby. "Hold Anna while I make sure everything is locked up."

He ran downstairs and checked both of the shop doors and the one window that opened. He double-checked the alarm. Back upstairs, he locked the door between his apartment and the bookstore. He checked the windows and the back door. Everything was secure when he returned to the living room.

"We're all locked up tight. Should I call Meri?"

"Laz said she would call her. Relax. There's nothing we can do. Besides, Laz has been wrong before. More than once. I remember when she had this horrid premonition that we'd all die in a car crash. That was the year that the traveling fair came to town. Turns out that we were on the bumper cars when the french fry vendor down the midway caught fire. Nobody was hurt. Not even the guy in the fry truck. Now, we listen to her warnings, and prepare for what might happen."

"So, what do we do?" He paced back and forth, too nervous to sit.

"Absolutely nothing. You've already locked us down. We keep our guard up for a day or two. She's certain it will be tonight...whatever it is. Just double-check before you answer the door, and make sure your phone is charged and the diaper bag packed and ready."

"You sound like we're going to have to flee." Panic welled in his throat. He swallowed hard and bit back on his fear. He wasn't a coward, but this whole premonition thing made him uneasy, and he could see that Cynth was more nervous than she let on.

"Honestly, I'm always ready to bug out. I keep my passport and ID on me at all times. I have a bugout bag in both my vehicles, along with a stocked medical bag, a flat of water, and a change of clothing. I keep cash in my purse as well."

He raised an eyebrow. "You sound like a prepper."

"I am a direct descendant of a Salem witch. Preparation is in our nature." She gently nuzzled Anna's sleeping head for its sweetness and comfort. "We protect ourselves and our loved ones. Family, friends, even acquaintances. Relax, Earl. It's going to be okay."

"I sure hope so." He wasn't even close to convinced, but he wouldn't let her see his fear. She probably sensed it with her witchy senses, but he would not show it. "I guess we have time to kill."

"I guess so. Anna's out cold. Why don't you bring her playpen out here?" She didn't add that it was for the baby's protection, but he knew what she was driving at and was impressed by her caution.

"I can do that." Moments later, the baby was fast asleep in the corner of the living room. They had to move an end table to the bedroom, so she'd fit, but he felt better knowing she was right at his side.

The alley doorbell rang. It was his main entrance for deliveries. He didn't run his personal shopping through the bookstore. "That'll be the food," he said unnecessarily.

"Do you want me to get it?"

"No, thanks. I can do it. My house, my bill. When we eat at your place, you pay." He hurried to the door and looked out the peephole before opening it. Nobody there except Jamal, his usual delivery driver.

"Hey, Jamal. How's your night?" He reached out his hands for the pizza box and the bulging bag on top of it. The teen handed them over. He set them on the kitchen counter.

"Good. Busy. Lots of orders. I'm swamped. Sixty-seven-fifty, please." Earl paid him and added a generous tip. Jamal turned to go. "Oh, ya. A lady gave me this for you."

Earl stared in horror at the innocuous envelope. "What lady?"

Jamal shrugged. "I dunno. White chick. A ginger. Crazy red hair and a weird accent." He thrust the envelope at Earl. "Paid me fifty bucks, said it's important. Seemed sus. But I need the money for uni."

Earl banked a shudder. He gave Jamal another five bucks. "Next time, just refuse and tell me about it. I'm not friends with that woman."

"Cool." He pocketed the money and loped down the stairs. "Later."

Earl dropped the envelope on the counter and locked the door.

"What did you get us?" Cynth asked as she came into the kitchen. "Geez, what's wrong with you? You're as white as a ghost."

He pointed at the envelope.

"What's that?" She moved toward it and backed up immediately. "Whoa. That's not good."

"It's from Rylie. Or rather a sus redheaded woman, according to Jamal. She paid him fifty bucks to drop it off."

"Don't touch it. Where's the salt?"

"In the end cupboard. Second shelf. Why?"

"That envelope reeks of dark magic. We need to cleanse your hands." She rummaged in the cupboard and grabbed the salt. She poured a generous circle around the envelope. "Over here." She turned on the tap. "Running water can cleanse negativity. Start washing, but don't touch anything."

He responded instantly to her calm tone, instinctively knowing it was an order, not a request, despite her calm tone. He thrust his hands under the streaming water. She poured dish soap, lemon juice, and half a box of salt over his hands.

"Scrub up to your elbows while I arrange for someone to check on Jamal. We want to make sure none of the evil transferred to him."

"Will anything happen to him? Does he know about you guys?"

"We'll make sure he's safe, circumspectly. He doesn't know, but his boss is one of us." She made a call and was back in under a minute. She stood beside him. "Take your hands out. Let me see them." He held them over the sink to drip, and she studied him from all angles. "You're clean. I don't see any more residue. But that envelope is a different story."

"Should we open it?"

"We will. But first, it needs to be cleansed, and checked over by Leticia."

"Because she's a cop?"

"And on the Witch's Council. We know it was Rylie, based on the description, but there could be others involved. We'll need prints and someone with more skill at reading residue. Like fingerprints, every magical person's residue is slightly different."

"I feel like a toddler in an advanced physics class. I know absolutely nothing. What can I do?"

"The food is clean, let's go eat and I'll get Leticia to swing by." She double-checked the back door, beating him to it by half a second and they went into the other room, leaving the envelope behind.

He dished up sushi, shrimp and mushroom pizza, cheesy bread, and chicken wings while she made another call.

"Leticia will be here as soon as she can. She's dealing with a three-car accident west of town. She said not to touch it or call anyone else until she has a chance to do her thing."

Resigned, he picked up his plate. His appetite had fled, but he had a feeling he'd need his strength to keep going later. No way was he going to sleep until he knew the foretold danger was past. He'd be brewing high-test coffee as soon as he was done.

Cynth settled beside him, the plate on her lap. "Have you read any more of your mom's diaries?" She bit into a honey garlic rib.

"I have. I read a bit every night. There's very little about magic, but lots about family life and her slow reconciliation with Dad. Her excitement over being pregnant with Meri was over the top. She wanted to teach her everything about magic."

"You sound disappointed."

"I'm annoyed. I'm not magic. I don't have the genes. But I would have liked to know about it. She told Meri because she hadn't promised Dad not to. It's kind of dishonest, but I can see why she did it. If I had those skills, I'd want to share them with my kids."

He ate half a slice of pizza and three pieces of sushi before he spoke again. "There's some weird stuff in the diaries. Things that don't make sense. Single lines here and there that seem out of place."

"Like what?"

"Nothing I can recall off the top of my head. I just remember thinking they were out of place. There was even some really bad poetry." He shook his head. "Verses that didn't rhyme and that were cryptic and weird. The strangest thing is that she knew about your talisman. At least I think she did."

Cynth perked up and stared at him. "How so?"

"She talked about having a vision, which I had no idea she could do. Then she mentioned a picnic at a waterfall. At first, I thought about the big falls, but later she mentioned Chickadee Falls by name. She said she found something and uncovered it. She put it back right away because she knew it had powerful magic."

"That does sound like she knew about the necklace and sensed its power. She must have been a strong witch to have that vision and then find it. I wish I'd known her better."

"She would have liked you."

"Thanks."

"What's Pearl's power?" He'd been wondering and decided that since they were confessing family skills it was a good time to ask.

"A little of everything. Every generation has one witch with talent from all the magic stacks. She's not great with fire, but with enough concentration, she can wield it. She's really great at sensing emotions. Especially guilt." She laughed. "If we were up to no good, she caught us every time."

"Mom too."

They shared a commiserating smile.

"I wonder what skills Anna will have." Cynth mused.

"You think she'll be magic?" Genetics said the odds of her being magical were high. He just hadn't really considered the idea.

"More than likely, yes."

His mind approached an idea and veered away. Like a thought on the tip of his tongue, he couldn't quite reach the idea. This often happened when he researched. An idea would lurk in the back of his mind for days before it came to light.

Anna started fussing. He took another bite of his pizza and set it down to pick her up. "Hush, little one. Uncle Earl is here." Her wails grew louder, and her face scrunched up in pain. He rocked her and paced.

"Maybe she's hungry. I'll get her a bottle."

The bottle did nothing to soothe her. She spit it out as soon as they put it in. "She doesn't seem to need burping and her diaper is clean and barely wet. I'll change it anyway." He made quick work of the damp diaper, replacing it with a clean one. He cuddled her close and walked back and forth.

"Let me try. There's a hold for colicky babies." She took Anna and held her with Anna's head by her elbow, face down. She gripped one small thigh in her hand and used the palm of her hand to press lightly against Anna's tummy. It was a position which often eased colic, though she didn't think this was colic. She had no idea what was ailing Anna. She walked around and around the coffee table. Earl stayed out of her way but didn't sit down. "I don't know what this is," she said as Anna's cries intensified.

"Is she okay?" He couldn't keep the worry from his voice. "I don't like the way she's crying."

"Babies cry. Sometimes it seems like there's no reason."

"Can't you scan her or something? Use your magic to figure it out."

"Are you sure?"

"I think Meri would if she was here. Go ahead. I know you don't like to use magic without the permission of the recipient. I give you my permission. Please." Anna's tiny face was scrunched up in a ball as she gasped between wails.

Cynth laid Anna on the couch and sat at her feet, her hands on the baby's belly. He hovered behind them. Watching. Waiting. Hoping.

With one hand still on Anna's belly, holding her on the sofa, she turned to him. "Come over here and hold her. I don't want her to fall off and I need both hands."

He replaced Cynth's hands with his own and held Anna with just enough pressure to keep her squirming body from falling.

Cynth took Anna's feet in her hands and carefully worked her way upward. Her eyes were closed, and her lips pressed together like she was straining. When she got to the abdomen, he shifted his hands to allow her access.

"Anything?"

"Not yet." Her words came out with a grunt.

She touched up Anna's body and arms, her neck, and her face. When she reached her ears, Cynth gasped. "Son of a bitch!"

"What?"

"Call Pearl. Get her here now. Call my sisters."

"What?" His voice cracked with tension.

"Someone is attacking her. They're in her mind. Get Meri too."

Thank the Goddess he had her family's numbers in his phone. "What can I do?" Panic was stealing his strength and logic. His fight or flight kicked in and he had nothing to fight.

"Give me your strength." Her tone wouldn't have let him argue, even if he wanted to. He hopped on the couch behind her and pressed his chest against her back. He wrapped his arms around her and held Anna.

Hyacinth's body trembled against him. Recalling Anna's birth, he pushed his energy into Cynth. He had no idea what she was doing, but if she needed his strength, he'd give it.

Chapter Twenty-Nine

C ynth struggled against the power that lurked in Anna's mind. It was dark and seemed to be searching for something. She'd never encountered a power like this. It was dark and malevolent and left shadows in its wake. She pushed against it. It pushed back. She heard a sick, feminine laugh in her head.

"Rylie," she gasped. Earl grunted and a wave of energy flowed into her. She pushed back against Rylie and thought, "What are you doing? What do you want?"

The only response was evil laughter that chilled her to her soul. "I don't know how to stop her. I can only hold her back."

"Say this. *Goddess, strong and true. Bastet, we beseech you. Protect this innocent. Give her strength. Turn out evil. Make her strong. Save your child.*" He repeated the words, and she repeated them with him.

Over and over, they chanted the odd prayer. Rylie bucked and screamed and abruptly fled. Anna stopped crying. Cynth cuddled her close. "Hey, missy. It's okay now. The bad woman is gone."

She flopped sideways to rest on the couch. Earl panted heavily in her ear.

"Shit."

"Where did that prayer come from?" She looked at him over her shoulder.

"Mom's books. It was one of those weird things. She wrote about saying it over Meri when she was born. It just popped into my head. I'm not sure why it stuck."

"Thank the Goddess it did. Your mom was brilliant to ask a specific Goddess to watch over her." She pushed out an exhausted breath. "Can you reach that food?"

He snaked out an arm and dragged the coffee table tight against their legs. She snatched a sushi roll and stuffed it into her mouth. Fishy goodness tantalized her senses as rice dribbled out and she pushed it onto the floor before grabbing another.

The doorbell rang.

"I've got it." Earl struggled to his feet, grunting with the effort. He had to be exhausted after pushing so much strength into her. He'd done it better than the first time with Anna. Practice must make perfect. He was becoming an adept witch's assistant.

Amber rushed into the room, her leaf print skirt flowing behind her. "What the hell happened? You look like crap."

"Food." She didn't have the strength for anything else.

Amber took Anna out of her arms. "Hi, Anna. Come to Auntie Amber. Let's get you some food." She picked the bottle off the table and started feeding her.

"I meant me." Her sister smiled at the teasing comment.

"You've got food on the table. Anna is starving. I felt her hunger as soon as I came in."

That was unusual. Laz was the psychic, though all of them had a bit of psychic talent. "Thanks." She finished the sushi. Earl hadn't come back. "Earl, are you okay?"

"Eating," he mumbled. "Waiting for the others."

Hazel and Dennis were next to arrive. Then Pearl and Abigail, with Kody hot on their heels. Laz came in covered in sawdust. She must have been in her workshop when Earl texted. Leticia was next, looking serious and official in her RCMP uniform.

"I'm putting an officer out front, and one out back," she declared after hearing their story.

Meri and Chen burst through the doorway. "Where's my baby? What happened?" She snatched Anna from Amber's arms. Amber smiled, clearly amused, and impressed by Meri's mama bear attitude.

Once again, they related the attack while Cynth's grandmother and sisters retreated to the kitchen. The apartment was too small for so many people with riled-up emotions. Even Cynth felt them bouncing around unchecked. "It was definitely Rylie. She even admitted it while we fought."

"How did you fight?" Pearl asked. "I didn't think you had that power."

"I didn't. But when I sensed her in Anna's brain looking for whatever she thought she'd find, I pushed at her. I gave her a mental shove and her presence backed away. She's stronger than I am. It wasn't until Earl remembered Bastet's blessing that I was stronger. I don't know what it is about Anna, but this is the second time she's attacked her. The third, if you count the night she was skulking around the alley."

"Something needs to be done about Rylie." Earl slammed his right fist into his left hand. He whirled to face Leticia. "You're the chief of police. Can't you arrest her?"

"I can't. Think about it going to court. Try telling the judge she magically attacked a baby. We'd be laughed out of court. The Witch's Council doesn't move fast, but they'll know about this"

"It sure as hell better be before my baby is hurt." Meri's glare could have cut stone.

Leticia whirled around to face her. "Don't take that tone with me. My hands are tied. I've got officers here and one at your place. I think this ties into everything else that's happened with Keres, Brown, and Natalia. We'll get to the bottom of this."

Cynth was glad she didn't mention the pendant. The fewer people who knew about it, the better. As it was, too many people knew.

Pearl came in carrying a hastily assembled charcuterie tray. Laz brought in fruit and nuts. "I think we need to make better wards for this place, and for Meri's home. Can we concoct a spell to protect Anna? Something more than the simple Bastet ritual. Though I still don't understand why she's being attacked.

Meri dropped into a chair and started weeping. "I do," she blubbered.

In unison, they spun toward her.

"And you never told me something might happen?" Chen's voice rose to a near shout. "I trusted you, Meri."

"Tone it down," Laz snapped. "The emotions rocketing around in here are like physical slaps to us psychics." She kneeled before Meri. "Tell us, Meri. We've been friends for years. We can help."

"I...I...I didn't say anything because it might not happen." She swallowed hard. "One in every hundred babies in our line, always a girl, is destined to be special."

"What the hell does that mean?" Chen snapped.

Cynth wondered the same thing as she and Earl dove into the food.

"Shut up and listen." Meri glared at her husband. "They'll be stronger than other witches, with extra powers. They're stronger psychically and physically, which means they'll be able to do more with less physical cost."

"Shit." Crumbs dribbled out of Earl's mouth, and he hastily cleaned them up.

"Double shit," Cynth agreed. "With someone out to get us, this could be brutal."

"I was waiting until she showed magic skills. That won't happen until she's at least five. In the same generation as the strong one, there is her counterbalance with a completely non-magical one. Usually in the same family. They keep the magical balance. If they're trained right, they don't go rogue. I didn't think it was worth bringing up because Anna could just as easily be the non-magical baby. If it even happened."

A rumble of comments went around the room, but Cynth was too tired to separate one from the other. "Rylie must have found out about this somehow. It doesn't seem like it would be common knowledge. Not the power or the counterpower, or even that it would be your family."

"The council would have records, though they're hard to access. I can check if they've been breached recently. Although I'm certain the council would have let me know."

Cynth looked at Leticia. She seemed to be telling the truth, but she was one to hold her cards close to her chest, which was why she was good at both her jobs. Chief of Police, and Witch's Council Police.

"Do you know where Rylie is staying?" She stabbed a piece of pineapple with her fork and nibbled on it. She was finally filling up, though the food hadn't done much for her exhaustion and certainly hadn't soothed her frayed nerves. Earl was still completely white.

Anna burped with such force against Meri's shoulder that everyone laughed.

"I'm taking charge here." Leticia looked each of them in the eye. "Abigail, you stay with Meri, Chen, Anna, Earl, and Cynth. You are their protection until we get this place properly warded. The rest of you go to the shop and make the appropriate wards for both homes. The Council will pay for the supplies. When that's done, we'll do a protection ritual for Anna. This will not happen again."

"What about Rylie's place?" Cynth asked.

"We'll be taking a team over to check it out. Unofficially, of course. Just a visit by friends as far as the RCMP is concerned. But that's for another day. We all need to be at our best and on high alert. I have a team watching her apartment. We'll go in when she's out."

"Couldn't they have warned us that she was out and about?" Earl snapped. "A heads up would have been nice."

"I'll be finding out why the man tailing her, who's not police, didn't report that she was on the move. I need to be certain he isn't working with her, or with someone higher up." Cynth could almost see the consequences of Leticia's words. It was like her own psychic skills had taken a massive boost. She wasn't sure she liked being so susceptible to the feelings of others. How did Laz manage to live like this? Obviously, spending most of her time alone in her workshop helped.

"I have to get back to the office. We're still dealing with the aftermath of that accident. I'll be back to escort Meri and Chen home. Call me when the wards and spell are ready." She headed for the door and turned back. "Listen, I think you should consider pulling in more muscle. People you trust. Danica, Kody, Mayor Quinton, Jerry and Mel. Maybe some relatives." She turned to Earl. "Jeri who works for you would be an asset. She's a literal encyclopedia of gods and goddesses. There isn't anything she doesn't know."

"How the hell did I miss that?" His mouth gaped open.

"Bro, you were blind to all things magic. You refused to see." Meri grinned at him.

"Apparently. Well, I'm awake and all in now. Let's fight this bitch."

Four hours later, they were back together again. "We've worked up a spell to protect Anna," Cynth said. "Jeri and I put our heads together and consulted some of her family's books." She looked at Earl's staff member and Jeri took over speaking.

"My family has a similar situation. In ours, in every seventh generation, twins are born who are powerless alone, but when paired together, have more natural skills and knowledge than any five other witches. Only once in our history has a pair gone rogue. That was centuries ago. It's the family policy that all twin births are presided over by the strongest of the family who are still alive. They cast the protection over the infants at birth and again every year until they are in full control of their powers."

Cynth took over. "We've modified that spell for Anna. Expanded it to include Bastet, who is clearly her protector, as well as Aphrodite, the Greek Goddess Soteria, Hindu's Green Tara, Athena, the Celt's Brigid, Chinese Buddhist's Guan Yin, Hindu's Durga, Norse Goddess Freya, and even Mother Mary and Jesus of the Christian faith. We're going wide here."

"Holy shit." Earl looked gobsmacked. "That's a lot of power."

Mel and Jerry stood holding hands and echoed Earl's surprise. Danica with her short pixie cut green spiked hair fist pumped. "Girl power. But you should add the Roman Goddess Salus. She's badass."

"That's a good point." Jeri nodded at Danica. "We shouldn't forget any pantheon." She pulled out a leather-bound book. "Let me modify this spell with a wide invitation to all Goddesses inclined to add their protection, and a block to those deities intending harm and the mischief makers like Loki." She made some frantic notes. "Okay, all set."

"I'll just stand over here while you guys work your magic." Earl moved to the corner.

"I'll join you," Dennis, Hazel's fiancé said. "I don't have magic either."

"Don't be silly. You both have good hearts and love to spare." Cynth waved them back. "Besides we need your muscles to clear the room. We'll need a large empty space."

Earl, Dennis, Kody, Mel, and Jerry made quick work of clearing tables and lamps to other rooms. The sofa was tilted on end and shoved into a corner, and the chairs moved to the kitchen.

Cynth handed small bells to everyone. "Keep a rhythm with the music we play and focus on good thoughts. After we cleanse the room, we'll begin." Pearl saged the apartment while Lazuli swept the floor to remove any lingering negativity.

Jeri used a red chalk marker to draw a circle that encompassed the entire room and lined that circle with a circle of salt. She left a two-foot gap in each circle. "Step inside and I'll close the protective circle." Bells in hand, everyone except Leticia, who stayed out to guard the door, trooped inside and Jeri completed the circles.

Cynth addressed everyone. "Meri, you go to the center with Anna. Everyone else, make a circle outside the candle ring Amber is making. Try to stand family next to a friend." She came up with the idea to separate family members on impulse. Instinct told her it would make the circle stronger, so she went with the idea. She passed out papers with the ritual words on them and explained the pronunciation of each deity's name.

"You'll repeat the spell with us three times. Focus on the protective intent and try to stay positive. Everyone ready?"

In unison with Jeri, Cynth invoked the deities they'd chosen by name and then welcomed others who wished to help.

E arl could have sworn he felt a shift in the energy of the room. *This magic shit was powerful. Was this power why covens existed?* A breeze drifted through, though the doors were closed and he'd swear someone caressed his hair. He glanced at the people beside him, but Jeri and Amber were fully focused on the circle's center, Meri, and Anna. Soft chiming music, similar to when Cynth healed him, floated on the air. One by one, the others added their bell's chime and began to hum softly.

The hair on the back of his neck lifted. Electricity raced across his skin, and he smelled jasmine, cinnamon, and something earthy and exotic. His heart thumped into overtime and with effort, he managed to slow it back to near normal. He focused on the music and his heartbeat began to beat in time. *Crap on toast and holy bent book corners. This shit was real!* Nervous though he was, he was astounded at how many times he was shocked by magic.

"Now," Cynth called out, her voice a pleasant singsong. She began singing the words on the page. Abruptly, he realized she'd turned the simple words into a song that matched the music. He played his bell and joined the chorus. The voices rose together in harmony like a practiced choir. Despite the urgency of their mission, he was drawn into the beauty and pageantry of it all.

An enormous bang rang out, and the apartment shook. The group hesitated.

"Don't stop," Leticia commanded.

What the absolute hell on a skateboard was going on? His knees shook and for a moment, he felt like he'd lose his balance as the room bounced under him. Cynth kept going with her ritual and, relying on her good sense, he joined in once again. She gave him a proud smile that strengthened his resolve. Though he was unaccustomed to being less than the man in charge, he was happy to let her lead their charge.

Another boom. An explosion? The room shook. Someone or something was seriously pissed. From where he stood, he saw water spraying from the tap in his kitchen. Leticia spoke into her radio, demanding that someone shut off the building's water. He could do it. He knew where it was, but he'd been warned not to break the circle.

Abruptly, the water stopped flowing and the room stood still. Peace washed over him. Meri kissed Anna's head. Cynth kept going, but her singsong voice slowed, and her voice became a whisper. She paused at the end of the verse and smiled before thanking the deities and bidding them goodbye.

Earl found himself echoing her thanks and farewell aloud along with the others. The circle was cleared, and the chalk and salt residue washed down the drain like they'd washed the evil from his hands earlier.

Holy broken bindings. It was inconceivable that they'd done that earlier tonight. Or rather last night. Outside, dawn was lighting his windows.

Wards were hung and his windows were marked with protective sigils. "Didn't you do that already?" He looked at Cynth.

"We did, but after the magic thrown at this place tonight, we need to reinforce them. Like rearming an alarm or strengthening a weak link in a chain."

They said their goodbyes, and Leticia scooped the letter Rylie had sent and put both it and the salt surrounding it into a container. "I'll let you know what we find."

After the others left, he and Cynth cuddled on the couch.

"Well," she said, "that was interesting."

He burst into laughter. "You can say that again."

"That was interesting."

He dove at her, reaching for her ticklish sides. She'd intended it as a diversion, but he was more than happy to be distracted from the questions and concerns in his mind. They made love on the wide sofa. As he drifted into sleep, he wondered why he wasn't angry with Cynth and her family for bringing evil right to his door. Had she influenced his mind to keep him calm?

He didn't sleep long and woke with a sense of urgency that wouldn't let him rest. He crept into the kitchen and started coffee before going to shower. He was barely wet when Cynth slipped through the curtain.

"You left me alone." It was more a question than accusation.

"You needed to sleep. Last night was hard on you." He caressed her cheek. "You still have dark circles under your eyes."

"Way to charm a girl." Her voice brimmed with sarcasm as she stepped past him to hog the hot spray.

"Believe it or not, that was a total compliment. You're badass in the extreme. I nearly shit myself when those explosions started. And the earth shakes? I may have wet myself. But you, you just kept going like it was choir practice. You have a lovely voice by the way. You should sing more often."

"Nope. If it's not a spell, my singing is like two cats fighting in a bucket. Loud, screamy, and deafening. I have no idea why, because if it's a spell, I'm told I have near-perfect pitch."

He soaped up her back and pivoted her so he could pay close attention to cleaning her front. "Did anyone ever tell you that this magic shit is insane? Like crazy, and scary, and weirdly fun."

"Ya? Watch this?" A shampoo bottle floated toward her, opened up, and poured the exact right amount on her head before closing and floating back to the shelf.

He'd seen it before and was still impressed. It brought to mind his earlier concern. "Can you control my mind? Is that why I'm not pissed at you bringing evil to my door?"

She was silent for a long time. At least seven emotions crossed her face. Surprisingly, none of them was anger. "Some people can. I can't."

She paused and scrubbed her hair. "And I wouldn't even if I could. I am sorry this is happening to your family. Meri's been a friend for decades. We never ended our friendship when you and I broke up. We just didn't tell you." She rinsed and turned to face him.

As she lathered his chest she said, "I do regret keeping that secret, but she was afraid you'd go all big brother and pitch a fit."

"And I would have." He managed a chuckle. "You did the right thing. Meri told me, just last week, how much your friendship meant to her after Mom and Dad passed."

She nodded, and they continued their shower.

"I made you coffee." He toweled her back dry. Her sweet curves tempted him to start something neither of them had the energy to finish.

She laughed. "You made *you* coffee. Don't try and fool me."

"I made us coffee. We need to be awake if Leticia calls us to storm Rylie's place." They drank their coffee, ate breakfast delivered by the local pancake house, and curled up on the sofa together. He drifted in and out of sleep as she made her morning check-ins of her patients. He woke to the sound of his phone ringing.

Chapter Thirty

Cynth and Earl climbed into Leticia's cruiser just before five. The fewer people traipsing into Rylie's suite, the better. She lived on the top floor of the only building in Three Moon Falls that was taller than three floors. They took the elevator to the eighth floor and knocked.

Nobody answered. Leticia muttered a few words and the door popped open. "Police. We're coming in for a wellness check." Her voice carried far enough that the neighbors had to have heard it.

"And we hope you're not well," Earl muttered. Leticia glared at him.

A wave of stench hit Cynth. Dirty socks, skunk, rotting garbage, and sage. "Gross." They entered, closed the door, and donned latex gloves. Leticia opened the patio door, letting in some fresh air. "Ugh. My nose is destroyed. I'll never be able to smell properly again."

Tattered brown tweed furniture and abused pine tables dominated the small room. Dirty laundry and blankets littered the floor.

"You take the kitchen, Earl. The first bedroom is yours, Cynth. Report back anything you find. Magical or mundane."

Five minutes later, he was at her side. "Nothing in the kitchen."

The bedroom was a bust. The only upside was that it wasn't as disgustingly dirty as the rest of the house. The bed looked like it had clean sheets. Cynth eased open the second bedroom door, Earl at her heels.

"Bingo!"

"What?" Leticia called from the living room.

"It's her office." In direct contrast to the living room, bathroom, and kitchen, the space was spotless. A laptop sat with the top open. Three floor-to-ceiling shelves were filled with books. Some old, some new, and some ancient. "Earl, you check the shelves for anything that might be a clue. I'll check the desk."

"I'll take the computer." Leticia sat at the desk and muttered again. The screen brightened and the computer greeted her with Rylie's name. "Wow, that's creepy." She began searching computer files while Cynth finished a fruitless search of the desk and moved to a filing cabinet near the window.

"It's locked."

Leticia got up and muttered over the cabinet, and the lock popped open.

"I need to learn that trick." Cynth opened the top drawer and flipped through the few files she found. "Hm. This one says Keres." She pulled it out and opened it on top of the cabinet. "Holy moly. This is a dossier on Keres. His birth certificate, and his wife's death certificate. A list of places he's lived and who he had relationships with. Even the people who used to be his friends. Earl, you were right. The address you found for him is listed here."

Leticia whirled around to stare at them. "You have his address? Why didn't you share it with me?"

Cynth winced. "I forgot? Earl and I were going to check it out."

"I didn't hear that," Leticia mumbled. "Bring the file to the desk and I'll take pictures. I'll send them to you later. I don't have enough manpower to study them."

As Leticia snapped photos of every page, Earl cried out. "Jeez. Necromancy? Really? Is that a thing? Tell me that isn't a thing."

"There are lots of stories of it, but no evidence that I'm aware of. Relax, hun. Just keep looking."

"I'm not sure I want to."

Cynth was about to offer encouragement when he turned back to the shelves. He wasn't the only one creeped out by raising the dead. Just the thought made her skin crawl. She returned the Keres file to the cabinet and brought back one on Earl. It was short with almost no information, but judging by the one she found on his sister and Chen, it was as if Rylie didn't consider Earl of any importance. "She's got everything on your sister. Her birthdate and skills. Stuff about your mom. Info on Meri's pregnancy and your family history of magic."

After they copied those files, she traded them for one on Leticia, but didn't open it. "You don't want me prying into your life. I'll leave this one to you." She opened the one on her family and flipped through. Nothing there that she didn't already know, but she photographed the pages anyway and passed it to Leticia so she could do the same.

The thickest file was on a man named Vance MacElroy. "You ever hear of Vance MacElroy? Ma-Kell-Roy. Mac El Roy. Mackle Roy...however you say it."

Leticia froze. "Lance Ma Kell Roy?" She slapped her hand on the desk. "That son of a dog turd escaped council custody ten years ago. They've been looking for him since. He's gone dark. There's no evidence of him or his magical signature anywhere."

"What did he do?" Earl walked over to the desk.

"He was on the council with access to everything. Until he went rogue and blew up an airplane and torched an elementary school with fireballs. Luckily, no one was hurt in the school. But eight people died on that private plane. All of them magical. Three were on the council. Things were in disarray for years afterward. He was caught, served eight years, and broke out a decade ago." She took the file from Cynth and studied every page.

"Holy busted wands. There's stuff in here I'll bet the council probably doesn't know about him. Recent stuff. They copied the rest of the files and turned their attention to the bookcases, which contained everything from basic Wicca to the history of the witch trials worldwide. There were spell books, grimoires, and reference tomes. They ranged in age from last year to undated museum-quality books.

"What's this doing here?" Cynth noticed a contemporary fiction novel that had fallen short of its publisher's hype and bombed epically. She reached for it and instantly pulled her hand back. "Whoa. That's no ordinary book. I can feel the evil in it. Where the hell did she find something so evil?"

Leticia pulled it out and flipped it open. "It's in some other language. I don't recognize it. She flipped a page or two. "Judging by the pictures it's about blood magic and necromancy." She slammed it shut with a shudder. "I'm voodoo and many of us walk on the darker side of light magic, but I've never seen anything like that."

"Should we take it?" Earl asked. "I mean it would keep her from using it."

"We can't," Cynth said. "She'd know someone was here."

"As soon as I have council go-ahead for the raid, I'll get it back to council hands. I'm sure it was taken from the archives."

"How did Rylie get it, and why didn't she ward her apartment? We came in without any trouble at all." The question had been nagging at the back of her mind since they arrived.

"Stupidity? Arrogance?" Leticia frowned. "I'm getting the idea that she's not acting alone, and neither were the others. There's something larger in play and we need to stop it."

The rest of the search turned up nothing but general-purpose magical items like tools and herbs. A quick double-check ensured everything they touched was put back where they found it. Leticia closed the windows, and they stepped out into the hall. Leticia said a reversal spell, and the door closed itself and the lock clicked.

"Earl, you need to know that even though we put everything back, Rylie will undoubtedly know someone was there, and maybe even who it was. You and Cynth have to watch your backs. We stopped her attack on Anna and broke into her apartment. She's going to be gunning for blood and more dangerous than she was before. She'll want vengeance, along with her search for the talisman. Be careful." On the ride back to Earl's, she reminded them repeatedly to be careful.

"Take this card. John is private security, and he knows what's up. You might want to hire him to watch Meri. And maybe yourselves. His guys are the best. I'll send those photos as soon as I'm back at my desk."

"Well, doesn't all this just rot your socks." Earl grumbled as he climbed the steps to his suite behind her. "What comes next?"

"I wish to hell I knew. Halloween is only days away, and the veil is thinnest, almost non-existent then."

"What does that mean?" He unlocked the door and waved her inside. "The veil is thin?"

"The veil between the worlds. Living and dead. This is when spirits can cross over or communicate with the other side. If I were going to try necromancy, I'd do it on Halloween. Luckily it isn't the full moon. It's nearly the new moon. Of course, that's a great day to cast spells for things you wish to increase or grow." She stamped her foot. "Broken wands and fairy wings. We don't know nearly enough."

"Bringing back the dead. Veils between worlds. Your life, and by connection, my life, get crazier every day."

"If it's any consolation, I don't believe bringing back the dead is possible." She sure as burned herbs hoped it wasn't.

"What's on for tonight?"

"I could go home since Hazel and Dennis moved the pendant to safety."

"You don't sound certain." He plugged in the kettle and pulled down two dark green mugs with lighter green leaves on them. The pattern matched the rug he had in front of the sink. "You're more than welcome to stay. I won't even ravish your exhausted body."

"Maybe I should go then." She winked. "Honestly, being with you is comforting. I'd like to stay if you don't mind. You don't need to sleep with me." *Even if I want you to.*

He pulled her close to him and leaned back against the counter. "Hyacinth, you're welcome to stay for dinner, the evening, and even the night. We'll take the whole ravishing thing as it comes. No pressure either way." He waggled his eyebrows. "But I might let you force me."

She elbowed him in the chest. "Just for that, you're buying dinner. And I'm starved."

"Girl, you eat like a horse."

She neighed and pranced into the living room to flop on the sofa. "I'm ready to strap on the feedbag, cowboy. Hook me up."

"What'll it be, filly?"

"Naw, not in the mood for Philly cheese steak. In an ideal world, I'd have Heaven's salmon with rice pilaf, and whatever the dessert special is. Beyond that, I'm not fussy."

"It's your lucky day. I know a guy. As it happens," he paused dramatically, "the owner is a very good customer and friend. I might be able to get takeout."

"Don't do that. You'd have to go get it. Just order in."

"I'll get Bill's taxi to bring it. Kind of like small-town Skip the Dishes."

She listened while he made several calls. First, the taxi to ensure they had time to run delivery, then to Heaven for food, the liquor store for wine and beer, then the grocery store for more food, and the bakery for a caramel cheesecake. After that, he called Bill's again and gave them the pickup order.

"You better tell that cop out back that we're ordering food. You don't want him to scare the pants off Bill's driver."

"Good point." He made another call and added food and coffee for the men watching his house and for the pair watching Meri. He snuggled in beside her and flipped on the television.

"Is it any wonder that I love you?" she asked. "You're a good man Earl Cooper. A really good man."

Before their food arrived, a uniformed officer stopped by with a large package for them. Inside was a binder with color prints of everything they'd found and photocopied at Rylie's, and a note asking them to start detailed reading for more information.

"I'm not reading anything until I fuel my brain. I'm running on fumes." She yawned. "I could sleep for a week."

"As long as you do it in my arms." He pulled her closer.

"I can live with that."

Chapter Thirty-One

For the next three days, Hyacinth and Earl spent every waking minute together, studying the photographs from Rylie's and scanning his mother's diaries. Earl had found clues there before. Maybe they'd find something again. Cynth wasn't just hoping she was counting on it.

As she dried the dishes he washed in soapy, lemon-scented water, she said, "I can't help but think this all boils down to Vance MacElroy. The pure size of Rylie's dossier on him and the fact that he's a convicted magical felon brings him to the front of my mind over and over. But if it's about him, why hasn't he shown up in town? Why work in the shadows? And how did he manage to recruit, Keres, Brown, Natalia, and Rylie? They were all gung-ho on getting the pendant, and on injuring my family." She set a dry plate in the cupboard and grabbed another wet one.

"What I want to know is why we haven't heart from Rylie since we protected Anna."

"I know, Earl. It doesn't make sense that she's been quiet for days. Nobody I know has even seen her around town. She hasn't gone back to her apartment either. I have this horrid feeling that the other shoe is about to drop. I'm tired of living in fear."

"Me too. Let's get married."

"What?" She stared at him until her eyes hurt. "Why would you propose now? Are you losing your mind? Do you need a doctor?" She was half giddy that he asked. She was praying for a long future with him. But now was not the time.

"Not exactly the reaction I was hoping for."

"It's just so random." *Scary random. What possessed him to propose in the middle of a crisis?*

"Cynth, I love you. I love you more every day and I know you love me too. I want to spend the rest of my life with you. I'd like seventy-five years together, but if all I have is until whatever this crap is goes down, I want to have you for my wife. We belong together. I want to go into this fight married to you."

"Oh, Earl." She had no idea what to say to him that wouldn't hurt his feelings. "I love you more than you'll ever know. I don't think I ever stopped loving you. I fell for you the first time I saw you and never unfell. But getting married in the middle of a crisis? Isn't that kind of crazy?"

"Not to me. But if you aren't sure, or you think the timing is bad, I'll wait."

He didn't sound angry, but beneath the obvious love, she felt the strong, dark emotions rolling off him. He really wanted to marry her. Her heart clenched with joy and sorrow. No matter how much she wanted to spend her life with him, she wouldn't commit during such unstable times.

"Promise you'll ask again when this is all over?" Her heart ached, knowing she might have scared him off forever. His nod of agreement did nothing to allay those fears. She tossed her tea towel aside and leaned against him, wrapping her arms around his waist. "I'm sorry. I can't leap right now, but know that I love you more than anything, or anyone else. Don't hate me," she added, feeling like a scared teenager all over again.

He tipped her head and stole her heart with a toe-melting kiss. "I could never hate you. I'm disappointed, but hatred? Never."

E arl hugged her until she fought to get away. Disappointed wasn't adequate for what he felt. He was terrified he'd lose her in the upcoming war. Judging by her stories of the previous fights, it was certain to be a war. His heart screamed that if they were married, she'd be safe. Totally illogical. But it was how he felt.

The hardest part was that this could go on forever. So far, three people had come after them. Four if you counted Natalia. Keres had tried to escape prison. MacElroy was in the wind. Who else knew about the talisman and what it might do? How long before they came calling?

Much as he hated to, he dropped the subject.

"I'm going to take another look at the note Rylie left us. I feel like that stupid poem must mean something. Why else would she have written it?" Leticia had returned the cleaned note that morning. They'd spent nearly two hours puzzling over the cryptic poem and come up dry.

She was beginning to think the poem was designed to throw them off somehow. It didn't make any solid sense. Granted, poetry was often confusing to her.

"I'm going to read my family grimoires to see if there are clues to what the pendant can do. And maybe I'll take another peek at your mom's diary."

"We're missing something big. Laz called me with another warning today. I swear I'm going to stop answering your sister's calls and block her. It's bad news all the time. My nerves are twitching like a rabbit's whiskers."

"Mine too. And trust me, she's calling me way more often than she is you. She gave Rosie her phone number and Rosie's been calling her with warnings and that's amping up Laz's concern."

"Rosie has magic?" He felt like he was the only person in town without magic.

"Just premonitions as far as I know, but there's a chance that she's our Great-grandmother Rosie reincarnated. If so, she might have substantial skills. She could manifest her skills any day now."

He stared at her incredulously. "No way."

"Maybe, maybe not. Until recently, I didn't fully believe in reincarnation. We've been known to talk to our dead relative's spirits. That led to disbelief in coming back. But Rosie says and does things that our Gramma Rosie used to do."

"I've heard stranger things." He shrugged. At this point in their relationship, nothing could surprise him. "Let me guess...vampires and demons are real."

"Vampires, I've never seen one, but I'm damn certain demons are real, but perhaps not what Christians tell us they are."

"Why am I not surprised?" And he wasn't. Not in the slightest.

"Because you're a very smart man."

"Enough compliments. I've already agreed to sleep with you. Now, back to research."

"Earl, are you ready? It's time to go." Cynth stood waiting at the front door of the bookstore. "Dude, it's Halloween. We have a family dinner at my place. We're already late."

"I'm coming," he shouted from somewhere near the back of the store. "Just a couple more kids."

Her man was an enigma. Until a few weeks ago, he believed magic didn't exist. Yet all the while, he had Halloween parties for the local kids. Now that he knew the truth, she couldn't drag him away from his party. Laughing to herself, she stormed to the back of the store and grabbed him by the arm.

"Sorry kiddos. Mr. Cooper has to go. He's late for a very important meeting. Miss Jeri and her assistants will take over. Say goodbye."

Two dozen kids screamed goodbye in unison and she barely resisted wincing. With the long hours they'd been putting in on fruitless research, she was overtired and getting run down. Tonight was her favorite holiday, with all her favorite foods. She was sure to come out rejuvenated. If they ever got there. Earl's shop ghost, Mila, waved goodbye. That was new. Before now, she hadn't been much on voluntary communication and rarely showed herself. Cynth waved back.

"Wait. I have to run upstairs and grab something." He raced off, and she stood, tapping her foot until he came back. Mila hovered around, her mouth moving without sound, and her hands flying urgently.

"What's up, Mila?"

The ghost frowned and flew away. Intrigued, Cynth followed her to the paranormal section Earl had recently added. Three books fell off the shelf in succession. A nearby patron glared at Cynth. She squatted by the books and pretended she was going to reshelve them. Pages flipped in one, then another. The pages came to rest. The first was a ghost story about helpful ghosts. The second was an essay on why spirits were stuck on this side of the veil. The third was a book aimed at teens with instructions on how to talk to ghosts.

"I don't understand, Mila." She snapped pictures of the pages to study later.

Mila crossed her arms over her chest. Cynth took the books to a corner reading nook to look at them further. Mila hovered over her with a disapproving frown. "Sorry, Mila. I'm not getting it. I know it's important. Hazel and I will come back after dinner and see what we can work out."

Mila rolled her eyes and shook her head and vanished with an audible pop.

"There you are," Earl exclaimed entering the secluded reading corner. "I've been looking all over for you."

"Mila wanted me to look at these books. I can't figure out why. She's really agitated. For a ghost who rarely shows herself, she was set on me seeing these pages and I can't figure out why. I'm coming back after dinner to look at them."

"I'll help. Not that I know anything about ghosts. I assume you'll bring Hazel. Isn't she the ghost whisperer?"

"She sure is."

He dropped a kiss on her cheek. "Come on, you're holding up progress." He winked as if it wasn't him who was running behind.

She broke a few speed limits on the short drive to Hawk Manor. The yard was lit with green, orange, and purple lights. Gramma Pearl had pulled out all the decorations. The inflatable dragon, vampire, and a Minion dressed as a ghost gave the place a playful air. Fifty pumpkins lined the driveway, each lit with a reusable light.

"That's a lot of pumpkins."

"Yup. We do this every year. Just for us, and for guests in years we have them. We make pies out of some, freeze some more, and feed the rest to the deer. They love them."

"Always the environmentalist. I love that."

"Thanks. Mother Earth needs our care."

Laughter spilled out of the house as they walked past the cats standing sentinel and climbed the stairs. The front door popped open on its own and closed behind them with a soft thump. Her entire family milled around the living room. Pearl, Amber and Kody, Hazel and Dennis, Lazuli, and Abigail, and now her and Earl. Everyone else held glasses of the family's traditional fruit punch.

"We're here!"

"Finally. I'm starved." Laz grinned at them. She ushered everyone into the kitchen where ten places were set around the enormous table already laden with food. The sisters bustled around dishing and bringing over the hot food, and cold side items like cheese and pickles.

"Who's missing?" Earl asked.

"Nobody. We set an extra plate on Halloween to welcome the spirits of those who have passed. It's how we honor our ancestors."

"Like the empty plate for fallen veterans at military functions. I like it. Where do I sit?" Pearl put Abigail and Laz at the back on either side of the empty plate, and organized them male and female, after that. She took the last seat at what could be construed as the head of the crowded table.

"Yum. My favorite." Cynth rubbed her hands together.

"Can you be more specific?" Earl poked her lightly in the side. "Turkey, potatoes, meatloaf, fresh veggies, ham, roast beef, or what?"

"All of them. I'm starved." Since everyone was looking at them, she said, "I'll do the blessing." She waited until everyone was ready before she gave thanks to the Goddess and to Mother Earth for the bounty they were about to eat. She ended with, "Keep us safe in the fight that's coming and guide us to victory. As we will it…"

Everyone chimed in, "So mote it be."

A massive thunderclap sounded outside.

"Holy smokes," Earl exclaimed. "That's a finale."

Cynth looked around the table. Everyone was as confused as she was. It was a cloudless night but the noise had sounded exactly like thunder. It wasn't anything like the explosions that rocked Earl's apartment when they fought Riley. "I guess the gods approve." She shrugged, though inside she was shaking.

Laz started to say something, then clamped her lips shut so hard her teeth clacked. Everyone stared at her. After a moment, nervous chatter started. It slowly morphed into normal conversation and family teasing.

"So, when are you and Earl getting hitched?" Hazel asked. Her wedding to Dennis was scheduled for Christmas Eve.

"I asked. She refused." Hurt echoed in his voice.

"My bad." Hazel mimed zipping her lips and then comically tried to put food in her mouth without opening them.

"When this shit with Rylie is over, I'll accept his proposal. Until then, I won't tie him to me when I know I'm going into a battle."

"A lot of soldiers used to marry before going into a major battle, to give them incentive to come home," Dennis said.

"See?" Earl's eyes pleaded for her to change her mind.

"We need to talk about this fight," Laz said, dropping her fork with a clatter. "It's coming. Soon. I can barely eat because I'm so jittery."

Everyone felt the same, though Cynth was certain she had it worse than the rest of her family. When they fought Keres, they fought as a family. Hazel and Dennis fought Brown and Natalia alone. Her intuition screamed that she'd be alone in this. Hopefully, with Earl far away. Having a mundane there would split her attention and she'd be protecting him instead of taking out Rylie.

Everyone was twitchy, jumping at the slightest sound. Cynth knocked over her water glass and Pearl screamed.

"Sorry, Gramma. I didn't mean to."

"No harm done, dear. I'm rather on edge." Her smile was warmly reassuring, though it had a hard edge to it.

"Who isn't on edge?" Earl asked. "I'm not even magic and I can feel the tension creeping in like a black fog. It feels like a horror movie looks."

"Boy's got some intuition after all," Pearl quipped, releasing the tension slightly.

Up and down, the tension ebbed and flowed without ever letting off entirely. Cynth knew tonight was the night. After dinner, while cleaning up she whispered to Laz, "It's tonight, isn't it?"

"Pretty sure, yup." She frowned as she rinsed plates before loading them in the dishwasher. "I can't figure out why she hasn't attacked already."

"Maybe she's waiting for midnight? You know, for dramatic effect."

"You guys should stay here tonight. We all should. I think there's strength in numbers."

She won't attack until I'm alone, or nearly alone. I know I pissed her off when I chased her out of Anna's head."

"Who's watching Anna tonight?" Hazel joined the conversation.

"Leticia assigned two magical cops to them and has patrolmen doing regular drive-bys. She'll be fine. There's no way for Rylie to penetrate that spell. Nobody could. Earl texted them every few minutes, just in case you didn't notice his preoccupation with his phone during dinner."

"I had wondered." Hazel dropped the beef and chicken bones into crock pots to simmer overnight for soup broth. "I'm going to bed.

Dennis and I are staying in my old room. Amber and Kody are staying in hers. Abigail will take the guest room. I really think you and Earl should stay too."

Laz shook her head. "I thought so too, but Cynth is right. This won't happen with us around. It would be better to get it over with. Besides, we're not far from the shop, and if shit gets real, she can holler over our psychic connection, like you did from the island. Though you could have given better directions, not just shout for help."

"She shouldn't have gone alone," Cynth corrected.

"And yet, you're going to take on Rylie alone." Hazel's glare would have cut granite.

"It's inevitable." Laz dropped to her knees, clutching her head. "Ooh," she moaned.

"Gramma!" Cynth called. Pearl came running. "She just groaned and dropped."

Laz looked up at them, grunted, and fell over as her eyes rolled up in their sockets.

"Crap." Cynth straightened Laz, so she was in a comfortable position though she kept writhing around. At least she was in the center of the room and wouldn't bang into anything with her gyrations.

"What the hell?" Earl stared at Laz, then and Cynth.

"A vision, I think. She's had bad ones before, but never like this." She held her sister's head in her lap and stroked her brow to ease the pain she saw in Laz's brain. She couldn't heal her mid-vision if she needed healing at all. Sometimes visions were just painful and left no trace afterward.

A full minute later, Laz opened her eyes. She looked straight at Earl. "Sorry about the bookstore." She closed her eyes again. "I need a drink."

Hazel brought a glass of water as Cynth and Earl helped Laz to the sofa. Everyone else huddled around anxiously, waiting to hear what she saw. She sipped the water.

"What happened to my store?" Earl asked, panic heavy in his voice.

"Nothing. Yet. But it's going to burn tonight. I need wine."

"How?" he demanded.

"No idea. All I see is the books on fire, and you and Cynth in the background." She winced in apology. "You should go and move some of those antique and rare books out of the shop. It won't be totaled, but you'll lose a lot. I hope to the Goddess that you have insurance."

Chapter Thirty-Two

With rushed calm, Cynth and Earl loaded his more valuable books into boxes and onto a dolly. They'd store them in her family's shop until it was safe to bring them back. Once they were all safe, they began moving his other stock.

"We should have brought your family," he grumbled. "They could have helped.

It was his fear talking, and she knew it, so she cut him some slack. "You heard Laz. It has to be just us."

"Is this like a *Matrix*, prophecy thing?"

Goddess, save her from uneducated mundanes. "It isn't a prophecy. Just a vision. But my intuition tells me she's right."

"So why aren't we calling Leticia or the Army or someone? Why not have your family in the shop ready to fight with us? Maybe she's wrong." His voice cracked with tension and emotion.

"Altering the circumstances will only delay the inevitable."

"So, we delay it forever? That works, right?" He opened the book-store door and let her go in first.

"Hun, when this is done, and we're married, there's a lot I have to teach you."

"Are you accepting my proposal?"

She rolled her eyes and walked toward the back of the shop. "Come on, Earl. Let's just go watch television or something. It's late. I'm too tired to lug another book. A nap would do us both some good. It's after three. Come to bed and cuddle me."

"But my inventory..."

"Is covered by insurance."

"And how do I explain that some books aren't here?" He glared.

This was shaping up to be an epic fight between the two of them, and she didn't have the emotional fortitude to deal with it. "Tell them you sent them out for historical evaluation, or that you loaned them to a research project. You do both things all the time."

"How the hell do you know that? Have you been spying on me? Using your witchy skills to sneak peeks at me? Do you watch me shower, too?"

"Get real, idiot. I can't do that stuff. I'm friends with your sister and half your staff. I shop here, and I'm not freaking blind. You mundanes are clueless." She snapped her mouth shut, unable to believe the hatred they were spewing at each other.

"Holy shit," she whispered. "Listen to us. Bickering like five-year-olds. She's close. She's manipulating our emotions. It never occurred to me that she's a vampire."

"You said vampires aren't real," he snapped.

"No, I said I've never seen one. I'm not sure they exist." She forced herself to be calm and began building a wall around her emotions. "But I meant she's an emotional vampire. They don't suck blood. They get their power from powerful emotions. She wasn't just after

Anna's potential magic, she was manipulating her, scaring her. Infant emotions are completely primal, probably the strongest emotions of all beyond hatred."

Earl clenched his fists, and his jaw muscles flexed. He was always calm. Except for her first demonstration of magic, he rarely lost his temper. That time, it was fear-driven anger. It was hard for her to watch as he struggled for calm.

"Sorry. I'm afraid. Come here, Cynth." He waved her closer as he came toward her.

She stepped willingly into his arms. "I don't think you're an idiot," she whispered. "You're one of the smartest people I know. Although I wish you understood magic better."

"And I admire your talents. Though Amber's ability to throw fire freaks me out."

They stood wrapped in each other's arms. She rested her head against his chest and listened as his heartbeat calmed to near normal. "Sometimes it freaks me out, too. Are we good?"

"We're good. Scared, but good. It's going to be soon, isn't it?"

She hated how resigned he sounded, as if awaiting their deaths. "I think so. It won't be long, and Earl, we can win this. I don't know how, but we can do this."

In another aisle, a book thumped to the ground, and she let out a squawk. "You and I, and Mila, apparently. She's trying to tell us something like she was earlier. Let's go look."

They'd only taken two steps when the front window exploded into a million pieces. They were sprayed with shards of glass. "Get down," she screamed, but he was already tugging her toward the floor. Crouched low, they hurried toward the back of the store, and away from potential danger. She stifled a cough from the dust in the air.

Her heart thundered in her chest and her breathing came in gasps. Adrenaline coursed through her, making her fingers and toes tingle. Fight or flight kicked in. "Get behind me!"

He didn't move.

"Earl, I need you to listen. You're my conduit. I need you safe. Stay behind me and be ready to push your power at me." As she spoke, she screamed for assistance from her family. She didn't mean to. She knew they'd arrive too late, but instinctive fear overrode common sense. Earl shifted left and back so he was no longer blocking her view down the aisle toward the front windows.

"Come out, come out, wherever you are," Rylie's voice chanted.

"Screw you, beotch."

"Now, now, Hyacinth. That's no way for a lady to talk. And you, in the back, mundane, don't bother calling for help. I've got a signal jammer. No cell calls will go through and I've cut your phone and internet lines."

"Crap." She raised her voice. "Do your worst. You're nothing but MacElroy's bitch, anyway. You've got no actual power."

"Geez. Rile her up much?" Earl groaned.

"You can't fight or cast proper magic when your emotions are out of control. Things go awry. I'm throwing her off her game." *I hope.*

"I'm nobody's bitch."

The ground heaved. Tiles cracked off the floor and books rained down. Earl groaned in dismay. "Remember the insurance," he said aloud, though obviously talking to himself.

"Ha. That's all you've got?" Cynth taunted and sent back a return roll of earth. More books fell and another window burst. Rylie screamed in pain.

"Good one," Earl praised.

"Sneak left. Let's go see what Mila was throwing around." Without taking their eyes off the front entry, they inched backward and then left into the next aisle.

"Crap." The entire aisle was covered in books. Cynth groaned as Mila pitched books left and right, digging through the piles. "Let us know when you find it, Mila."

"Oh, my god. Is that her?"

Mila's head snapped up.

Cynth glanced at him. His eyes were wide, and his mouth was open.

"Hi, Mila." His voice trembled, and the ghost returned to her digging.

A blast of heat smacked into them, jerking Cynth's attention back to Rylie. "What do you want? Go home and leave those of us with genuine talent alone." Earl's hand was warm on her shoulder. His solid touch slid down her arm until their hands meshed together.

"Crouch down and stay low."

Small rocks flew past them from the back of the store.

"Those are semi-precious gemstones," he hissed.

"Earth magic. I can't control non-natural things, but I can throw rocks, and probably books." Rylie's squeals of complaint punctuated Cynth's statement.

"I've seen you lift dishes. Can't you throw other stuff?" He sounded puzzled.

"Not with accuracy over distance." They ducked as the rocks flew back at them. She threw up her hand, and they fell to the floor.

"Send them back," he hissed.

She closed her eyes and focused on the street under Rylie's feet. She felt for cracks in the pavement. There! She wiggled her power into it, splitting it wider and wider. The road cracked and the dirt and gravel beneath it spewed up over Rylie's feet. It wasn't easy to fight when you could only feel your opponent and not see them. She needed to get closer.

Tugging Earl's hand, she inched forward, crouched low, and peeked around a shelf. Perfect. She could just see Rylie's feet and the small gap she was making below her. She pulled back behind the protection of the bookshelf and took off her shoes and socks.

"What are you doing?"

"I need the connection to the earth. This is as close as it gets."

"You'll cut your feet to ribbons. Jeez, Cynth, be careful."

She popped a quick kiss on his lips. "Stay with me." Using a book as a broom she swept the glass away in front of her and focused on her connection to the ground. Minute bits of dust beneath her feet heightened the limited connection. "Okay, here goes."

Calming herself, she turned her attention back to the crack and, with one enormous thrust split it apart. Rylie crashed to her knees as earth flew in all directions and a water main burst spewing water high in the air.

"You bitch," Rylie screamed, scrambling out of the geyser and closer to the shop front.

"Duck," Cynth barked at Earl, and they dove to the ground just before a fireball shot past their heads.

Cynth's heart echoed every word of Earl's creative curse. Rylie was tough and had powers she couldn't compete with. Another fireball flew past and landed behind them with a small explosion.

"Shit. I'll kill that bitch for torching my store!" Fire crackled menacingly behind them. Smoke filled the room. "Ouch. What the hell? I just got hit by a book."

"Are you okay?"

"I'm good. Freaking Mila."

Cynth snickered at his rough proclamation. By the Goddess, she loved him. She looked up. Rylie was framed in the store's open door.

Power surged through her. She picked up a book and threw it at Rylie. She pelted every book within reach. Over and over. As fast as Earl handed them to her, she threw them, adding a magical boost of power to them.

Rylie cowered under the attack. She summoned a fireball, but it fizzled out.

Slapping her hand on the ground, Cynth sent a shockwave racing toward her enemy, knocking her to the ground. Rylie dropped and rolled left.

Cynth rushed outside, past the distracted Rylie, pulling Earl behind her. They dodged right, away from the empty holes that had been clear windows with creative displays. They ducked behind her SUV.

"Get back here! Coward." The earth shook. A fireball exploded against the vehicle.

Cynth rolled small pebbles and road sanding salt together to form dozens of projectiles. She pelted them at Rylie one after another. Her aim was off, but several of them hit home. One smacked Rylie hard in the head, making her scream in anger.

Cynth pulled in the power of the wind. It wasn't her best strength, but she managed a small twister of dirt and rock and swirled it around her foe.

Rocks rained back on them. Earl grunted in pain and dropped his grip on her hand. Amid the dust and smoke, she smelled the coppery tang of his blood. "How bad is it?" She didn't risk checking for herself.

"Scratch. Okay, big scratch. I'm good." The sound of tearing fabric rent the air. "Good now. Covered it." His voice was heavy with pain. He was hurt worse than he'd let on.

Her anger skyrocketed, and she leaped to her feet. With all her effort, she rained rocks, sand, and books onto Rylie's head.

Rylie countered by throwing a heavy chunk of the wooden window frame at her. She thrust her arm up to protect her face. The wood slammed into her forearm with a sickening crack. Blinding white agony dropped her to her knees. She groaned in anguish.

Chapter Thirty-Three

"**B**itch, you missed." Cradling her injured arm to her chest, Cynth urged Earl down the street. There were very few vehicles to hide behind. They lurched from her vehicle to the first doorway to the next doorway. They hurried down the street.

"Where are we going?"

"The park." Three Moon Falls was a beautiful town, but in late fall and early winter, it was barren of greenery. The park had large trees and several boulders she could grab onto and use to her advantage. She needed grounding. She was already growing weak, and Rylie showed almost no signs of losing power.

They huddled behind a birch grove, and she scratched the grass away from the raw dirt. Earl did the same, though she doubted he knew why. Panting in pained agony from her broken arm, she positioned her feet on the two places they'd cleared and rose to her feet.

"Eat this." He shoved one of his honey mint candies in her mouth. The honey bolstered her flagging energy, but not nearly enough.

Earl stood behind her, one hand on her shoulder. Like a wave of warmth, his energy flowed through her. Maybe they could do this. She sent another urgent call to her family. Why hadn't they arrived? Where were the police? Surely someone had noticed the fire and the earth shaking.

Rylie entered the park and strode toward them with the arrogance of someone sure of victory. Doubt filled Cynth's mind. Ruthlessly, she shoved it back. There was no time for fear or panic. This was a fight to the death. Her chest clenched. She didn't want to take a life. She was still stinging from her part in the death of Keres's minion. Though technically, Keres had ended the man's life. But if she had to, she would end Rylie's life to save Earl and Anna.

She humped up the ground at Rylie's feet, once again knocking her to her knees. A raven screamed angrily and flapped overhead. Mother Nature was pissed. She didn't like people messing with the earth.

Rylie slammed her hands on the ground, sending a shockwave back toward them. Back and forth, they slammed each other. Trees shook. The park's inukshuk tumbled to the ground, the stones rolling away.

Cynth gave the rolling stones a nudge toward Rylie. They rolled down the slight incline, picking up speed on the way.

Rylie jumped aside and threw fireballs at them. They sputtered out on the moist grass. Thank heaven it wasn't in the heat of summer.

Trembling with exhaustion and agony, Cynth tried to shake the ground and failed. Even with Earl's support, she wasn't strong enough. There had to be a better way. She crouched behind the trees, gasping for air. One-on-one, she'd never defeat Rylie.

"I've got it!"

She whirled toward Earl. "Got what?"

"This book. The one Mila threw at me. I kept it. Or most of it. It's trashed. But there's something here that might help. She folded a page." He held out the open book for her to read.

"No way!" Elation coursed through her, and then she crashed. "Shoot."

"What? It's perfect. You could do this, right?"

His confidence in her was overwhelming. "Could being the optimum word here. I could have done it. Look at the hand gestures." Her instincts screamed, and she pushed him left, just before a hail of small rocks assaulted the spot they'd been standing on. On the front and back of the page was written a poem with accompanying hand gestures shown in pictures, and by numbers within the text. Someone went to a lot of trouble to put it together.

"My arm is smashed."

"When did that happen?" His voice rose in panic. "We're doomed. Where's your family? Where are the police? Shouldn't Leticia be here?"

His out-of-control emotions battered her. "Chill out. You're beating my senses up with your potent emotions."

He took four deep breaths, and the battering eased up.

"Laz's premonitions said nobody but us. Alone." Sparks flew over their heads, though weaker than the last batch. Maybe Rylie was tiring.

Cynth shouted, "Tell your master you failed. Go on home now, little witch. You lost." She peeked around her tree to see the effect of her words. Rylie stamped her foot like a petulant toddler and the earth shook. Trees swayed and branches rained to the ground. Okay, maybe she wasn't that tired.

"There must be a way to do this spell. Mila knew something." He paused. "I can't believe I'm suggesting taking advice from a ghost."

"It takes two arms." She rolled the spell over and over in her mind, searching for a way to make it work. The gestures painted two-handed sigils in the air. Sigils of destruction and protection. Without them, the spell would fail.

She split the ground beneath Rylie's feet, creating a deep pit. The city was going to be pissed at the destruction. *Irrelevant, Cynth. Keep your mind on the goal.* She hated it when she was tired, and her mind went off on tangents.

How much earth could she move? Could she bury Rylie? Maybe just break her legs with the rocks?

She lifted and heaved a large, sharp-edged rock Rylie's way. As her vision faded, she heard Riley shout, "Missed me!"

"Cynth. Cynth. Come back to me." Earl's urgent voice and shaking brought her back from the impending darkness.

"Ya." She swallowed hard and winced at the pain in her arm. "I'm good."

"You're not good. You passed out on me." A wave of energy washed through her from his tight grip on her shoulders and he shoved another candy into her mouth.

"Thanks."

"I've got it." He released her and jumped to his feet. Gently, he helped her back up. "If I can push my energy into you, why can't you push your power into me? I could be your hands."

"It would never work. Magic doesn't work like that." She loved him for trying to find a solution, for trying to do more than just support her with his energy.

"Come on, Mila thinks this spell will work. She folded down this page and removed the pages before and after it. She wanted us to get the right one. I read the copyright. It's a reprint of a book from over three hundred years ago." He gave her a serious look and pointed at Rylie. "What have we got to lose?"

"It won't work." There was no way on earth.

"Okay then. What happened to the cheery Hyacinth? The one that always found the bright spot. Where did she go?"

"My arm is broken. I can barely see for the pain. Look at it." She lifted the hand holding her arm steady. "You can see the break. I'm lucky it didn't go right through the skin. How can I do magic like this?"

"You've been throwing stones and shaking the earth."

"That's my mind, not my hands."

"You once told me that spells are prayers with props. Cast it with your mind and your mouth. Say the words. I'll be in charge of props or, in this case, actions."

How did she explain that there was no way his idea could work?

The earth shook again, and the large stones rolled back toward them. She mustered the strength to stop them, but the effort knocked her onto her ass.

Earl hastily removed the T-shirt he wore beneath the dress shirt that had been torn to slow the bleeding from the sticks and stones that had hit him. He was still bleeding, and the makeshift bandage was stained red with blood. He stumbled unsteadily and then took out a pocketknife to cut the T-shirt into strips. With a short stick for stability, he wrapped her arm in a makeshift cast. Agony shot through her with every motion. With the last strip, he fashioned a poor substitute for a sling. It wasn't pretty, but it eased the ache enough that she was no longer in danger of bringing her supper back up.

Now he was bleeding, she was broken. They were both covered in tiny scratches from glass. She had glass embedded in her bare feet and dozens of scratches on her arms. She was peppered with burns from sparks. How could she possibly fight any longer?

Son of an evil wizard, and broken monkey balls!

Somewhere, not far away, a dog barked frantically. Lucky for them, she'd left Artemis with her family, and she didn't need to cope with that worry.

Counting on Earl to give her more energy, she poured her flagging strength into swirling the last of the damp leaves on the ground and pushed them into Rylie's face. A blast of heat and fire destroyed them before they got there. Heat singed the hair on Cynth's face.

Like a streak of golden lightning, Artie exploded across the park, leaping on Rylie, and knocking her to the ground. They wrestled back and forth, Artie growling and biting at Rylie's loose jacket.

"Artie, no!" Cynth screamed.

"We have to save her," Earl shouted.

"Give me that book!" Weaving back and forth, she struggled to stand and propped the book open on a branch of one of the trees shielding them. She read the spell again. "Shoot, we need a gold coin." Her knees wobbled and her vision faded to gray. She had to hurry, or she'd pass out before they finished the spell.

"I've got this!" He pulled a tattered pot-metal fair token from his pocket. "It isn't gold, but to me, it's more valuable than gold."

"Is that the cheap pendant we got at the circus?" Memories rushed in of standing, hand in hand, waiting for their matching four-leaf clover pendants to be engraved by the fair worker. "I can't believe you still have it."

She rummaged in the pocket of her jeans and pulled out the matching pendant. "I hope these will do."

"Come closer, stand behind me." He instantly complied, lifting her light turtleneck, and pressed his naked stomach and chest against her bare back. His skin was frigid, but a wave of heat ran through her. "Can you see the page?"

"Got it."

Rylie threw a blinding blast of yellow light past Artemis, right at their faces. Cynth slammed her eyes shut, but for a moment, she was blind. Blinking frantically, she cleared her vision.

She took three deep breaths. "Mother Goddess, hear our pleas. Come to us in our time of need. Help us defeat this evil. As we will it, so mote it be." Another deep breath. "Are you ready?"

His swallow was audible. "You betcha."

"Stop this woman, end this now..." Substitute coins in her hand, and focusing on her intent, she read the entire spell as Earl performed the actions. As instructed by the book, she read it a second time. Rylie's struggles against Artie weakened. The young dog stood on her chest, Rylie's jacketed arm in her mouth. The dog growled and showed her teeth without releasing her bite. Earl performed the actions, tracing the sigils in the air as Cynth repeated the spell a third time and tossed the coins over her left shoulder.

Thunder clapped. Lightning struck the ground. The smell of burned ozone filled her nostrils.

The earth heaved, and they fell to their knees.

Rylie went motionless.

Cynth and Earl stared at each other.

"Holy shit," Cynth whispered. "I think it worked."

"Is she dead?"

Artie barked twice and raced to their side.

"Good girl. You're such a good puppy." Cynth patted her on the head with what little strength she had left. "Guess we better check her."

Fortunately, Rylie wasn't dead. She was unconscious. "Now what, Earl?"

"How should I know? You're the brains of this operation."

She laughed. "Nope. You are. You convinced me to try that spell. I can't believe it worked." Disbelief gave way to giddy relief. Artie raced around the park, barking at nothing. When she passed Rylie, she growled before moving on to sniff and bark at the next thing. She'd gone from vicious fighter back to puppy in an instant.

Cynth's knees went weak. "Holy hell in a handbasket. We did it." She clutched her head. "Oh, I'm woozy."

"Food, you need food." He wobbled. "I'm not so steady myself."

She pulled out her phone and punched in Pearl's number. "Food. Park. We won." She flopped onto her back to rest. Earl sat beside her. "I should call Leticia. Rylie needs to be in custody before she wakes up."

Sirens wailed. A police cruiser, a firetruck, and an ambulance rolled up, lights blazing. Leticia climbed out of the cruiser and rushed over. "You have thirty seconds to give me the gist." She stared down at them.

"She attacked. We fought. We won." Cynth barely looked at her officer friend. "What are we telling the public?"

"I'll handle that."

"My shop's on fire."

"Got it." Leticia snapped her fingers. "The earth shake must have caused some sparks and the shop caught fire. This woman," she jabbed a finger at Rylie, "Attacked you when you raced from the shop." She grinned. "Close enough to the truth and easy to remember." She had an officer cuff Rylie and get her loaded into an ambulance. "You know what to do," she told the driver. "Keep her sedated until you get to the care facility."

"Care facility?" Earl muttered.

"Magical care and punishment. If she's injured beyond being unconscious, she'll be treated and then, after a full investigation by myself and the council, she'll be incarcerated."

"Oh. Magical incarceration," Earl said, his voice filled with wry humor. "Who knew?"

Epilogue

The next afternoon, after a hefty meal and solid sleep, Cynth looked around the living room, her heart bursting with love. Earl was laughing with Hazel and Dennis. Mel, Jerry, Amber, and Kody were deep in a game of Scrabble. All around her, her family and friends were having a great time. Laz sat with Rosie on her lap while Frank read them a story. Meri and Chen chatted with her cousin Cecily who held baby Anna in her arms. Gramma Pearl was deep in discussion with Leticia and Danica.

Life didn't get any better than this.

Earl smiled at her from across the room and her heart swelled.

This time around, their relationship had been considerably less rocky than before. They'd had some ups and downs but were standing strong together. Fighting Rylie and using magic together had been a bonding experience.

"Can I have your attention, please?" Earl's voice boomed over the general rumble of conversation. Everyone quieted and stared at him.

He walked toward Cynth with a soft look in his eyes and stood beside her, taking her hand in his. Nerves fluttered in her stomach.

"You guys know that Cynth and I have had our ups and downs. Most of them my fault, though she isn't entirely blameless."

Her family chuckled and she couldn't stop her grin. She'd dreamed of this last night. A tiny premonition of things to come.

"Cynth, I was an ass. I was wrong. Magic isn't evil. Like anything else, it's what you make of it. Together, you and I used magic, your magic, to counteract evil. You wouldn't be you without your magic, and I, for one, am glad you have it. I'm thrilled that you gave me a second chance."

He kneeled on one knee and held up a bright purple velvet box. "Cynth, I don't deserve you, but will you please give this mundane a chance and put me out of my misery? I'm nothing without you. We're stronger together. Will you marry me?" He flipped open the box, revealing a large, faceted malachite stone surrounded by small diamonds.

She gasped. Her heart stuck in her throat. She swallowed a lump of emotion and dashed away her tears. "Yes," she whispered. "A thousand times, yes!"

He slipped the ring on her finger, and it fit perfectly. She tugged him up into her arms where he belonged. She leaned into his warm embrace and whispered the secret she'd been keeping since the morning after they'd first made love. "Earl, you're going to be a father."

"Holy crap!" he shouted with a bright laugh. "I'm gonna be a dad!"

"I assume you'll move up the date of that wedding?" A deep voice said from the doorway.

"Daddy!" Cynth squealed and rushed into her father's embrace. "Mom. You're home."

Their party to celebrate Rylie's incarceration morphed into an engagement and coming home party that lasted well into the night.

Lazuli sighed as Frank and Rosie headed home. If he weren't her best friend's widower, she'd be all over him. Her honor and heart wouldn't let her pursue the man Celine had loved. She felt she had no choice but to watch him and his amazing daughter from afar. Her heart was heavy with melancholy, and she faked her best smile and laughed when she was supposed to.

She stood back in the corner, watching the victory celebration unfold. The high emotions rolling off her family and friends were as overwhelming as they were uplifting. Leticia stood with her. Neither said anything about the news Leticia had just shared with her.

In the wee hours of the morning, there had been a prison break at the magical facility. Keres, Brown, and several others were on the run. Dozens of people had been injured and two had died. It was only a matter of time before they came after her family. Again.

Rylie's poem had doubled down the certainty of another fight. While the words were vague and twisted, they told Laz that another, bigger battle was coming.

Her vision affirmed it. She was destined to lead the fight against the escapees and whoever set them free. She couldn't see the ending, nor could she see the fates of her family and friends. Overriding this was a desperate, sinking feeling that they might not all make it through the battle.

Love the novel you just read?

Be sure to check out the rest of the series!

Your opinion matters.

I'd love it if you would review this book on your favorite book site, review site, blog, or your own social media properties, and share your opinion with other readers.

Thanks in advance. Katie.

About Katie O'Connor

Best-selling author Katie O'Connor lives in Calgary, Alberta, Canada. She married her high school sweetheart and is living her happily ever after. She is the mother of two grown daughters and is extremely proud of her five grandchildren.

She is the founder of The Write Chicks, a private romance writers' group set up with the sole purpose of supporting each other's writing career. Currently, she is past president of the Calgary Association of the Romance Writers of America. In the past, she's been their secretary and has also served on the organizing committee for When Words Collide, a reader and writer conference in Calgary, Alberta. In 2025 she will be a Story Coach for the Alexandra Writer's Center Society in Calgary.

Katie's career path has been long and twisted, with most of her life devoted to her family. She's been a waitress, chambermaid, cashier, store manager, as well as a lab and X-ray technician. She's been a small business owner and is an avid quilter and crafter.

She's dabbled in writing since high school because something drives her to create stories. She swears it's impossible for her NOT to write. Unsatisfied with one genre, Katie writes contemporary romance, erotic romance, fantasy/paranormal romance, romantic suspense, and erotica.

She believes in all things magical, including dragons, fairies, UFOs, ghosts, and house pixies. But most of all she believes in love, romance, and hope.

Where to Find Katie

Website: https://katieohwrites.com
Email: katie@katieohwrites.com
Mailchimp Signup: http://eepurl.com/Q2nRr
Facebook: http://www.facebook.com/katieohwrites
Bookbub: https://www.bookbub.com/profile/katie-o-connor
Instagram: https://www.instagram.com/katieohwrites/
Goodreads: https://www.goodreads.com/author/show/5362469.Katie_O_Connor

Books By Katie

Their Christmas Heart
Their Christmas Love
Their Perfect Christmas
A Silver Fox Christmas Box Set
Heart's Haven:
Running Home
Building Trust
Saving Grace
Loving Winter
Heart's Haven Box Set
Three Moon Falls:
Fire Magic
Water Magic
Earth Magic
Midnight Magic
Air Magic
Stand Alone Books:
Carly's Heart
Matchmaker Christmas
Cupid's Charm
Gingerbread Dreams
Christmas in Silver Creek
Fake Dating at Half Moon Bay
Playing for Keeps in Half Moon Bay
Sleigh Bells Inn
Hearts in the Spotlight
To a Tea
Bulletproof Heart
Protecting Josie
Rekindled Fire
Winning her Love

Ticket to Her Heart
KO'd by Love

www.ingramcontent.com/pod-product-compliance
Lightning Source LLC
Chambersburg PA
CBHW030242030726
47493CB00023B/440